EXTRAORDINARY™

A STORY OF AN ORDINARY PRINCESS

BY
CASSIE ANDERSON

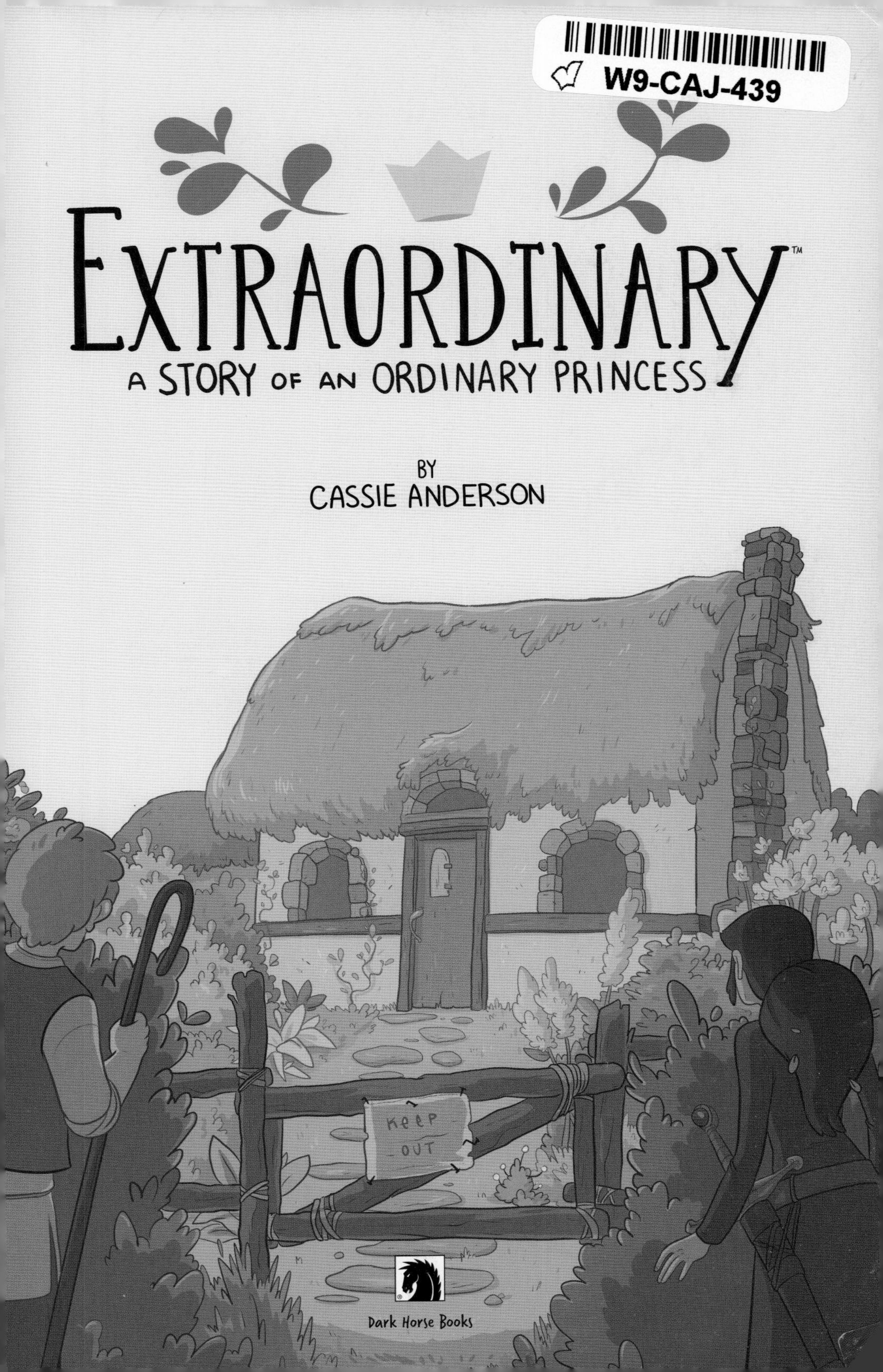
Keep
OUT

Dark Horse Books

President and Publisher
MIKE RICHARDSON

Editor
RACHEL ROBERTS

Assistant Editor
JENNY BLENK

Designers
PATRICK SATTERFIELD AND ETHAN KIMBERLING

Digital Art Technician
CHRISTIANNE GILLENARDO-GOUDREAU

Published by Dark Horse Books
A Division of Dark Horse Comics LLC.
10956 SE Main St.
Milwaukie, OR 97222

First Edition: July 2019
ISBN: 978-1-50671-027-3

10 9 8 7 6 5 4 3 2
Printed in China

Advertising Sales: (503) 905-2315
Comic Shop Locator Service: comicshoplocator.com

Library of Congress Cataloging-in-Publication Data

Names: Anderson, Cassie, author, artist.
Title: Extraordinary : a story of an ordinary princess / by Cassie Anderson.
Description: First edition. | Milwaukie, OR : Dark Horse Books, 2019. |
  Summary: After escaping a kidnapping, Princess Basil tracks down her fairy
  godmother and learns the solution to her ordinariness is going on quest
  for a magic ring.
Identifiers: LCCN 2019007211 | ISBN 9781506710273 (paperback)
Subjects: LCSH: Graphic novels. | CYAC: Graphic novels. |
  Princesses--Fiction. | Quests (Expeditions)--Fiction. | Magic--Fiction. |
  BISAC: JUVENILE FICTION / Fairy Tales & Folklore / General.
Classification: LCC PZ7.7.A474 E97 2019 | DDC 741.5/973--dc23
LC record available at https://lccn.loc.gov/2019007211

For Lola, and all the
ordinary princesses out there.

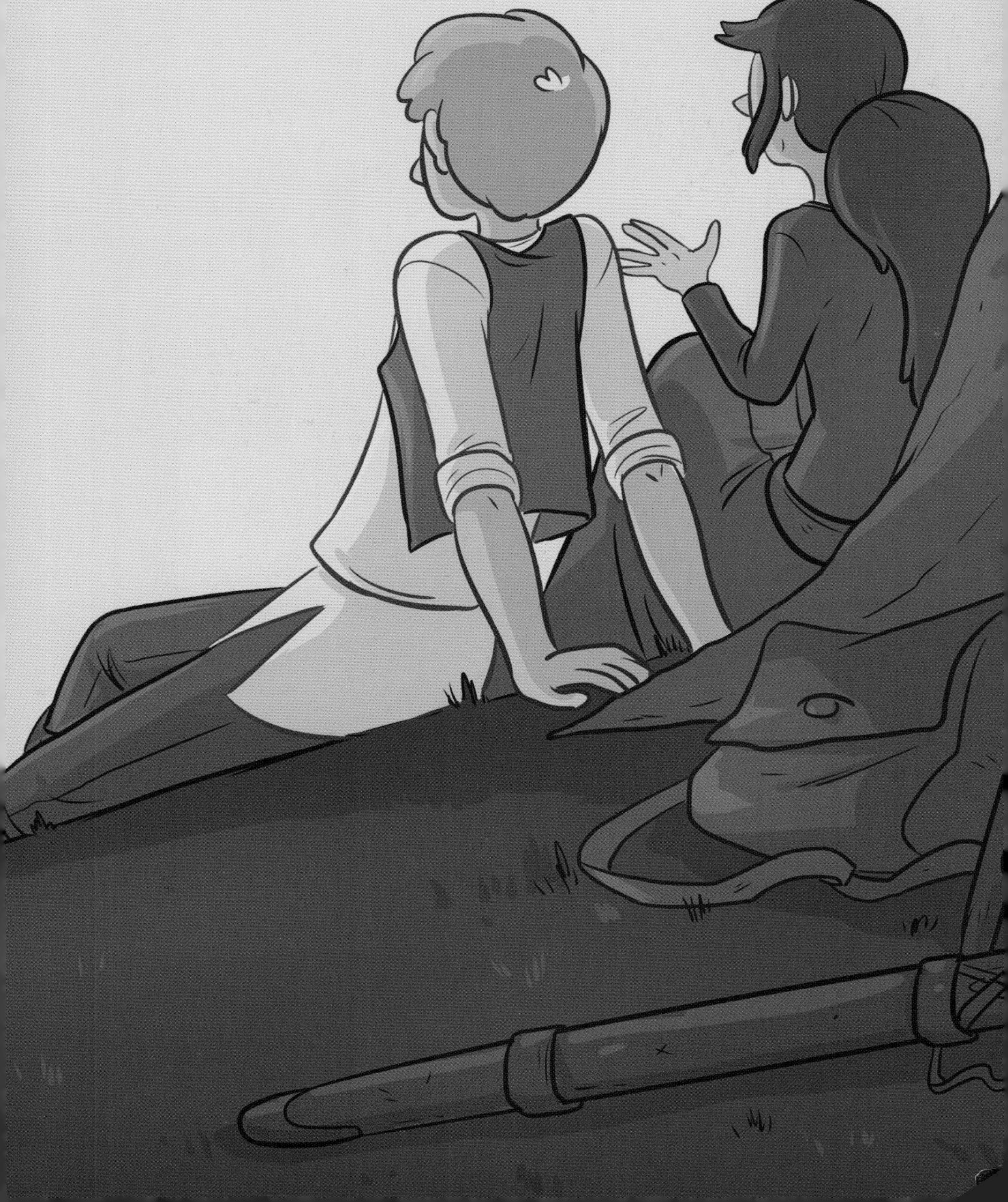

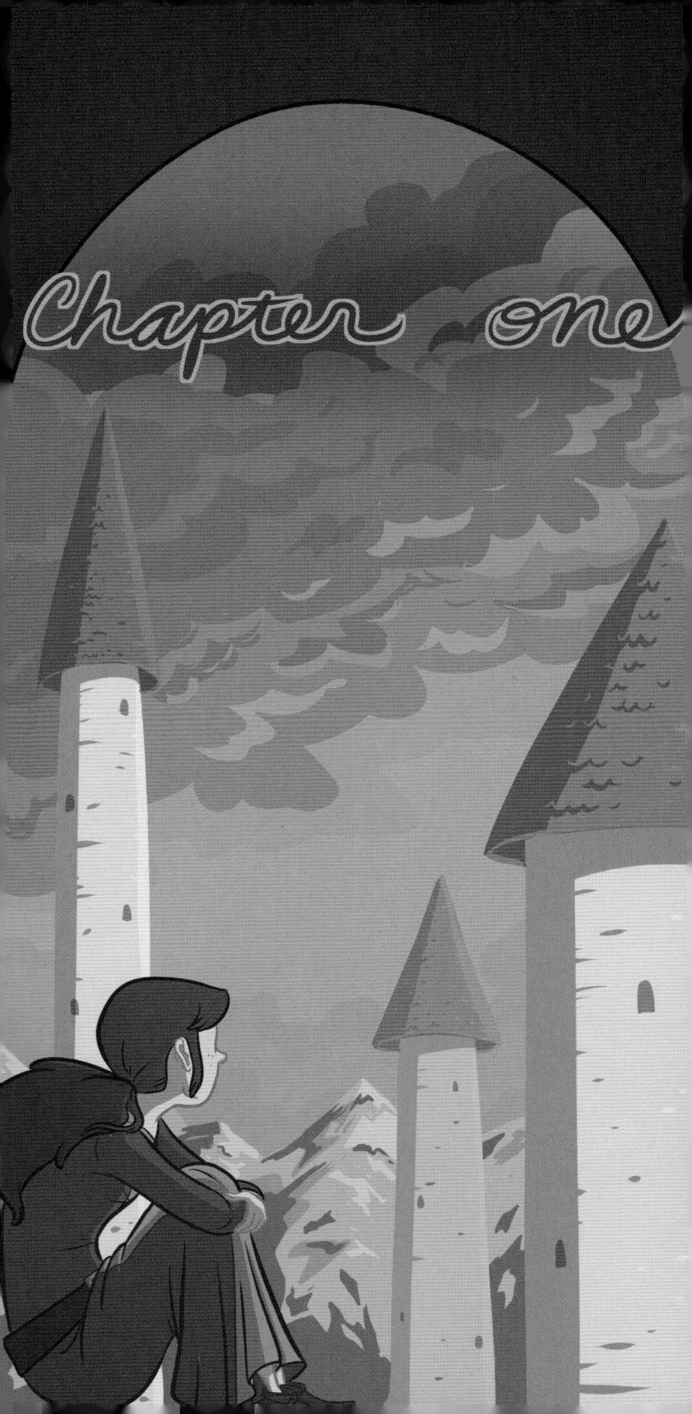
Chapter one

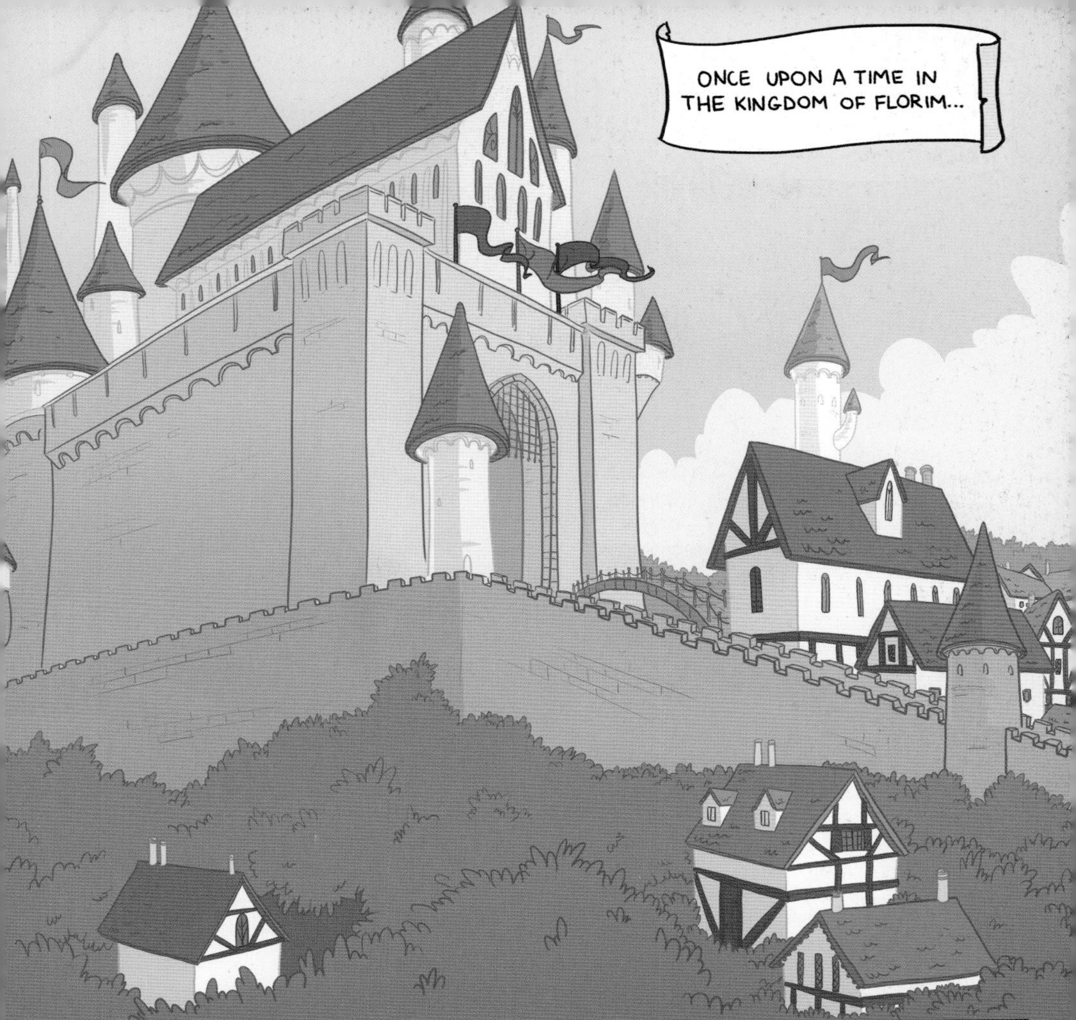
ONCE UPON A TIME IN THE KINGDOM OF FLORIM...

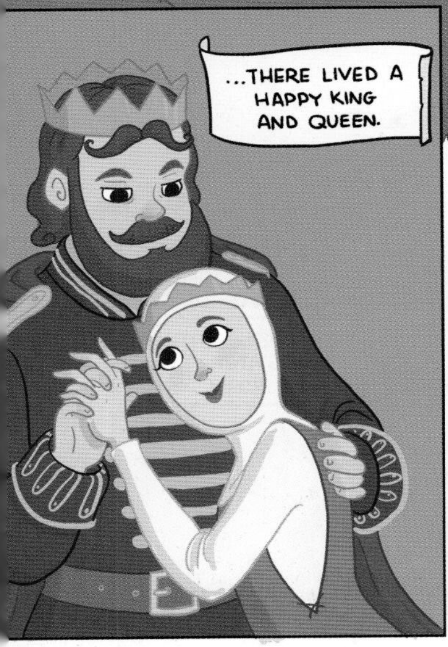
...THERE LIVED A HAPPY KING AND QUEEN.

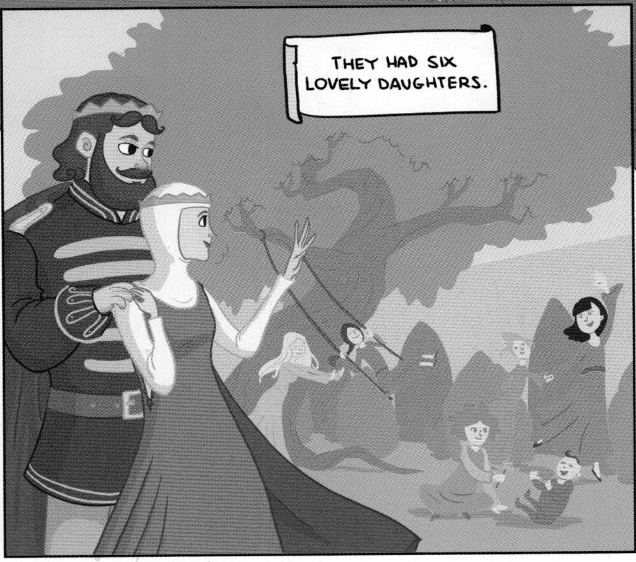
THEY HAD SIX LOVELY DAUGHTERS.

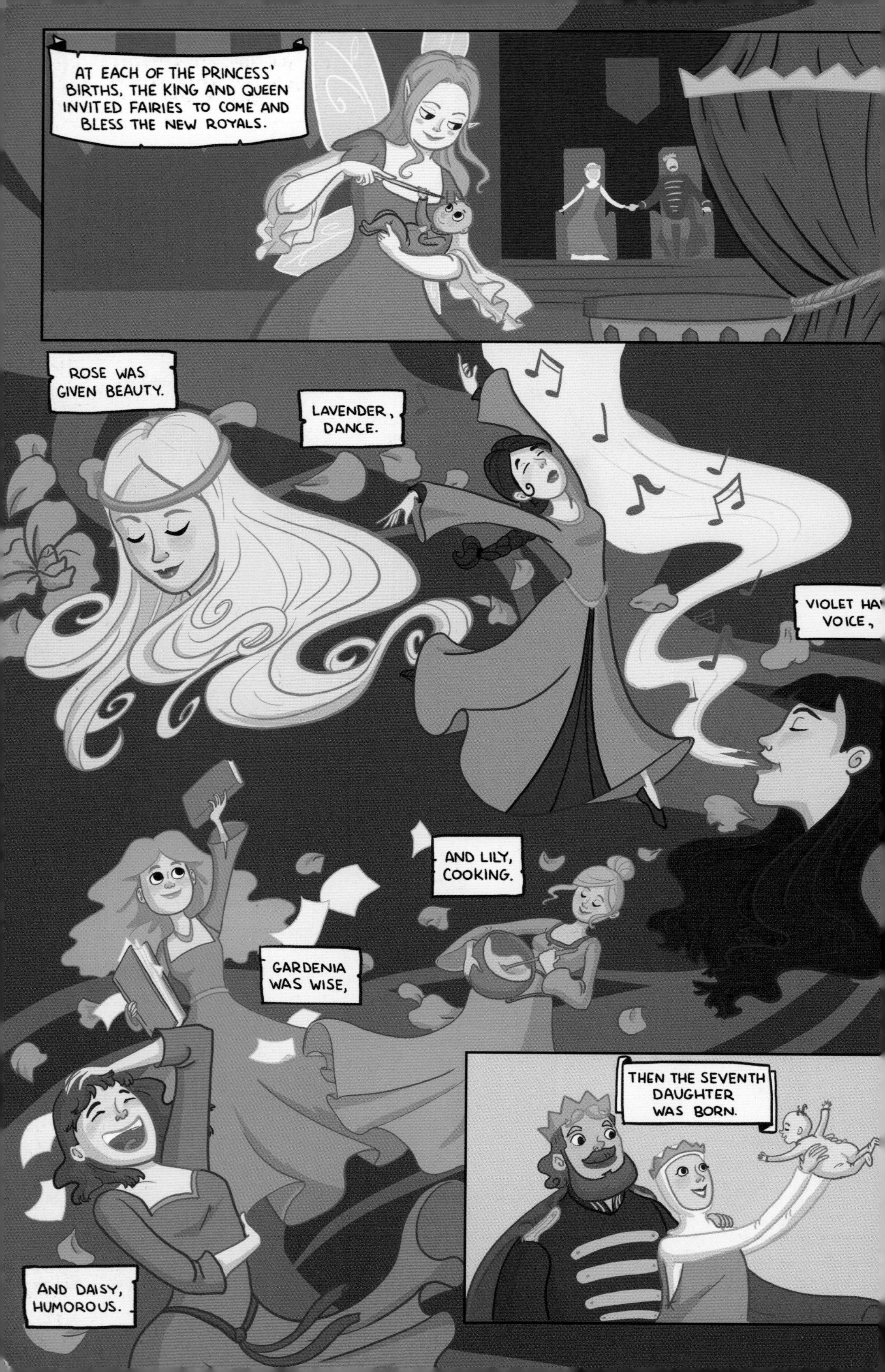

AT EACH OF THE PRINCESS' BIRTHS, THE KING AND QUEEN INVITED FAIRIES TO COME AND BLESS THE NEW ROYALS.
ROSE WAS GIVEN BEAUTY.
LAVENDER, DANCE.
VIOLET HA
VOICE,
GARDENIA WAS WISE,
AND LILY, COOKING.
AND DAISY, HUMOROUS.
THEN THE SEVENTH DAUGHTER WAS BORN.

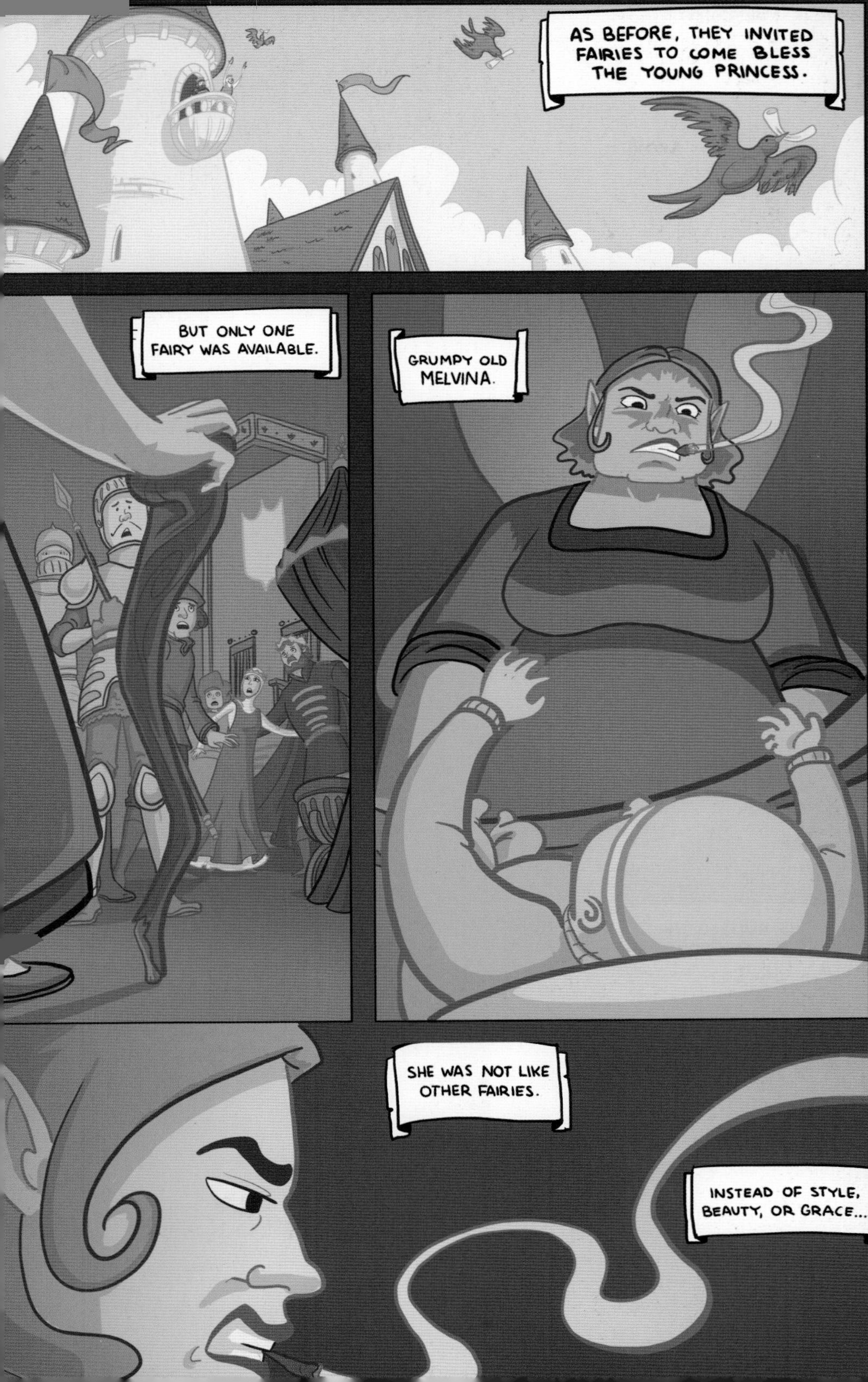
AS BEFORE, THEY INVITED FAIRIES TO COME BLESS THE YOUNG PRINCESS.
BUT ONLY ONE FAIRY WAS AVAILABLE.
GRUMPY OLD MELVINA.
SHE WAS NOT LIKE OTHER FAIRIES.
INSTEAD OF STYLE, BEAUTY, OR GRACE...

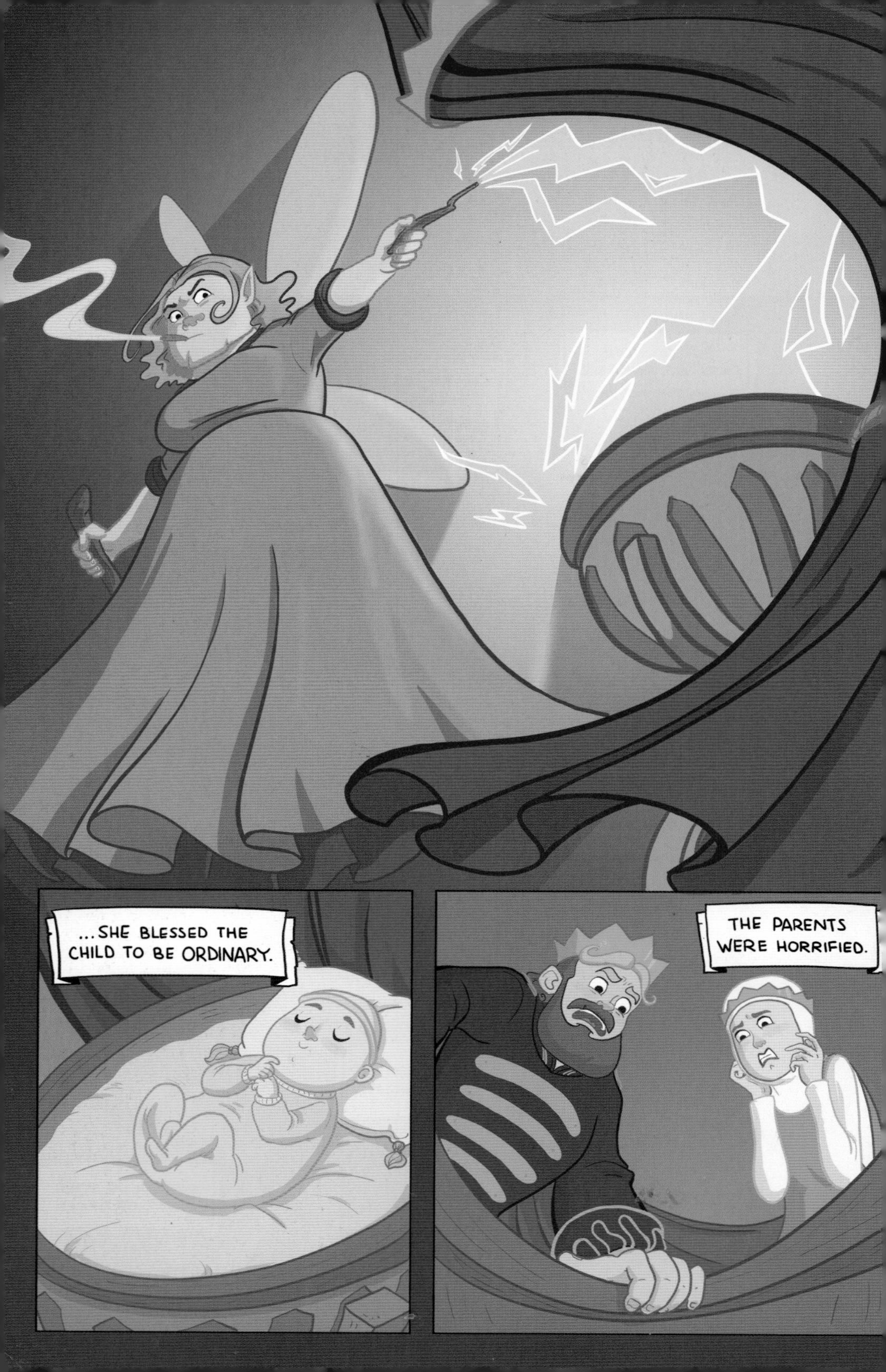
...SHE BLESSED THE CHILD TO BE ORDINARY.
THE PARENTS WERE HORRIFIED.

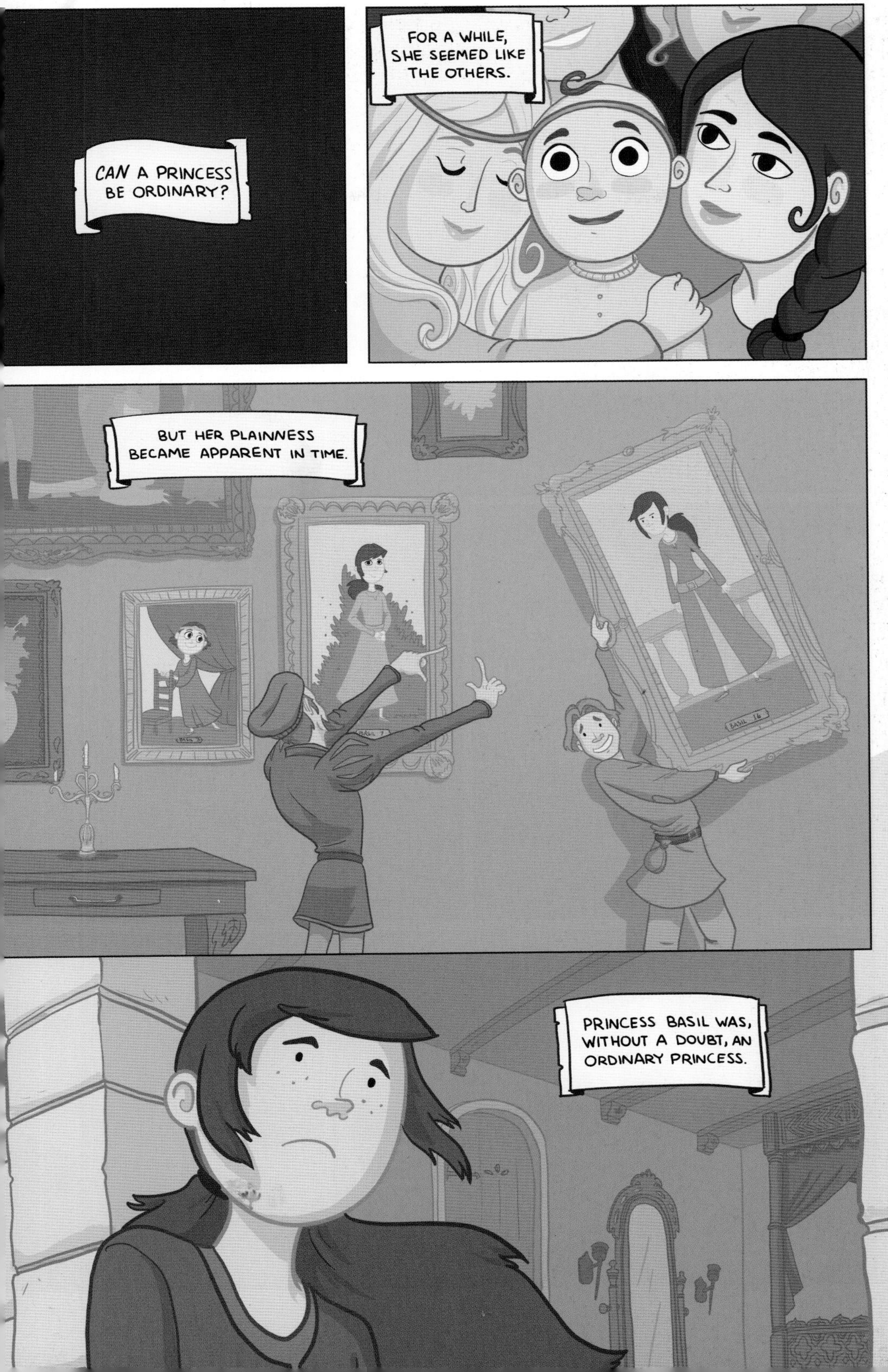
CAN A PRINCESS BE ORDINARY?
FOR A WHILE, SHE SEEMED LIKE THE OTHERS.
BUT HER PLAINNESS BECAME APPARENT IN TIME.
PRINCESS BASIL WAS, WITHOUT A DOUBT, AN ORDINARY PRINCESS.

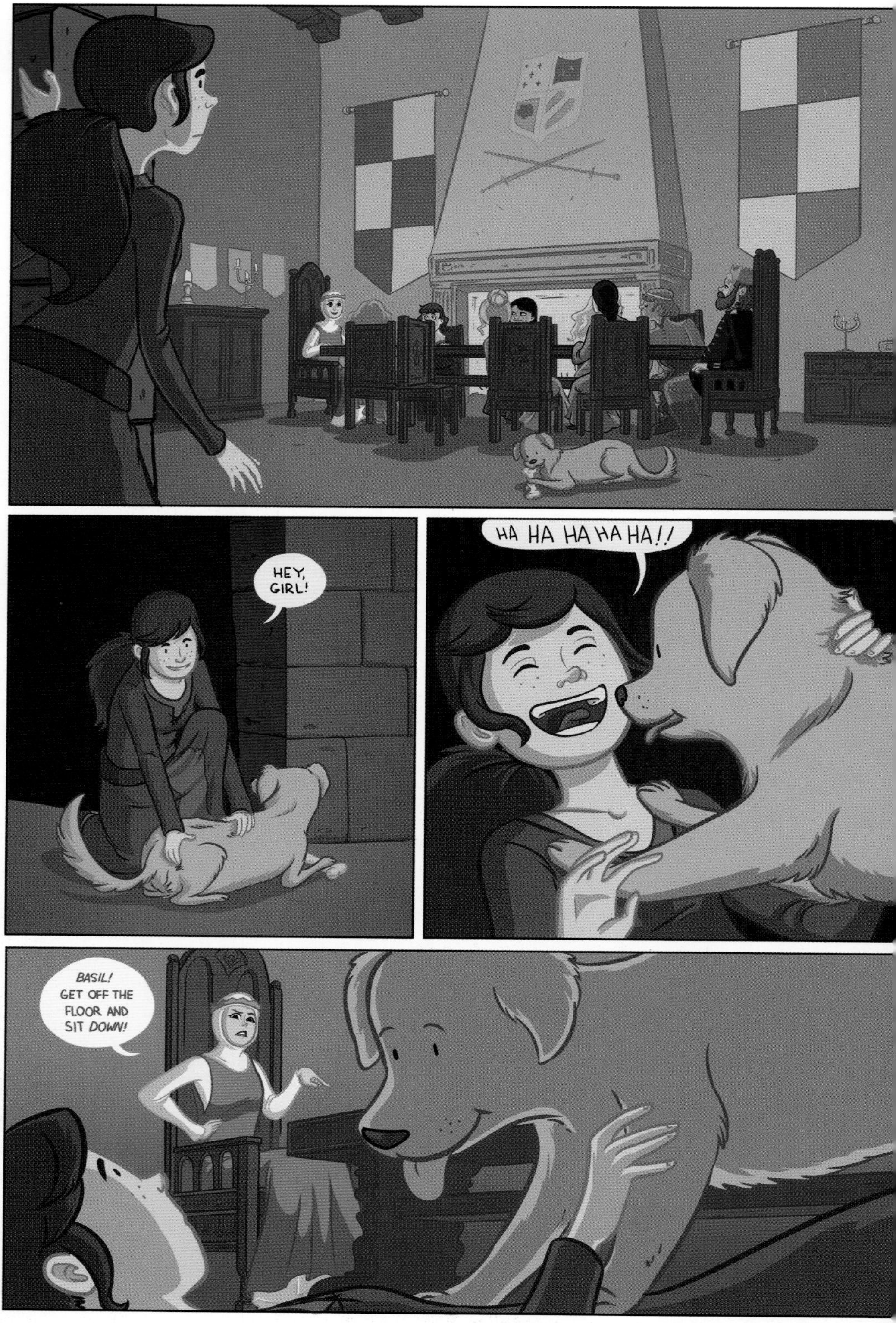
HEY, GIRL!
HA HA HA HA HA!!
BASIL! GET OFF THE FLOOR AND SIT DOWN!

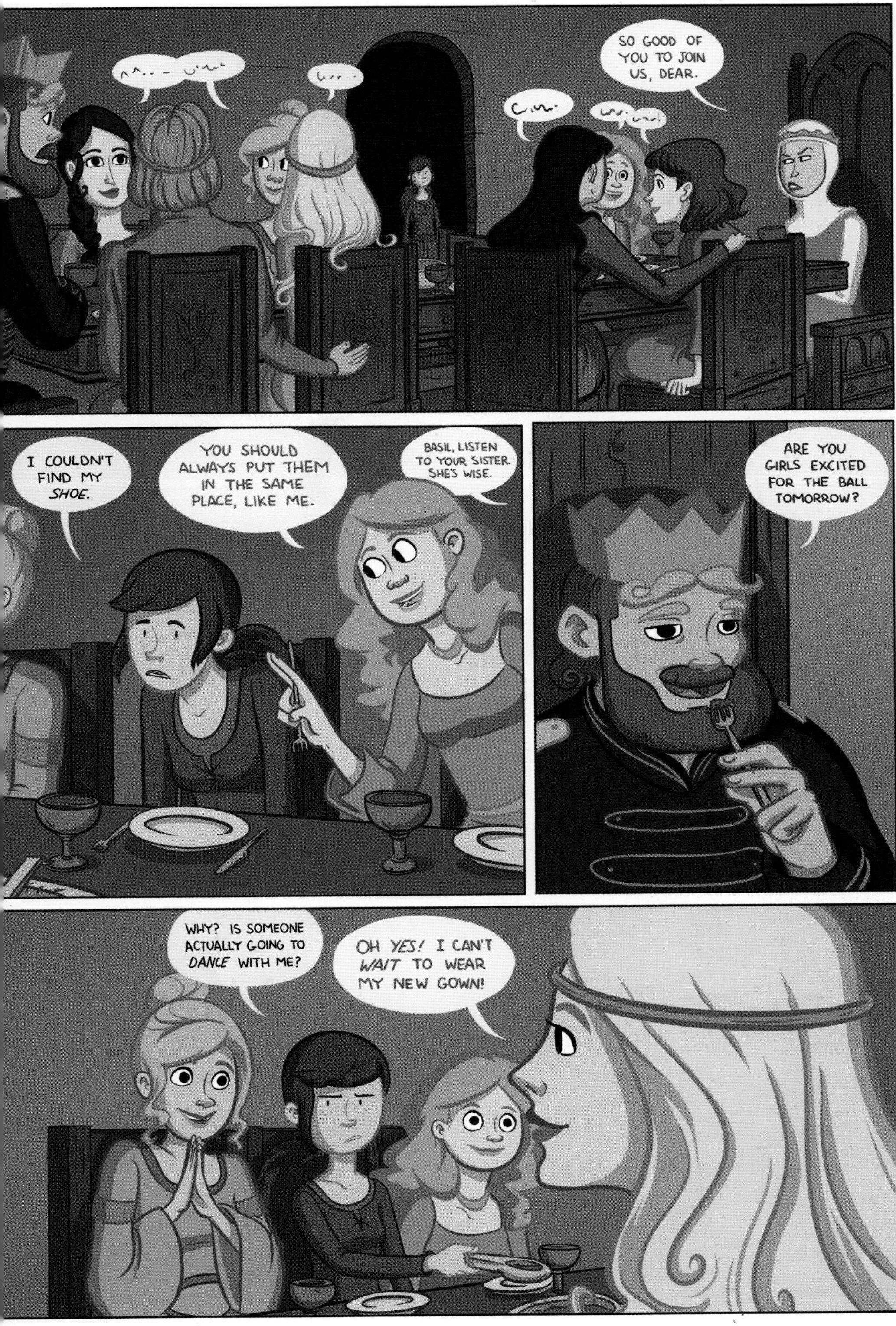
SO GOOD OF YOU TO JOIN US, DEAR.
I COULDN'T FIND MY *SHOE.*
YOU SHOULD ALWAYS PUT THEM IN THE SAME PLACE, LIKE ME.
BASIL, LISTEN TO YOUR SISTER. SHE'S WISE.
ARE YOU GIRLS EXCITED FOR THE BALL TOMORROW?
WHY? IS SOMEONE ACTUALLY GOING TO *DANCE* WITH ME?
OH *YES!* I CAN'T *WAIT* TO WEAR MY NEW GOWN!

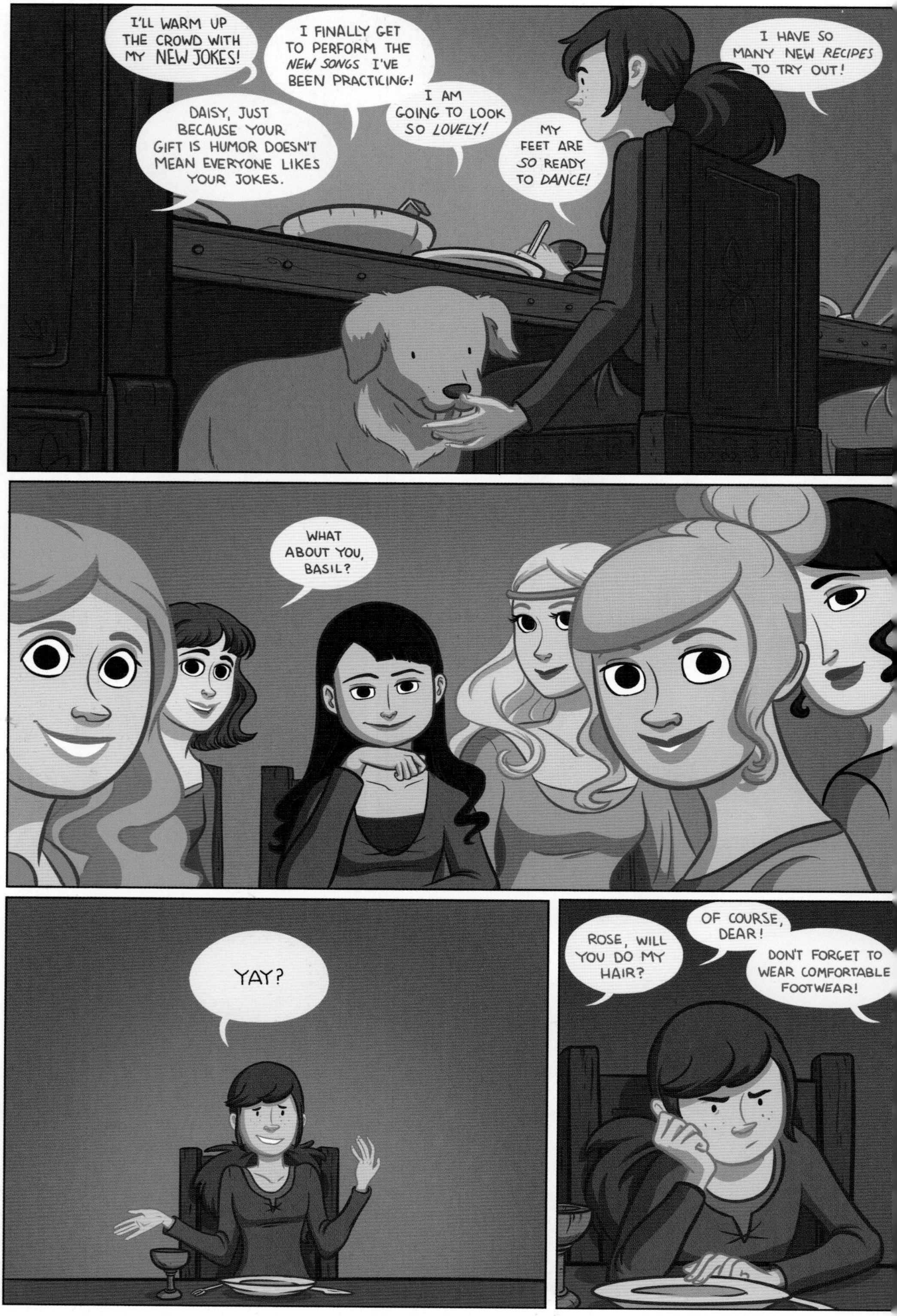
I'LL WARM UP THE CROWD WITH MY NEW JOKES!
DAISY, JUST BECAUSE YOUR GIFT IS HUMOR DOESN'T MEAN EVERYONE LIKES YOUR JOKES.
I FINALLY GET TO PERFORM THE NEW SONGS I'VE BEEN PRACTICING!
I AM GOING TO LOOK SO LOVELY!
MY FEET ARE SO READY TO DANCE!
I HAVE SO MANY NEW RECIPES TO TRY OUT!
WHAT ABOUT YOU, BASIL?
YAY?
ROSE, WILL YOU DO MY HAIR?
OF COURSE, DEAR!
DON'T FORGET TO WEAR COMFORTABLE FOOTWEAR!

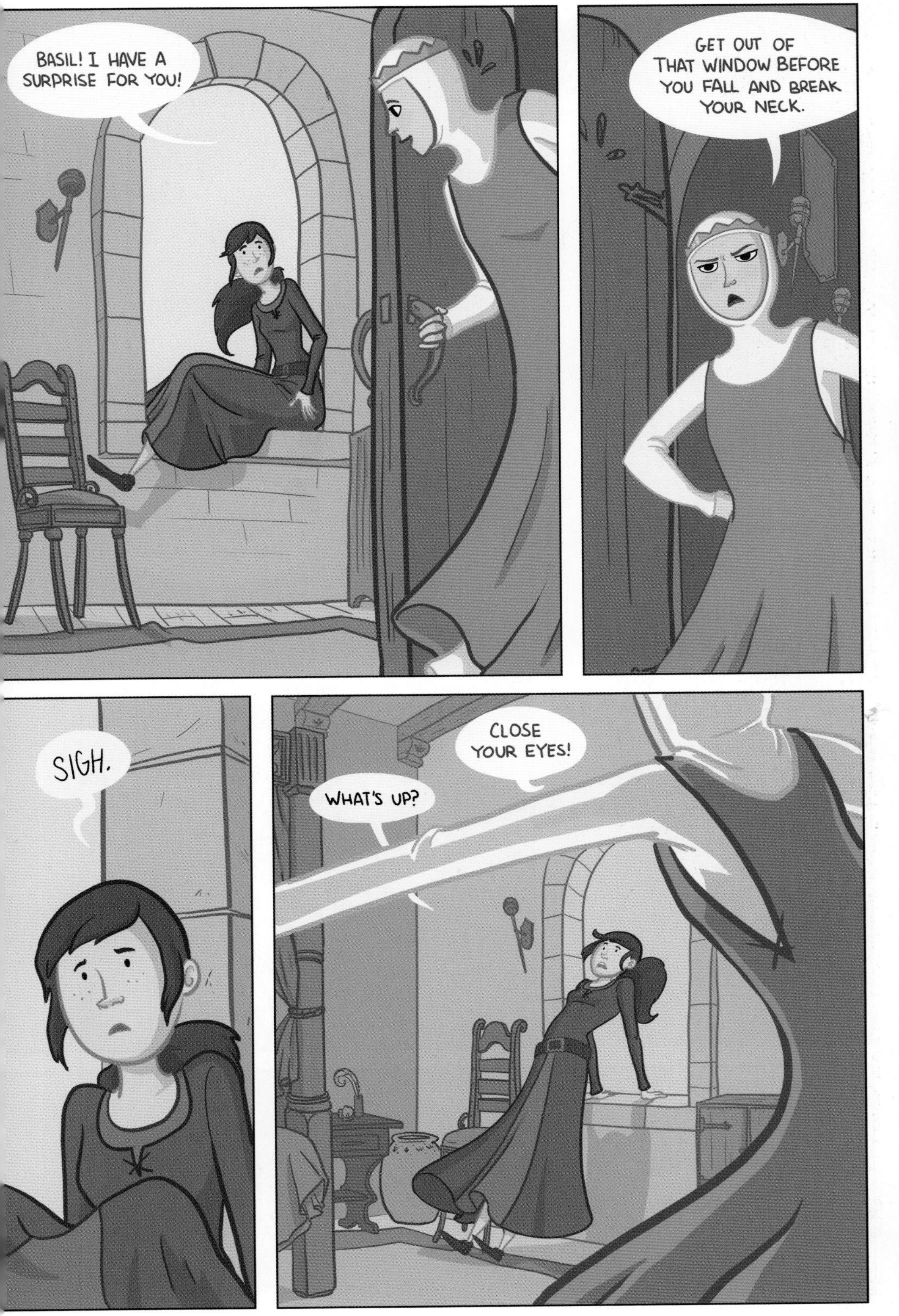
BASIL! I HAVE A SURPRISE FOR YOU!
GET OUT OF THAT WINDOW BEFORE YOU FALL AND BREAK YOUR NECK.
SIGH.
WHAT'S UP?
CLOSE YOUR EYES!

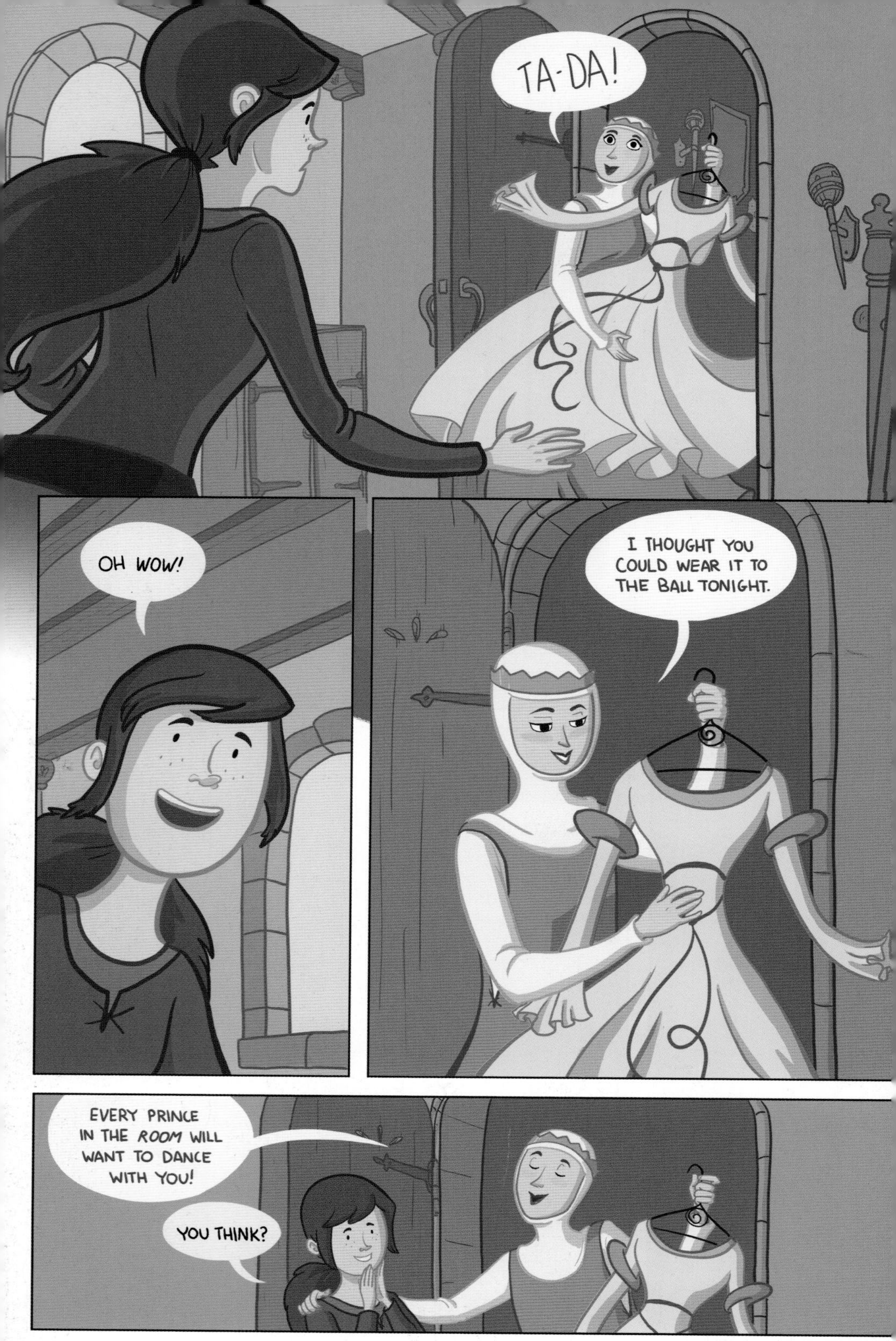
TA-DA!
OH WOW!
I THOUGHT YOU COULD WEAR IT TO THE BALL TONIGHT.
EVERY PRINCE IN THE *ROOM* WILL WANT TO DANCE WITH YOU!
YOU THINK?

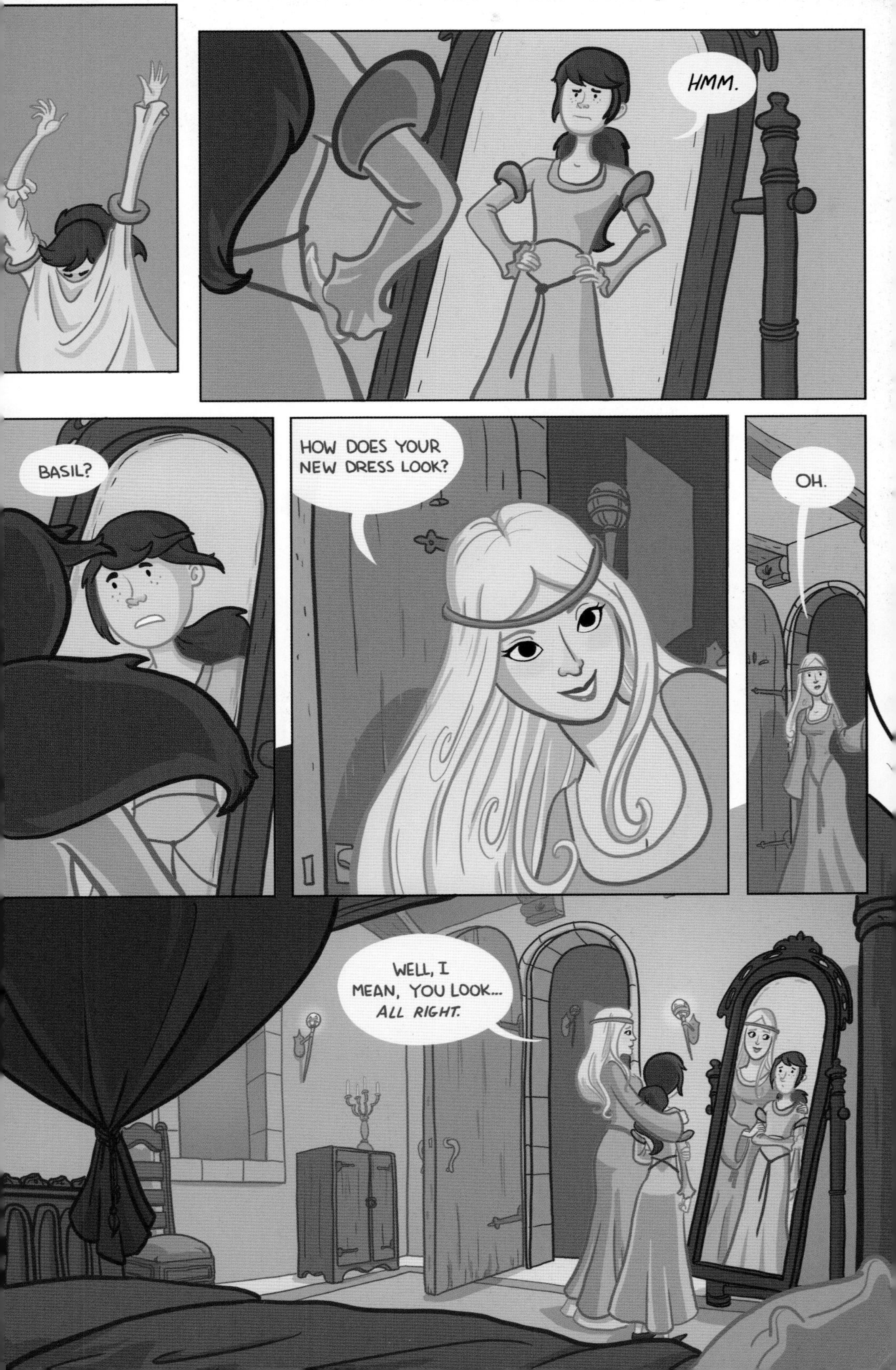
HMM.
BASIL?
HOW DOES YOUR NEW DRESS LOOK?
OH.
WELL, I MEAN, YOU LOOK... *ALL RIGHT.*

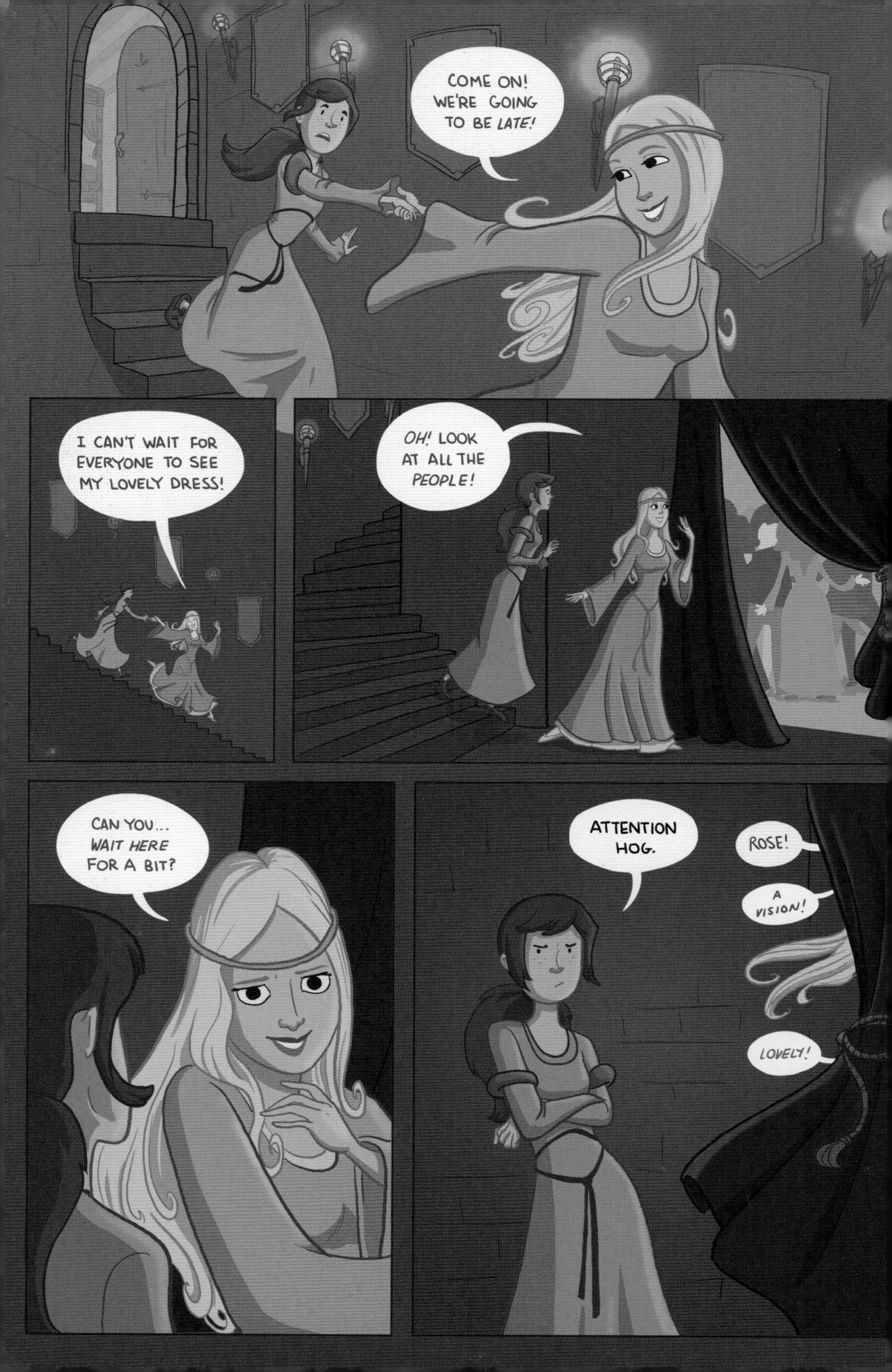
COME ON! WE'RE GOING TO BE *LATE!*
I CAN'T WAIT FOR EVERYONE TO SEE MY LOVELY DRESS!
OH! LOOK AT ALL THE *PEOPLE!*
CAN YOU... *WAIT HERE* FOR A BIT?
ATTENTION HOG.
ROSE!
A VISION!
LOVELY!

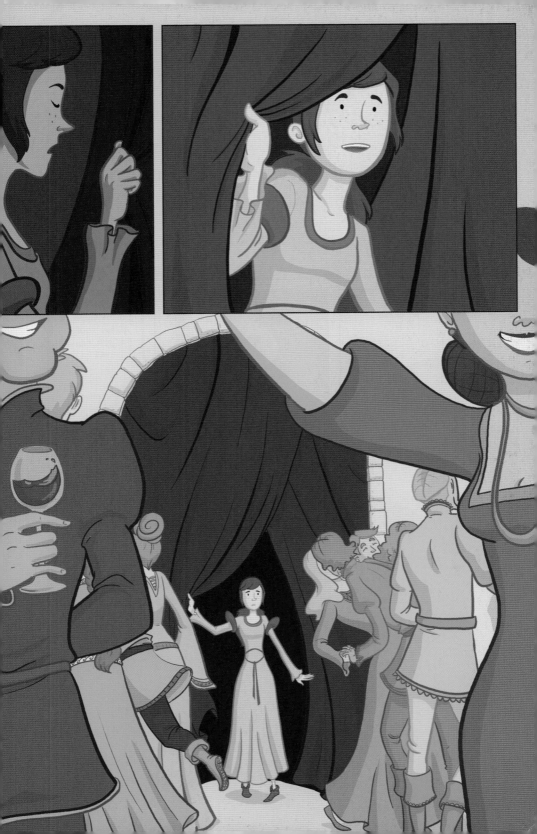

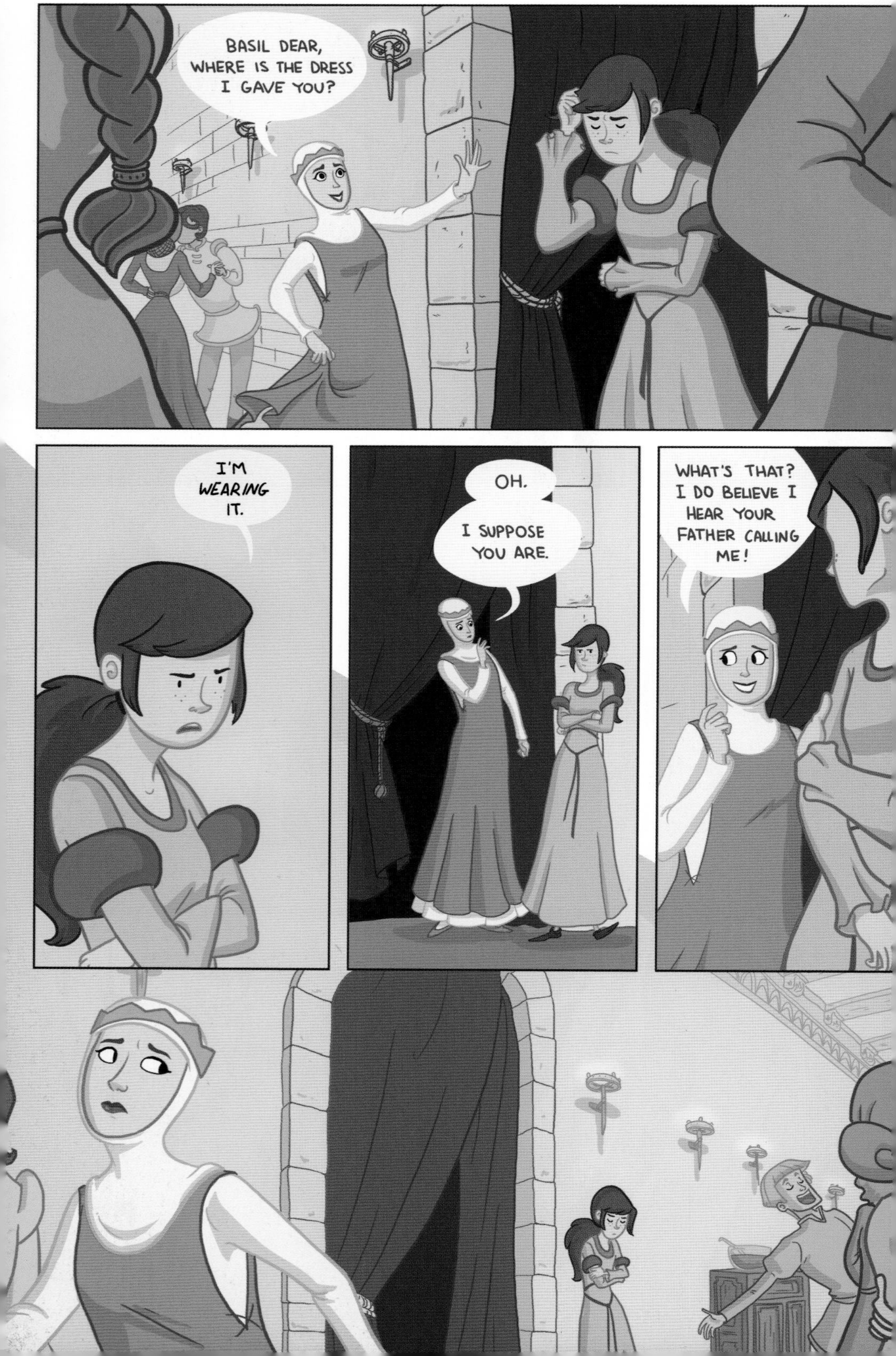

BASIL DEAR, WHERE IS THE DRESS I GAVE YOU?
I'M WEARING IT.
OH.
I SUPPOSE YOU ARE.
WHAT'S THAT? I DO BELIEVE I HEAR YOUR FATHER CALLING ME!

DID FRANCIS FORGET TO ADD THE FLOWER PETALS TO THE PASTRIES AGAIN?

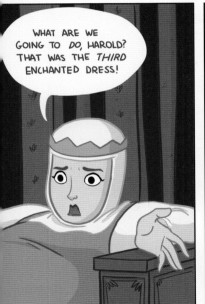
WHAT ARE WE GOING TO *DO*, HAROLD? THAT WAS THE *THIRD* ENCHANTED DRESS!

DEAR, MAYBE IT'S TIME TO--

I HAVE AN IDEA!

IT'S TIME FOR A NEW PLAN.

IF YOU'RE SURE...

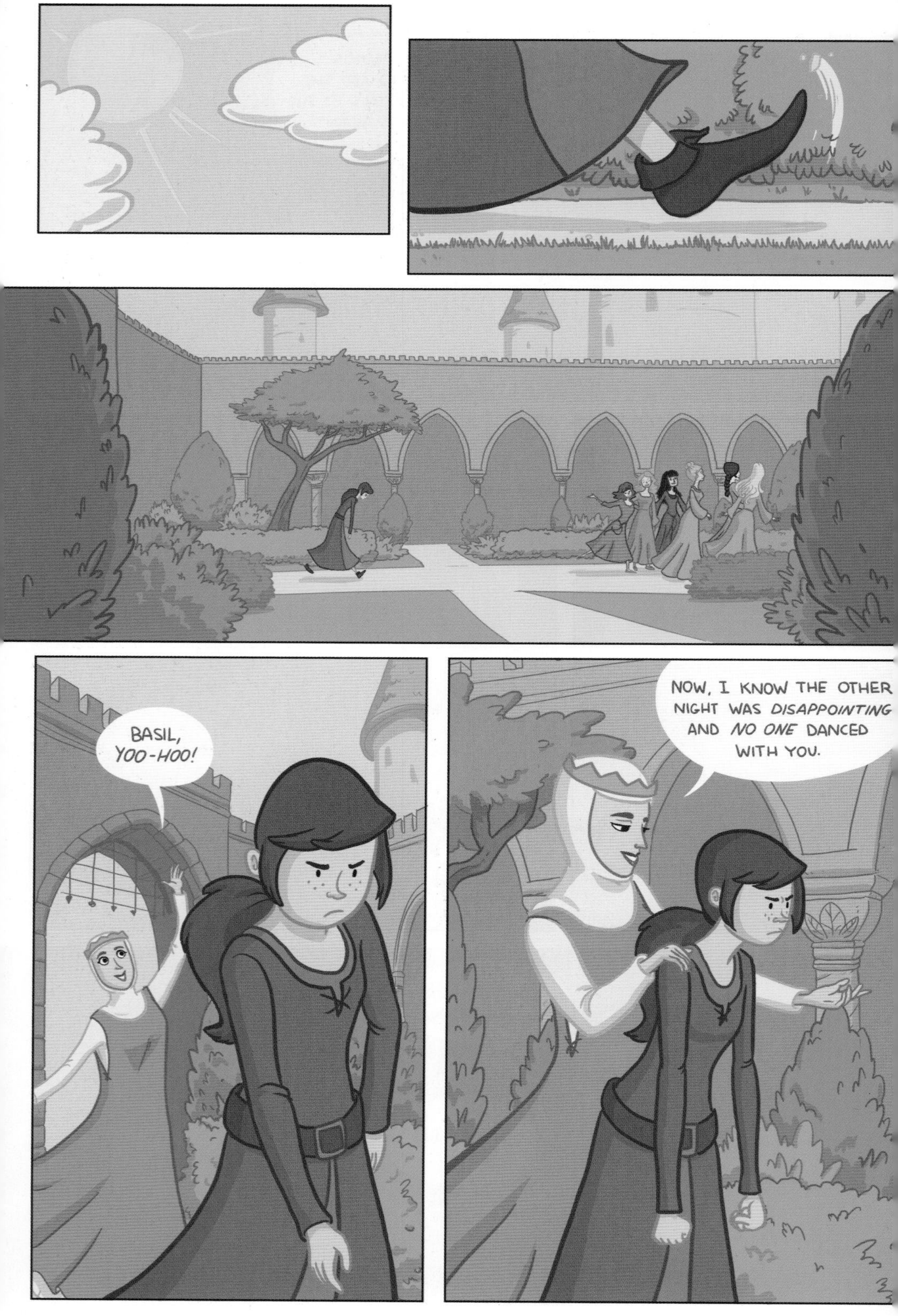
BASIL, YOO-HOO!
NOW, I KNOW THE OTHER NIGHT WAS *DISAPPOINTING* AND *NO ONE* DANCED WITH YOU.

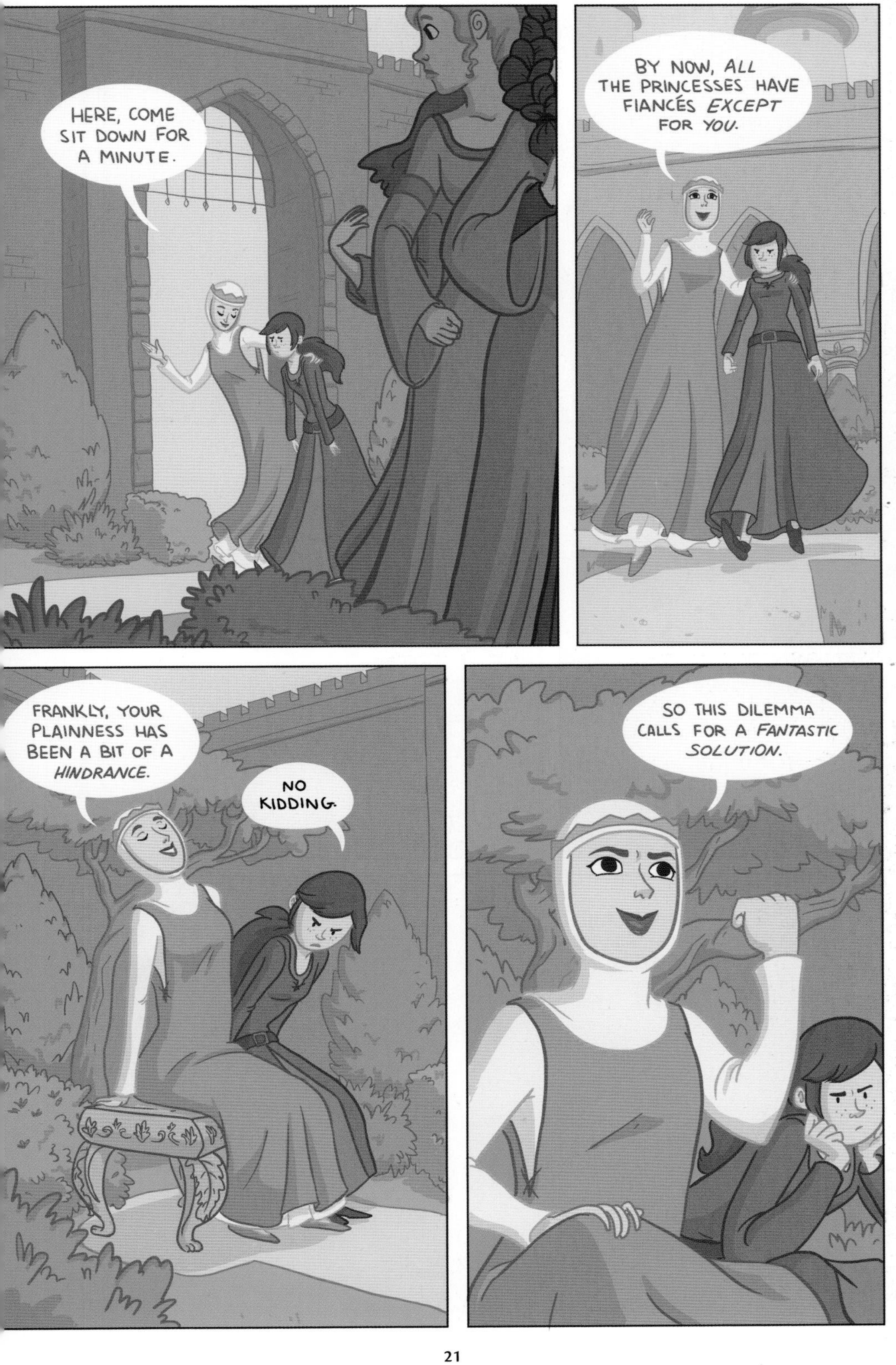
HERE, COME SIT DOWN FOR A MINUTE.
BY NOW, *ALL* THE PRINCESSES HAVE FIANCÉS *EXCEPT* FOR *YOU*.
FRANKLY, YOUR PLAINNESS HAS BEEN A BIT OF A *HINDRANCE*.
NO KIDDING.
SO THIS DILEMMA CALLS FOR A *FANTASTIC SOLUTION*.

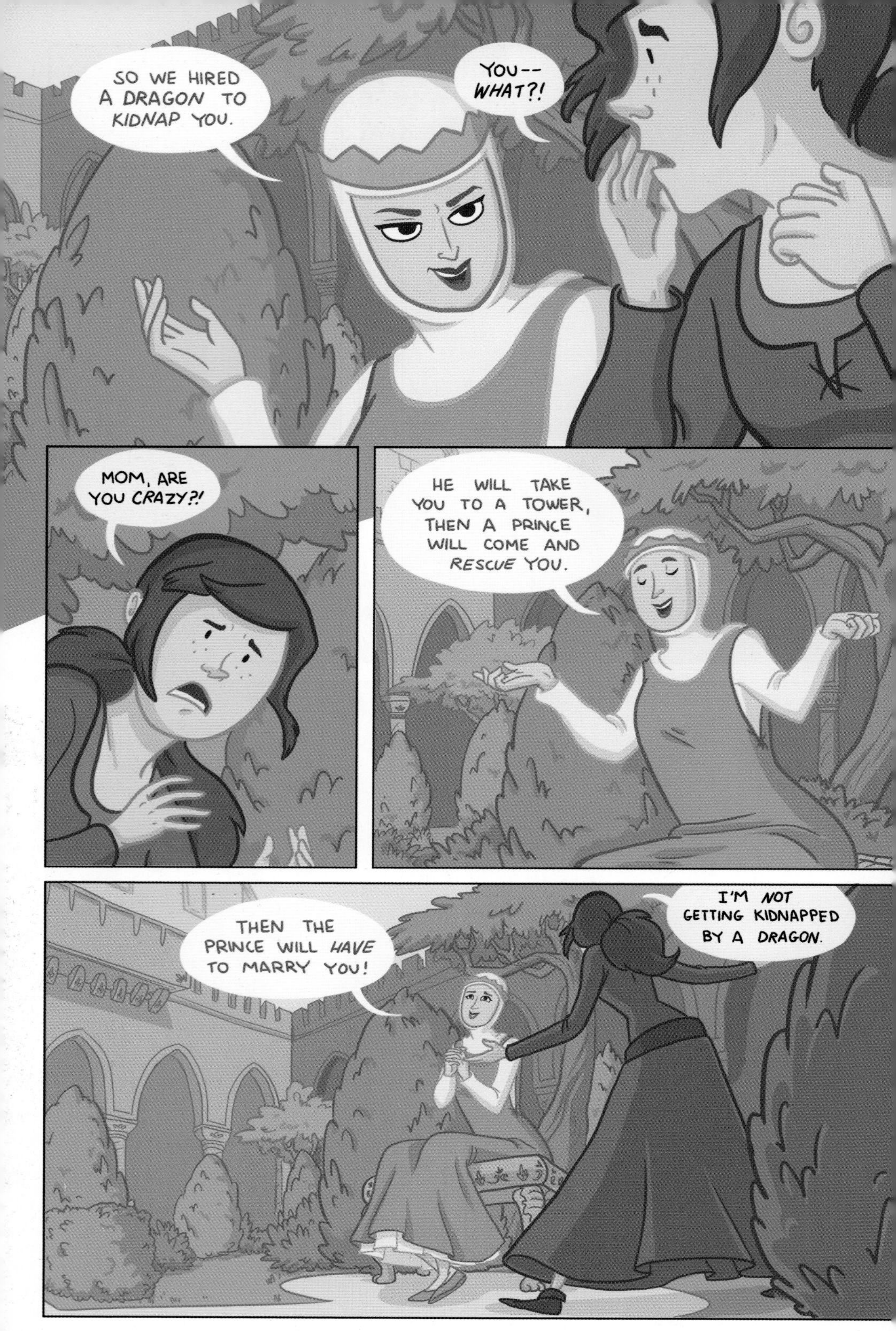
SO WE HIRED A DRAGON TO KIDNAP YOU.
YOU-- WHAT?!
MOM, ARE YOU CRAZY?!
HE WILL TAKE YOU TO A TOWER, THEN A PRINCE WILL COME AND RESCUE YOU.
THEN THE PRINCE WILL HAVE TO MARRY YOU!
I'M NOT GETTING KIDNAPPED BY A DRAGON.

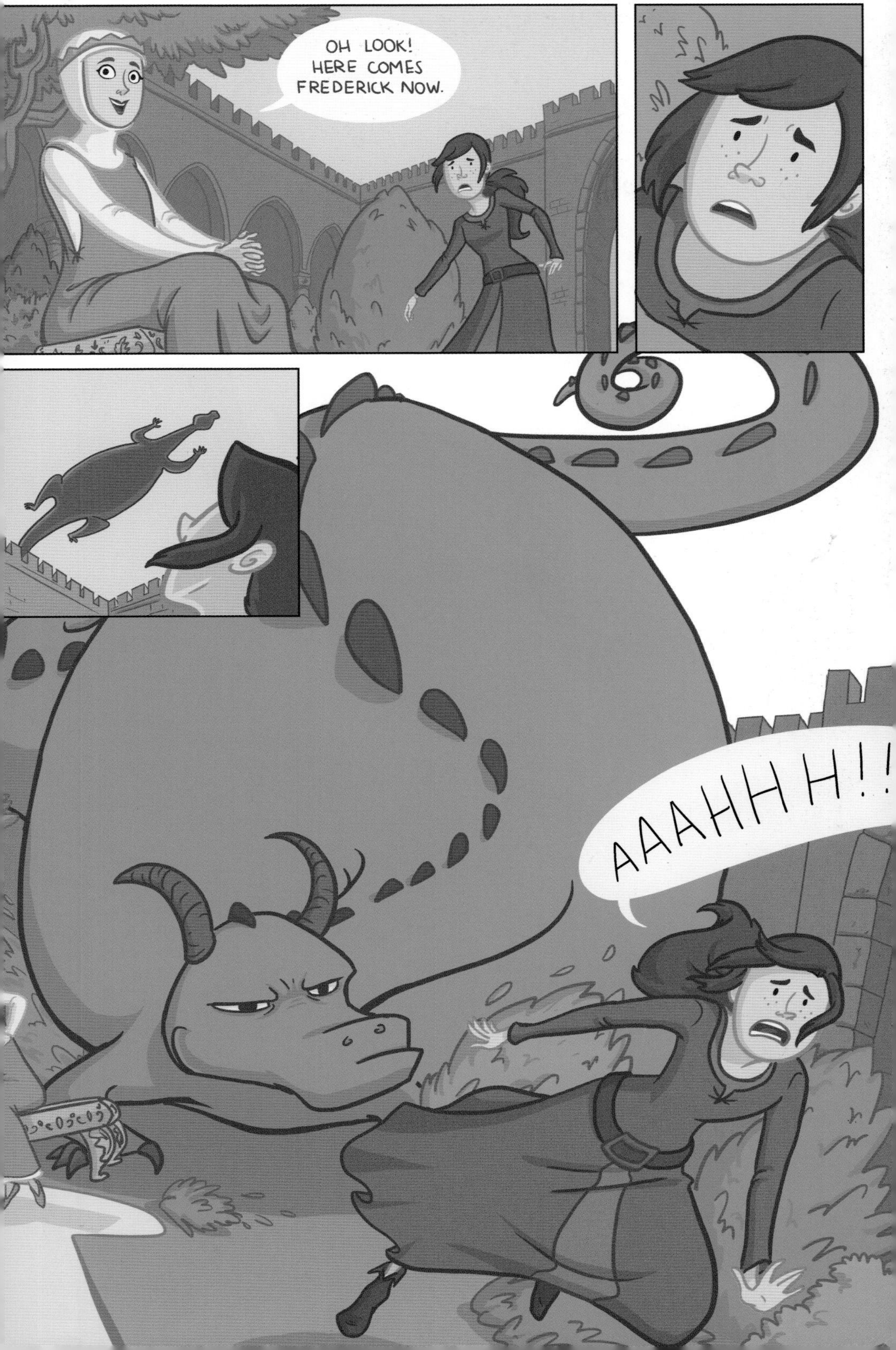
OH LOOK! HERE COMES FREDERICK NOW.
AAAHHH!!

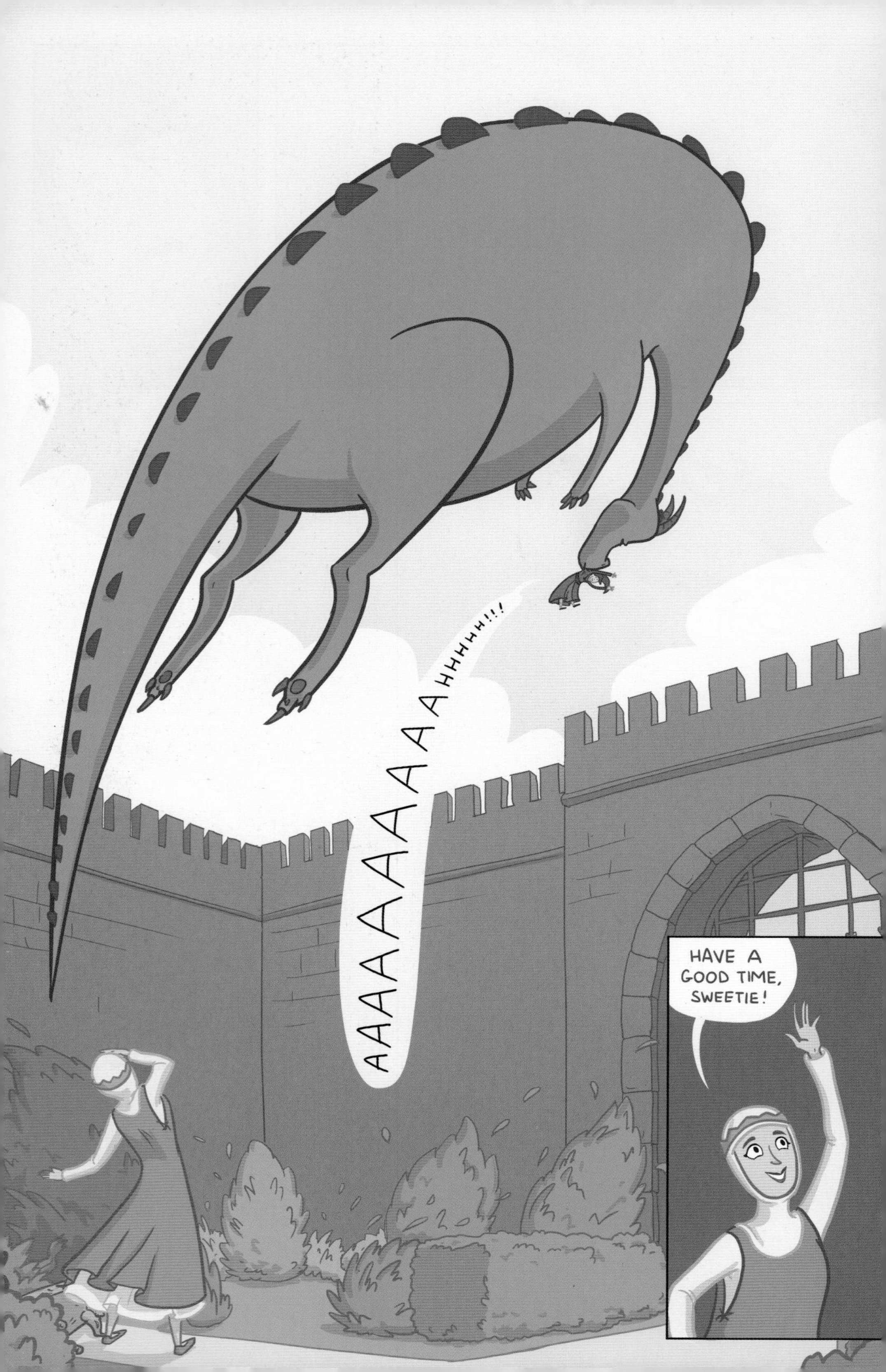
AAAAAAAAAAAHHHHHH!!!
HAVE A GOOD TIME, SWEETIE!

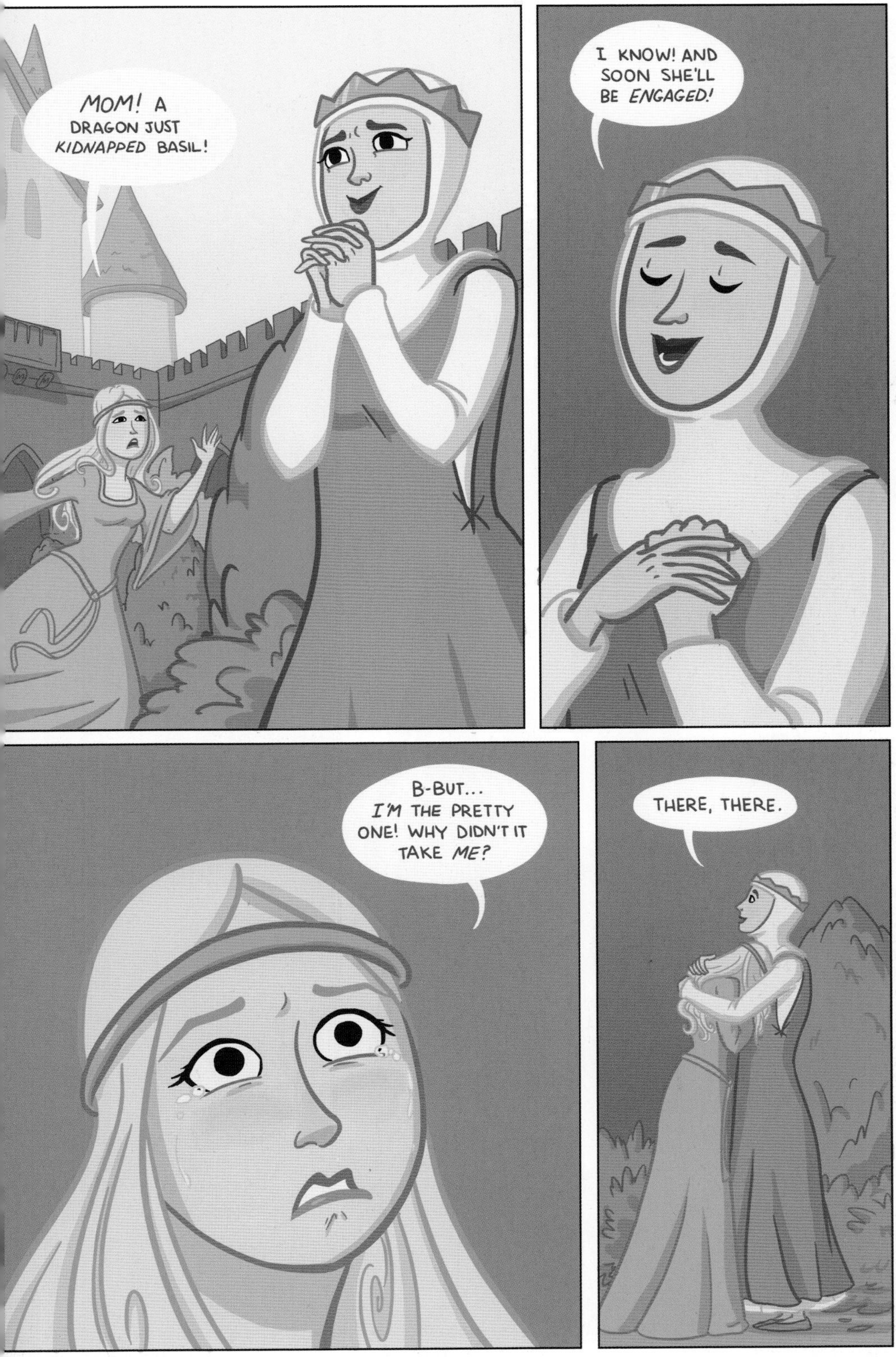
MOM! A DRAGON JUST KIDNAPPED BASIL!
I KNOW! AND SOON SHE'LL BE ENGAGED!
B-BUT... I'M THE PRETTY ONE! WHY DIDN'T IT TAKE ME?
THERE, THERE.

Chapter two

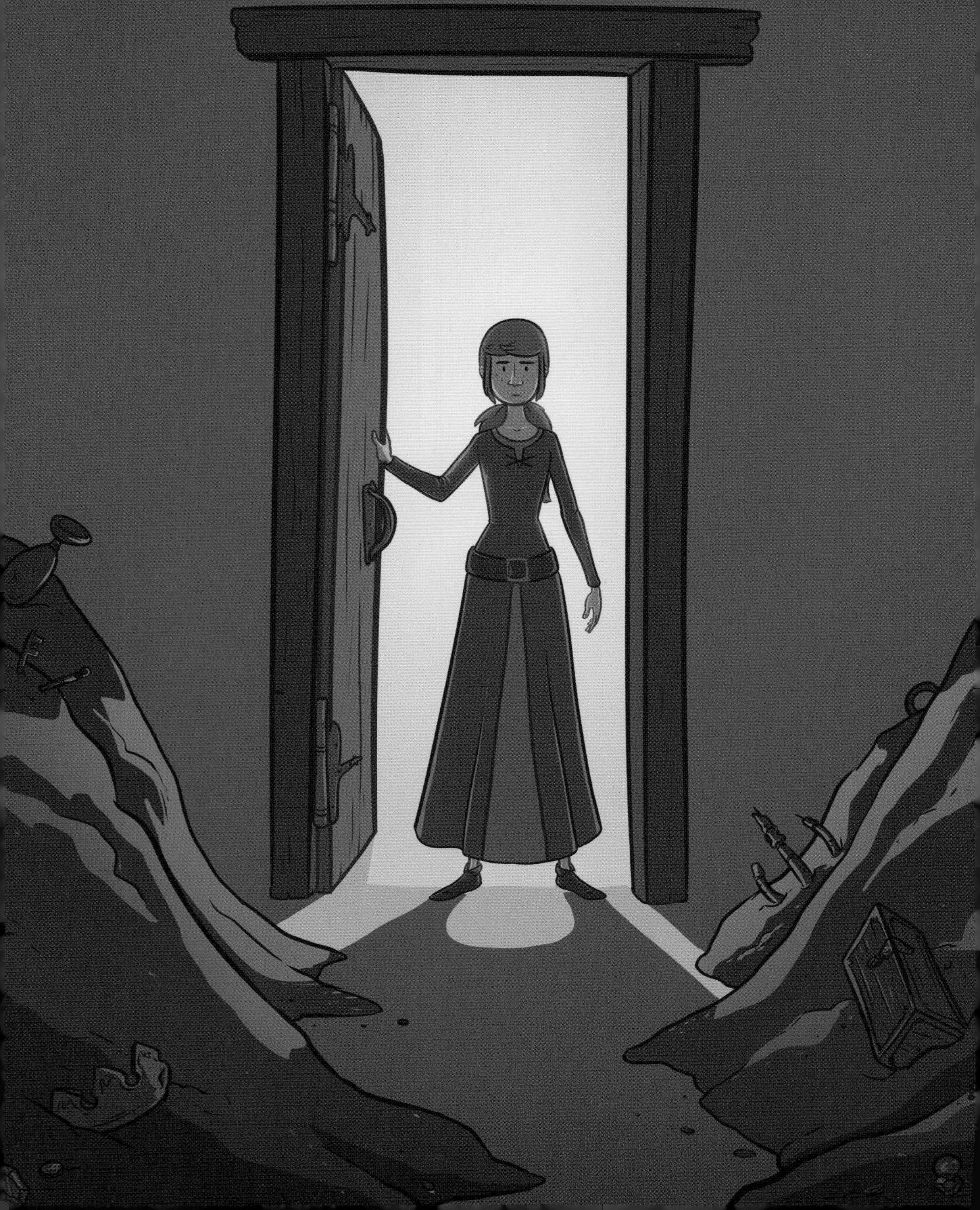

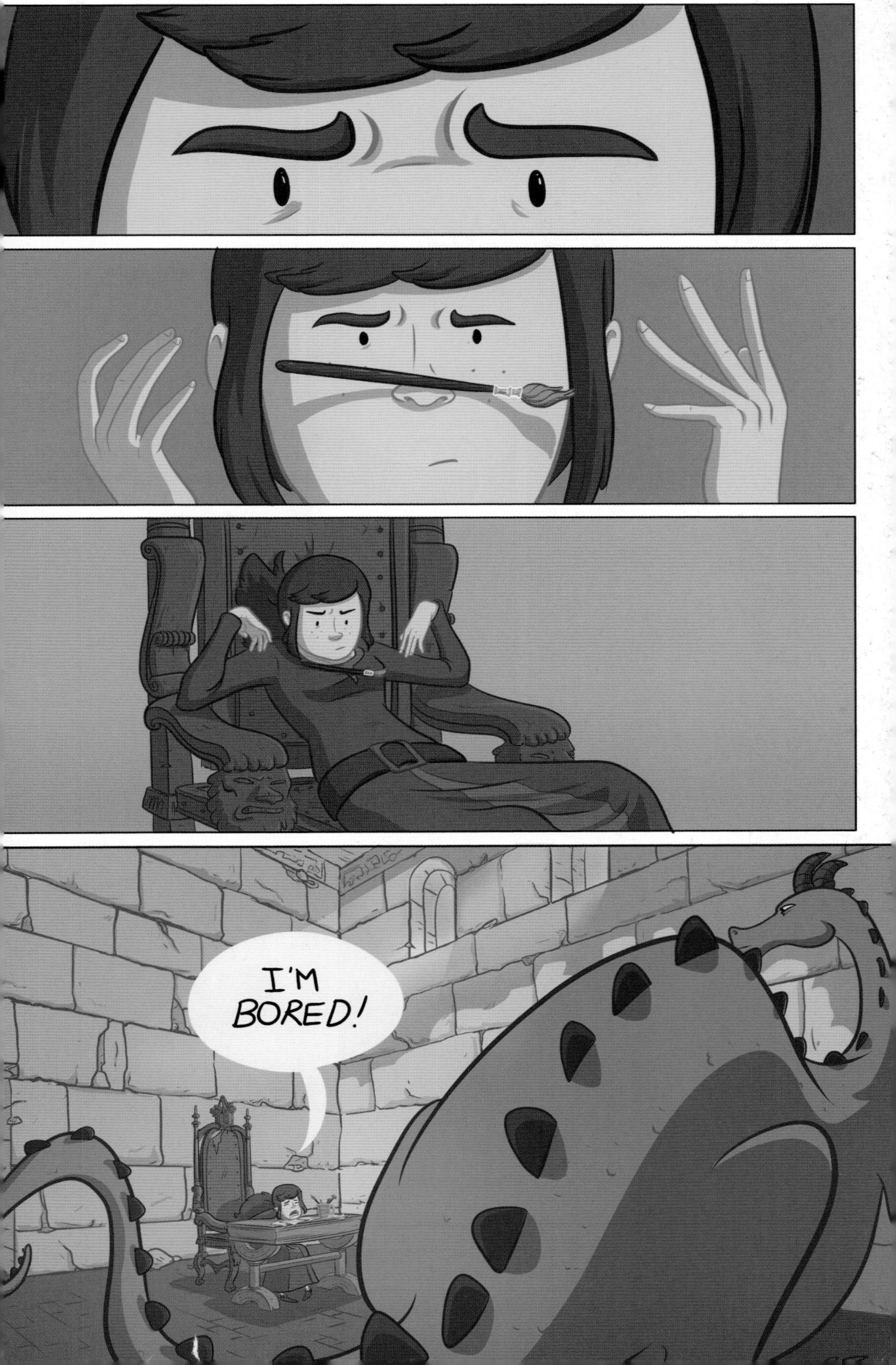
I'M BORED!

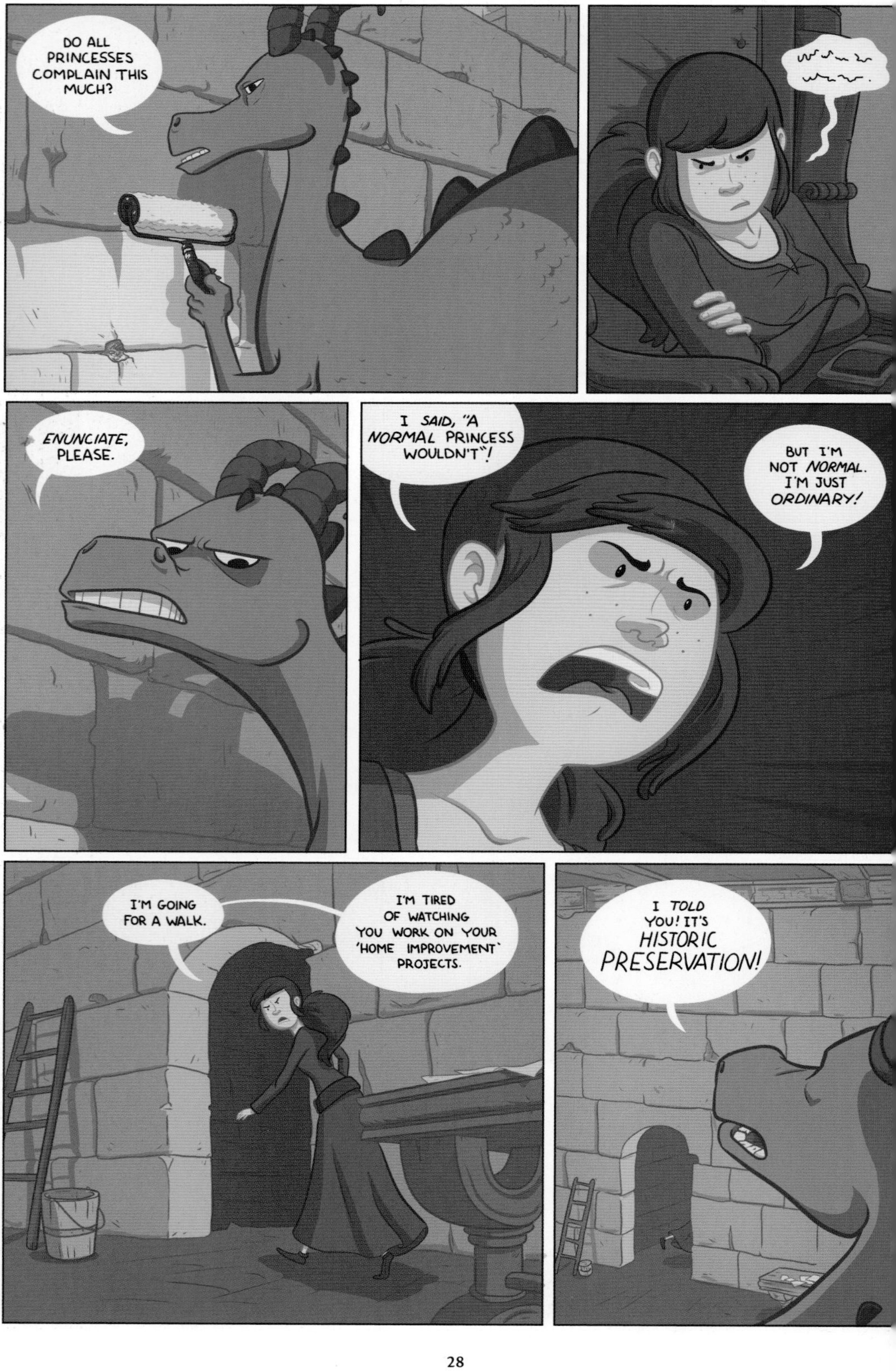
DO ALL PRINCESSES COMPLAIN THIS MUCH?
ENUNCIATE, PLEASE.
I SAID, "A NORMAL PRINCESS WOULDN'T"!
BUT I'M NOT NORMAL. I'M JUST ORDINARY!
I'M GOING FOR A WALK.
I'M TIRED OF WATCHING YOU WORK ON YOUR 'HOME IMPROVEMENT' PROJECTS.
I TOLD YOU! IT'S HISTORIC PRESERVATION!

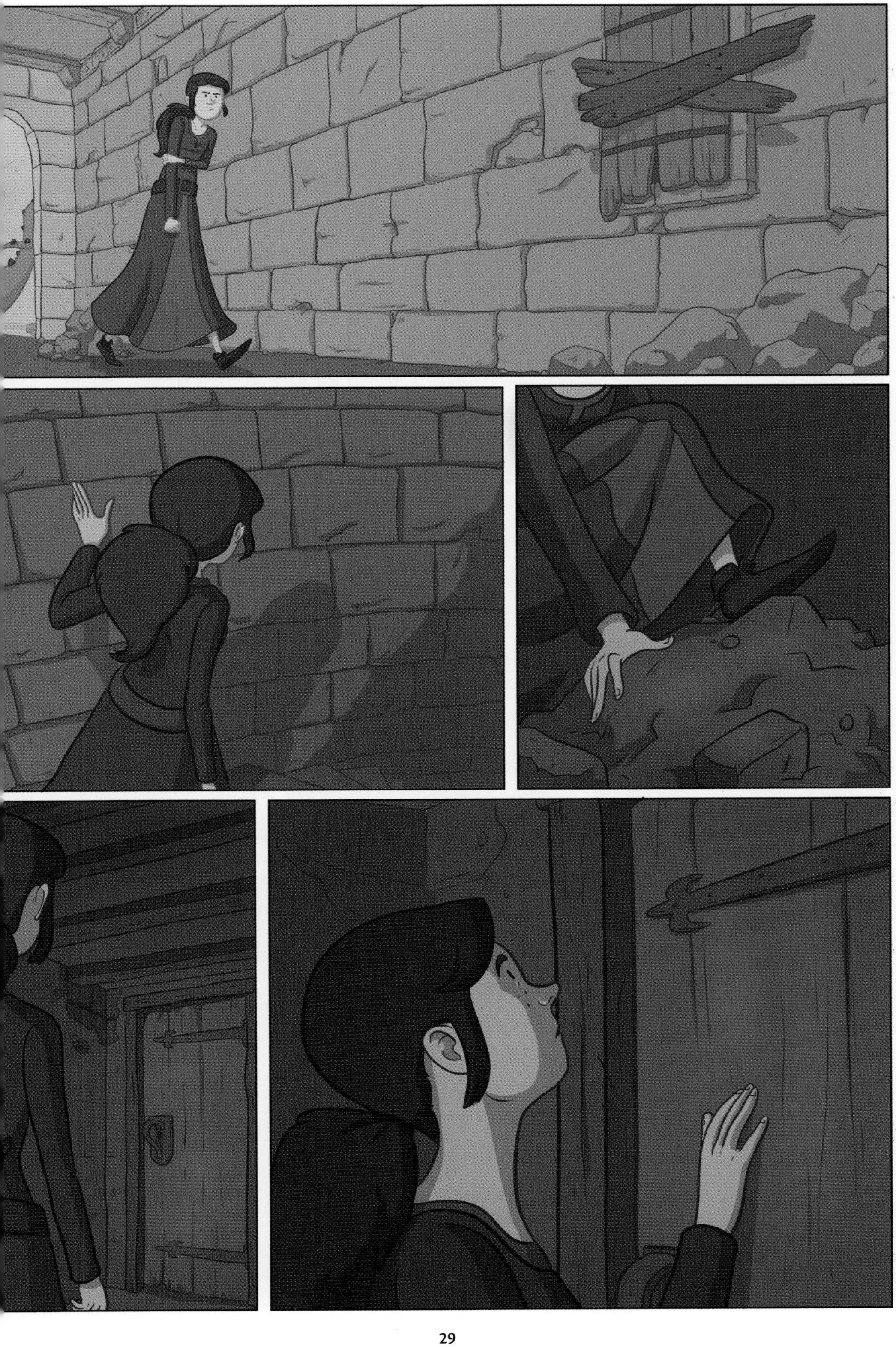

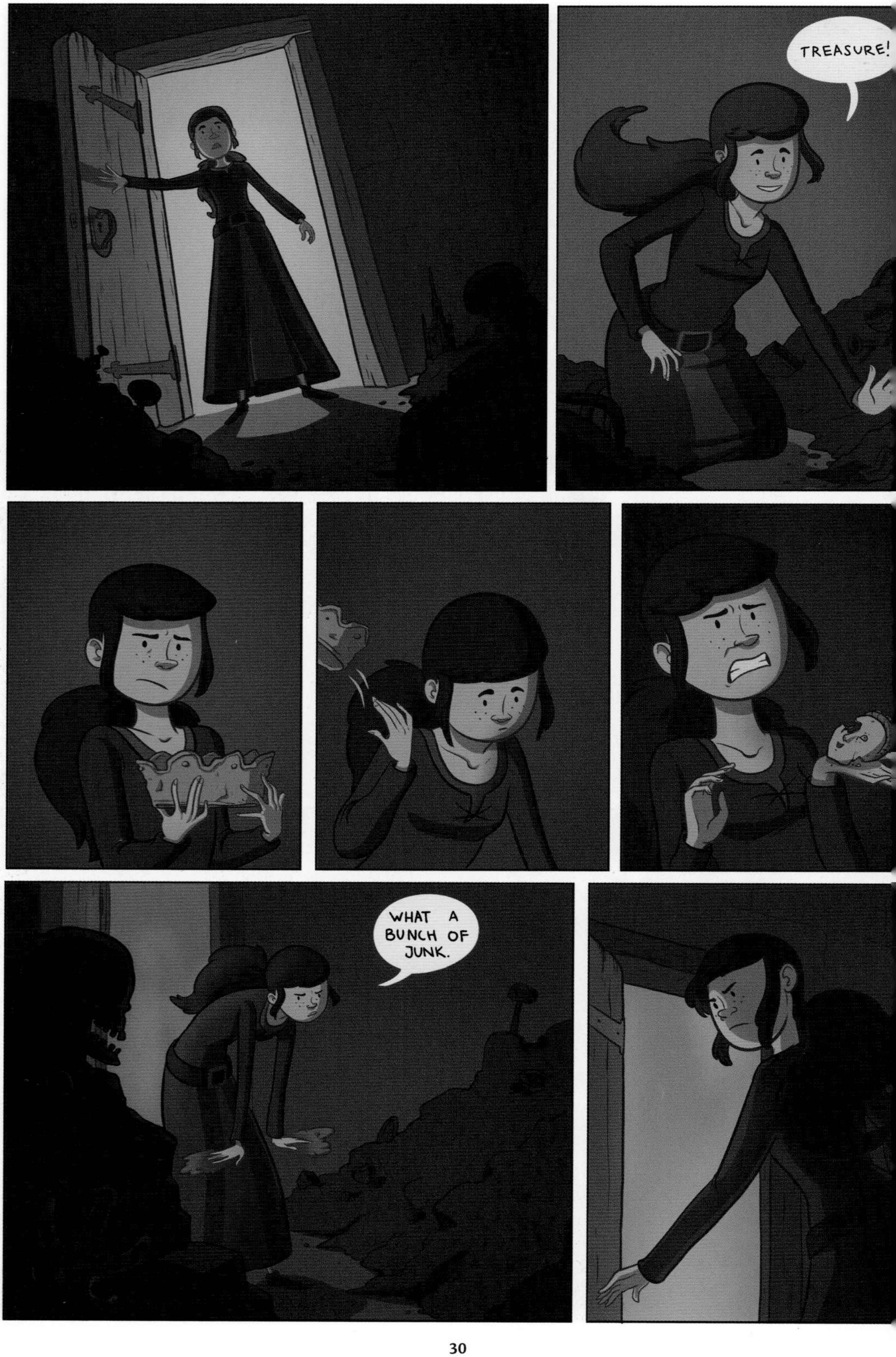
TREASURE!
WHAT A BUNCH OF JUNK.

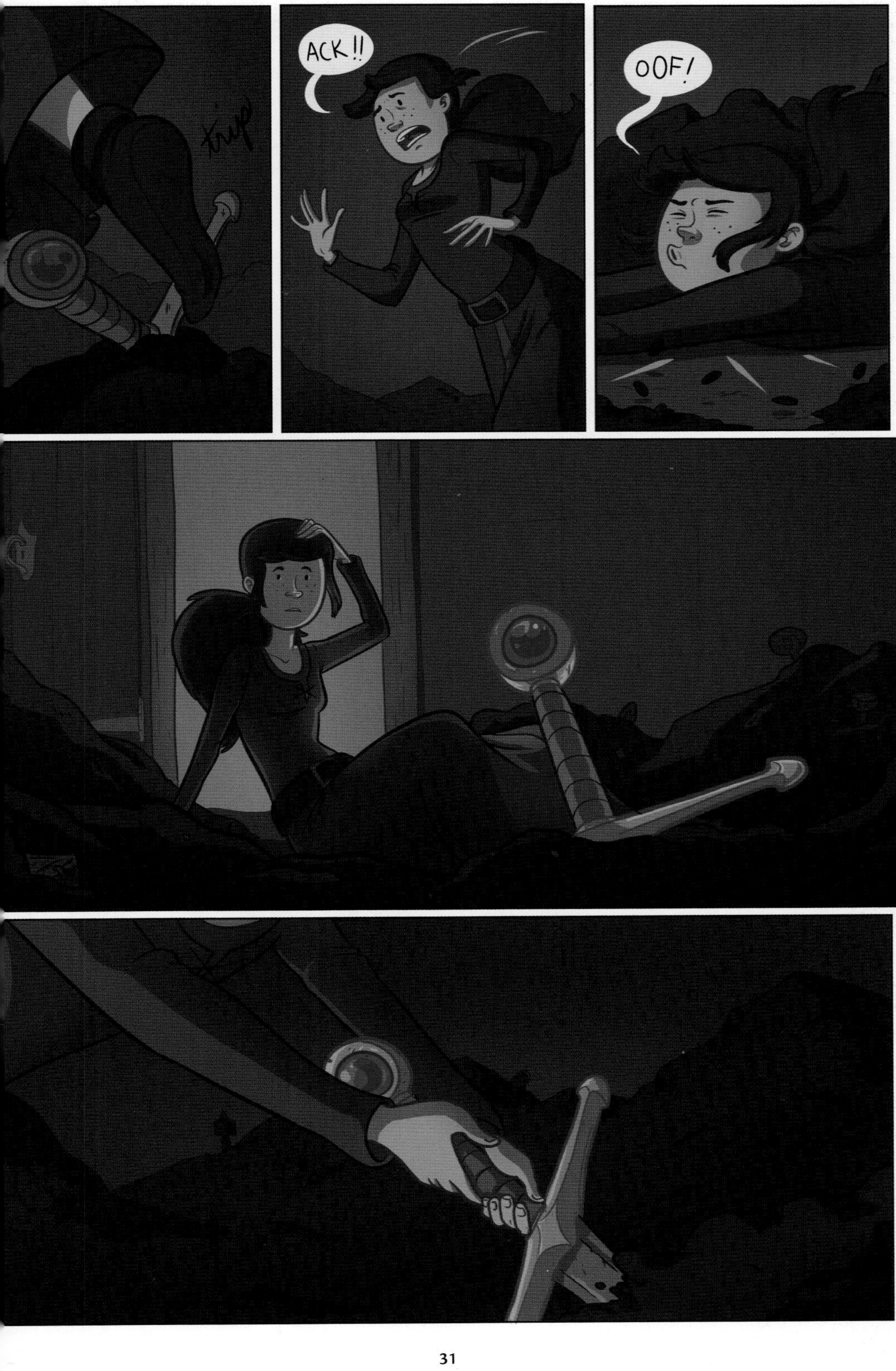
trip
ACK!!
OOF!

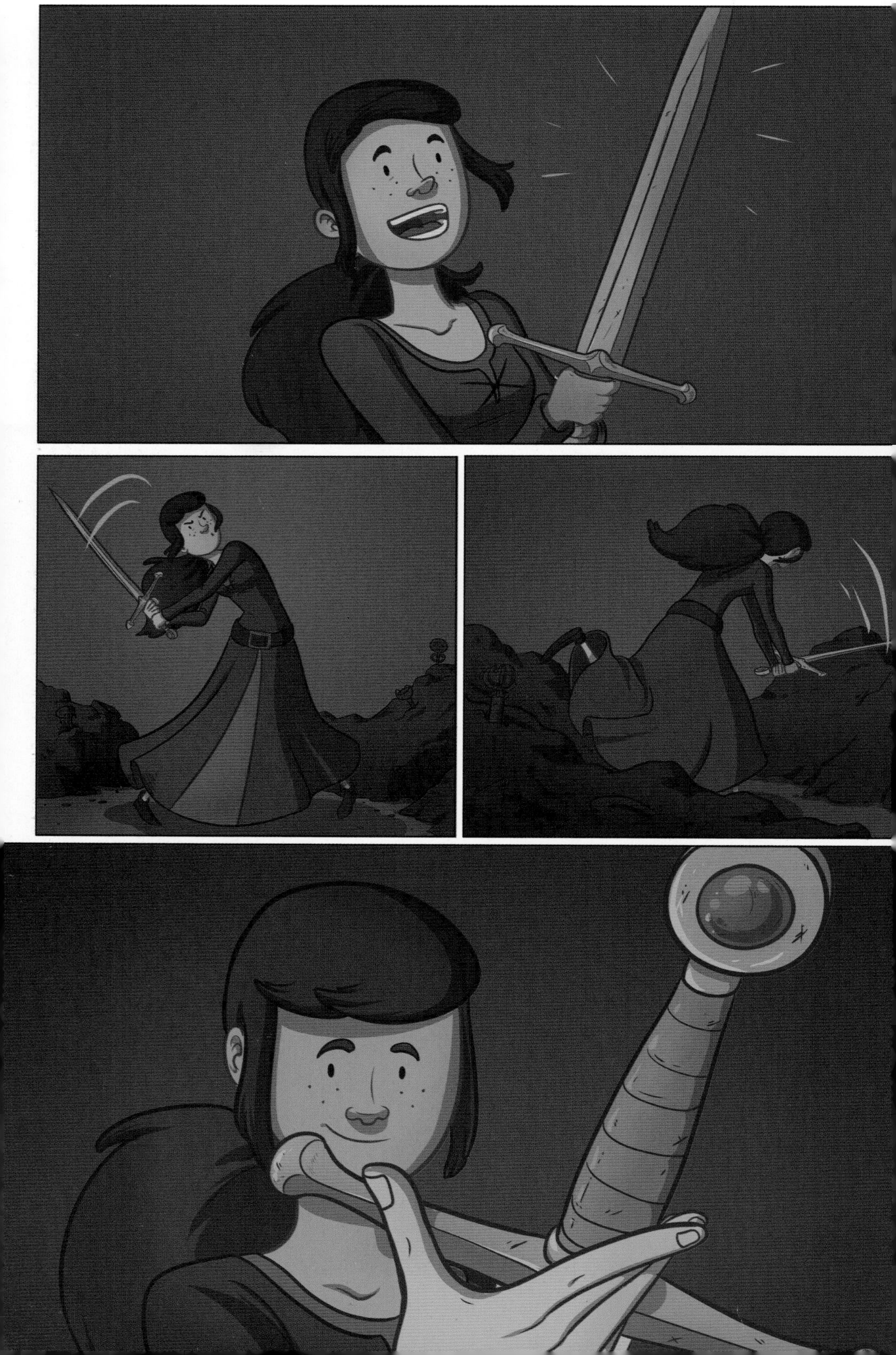

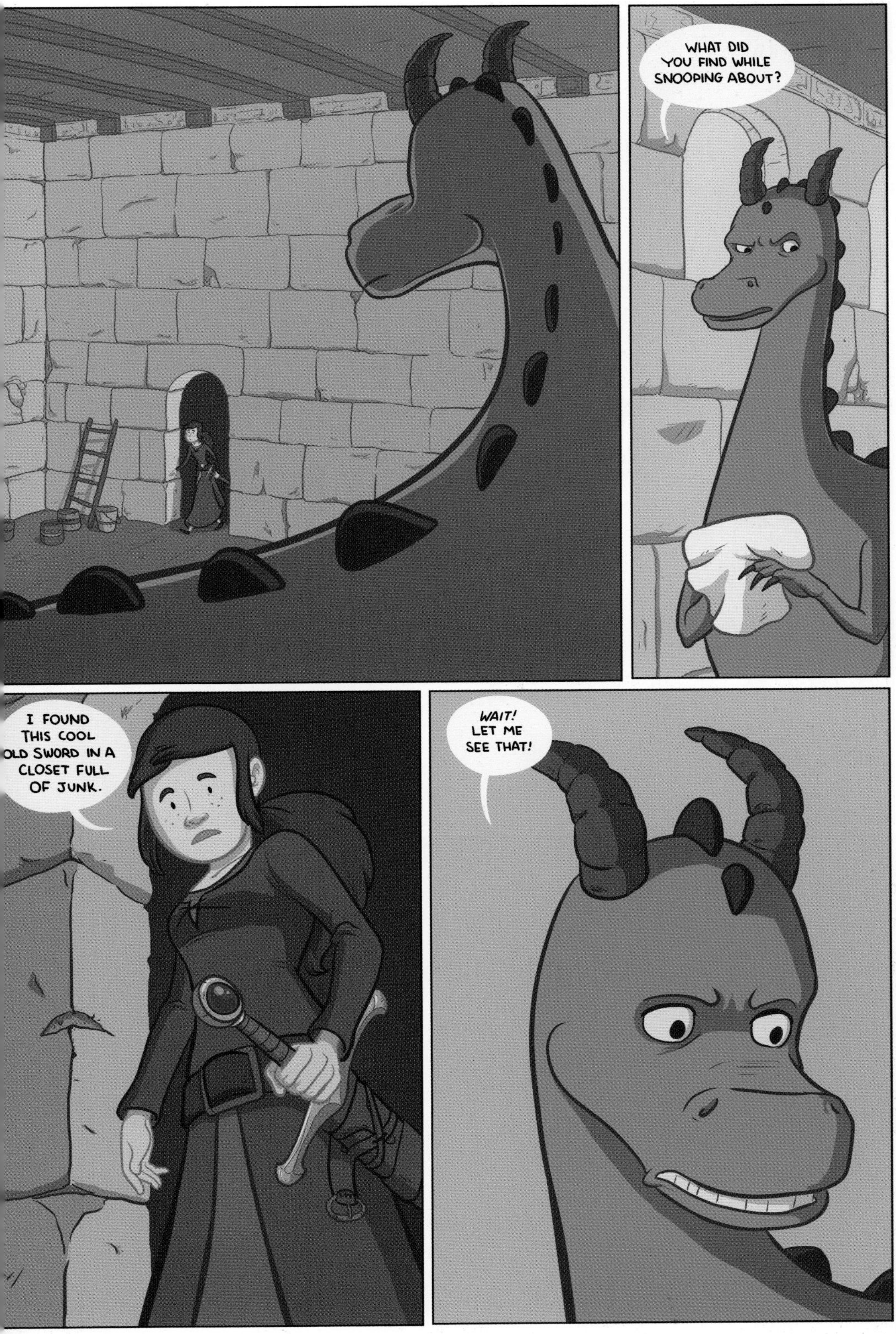
WHAT DID YOU FIND WHILE SNOOPING ABOUT?
I FOUND THIS COOL OLD SWORD IN A CLOSET FULL OF JUNK.
WAIT! LET ME SEE THAT!

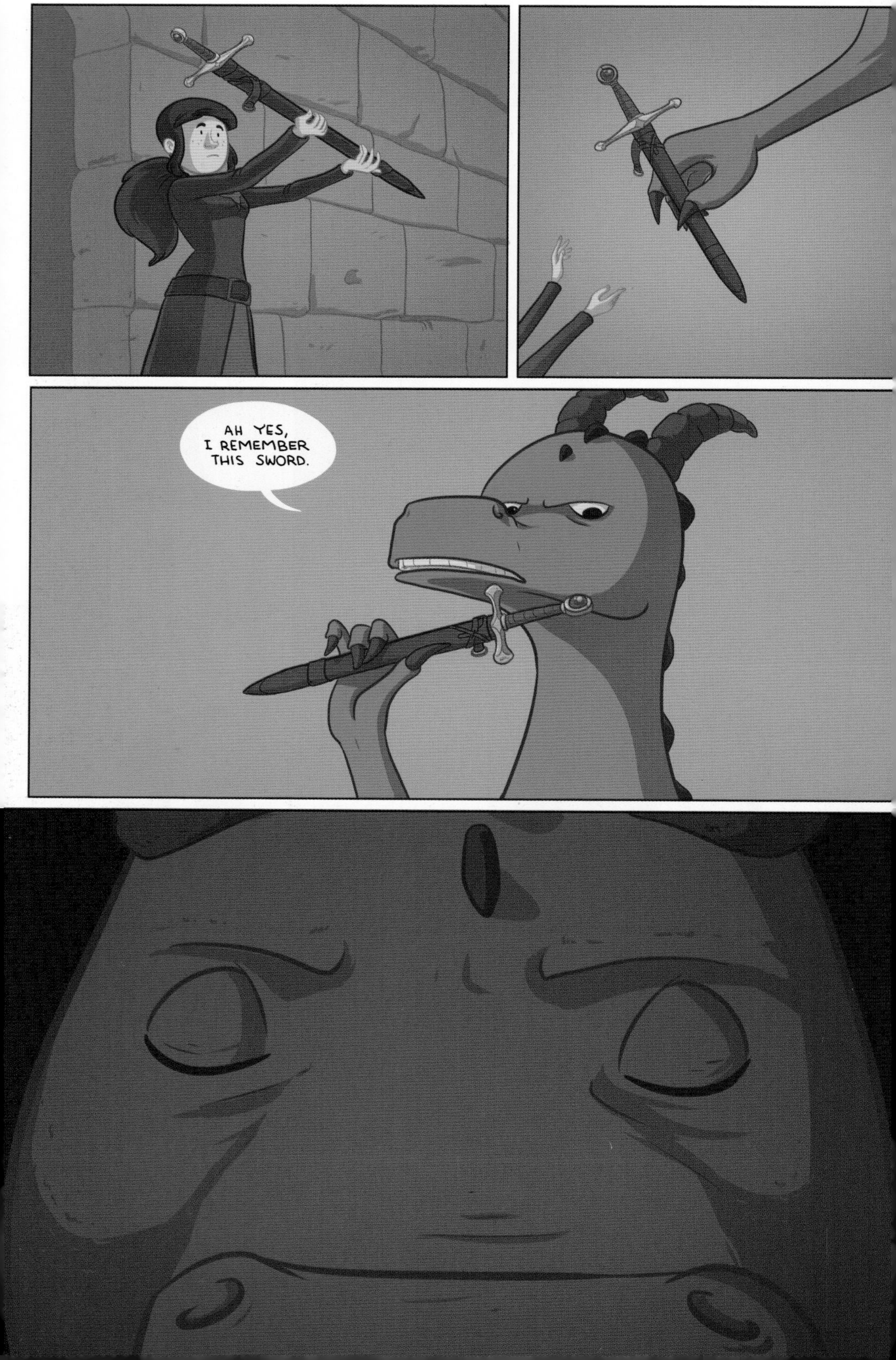
AH YES, I REMEMBER THIS SWORD.

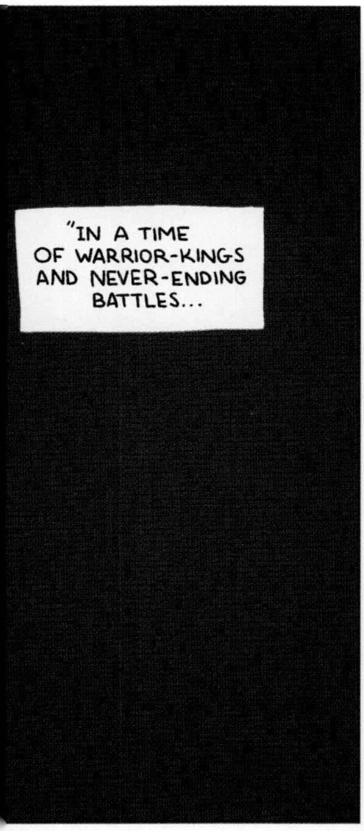
"IN A TIME OF WARRIOR-KINGS AND NEVER-ENDING BATTLES...

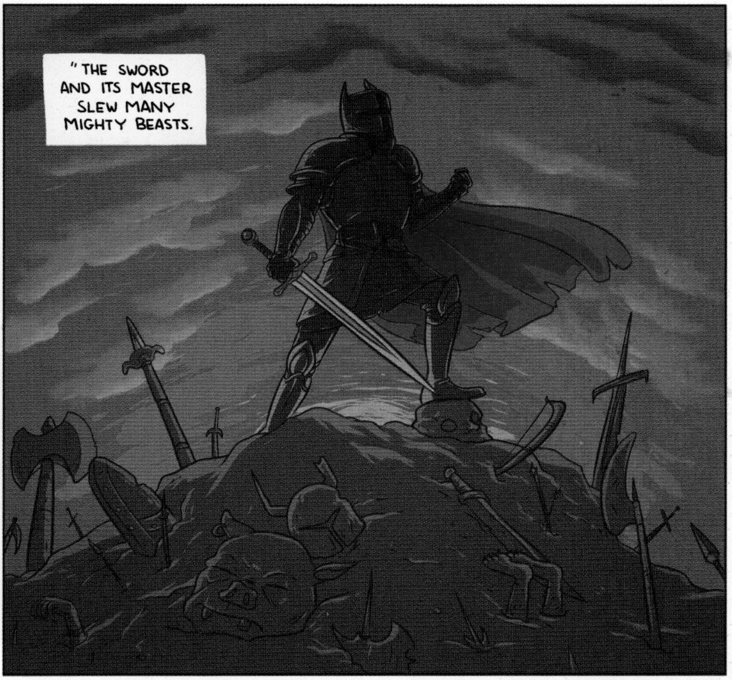
"THE SWORD AND ITS MASTER SLEW MANY MIGHTY BEASTS.

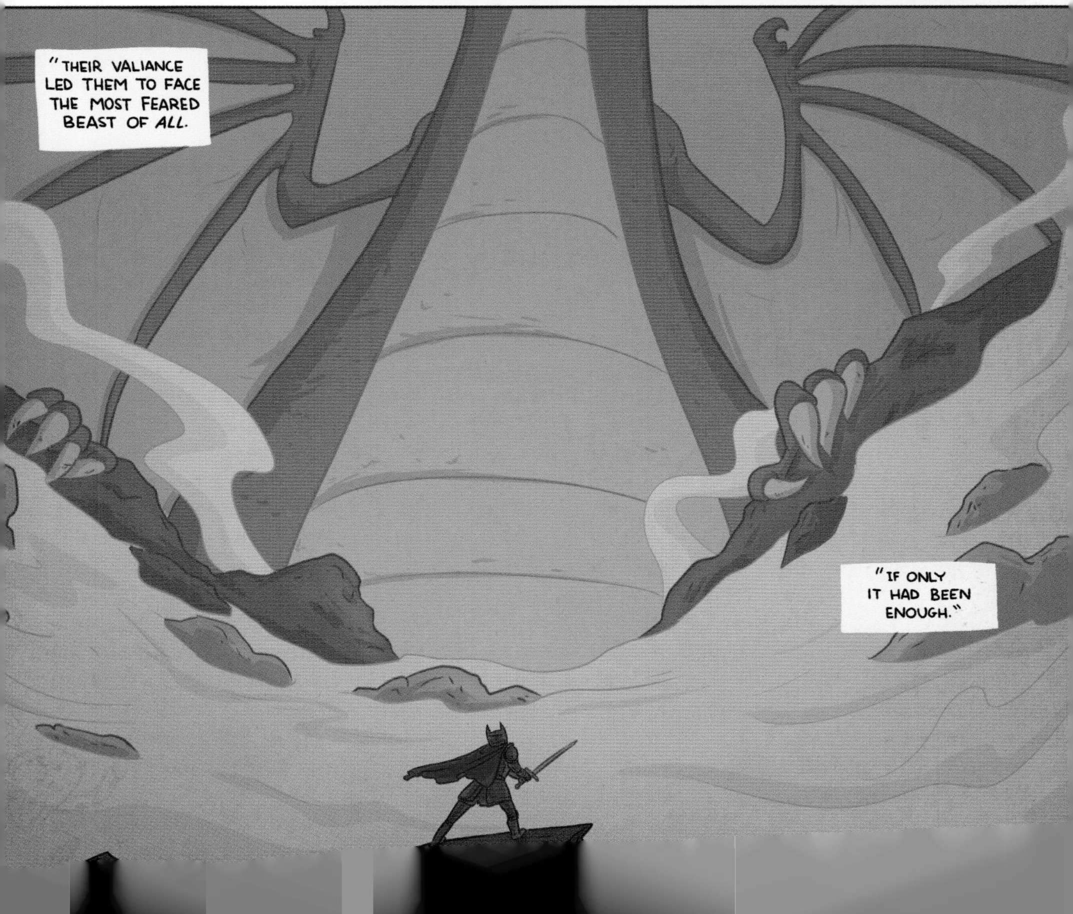
"THEIR VALIANCE LED THEM TO FACE THE MOST FEARED BEAST OF *ALL*.
"IF ONLY IT HAD BEEN ENOUGH."

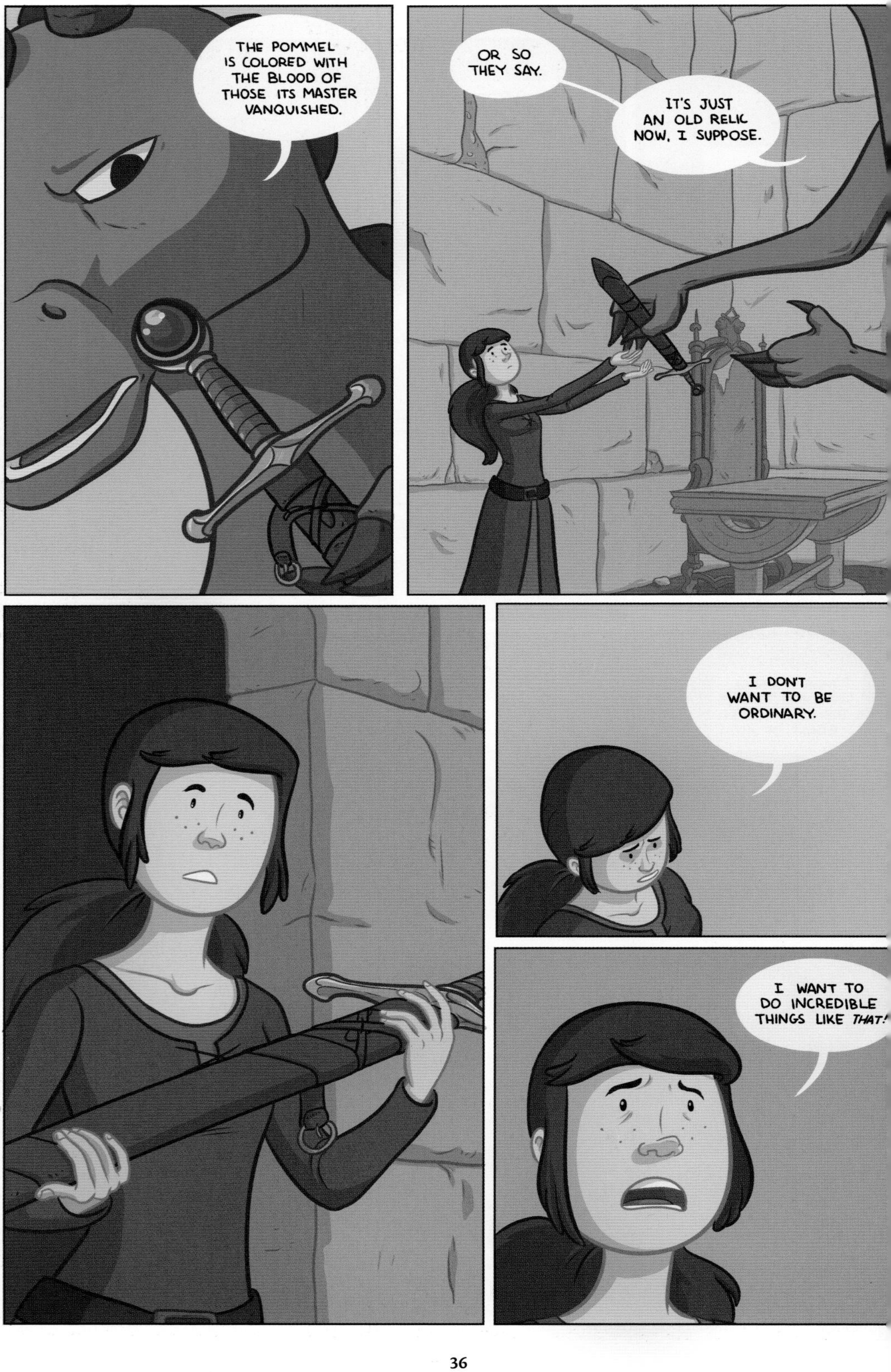
THE POMMEL IS COLORED WITH THE BLOOD OF THOSE ITS MASTER VANQUISHED.
OR SO THEY SAY.
IT'S JUST AN OLD RELIC NOW, I SUPPOSE.
I DON'T WANT TO BE ORDINARY.
I WANT TO DO INCREDIBLE THINGS LIKE *THAT!*

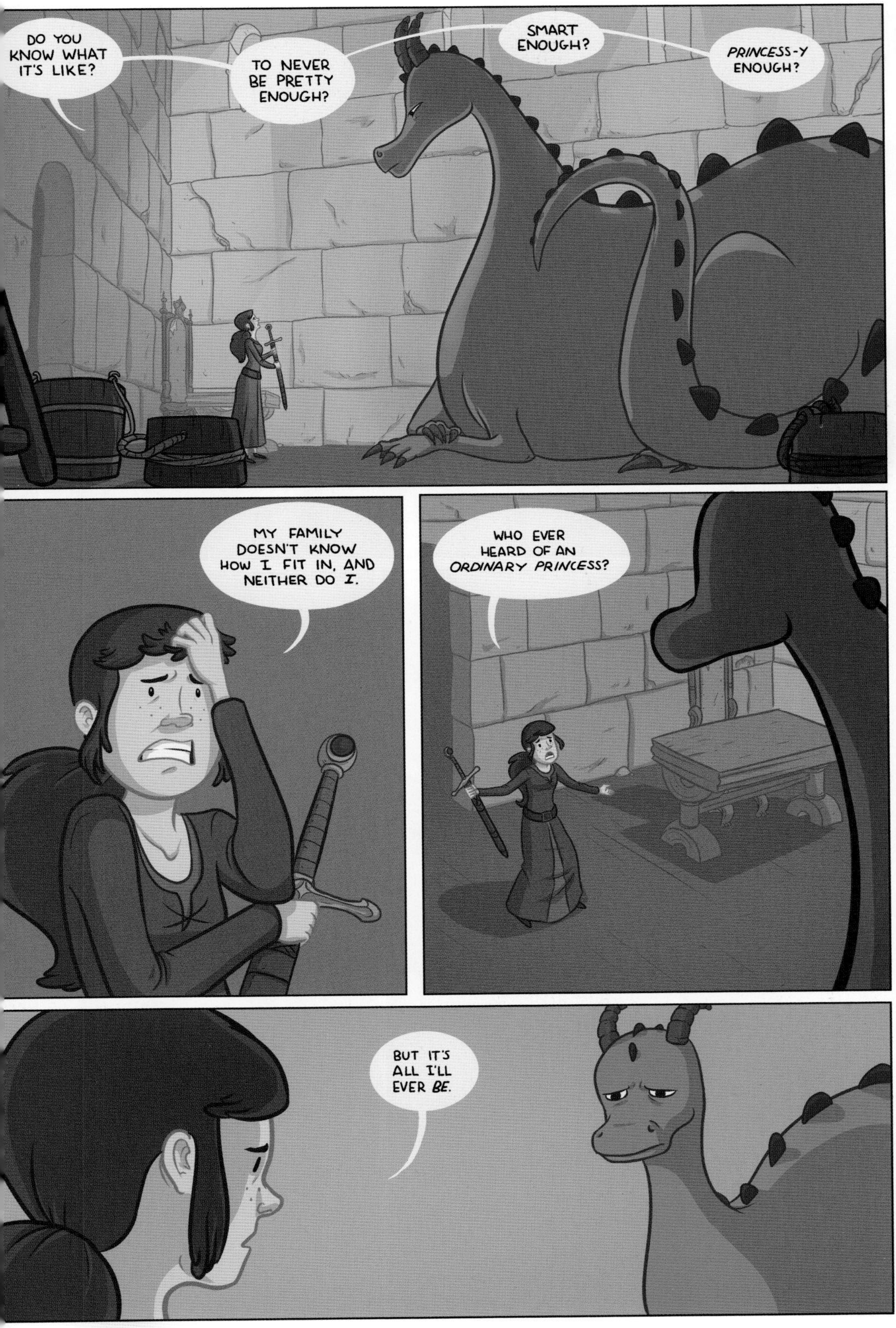
DO YOU KNOW WHAT IT'S LIKE?
TO NEVER BE PRETTY ENOUGH?
SMART ENOUGH?
PRINCESS-Y ENOUGH?
MY FAMILY DOESN'T KNOW HOW I FIT IN, AND NEITHER DO *I*.
WHO EVER HEARD OF AN *ORDINARY PRINCESS*?
BUT IT'S ALL I'LL EVER *BE*.

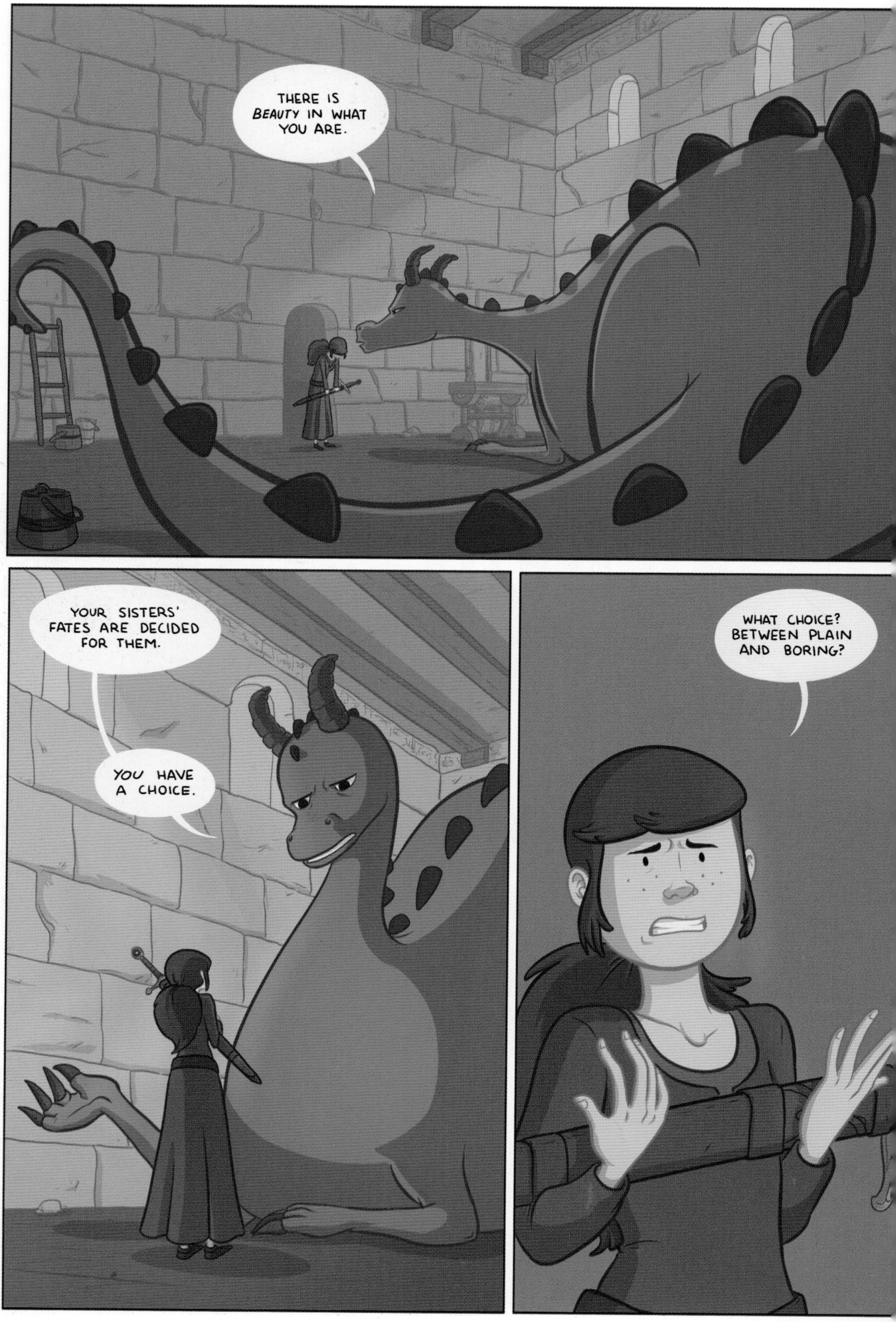
THERE IS BEAUTY IN WHAT YOU ARE.
YOUR SISTERS' FATES ARE DECIDED FOR THEM.
YOU HAVE A CHOICE.
WHAT CHOICE? BETWEEN PLAIN AND BORING?

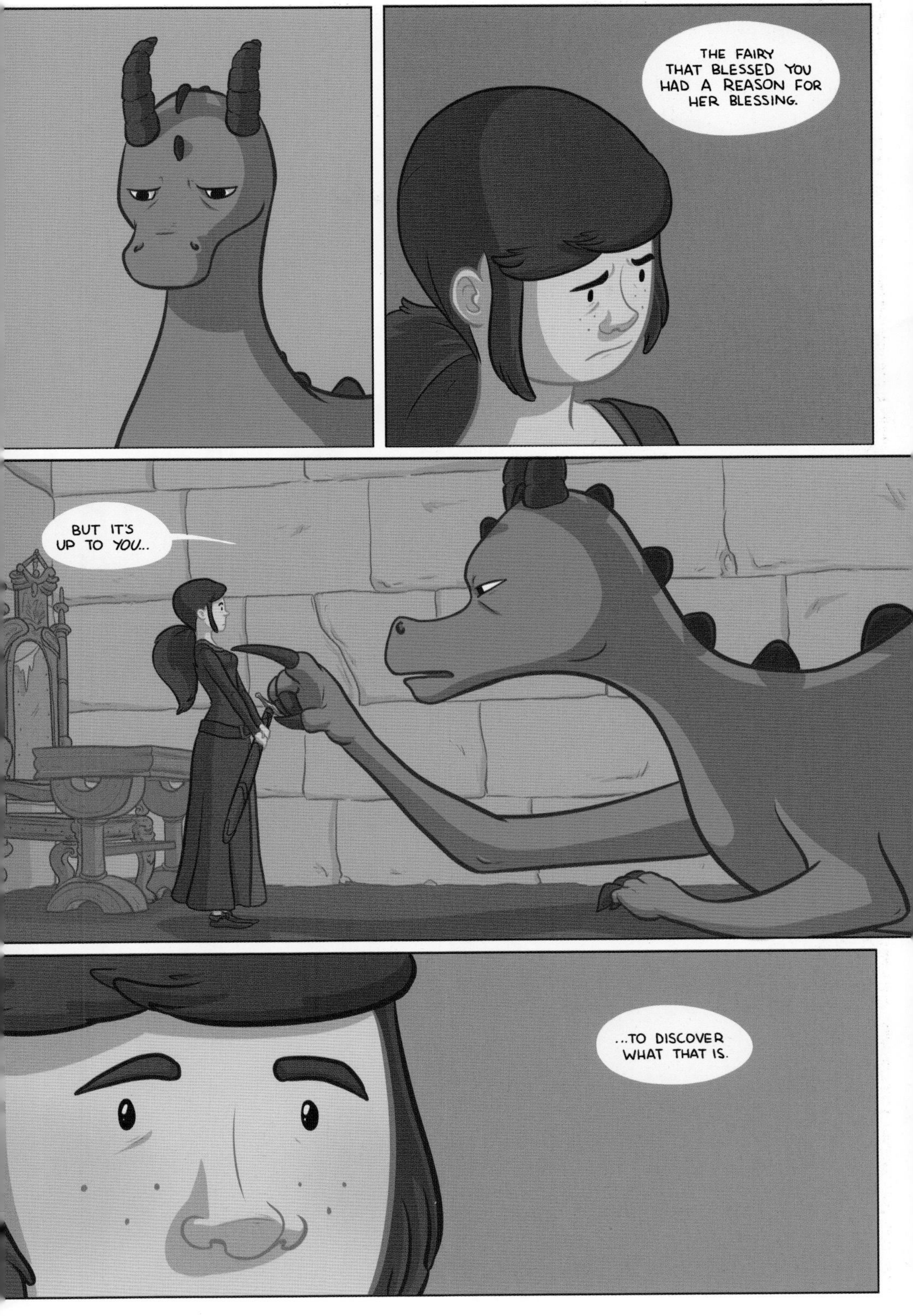
THE FAIRY THAT BLESSED YOU HAD A REASON FOR HER BLESSING.
BUT IT'S UP TO *YOU*...
...TO DISCOVER WHAT THAT IS.

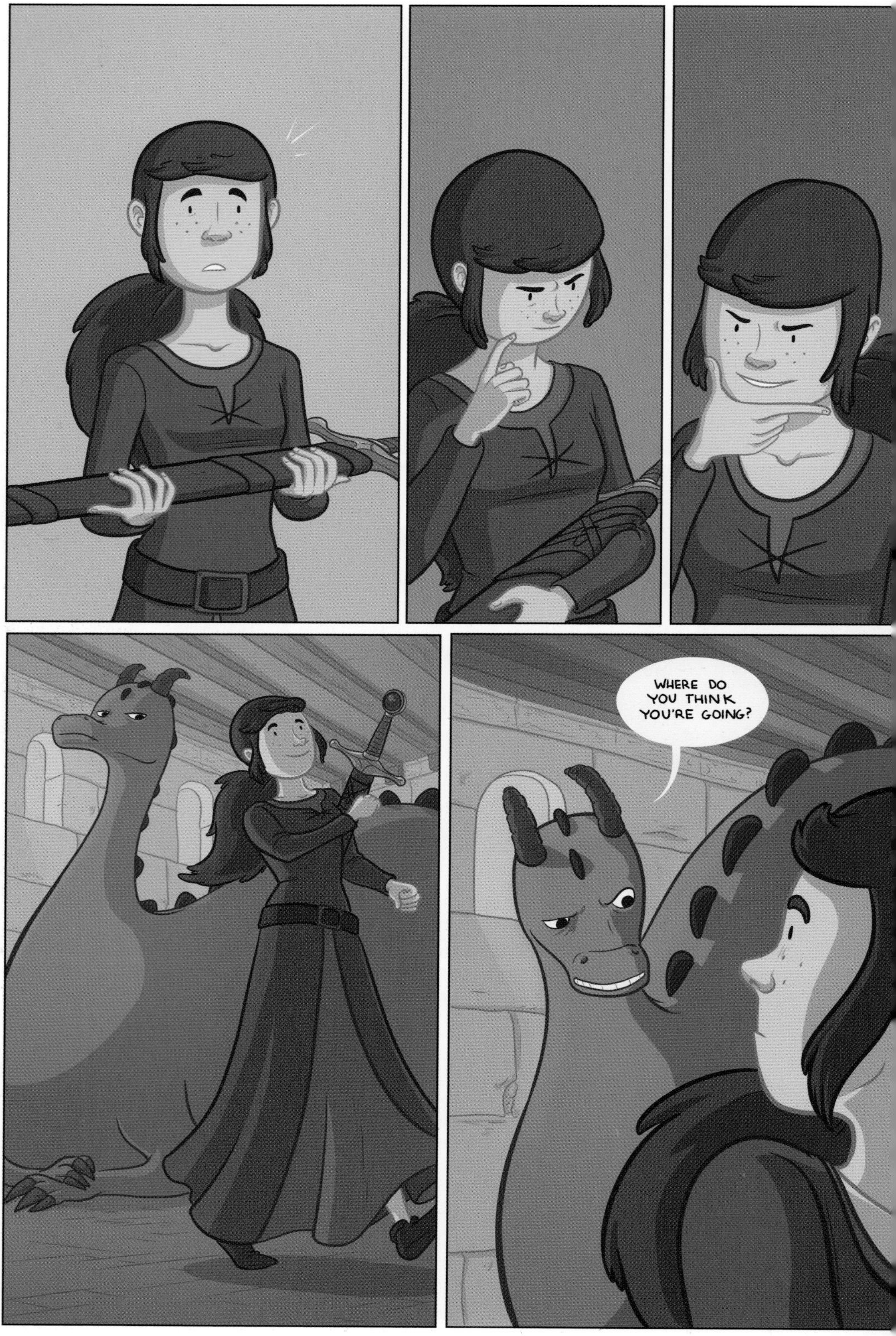
WHERE DO YOU THINK YOU'RE GOING?

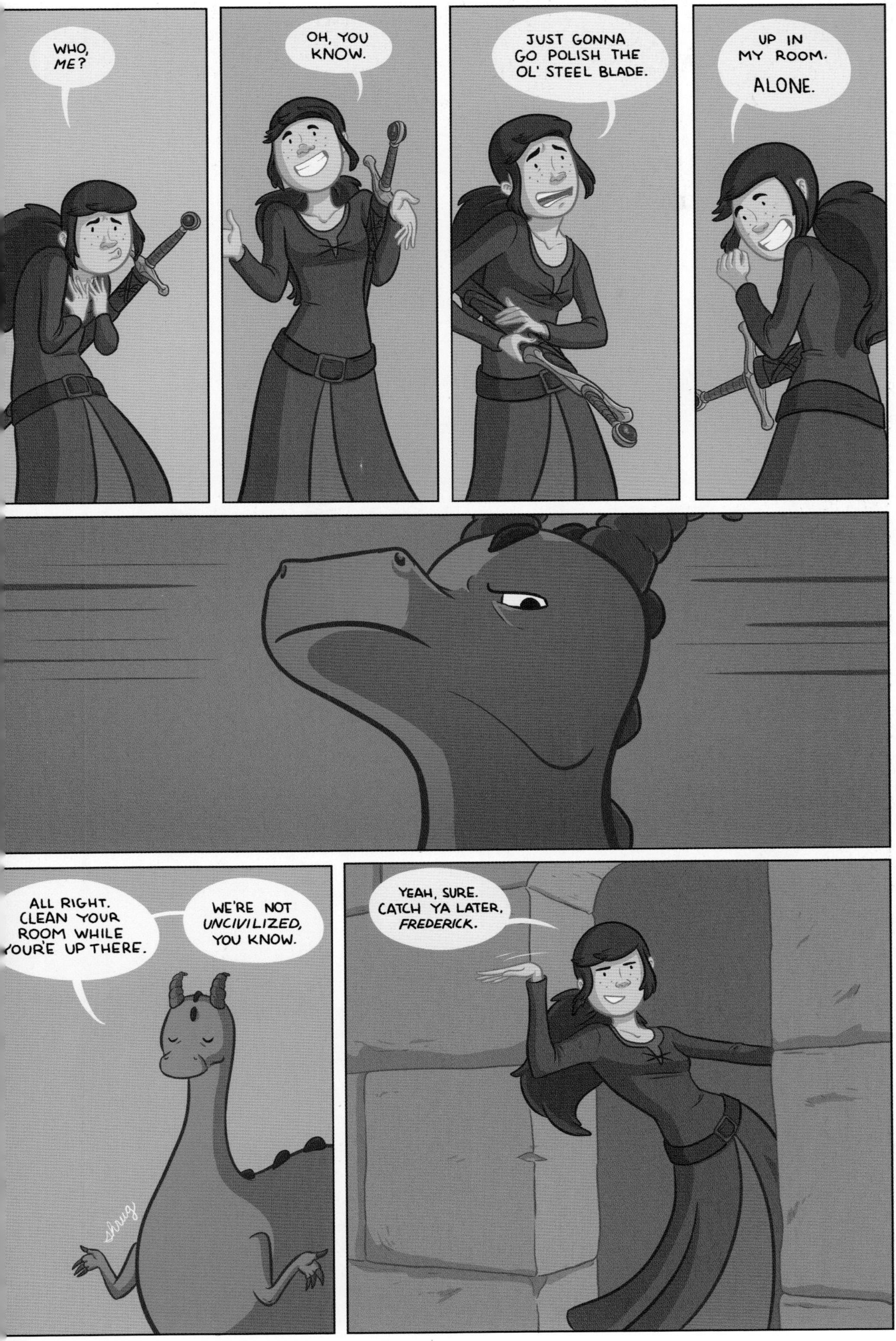
WHO, *ME*?
OH, YOU KNOW.
JUST GONNA GO POLISH THE OL' STEEL BLADE.
UP IN MY ROOM.
ALONE.
ALL RIGHT. CLEAN YOUR ROOM WHILE YOU'RE UP THERE.
WE'RE NOT *UNCIVILIZED*, YOU KNOW.
shrug
YEAH, SURE. CATCH YA LATER, *FREDERICK*.

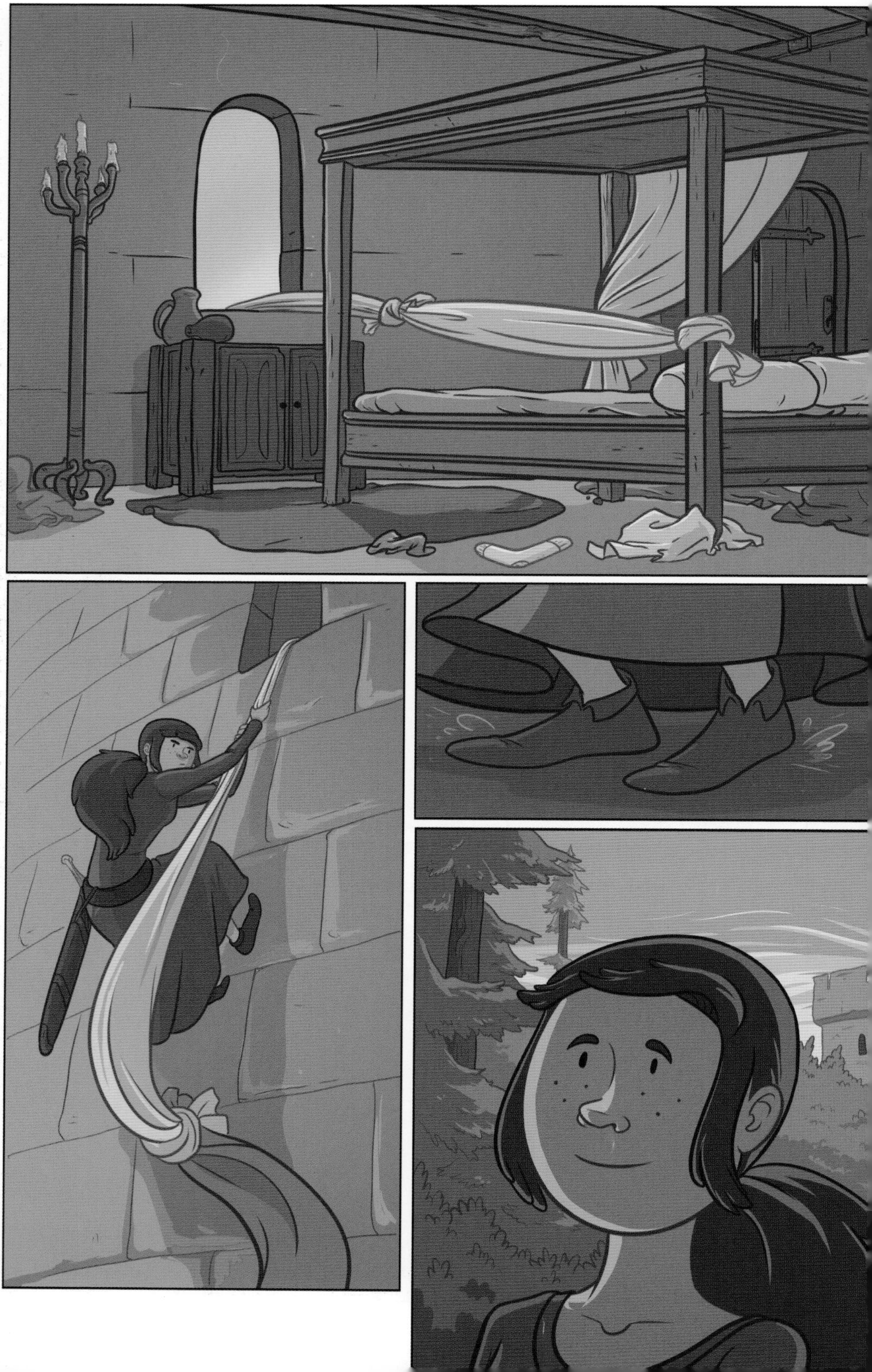

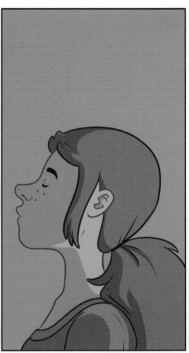

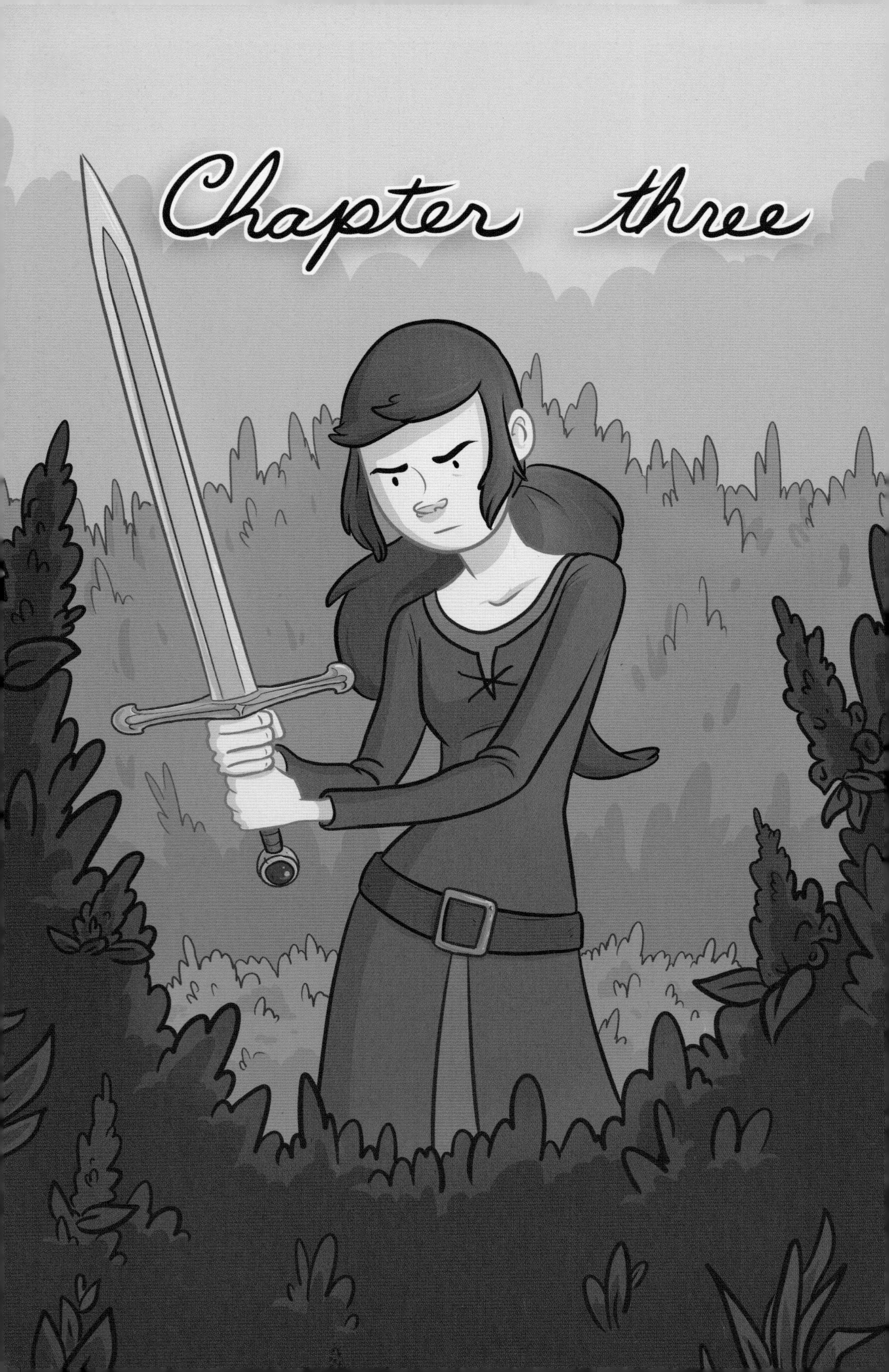
Chapter three

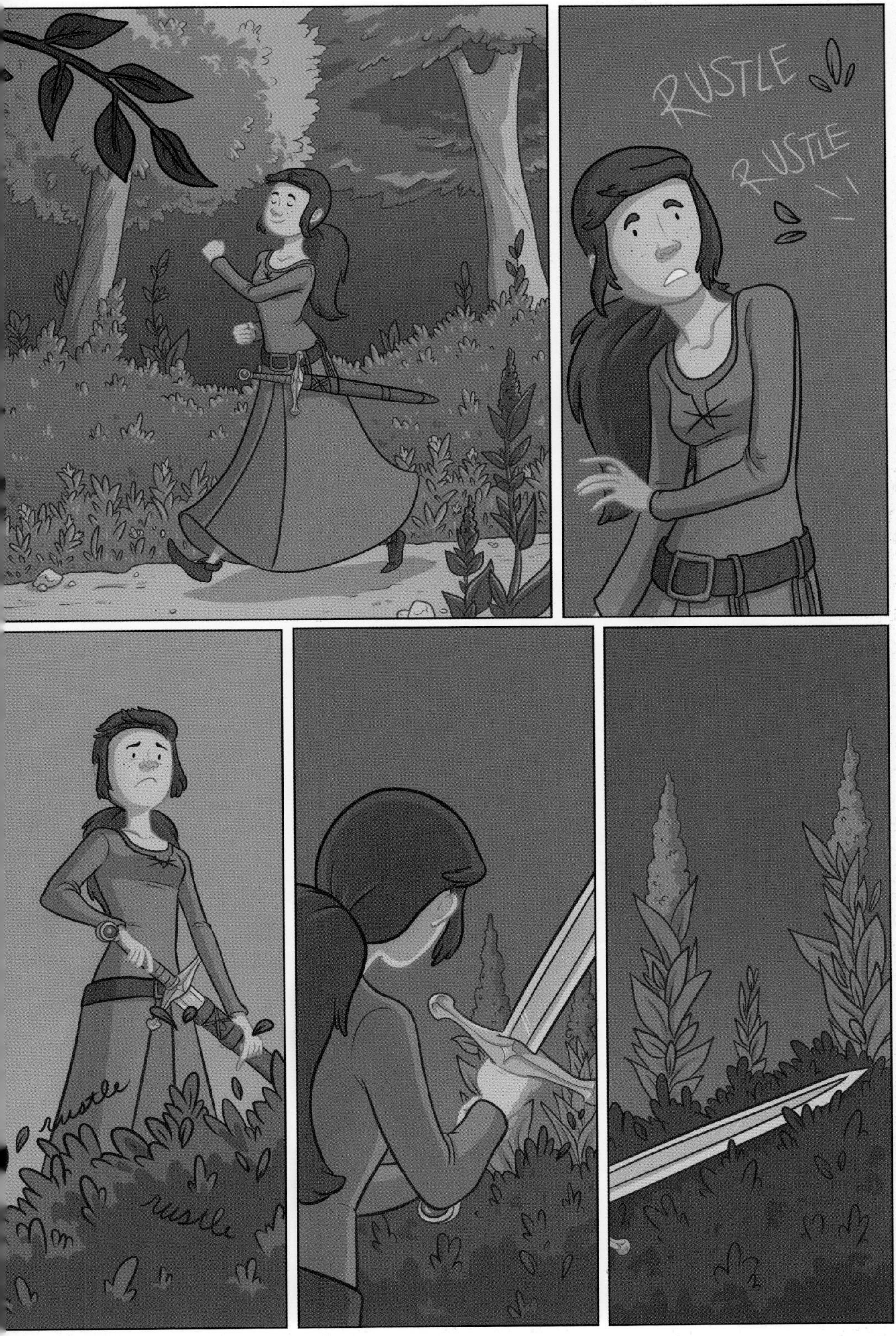
RUSTLE
RUSTLE
rustle
rustle

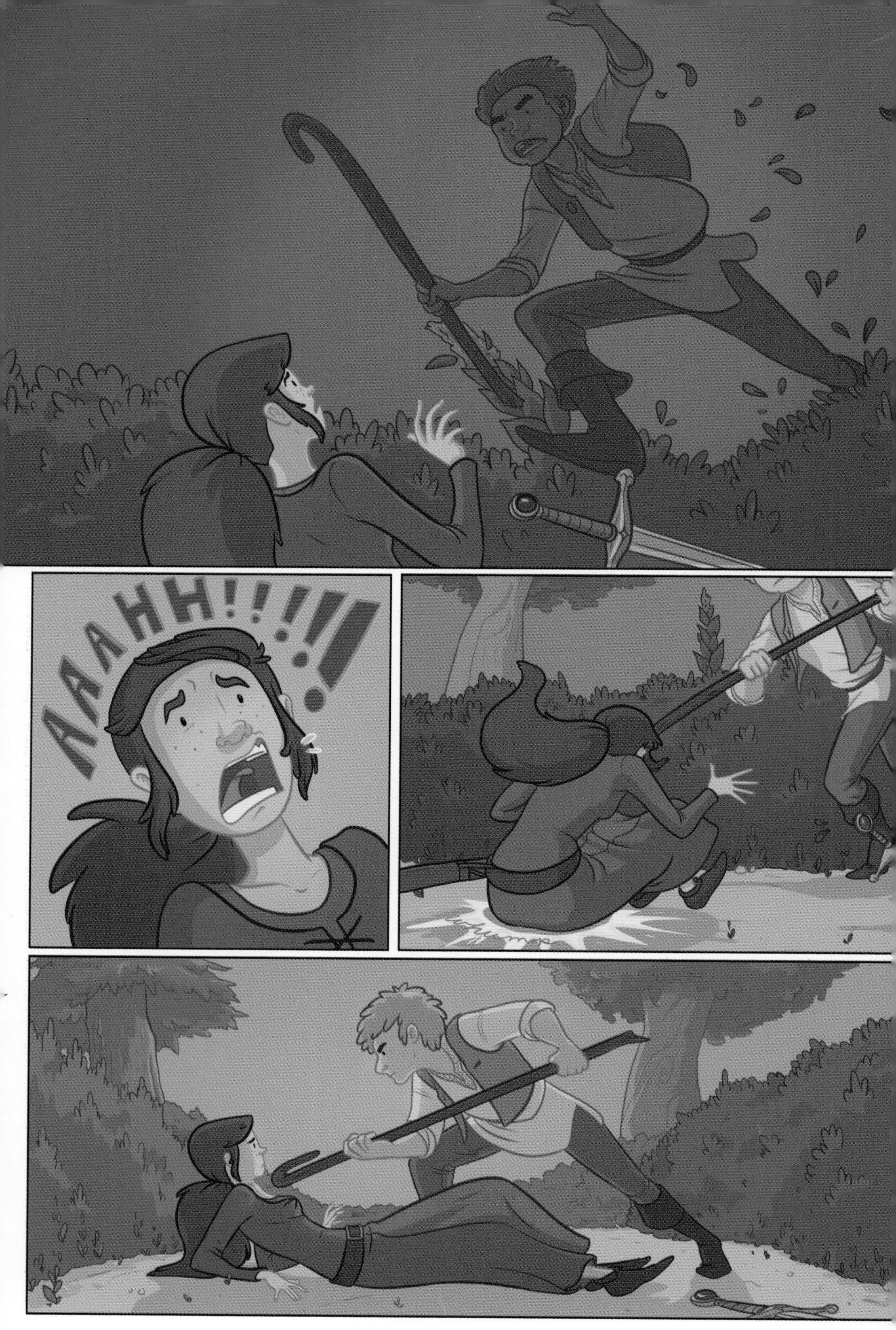
AAAHH!!!!!
whump

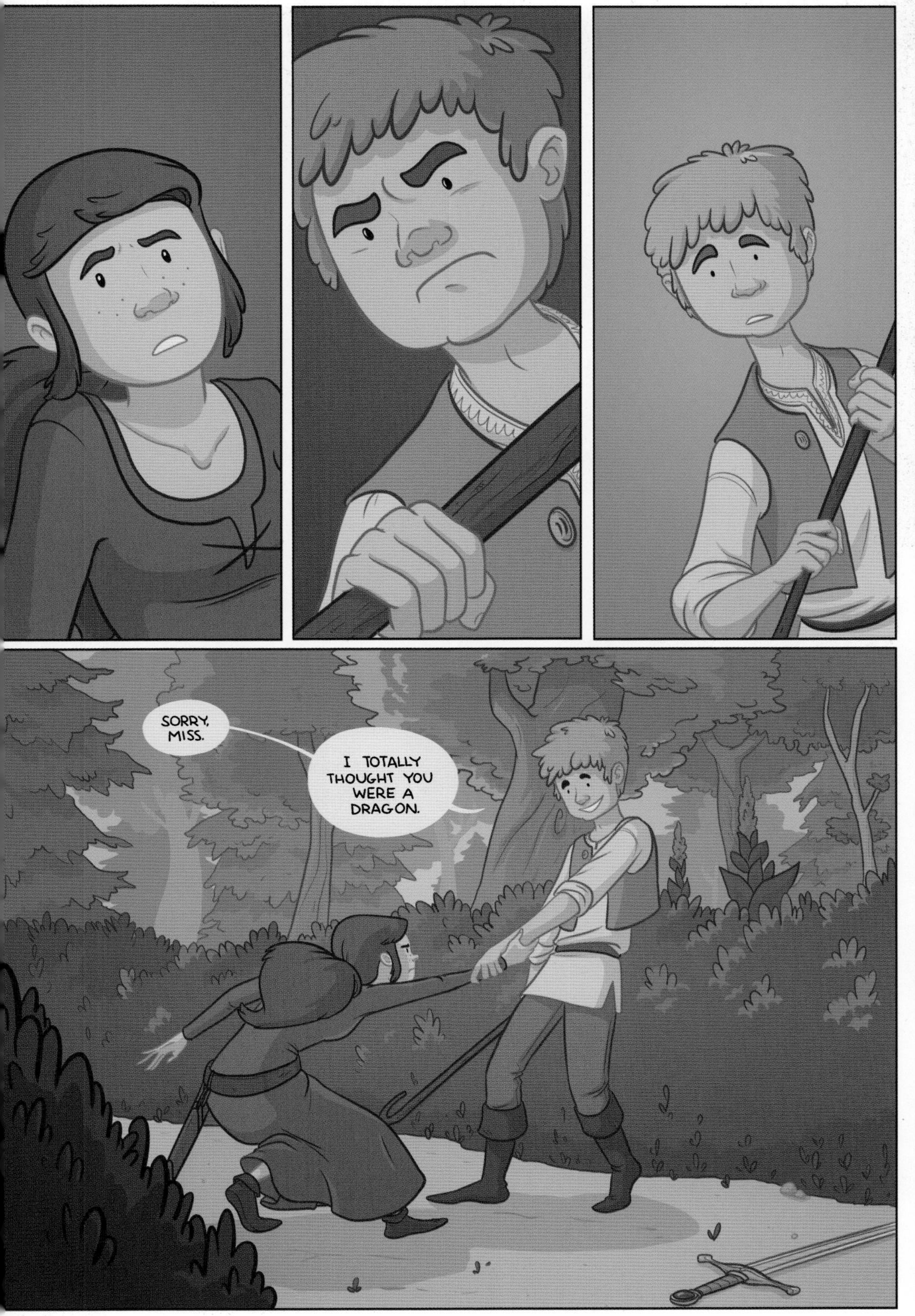
SORRY, MISS.
I TOTALLY THOUGHT YOU WERE A DRAGON.

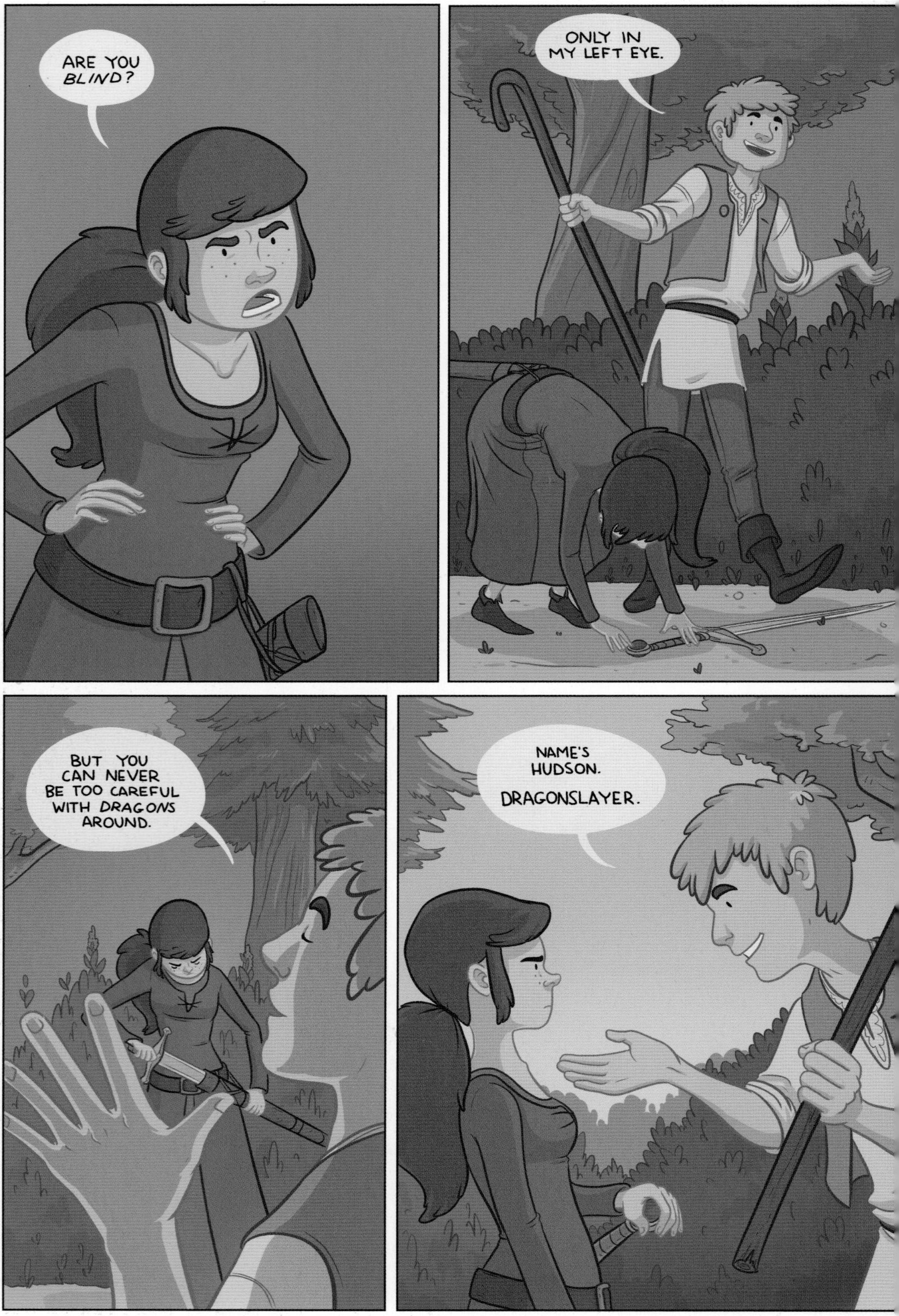
ARE YOU *BLIND*?
ONLY IN MY LEFT EYE.
BUT YOU CAN NEVER BE TOO CAREFUL WITH *DRAGONS* AROUND.
NAME'S HUDSON.
DRAGONSLAYER.

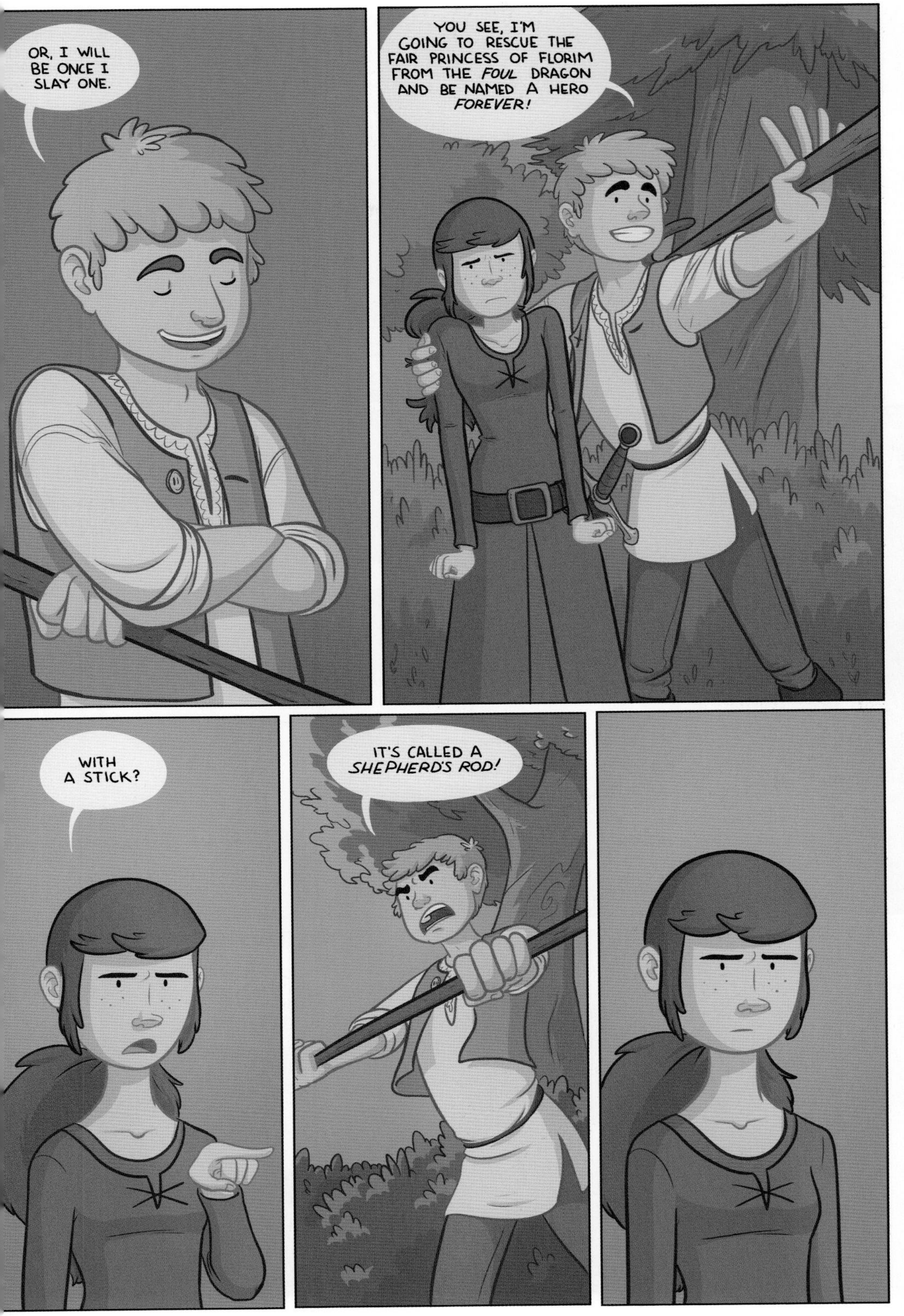
OR, I WILL BE ONCE I SLAY ONE.
YOU SEE, I'M GOING TO RESCUE THE FAIR PRINCESS OF FLORIM FROM THE *FOUL* DRAGON AND BE NAMED A HERO *FOREVER!*
WITH A STICK?
IT'S CALLED A *SHEPHERD'S ROD!*

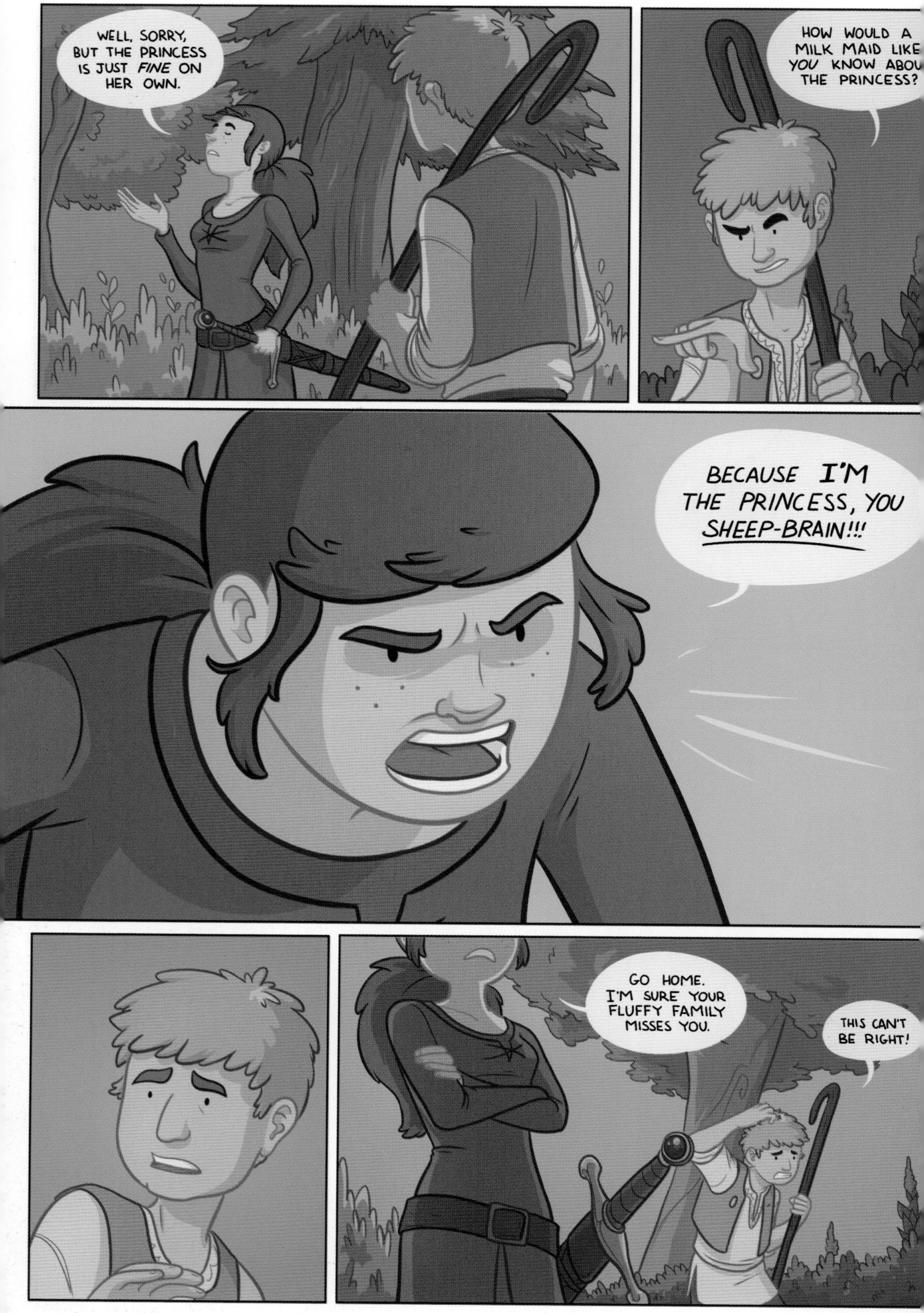
WELL, SORRY, BUT THE PRINCESS IS JUST *FINE* ON HER OWN.
HOW WOULD A MILK MAID LIKE *YOU* KNOW ABOU THE PRINCESS?
BECAUSE **I'M** THE PRINCESS, YOU SHEEP-BRAIN!!!
GO HOME. I'M SURE YOUR FLUFFY FAMILY MISSES YOU.
THIS CAN'T BE RIGHT!

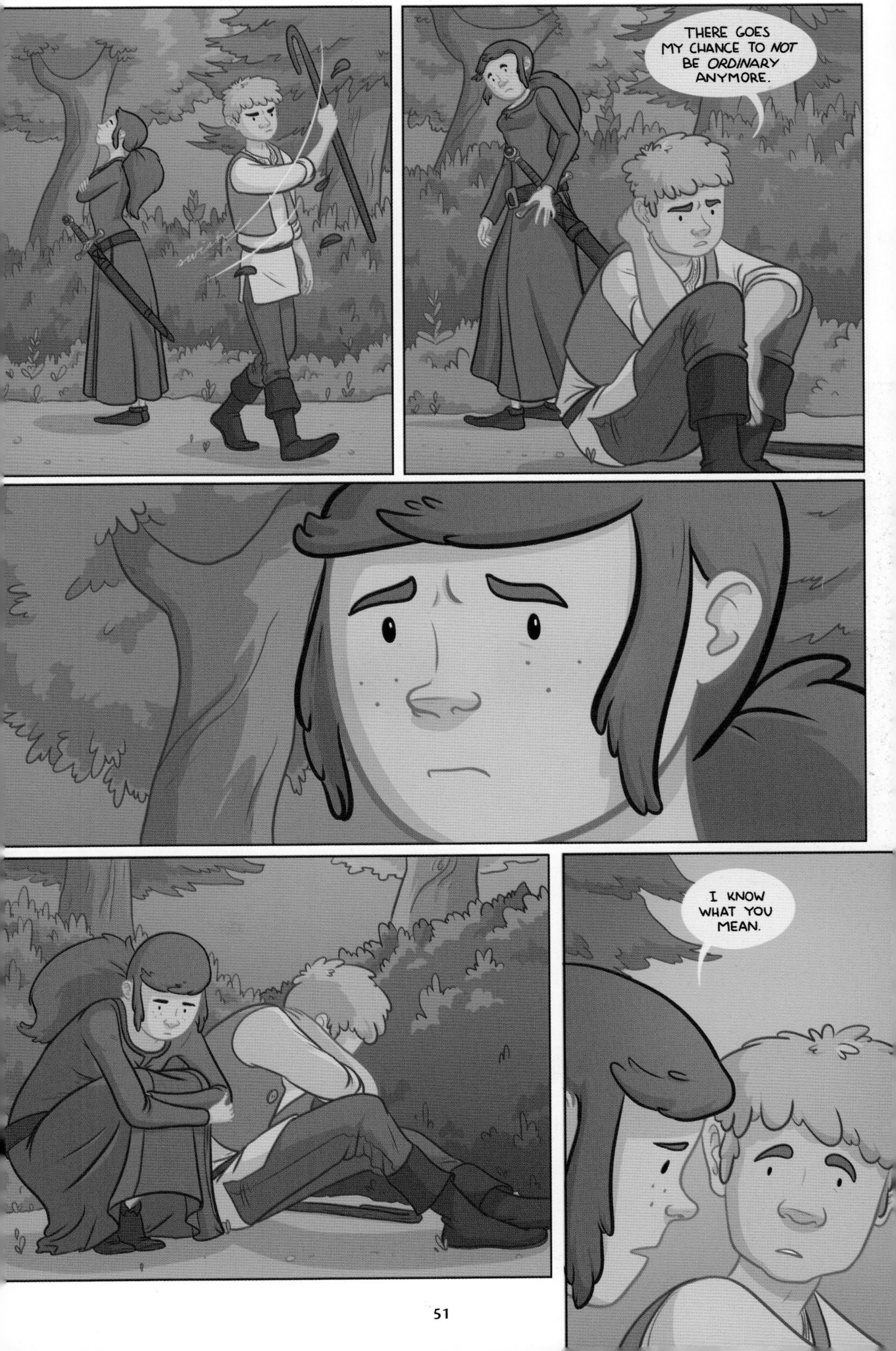
THERE GOES MY CHANCE TO *NOT* BE *ORDINARY* ANYMORE.
I KNOW WHAT YOU MEAN.

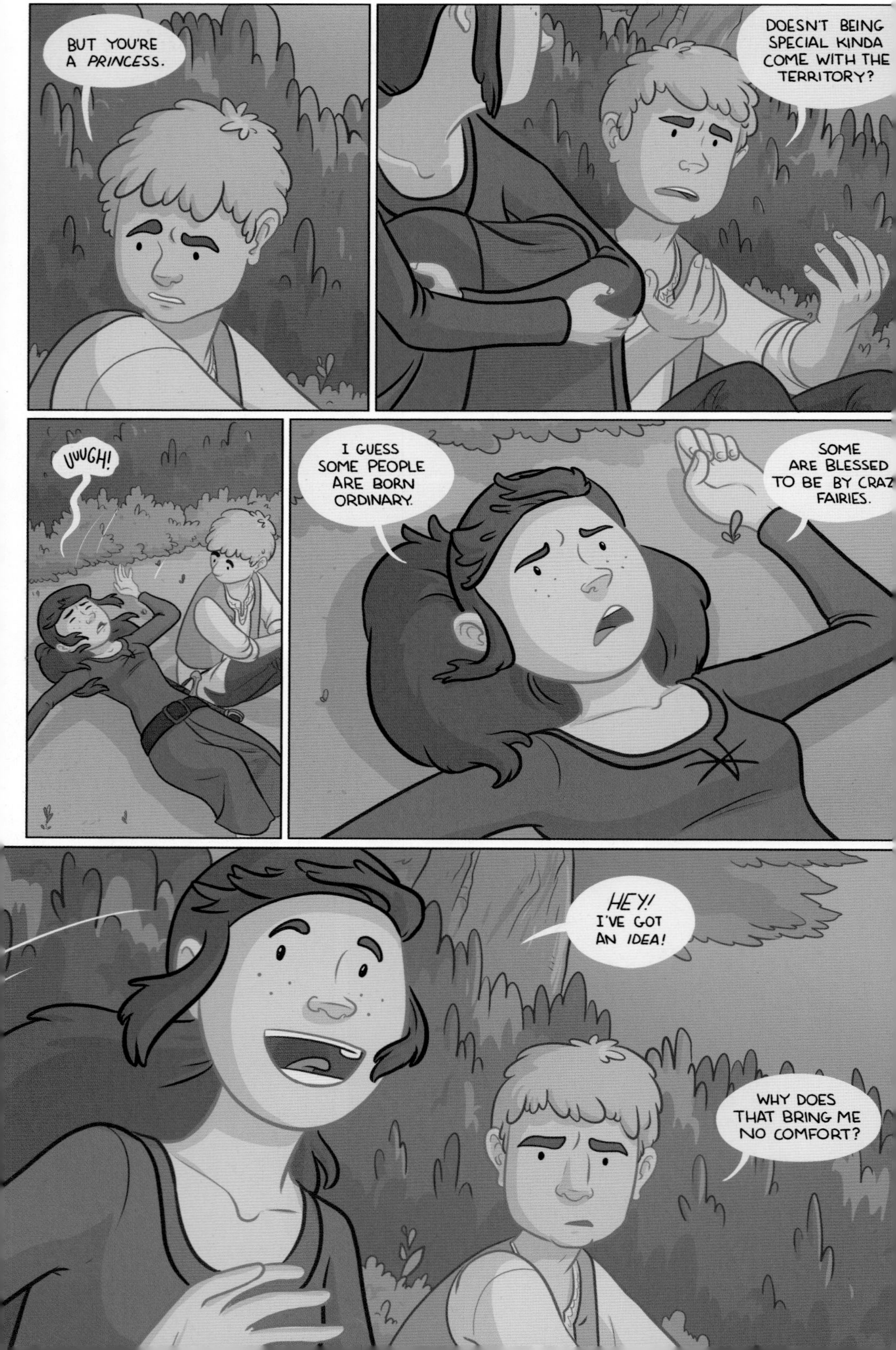
BUT YOU'RE A *PRINCESS*.
DOESN'T BEING SPECIAL KINDA COME WITH THE TERRITORY?
UUUGH!
I GUESS SOME PEOPLE ARE BORN ORDINARY.
SOME ARE BLESSED TO BE BY CRAZ FAIRIES.
HEY! I'VE GOT AN *IDEA!*
WHY DOES THAT BRING ME NO COMFORT?

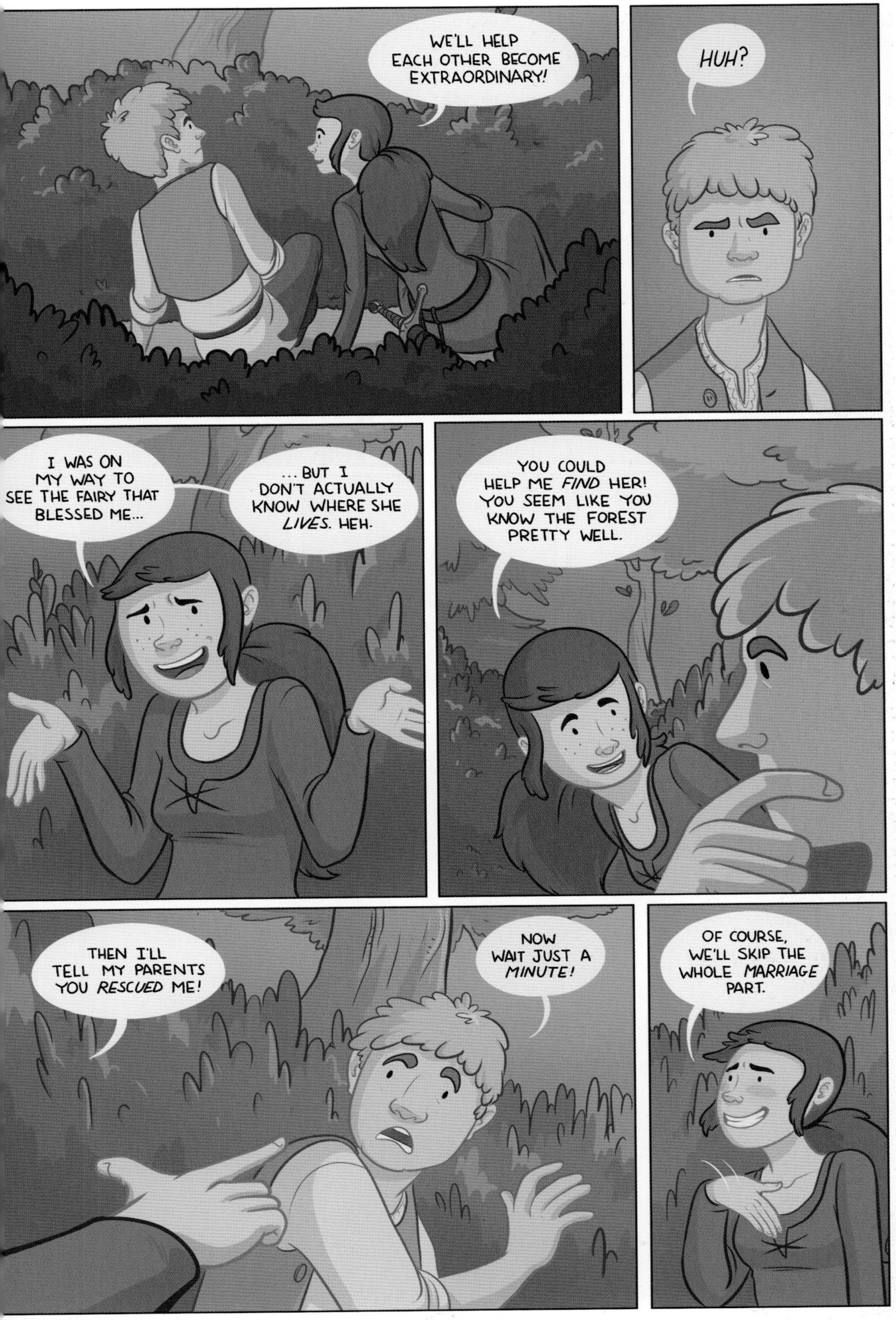
WE'LL HELP EACH OTHER BECOME EXTRAORDINARY!
HUH?
I WAS ON MY WAY TO SEE THE FAIRY THAT BLESSED ME...
...BUT I DON'T ACTUALLY KNOW WHERE SHE *LIVES*. HEH.
YOU COULD HELP ME *FIND* HER! YOU SEEM LIKE YOU KNOW THE FOREST PRETTY WELL.
THEN I'LL TELL MY PARENTS YOU *RESCUED* ME!
NOW WAIT JUST A *MINUTE*!
OF COURSE, WE'LL SKIP THE WHOLE *MARRIAGE* PART.

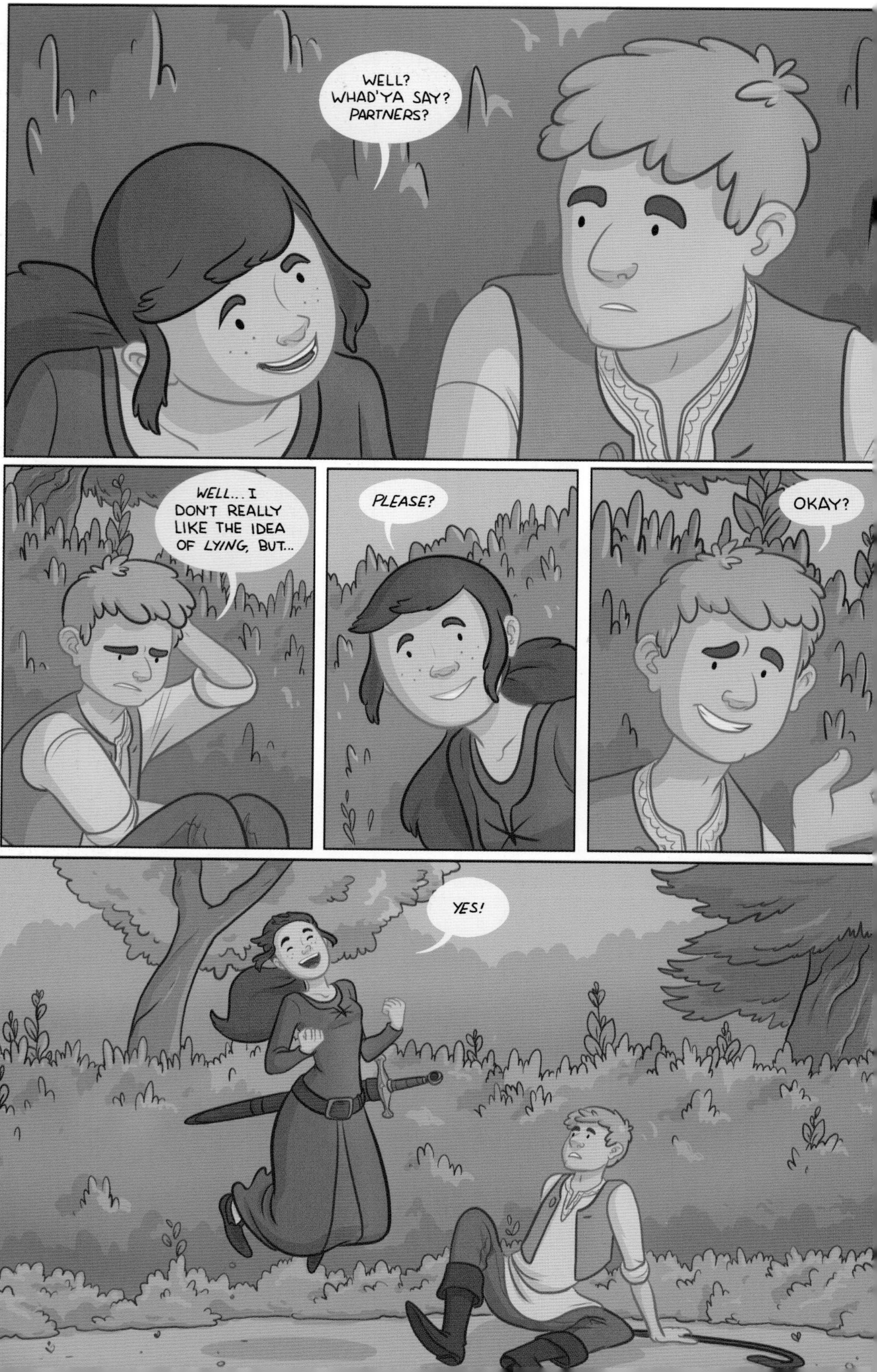
WELL? WHAD'YA SAY? PARTNERS?
WELL... I DON'T REALLY LIKE THE IDEA OF *LYING*, BUT...
PLEASE?
OKAY?
YES!

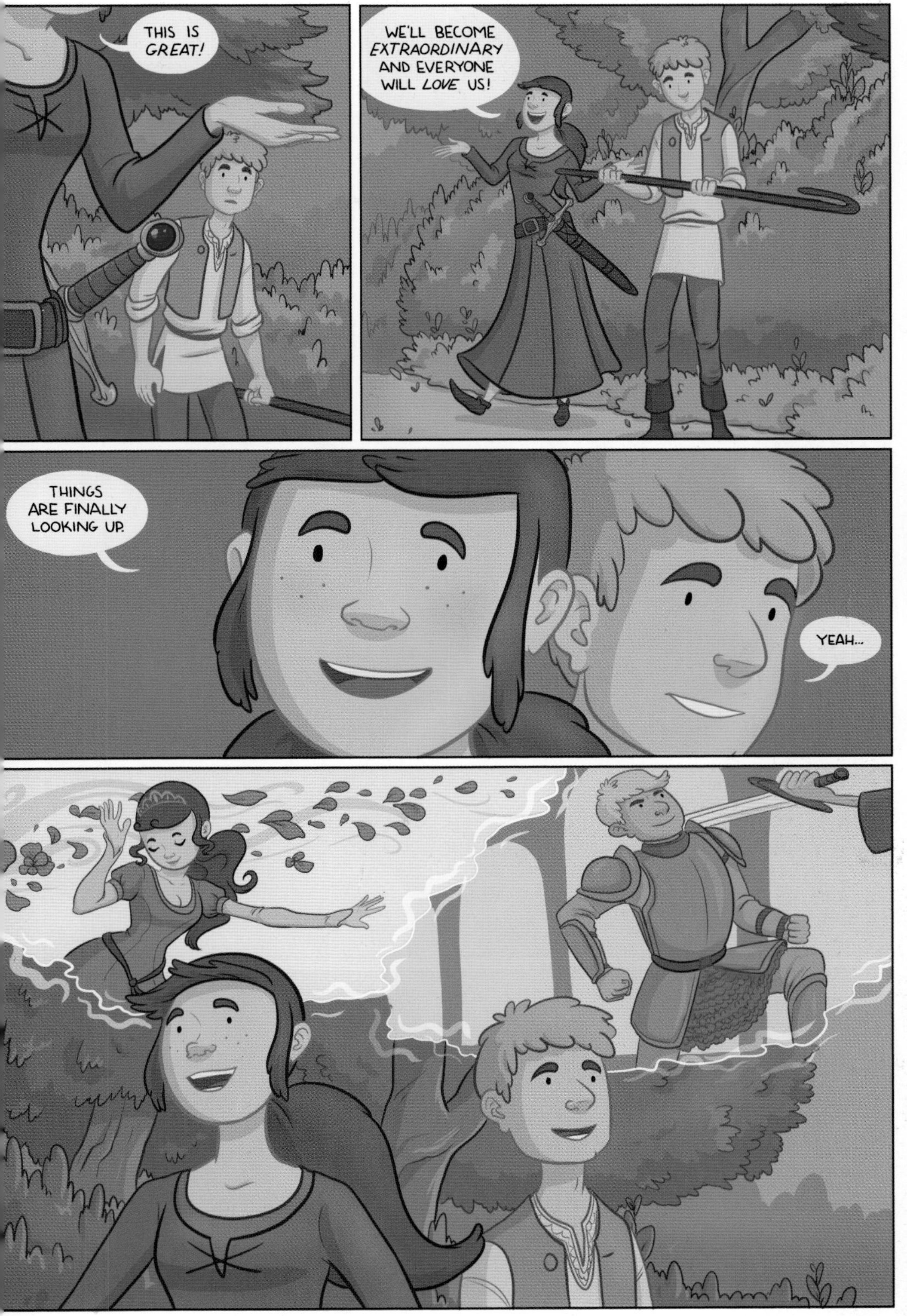
THIS IS GREAT!
WE'LL BECOME EXTRAORDINARY AND EVERYONE WILL LOVE US!
THINGS ARE FINALLY LOOKING UP.
YEAH...

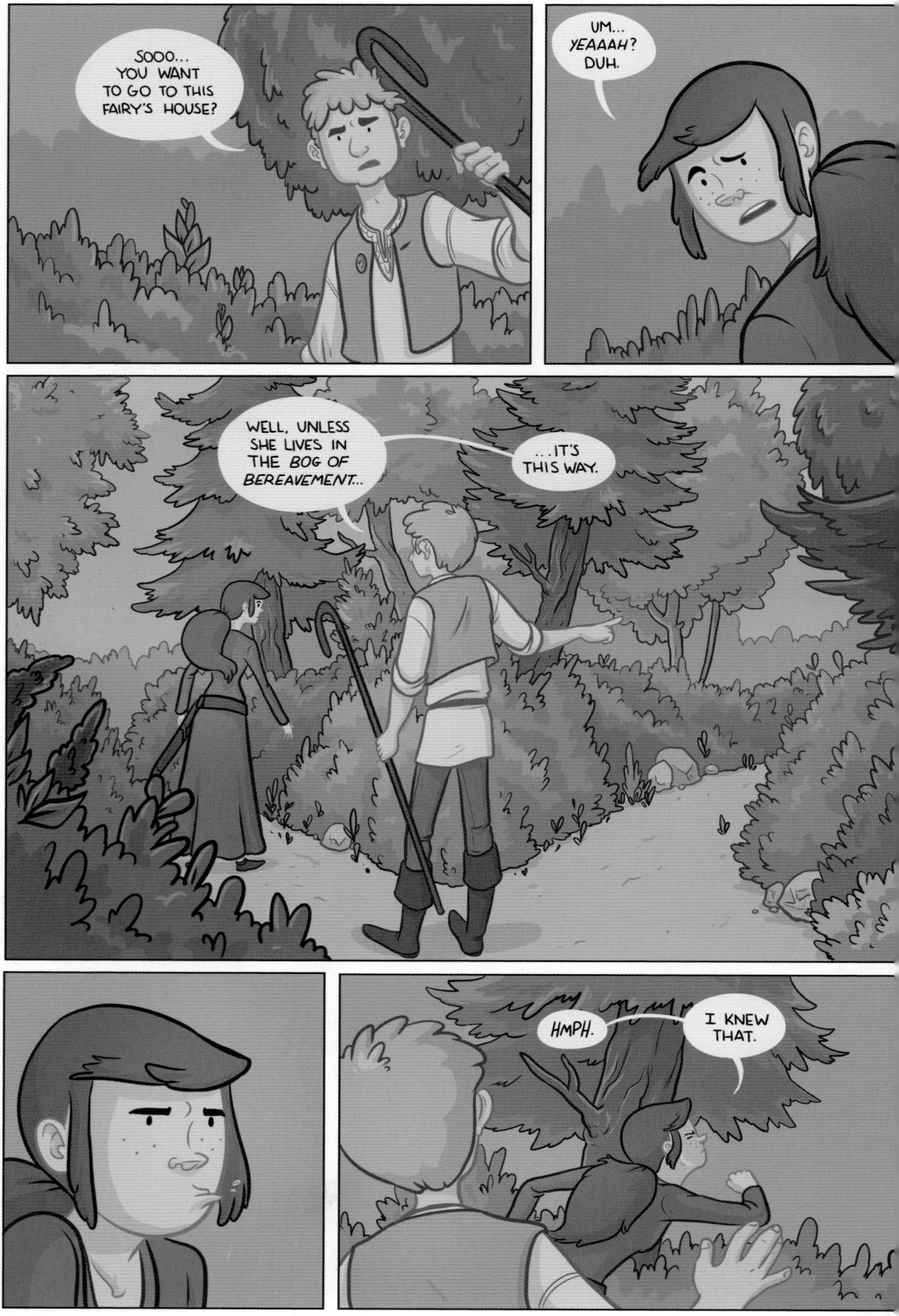
SOOO... YOU WANT TO GO TO THIS FAIRY'S HOUSE?
UM... *YEAAAH*? DUH.
WELL, UNLESS SHE LIVES IN THE *BOG OF BEREAVEMENT*...
...IT'S THIS WAY.
HMPH.
I KNEW THAT.

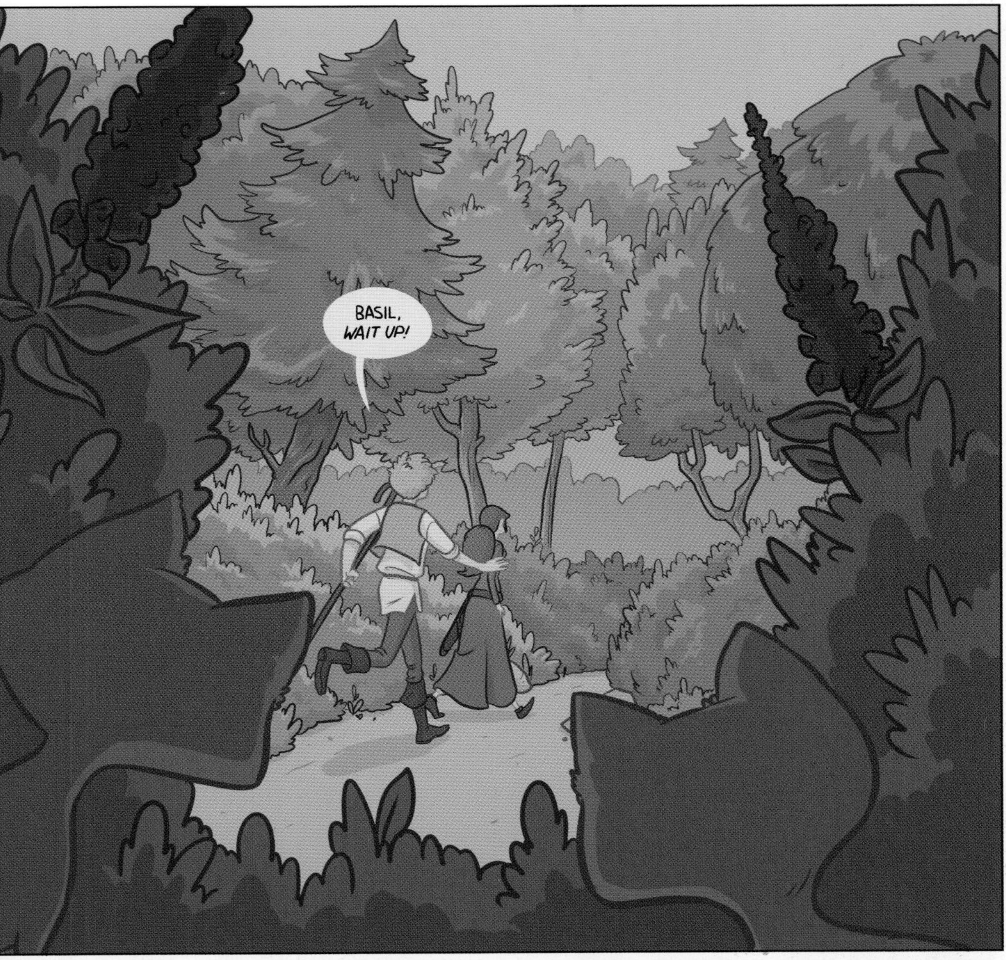
BASIL, WAIT UP!

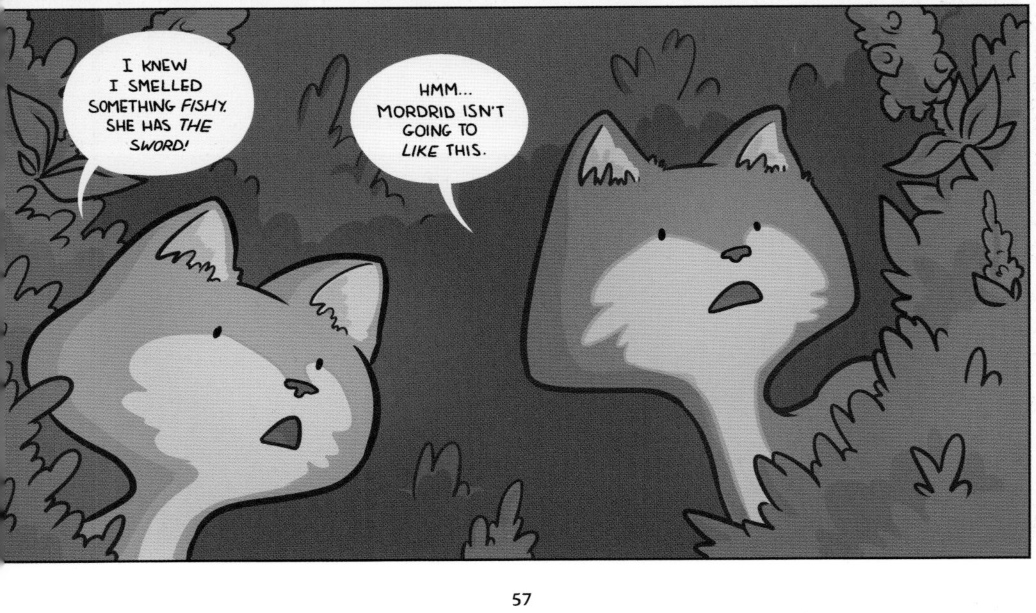
I KNEW I SMELLED SOMETHING FISHY. SHE HAS THE SWORD!
HMM... MORDRID ISN'T GOING TO LIKE THIS.

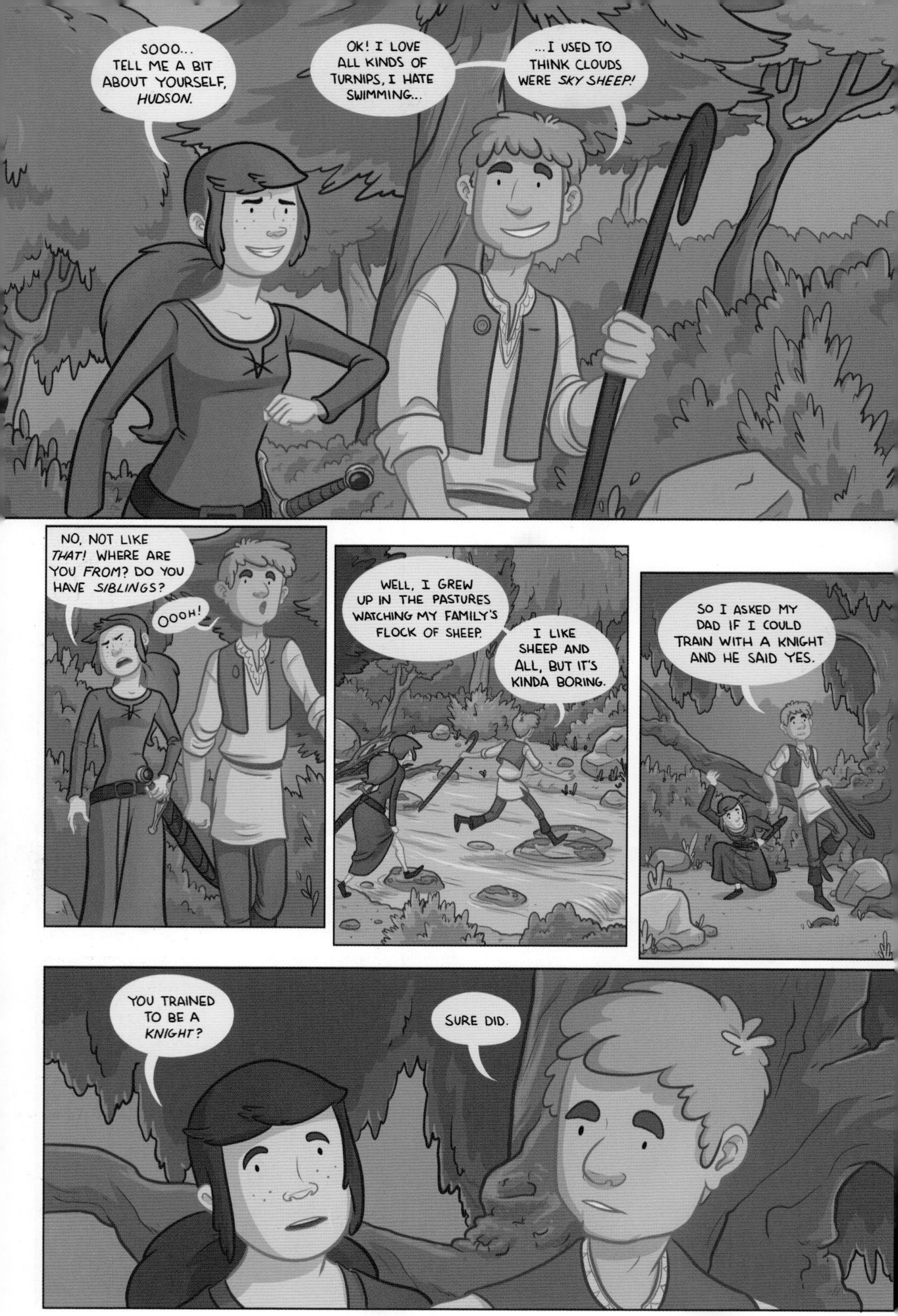
SOOO...
TELL ME A BIT
ABOUT YOURSELF,
HUDSON.
OK! I LOVE
ALL KINDS OF
TURNIPS, I HATE
SWIMMING...
...I USED TO
THINK CLOUDS
WERE *SKY SHEEP!*
NO, NOT LIKE
THAT! WHERE ARE
YOU *FROM?* DO YOU
HAVE *SIBLINGS?*
OOOH!
WELL, I GREW
UP IN THE PASTURES
WATCHING MY FAMILY'S
FLOCK OF SHEEP.
I LIKE
SHEEP AND
ALL, BUT IT'S
KINDA BORING.
SO I ASKED MY
DAD IF I COULD
TRAIN WITH A KNIGHT
AND HE SAID YES.
YOU TRAINED
TO BE A
KNIGHT?
SURE DID.

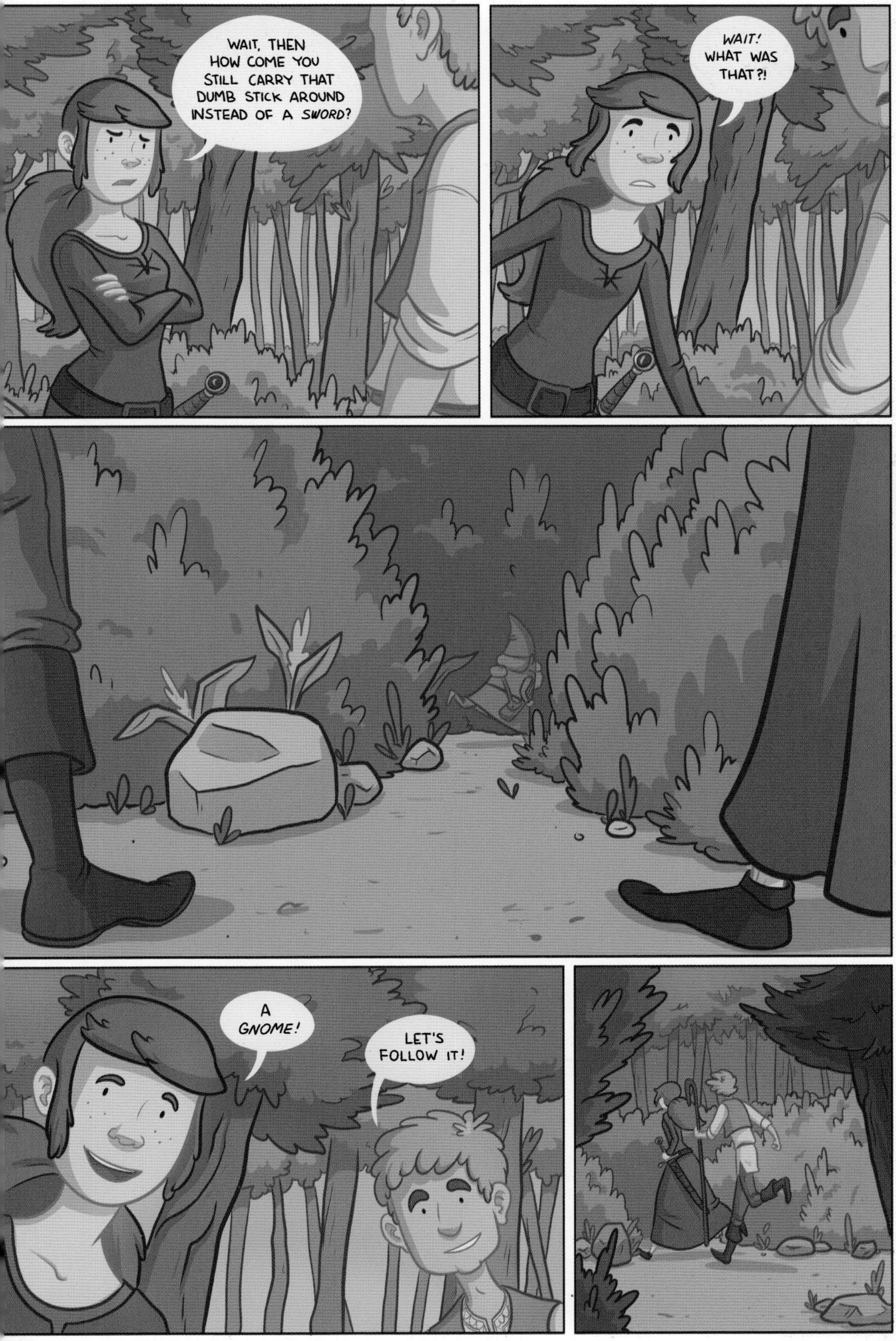
WAIT, THEN HOW COME YOU STILL CARRY THAT DUMB STICK AROUND INSTEAD OF A SWORD?
WAIT! WHAT WAS THAT?!
A GNOME!
LET'S FOLLOW IT!

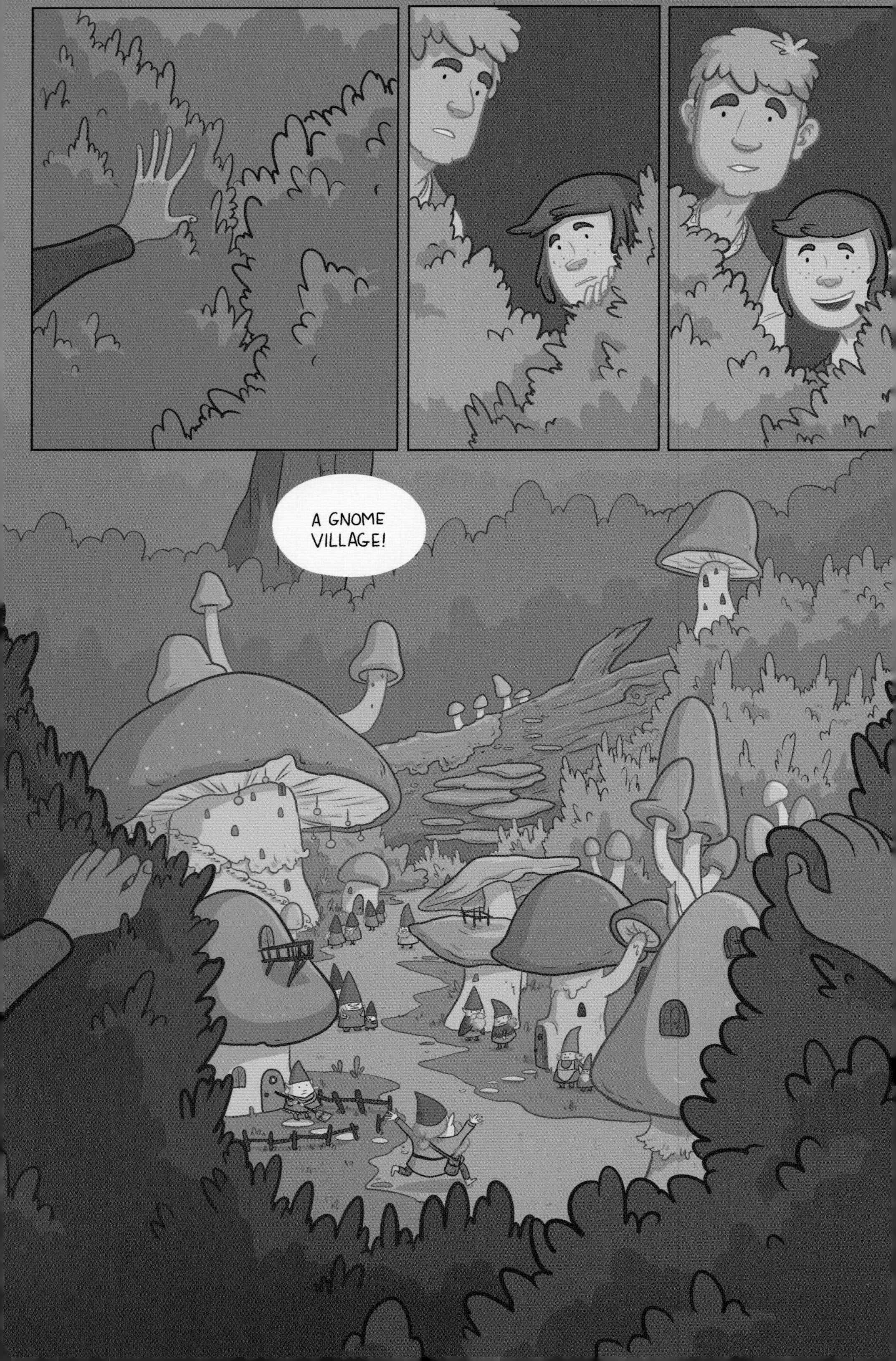
A GNOME VILLAGE!

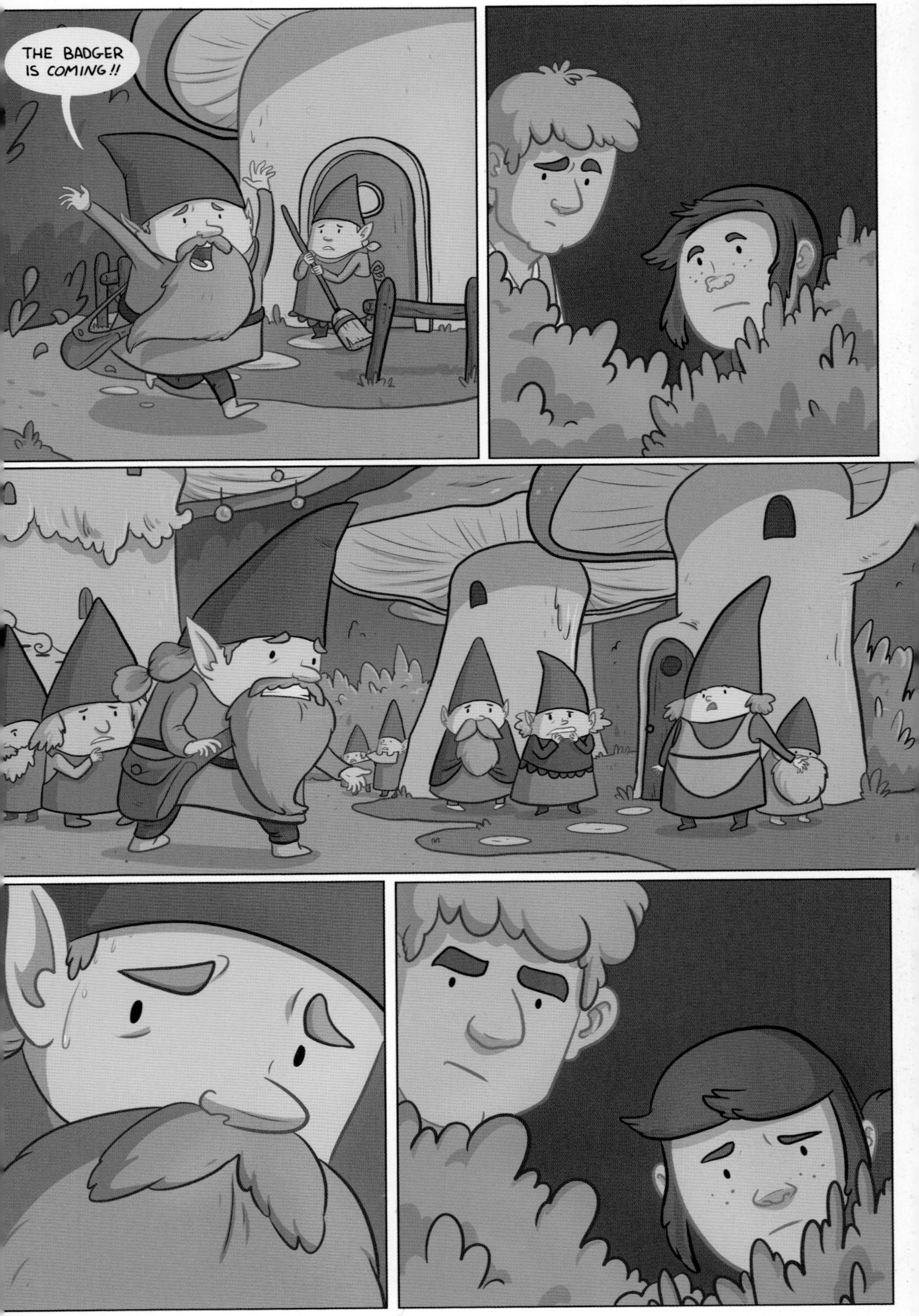
THE BADGER IS COMING!!

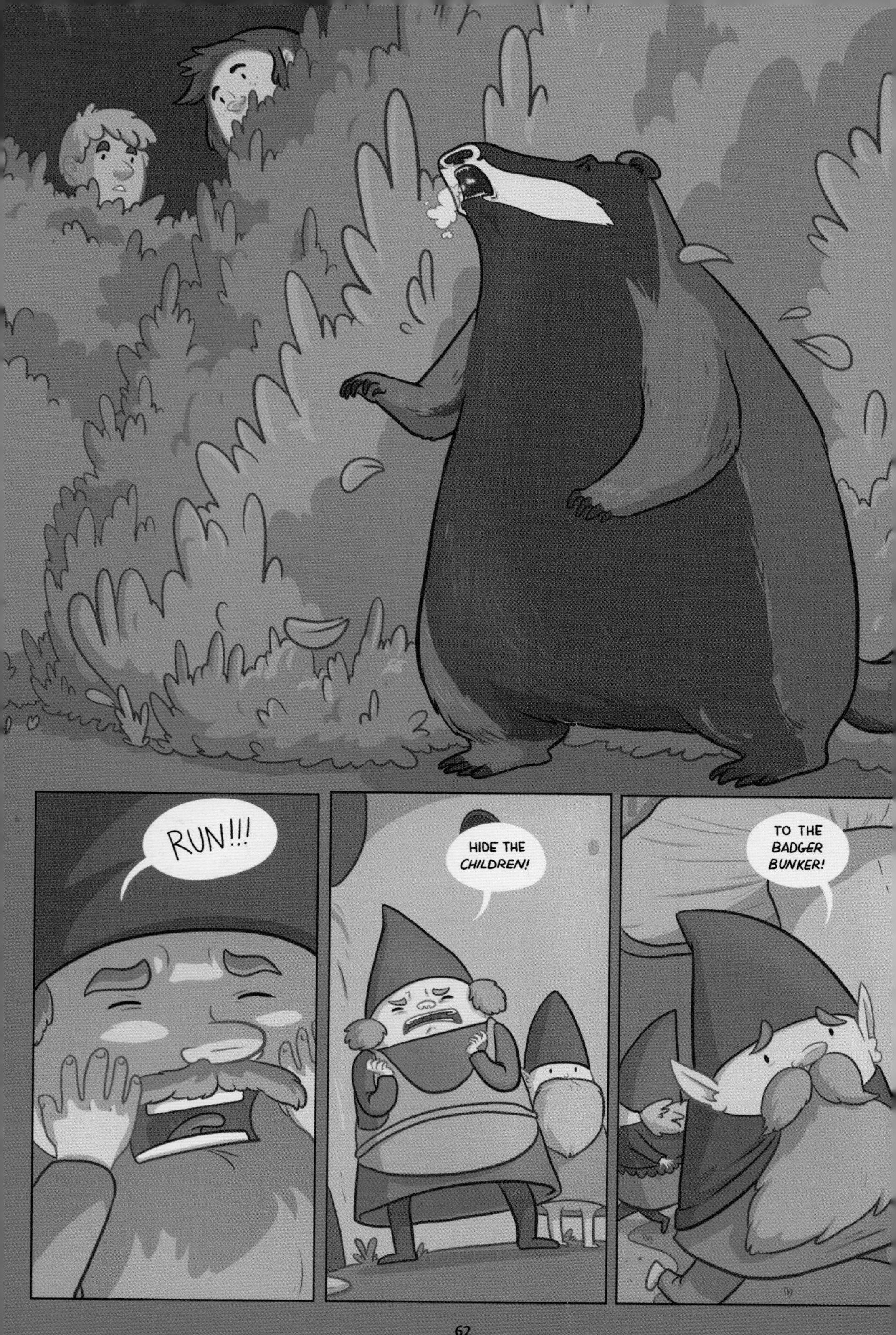
RUN!!!
HIDE THE CHILDREN!
TO THE BADGER BUNKER!

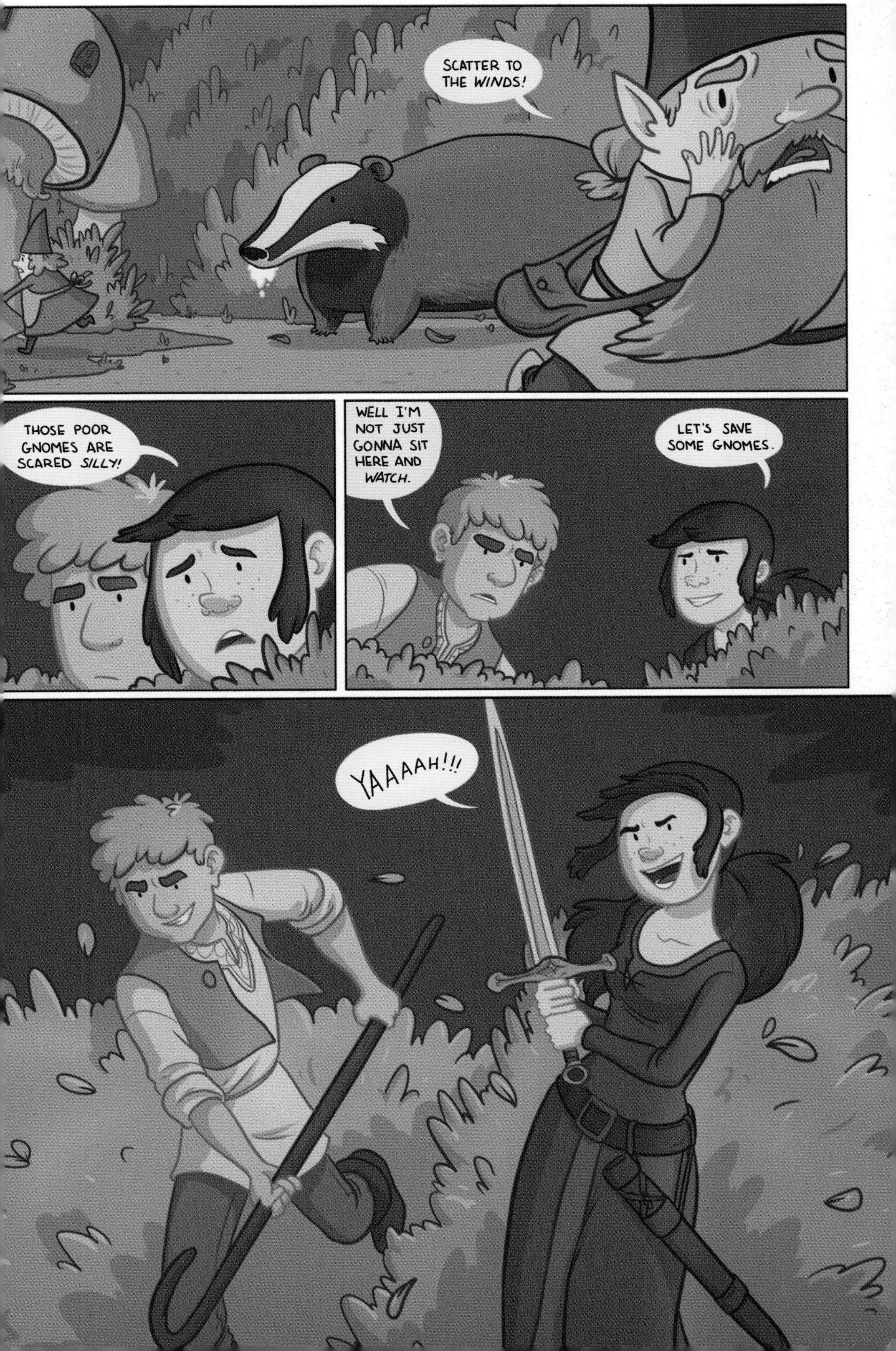
SCATTER TO THE *WINDS!*
THOSE POOR GNOMES ARE SCARED *SILLY!*
WELL I'M NOT JUST GONNA SIT HERE AND *WATCH*.
LET'S SAVE SOME GNOMES.
YAAAAH!!!

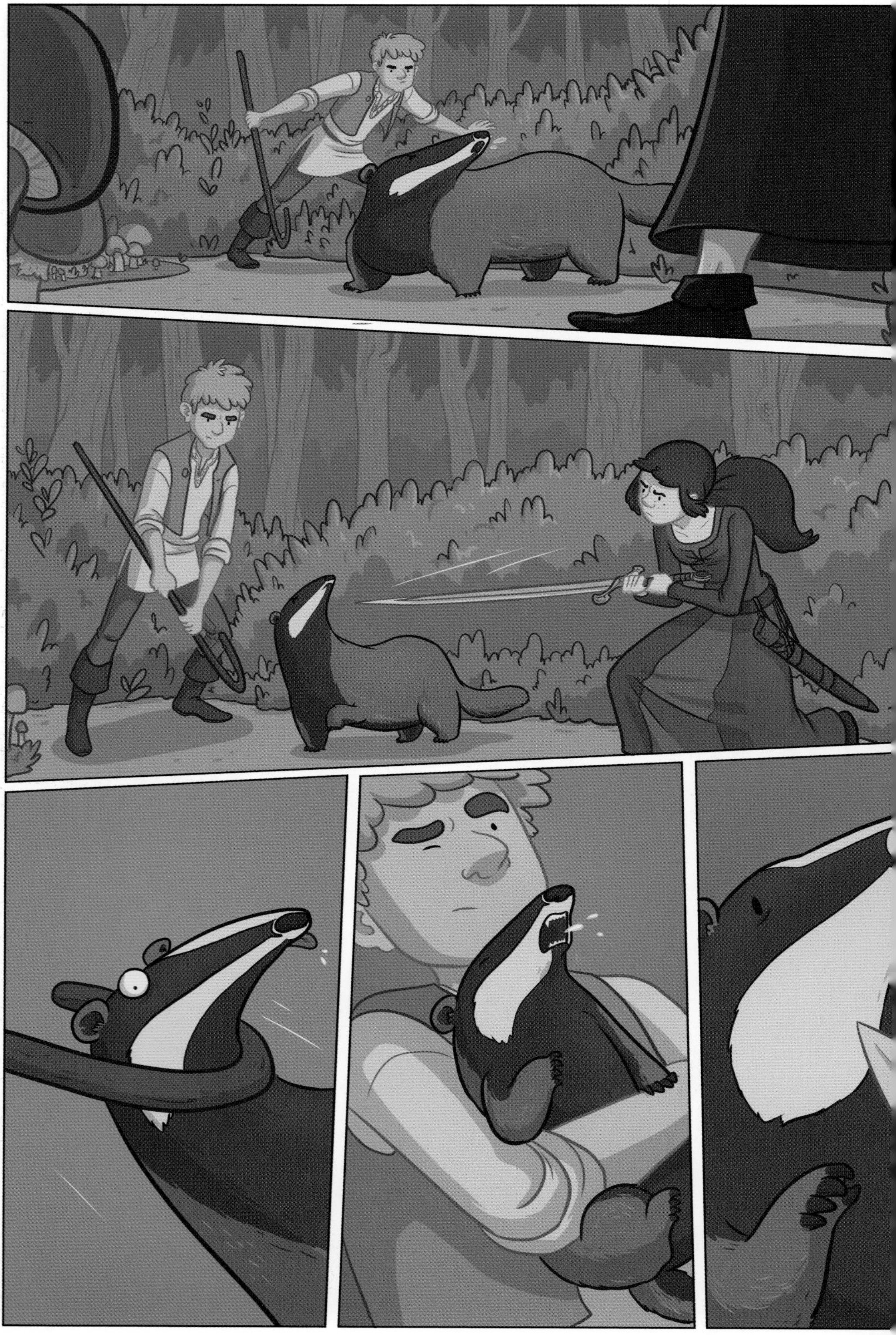

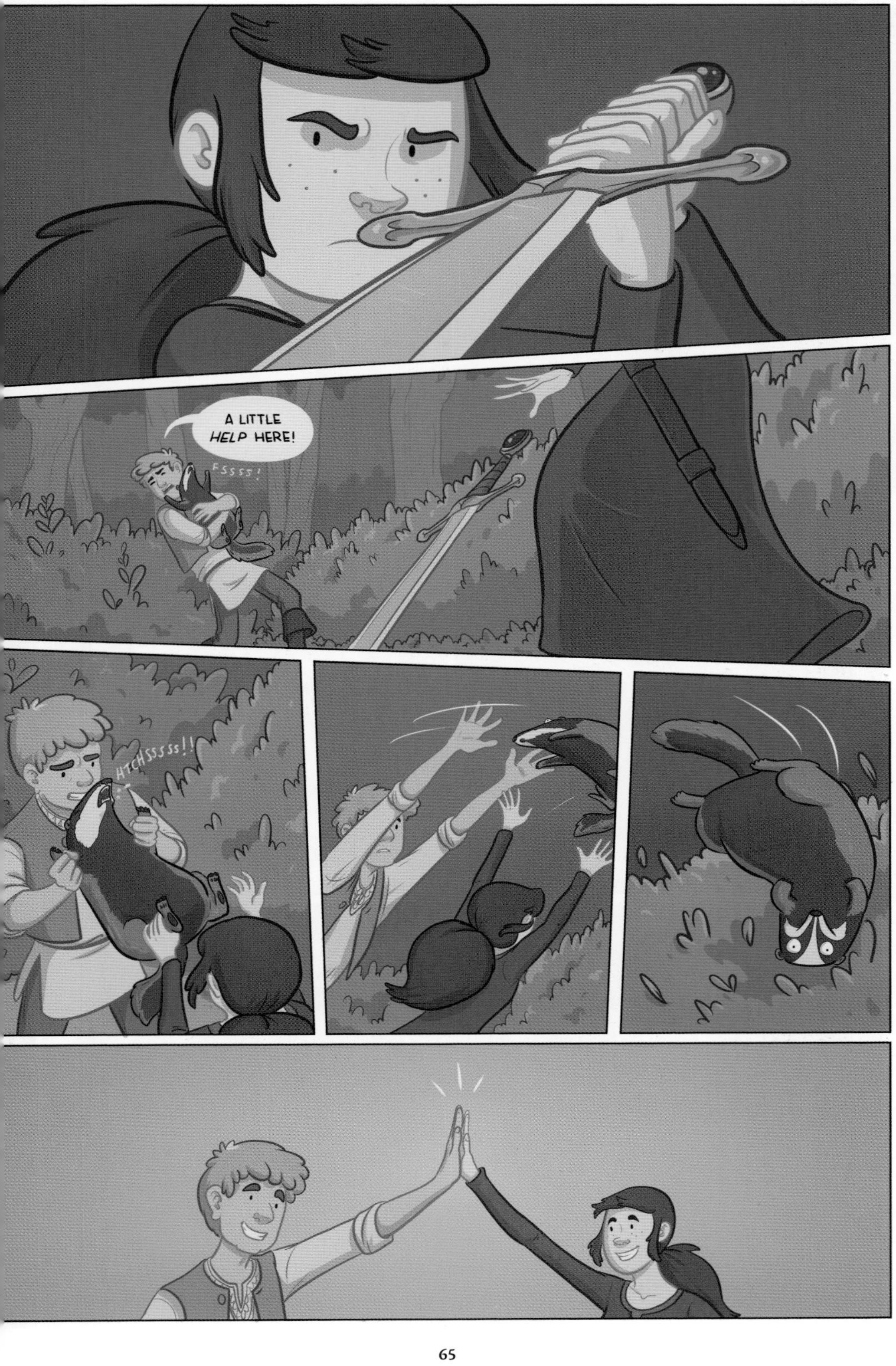
A LITTLE *HELP* HERE!
FSSSS!
HTCHSSSSSs!!

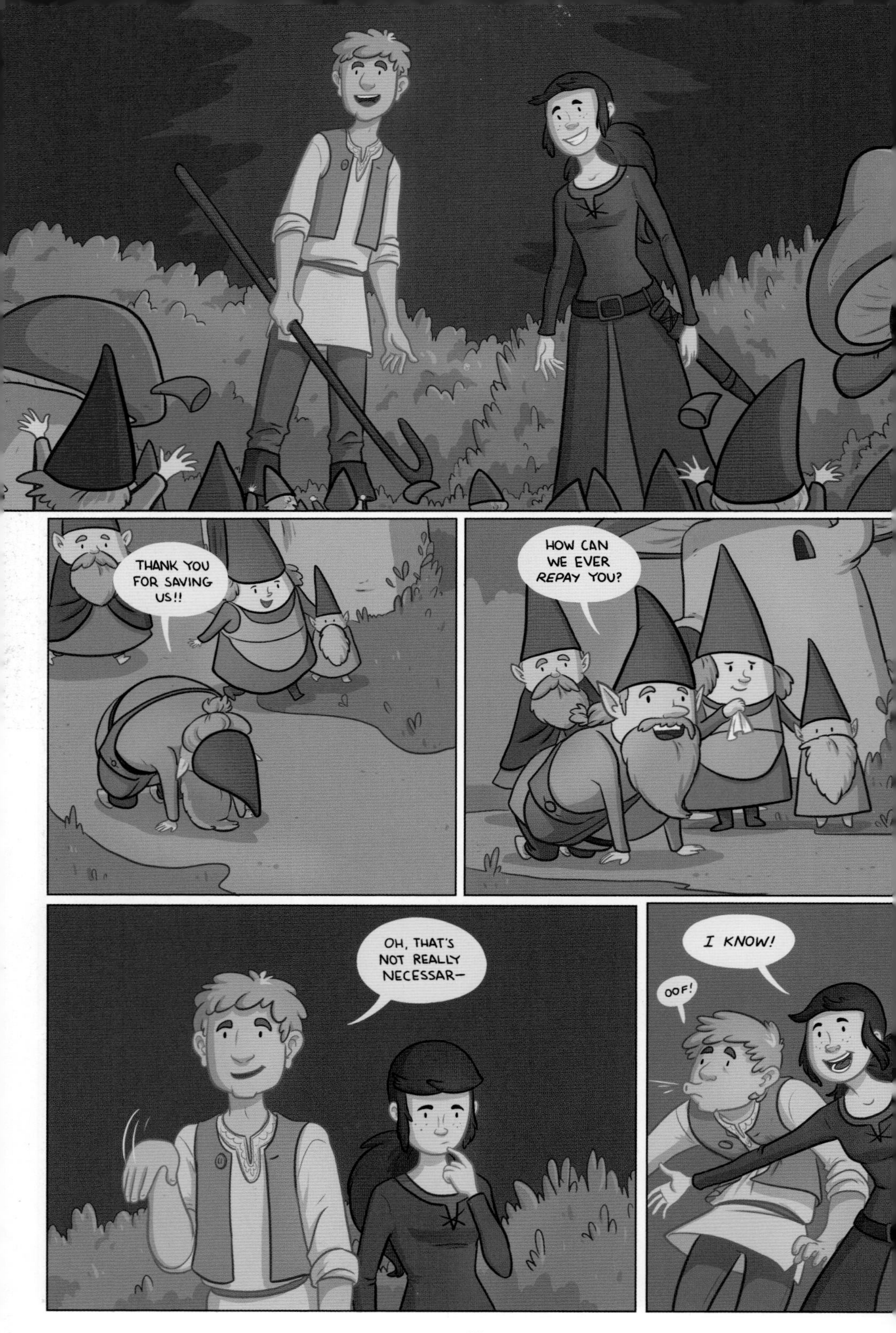
THANK YOU FOR SAVING US!!
HOW CAN WE EVER *REPAY* YOU?
OH, THAT'S NOT REALLY NECESSAR—
I KNOW!
OOF!

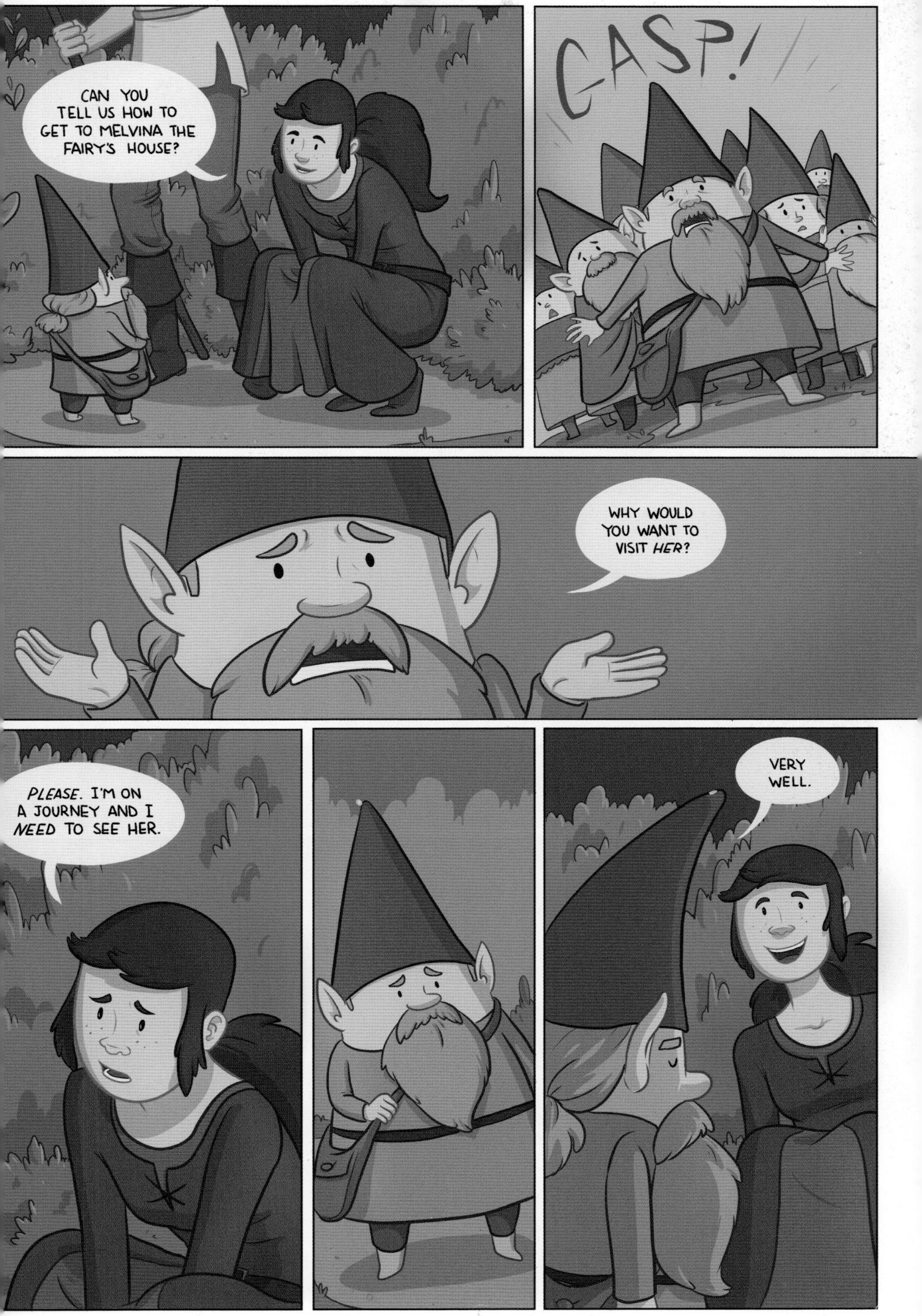
CAN YOU TELL US HOW TO GET TO MELVINA THE FAIRY'S HOUSE?
GASP!
WHY WOULD YOU WANT TO VISIT *HER*?
PLEASE. I'M ON A JOURNEY AND I *NEED* TO SEE HER.
VERY WELL.

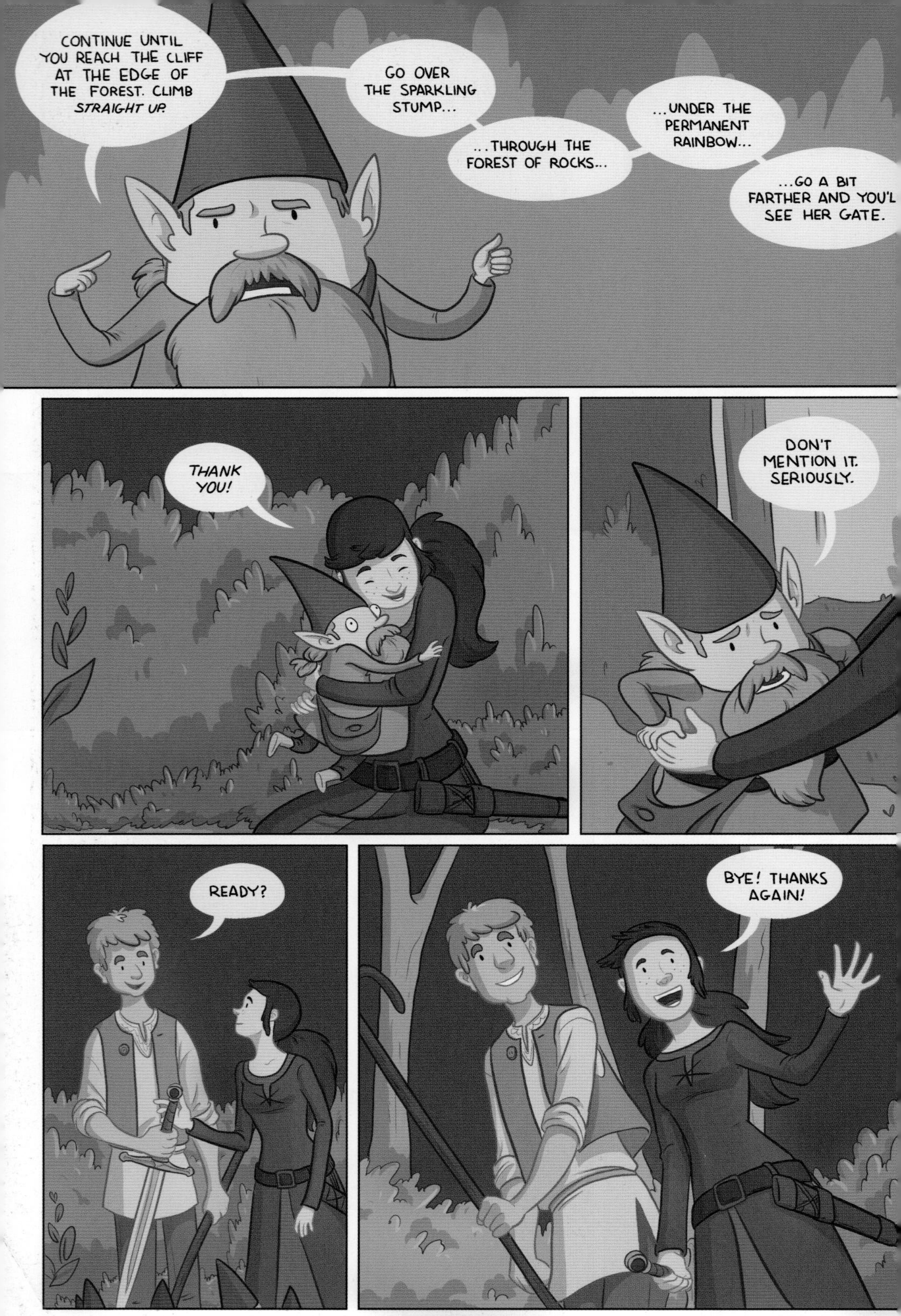

CONTINUE UNTIL YOU REACH THE CLIFF AT THE EDGE OF THE FOREST. CLIMB *STRAIGHT UP.*
GO OVER THE SPARKLING STUMP...
...THROUGH THE FOREST OF ROCKS...
...UNDER THE PERMANENT RAINBOW...
...GO A BIT FARTHER AND YOU'L SEE HER GATE.
THANK YOU!
DON'T MENTION IT. SERIOUSLY.
READY?
BYE! THANKS AGAIN!

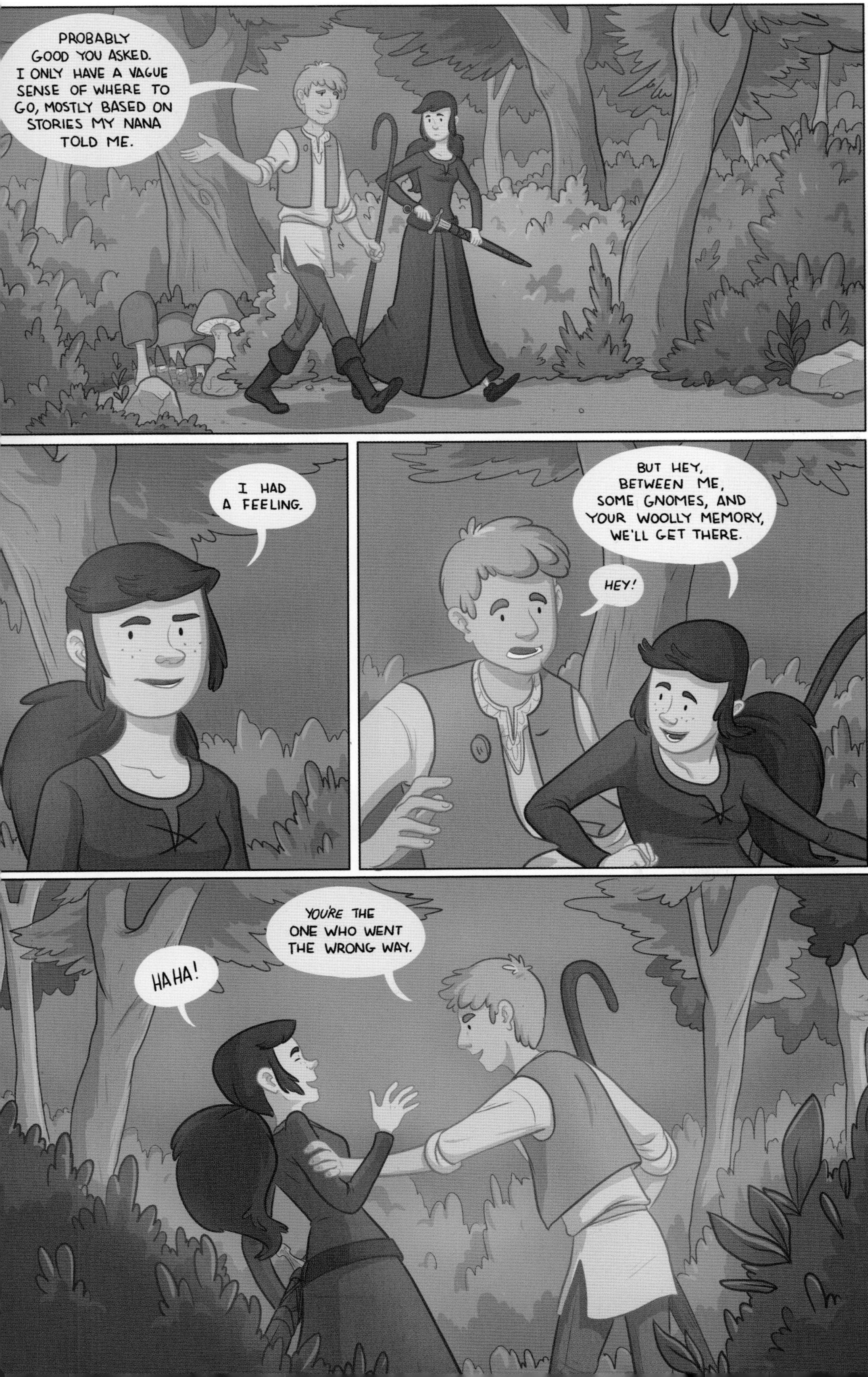
PROBABLY GOOD YOU ASKED. I ONLY HAVE A VAGUE SENSE OF WHERE TO GO, MOSTLY BASED ON STORIES MY NANA TOLD ME.
I HAD A FEELING.
BUT HEY, BETWEEN ME, SOME GNOMES, AND YOUR WOOLLY MEMORY, WE'LL GET THERE.
HEY!
YOU'RE THE ONE WHO WENT THE WRONG WAY.
HAHA!

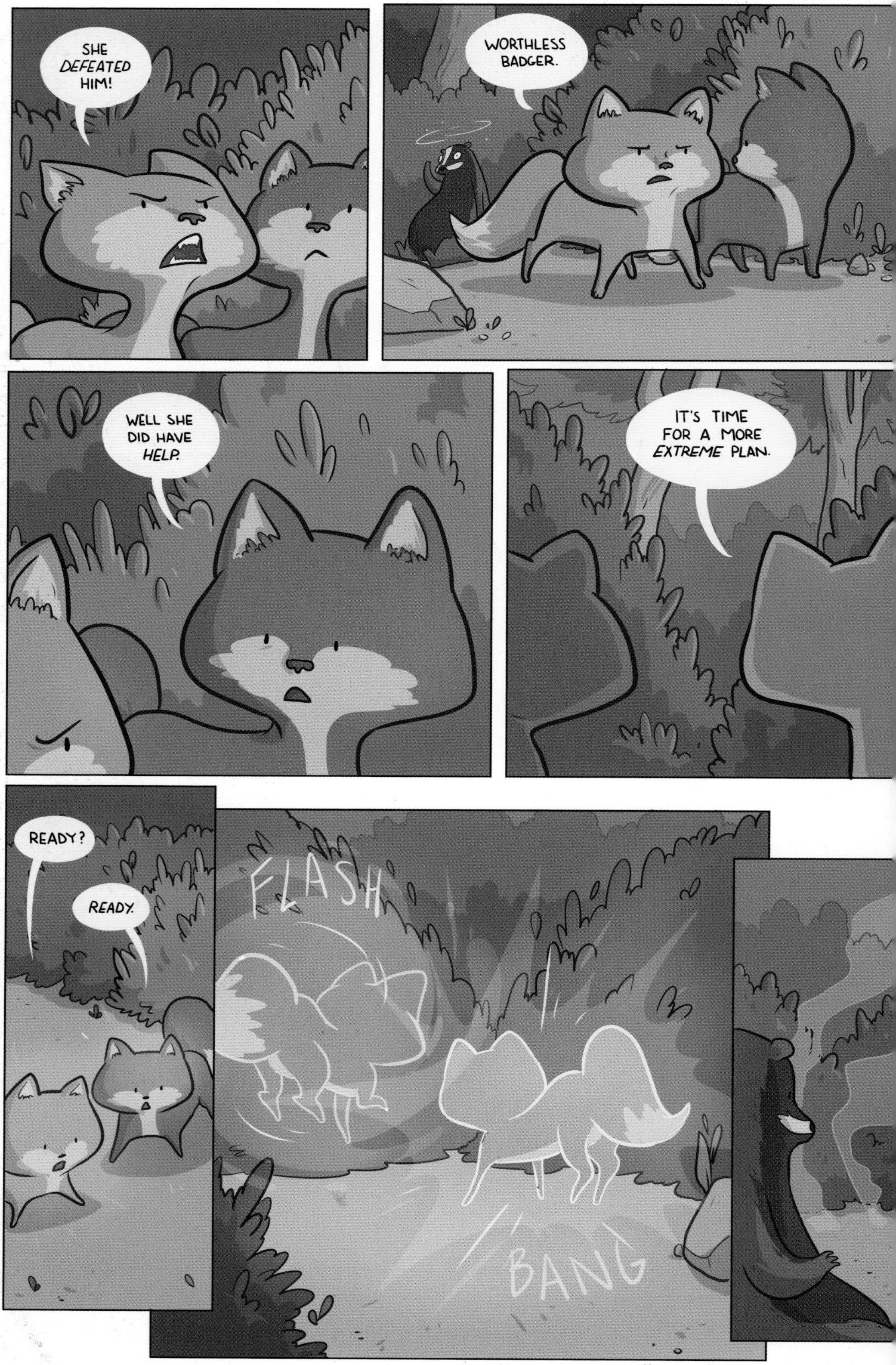
SHE DEFEATED HIM!
WORTHLESS BADGER.
WELL SHE DID HAVE HELP.
IT'S TIME FOR A MORE EXTREME PLAN.
READY?
READY.
FLASH
BANG

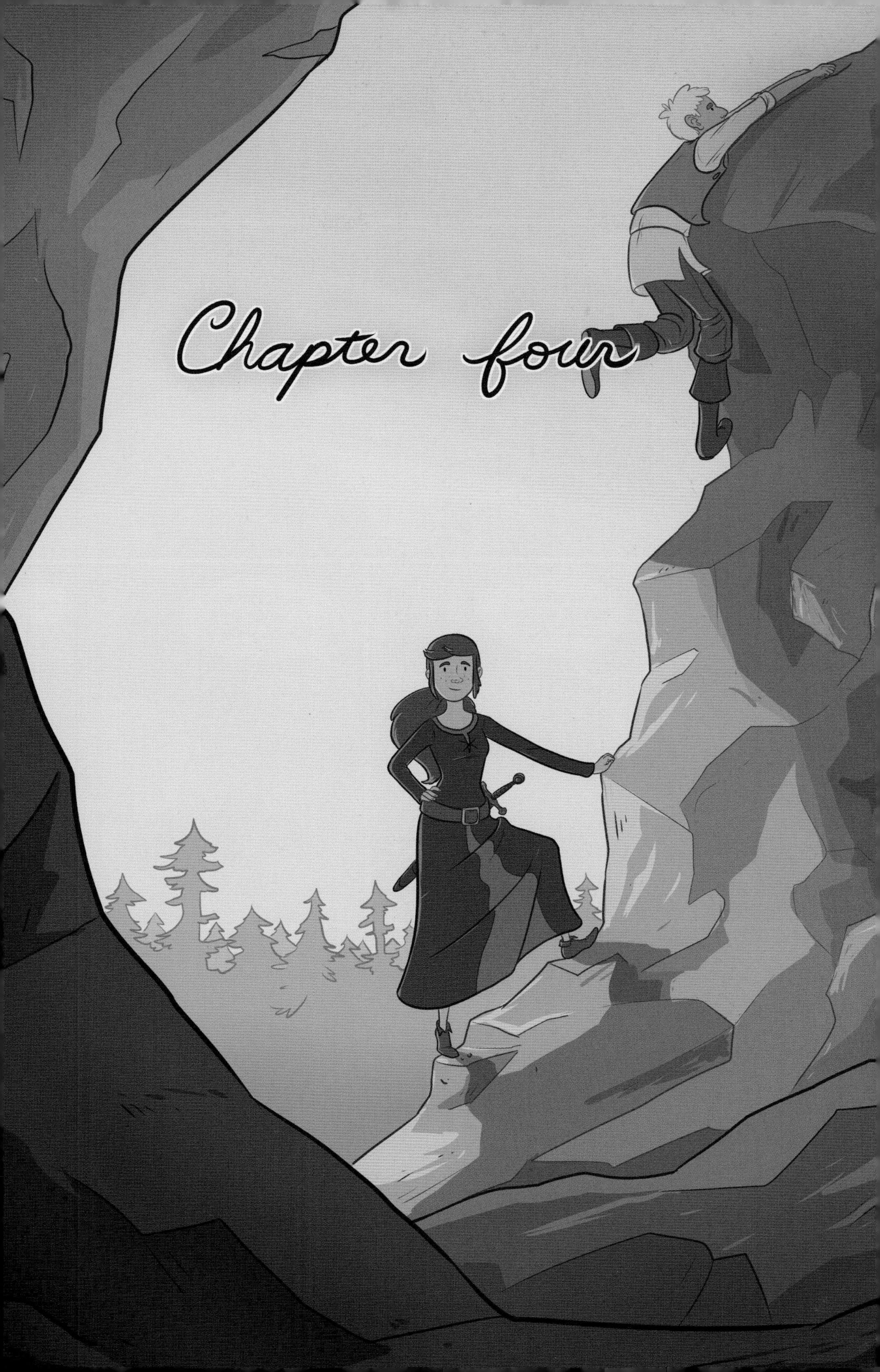
Chapter four

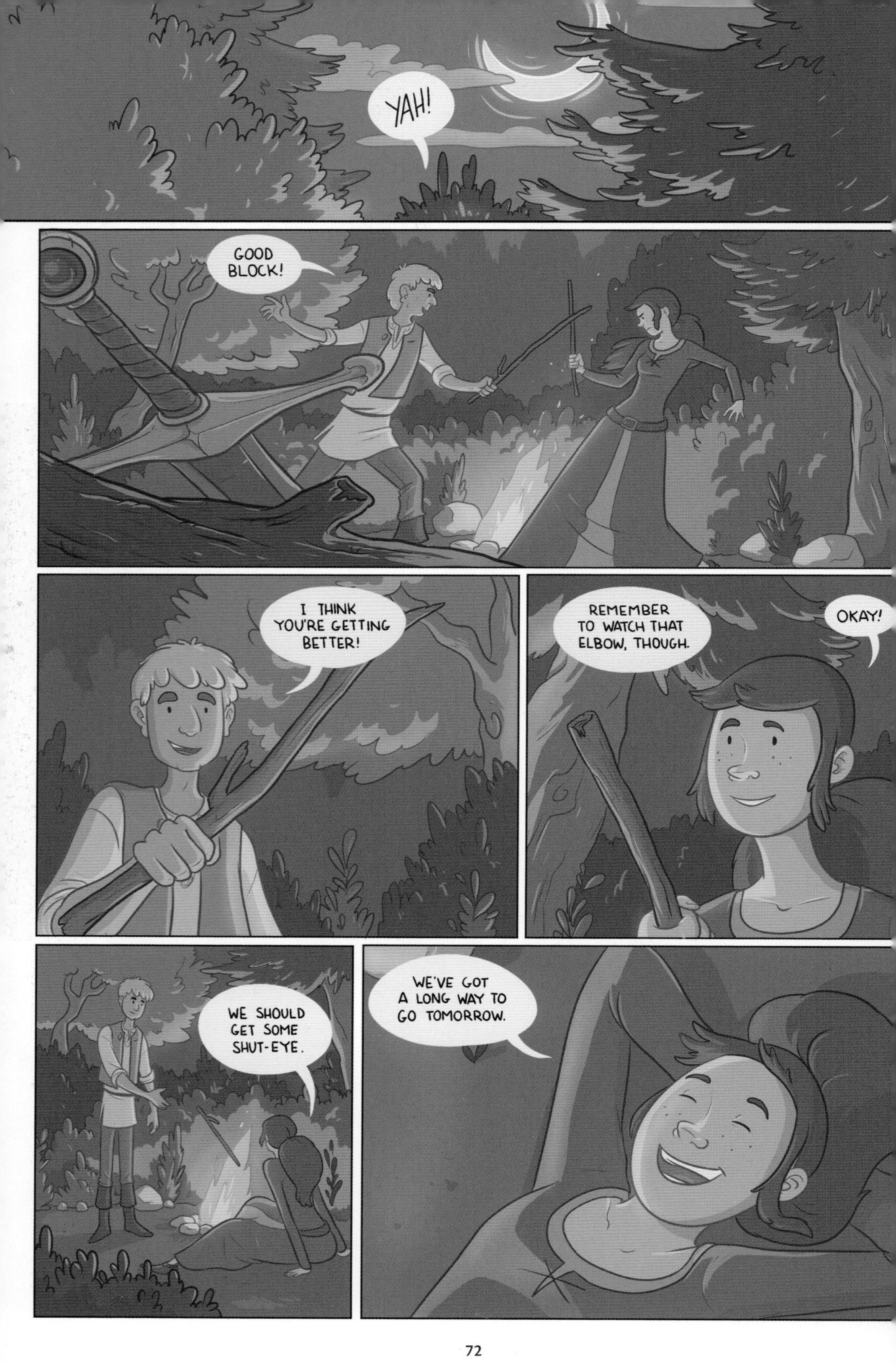
YAH!
GOOD BLOCK!
I THINK YOU'RE GETTING BETTER!
REMEMBER TO WATCH THAT ELBOW, THOUGH.
OKAY!
WE SHOULD GET SOME SHUT-EYE.
WE'VE GOT A LONG WAY TO GO TOMORROW.

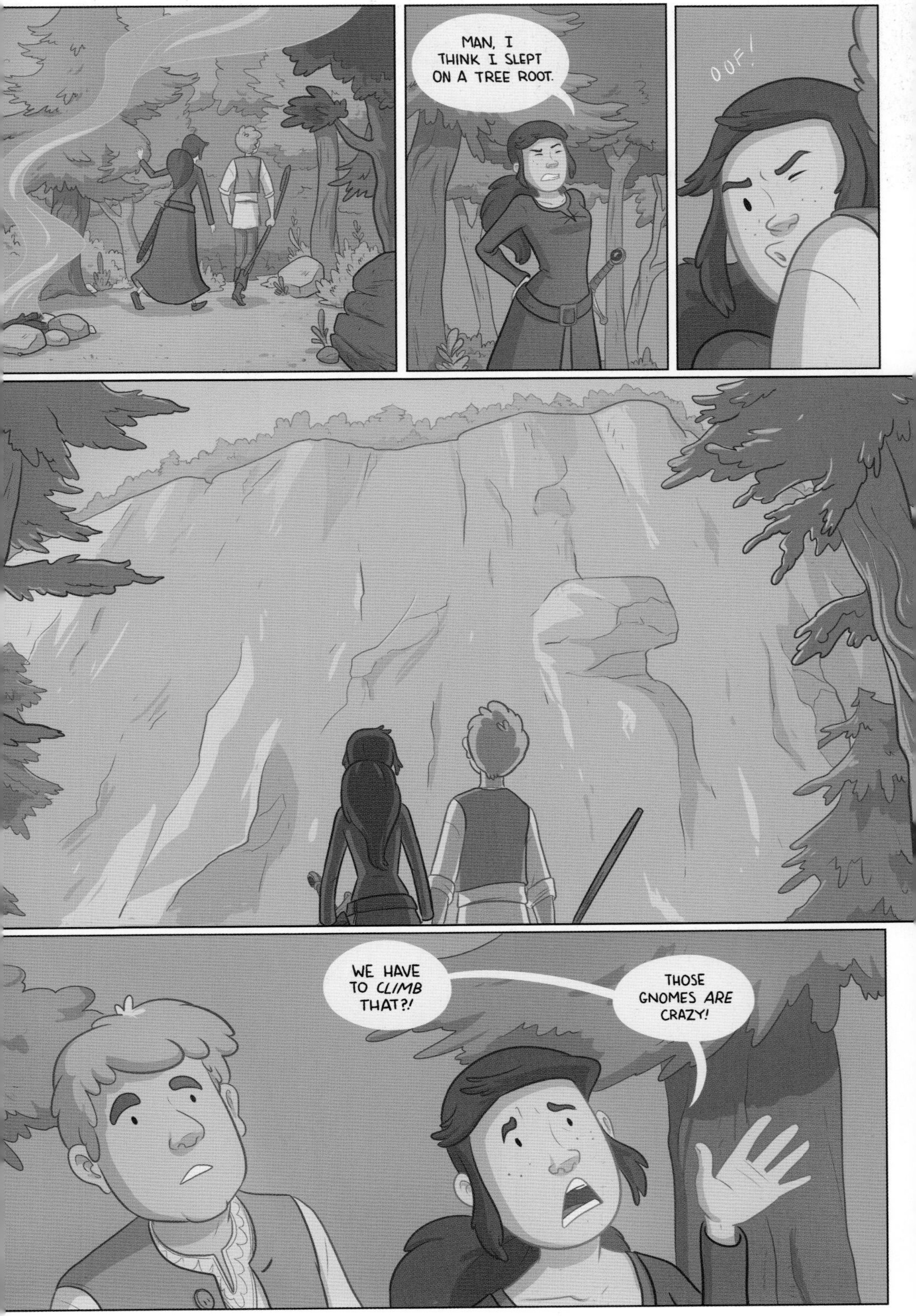
MAN, I THINK I SLEPT ON A TREE ROOT.
OOF!
WE HAVE TO *CLIMB* THAT?!
THOSE GNOMES *ARE* CRAZY!

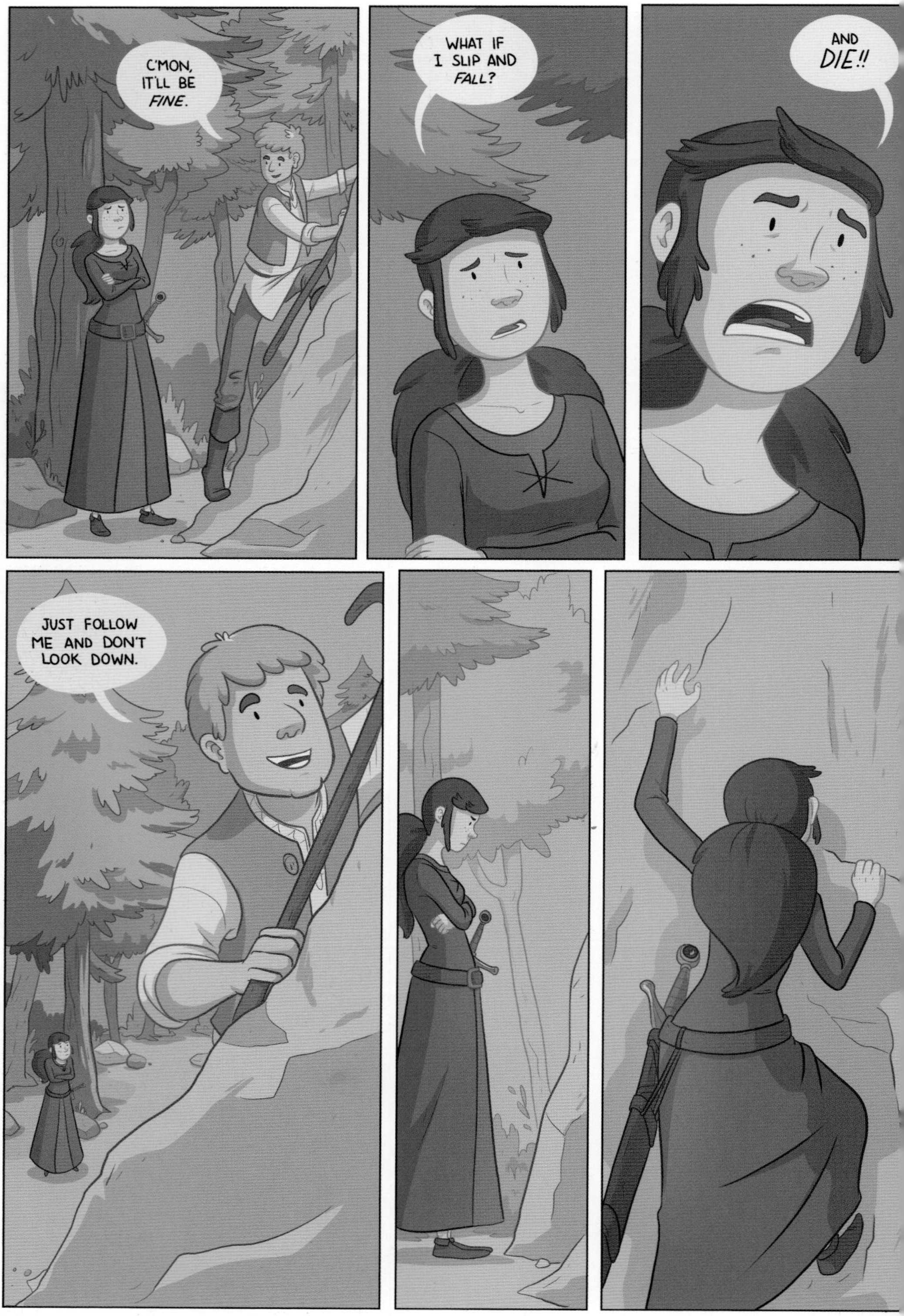
C'MON, IT'LL BE *FINE*.
WHAT IF I SLIP AND *FALL*?
AND *DIE*!!
JUST FOLLOW ME AND DON'T LOOK DOWN.

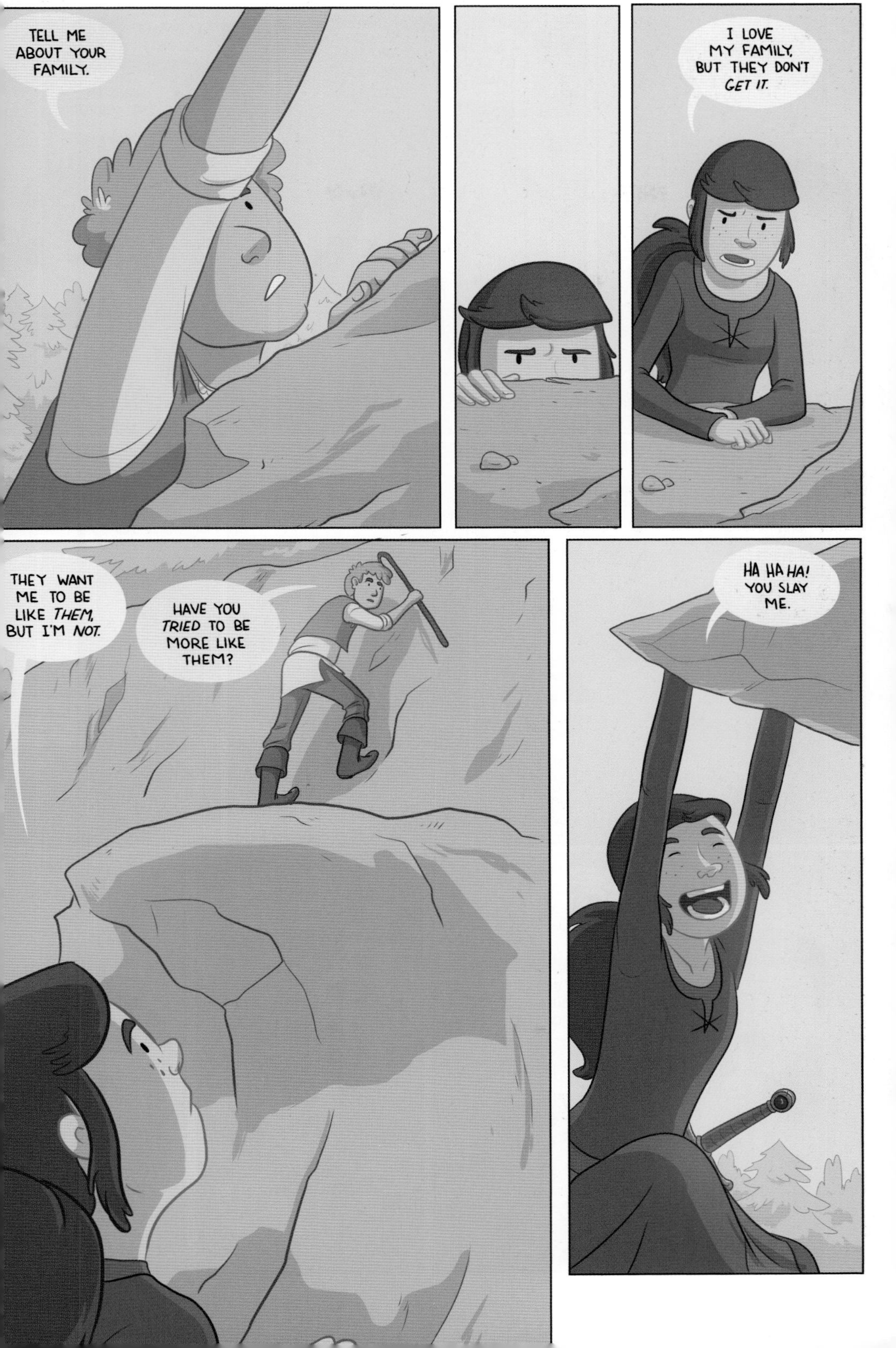
TELL ME ABOUT YOUR FAMILY.
I LOVE MY FAMILY, BUT THEY DON'T *GET IT.*
THEY WANT ME TO BE LIKE *THEM,* BUT I'M *NOT.*
HAVE YOU *TRIED* TO BE MORE LIKE THEM?
HA HA HA! YOU SLAY ME.

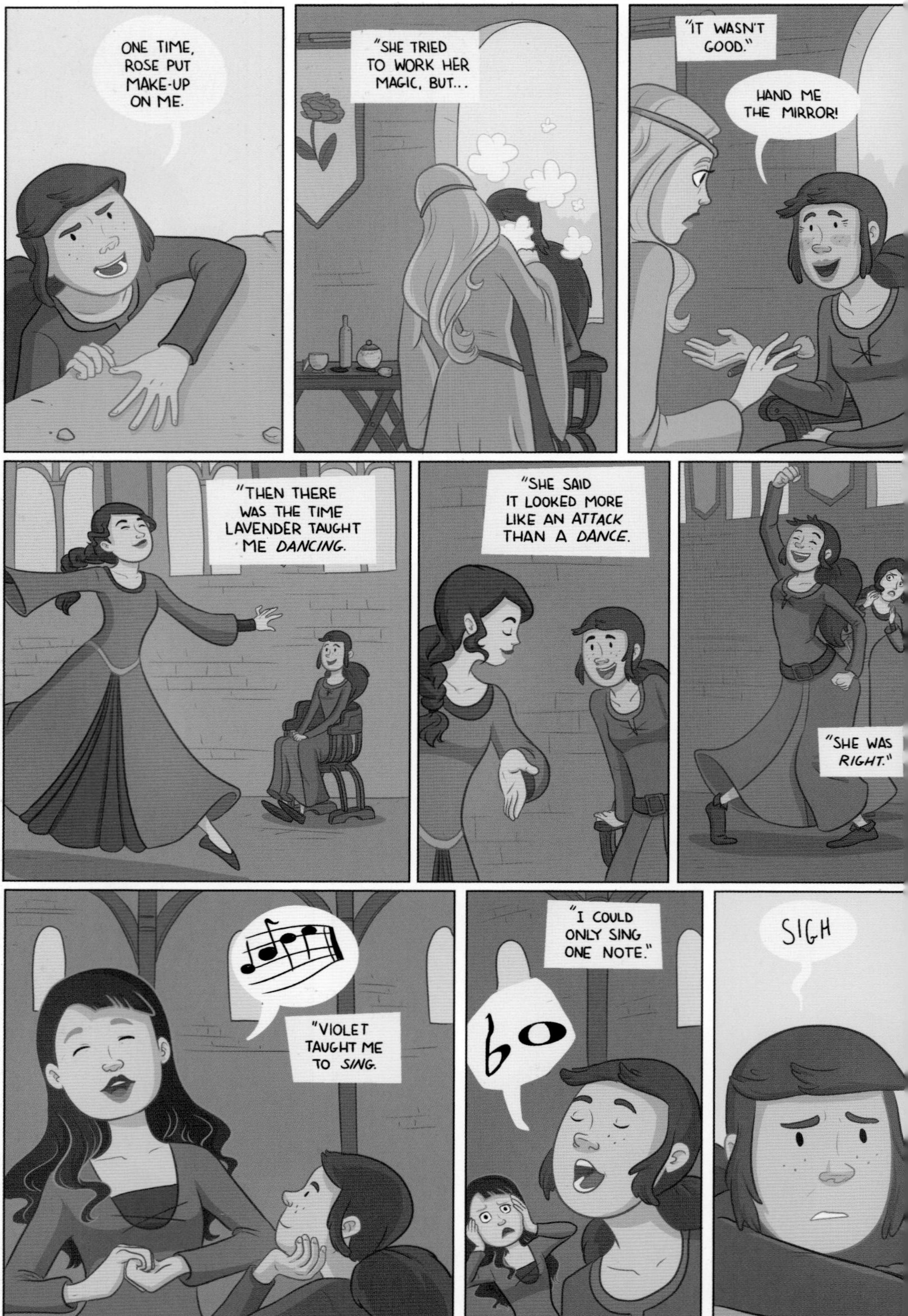

ONE TIME, ROSE PUT MAKE-UP ON ME.
"SHE TRIED TO WORK HER MAGIC, BUT...
"IT WASN'T GOOD."
HAND ME THE MIRROR!
"THEN THERE WAS THE TIME LAVENDER TAUGHT ME *DANCING*.
"SHE SAID IT LOOKED MORE LIKE AN *ATTACK* THAN A *DANCE*.
"SHE WAS *RIGHT*."
"VIOLET TAUGHT ME TO *SING*.
"I COULD ONLY SING ONE NOTE."
SIGH

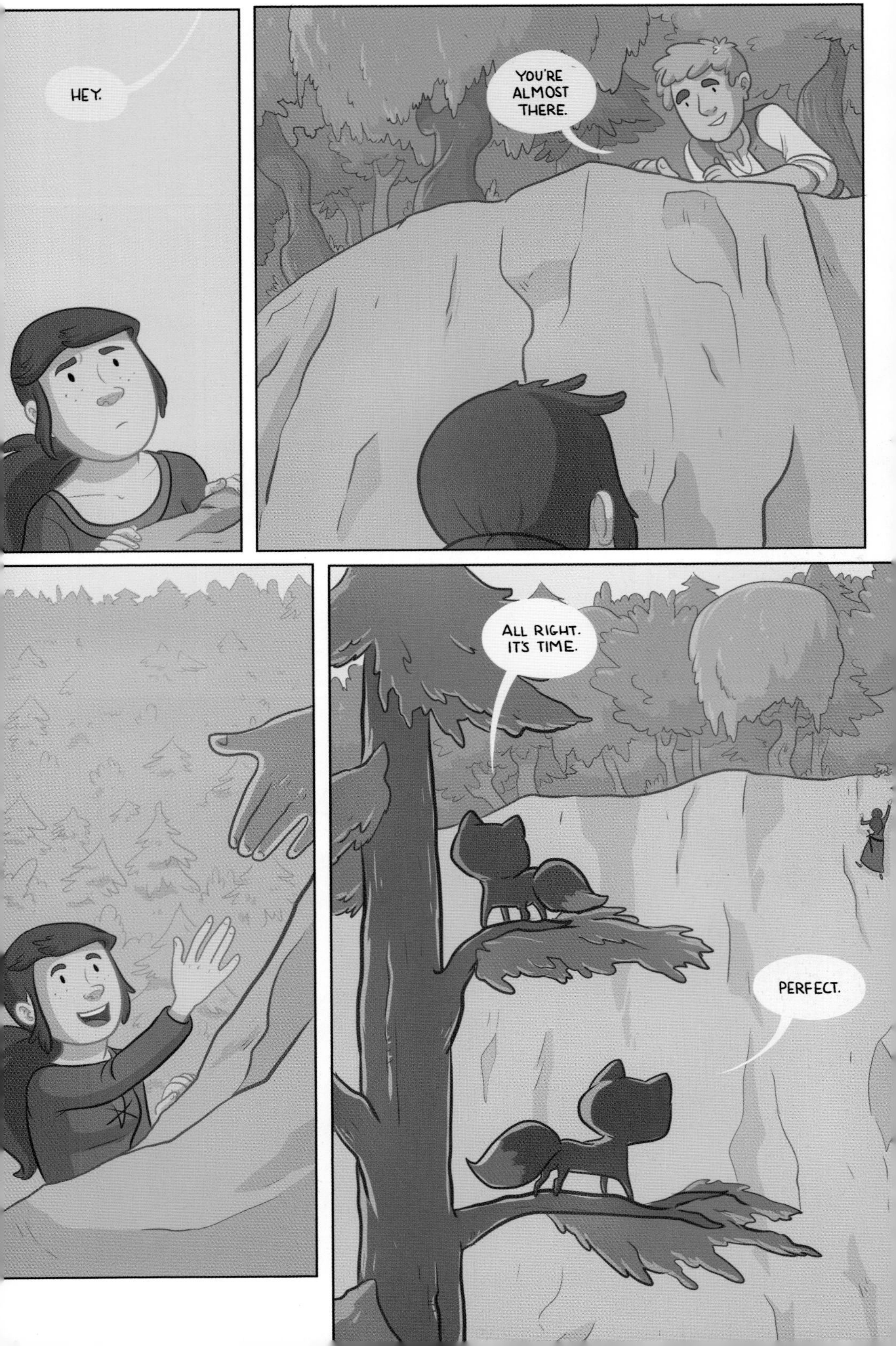
HEY.
YOU'RE ALMOST THERE.
ALL RIGHT. IT'S TIME.
PERFECT.

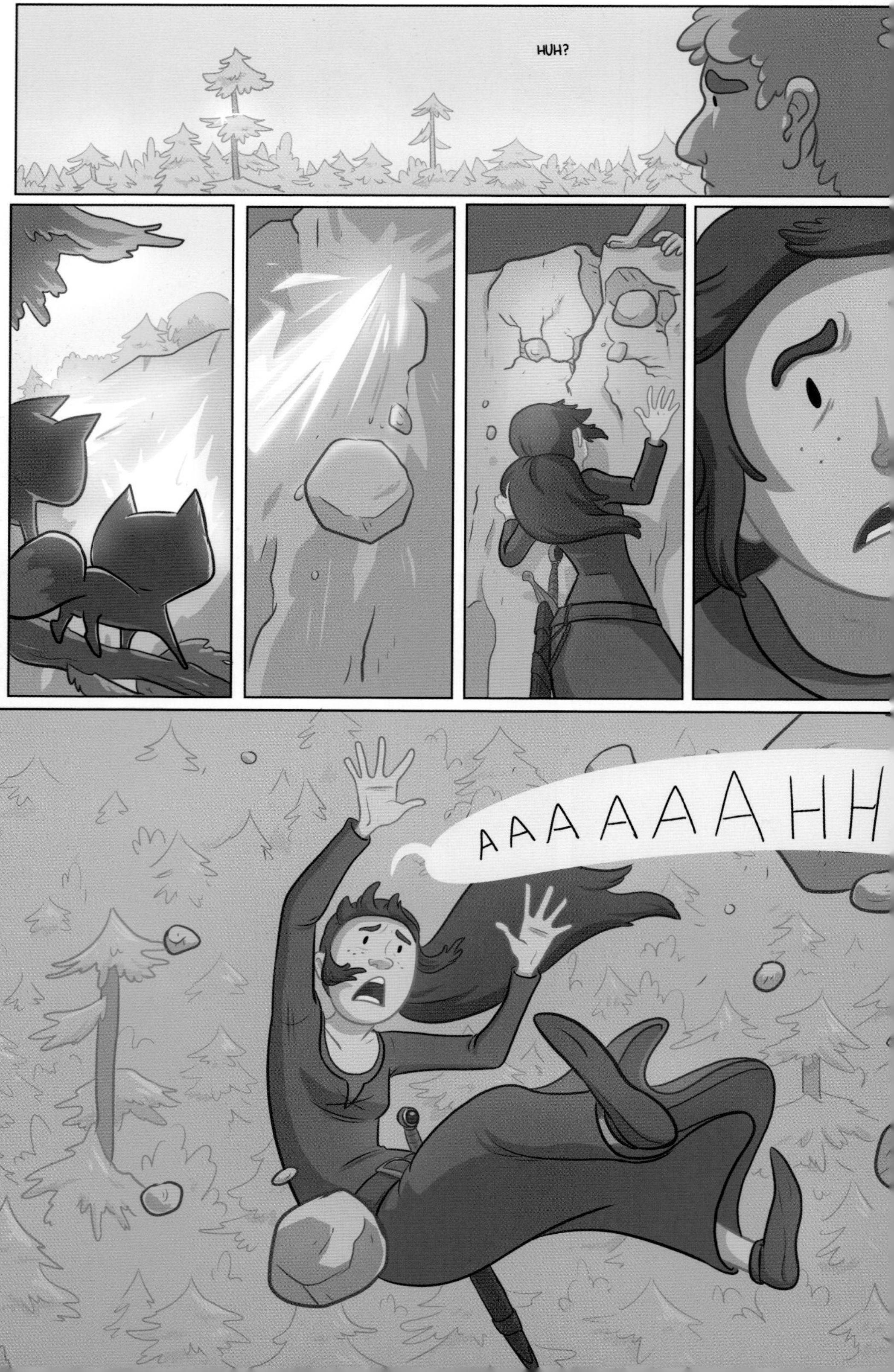
HUH?
AAAAAAHH

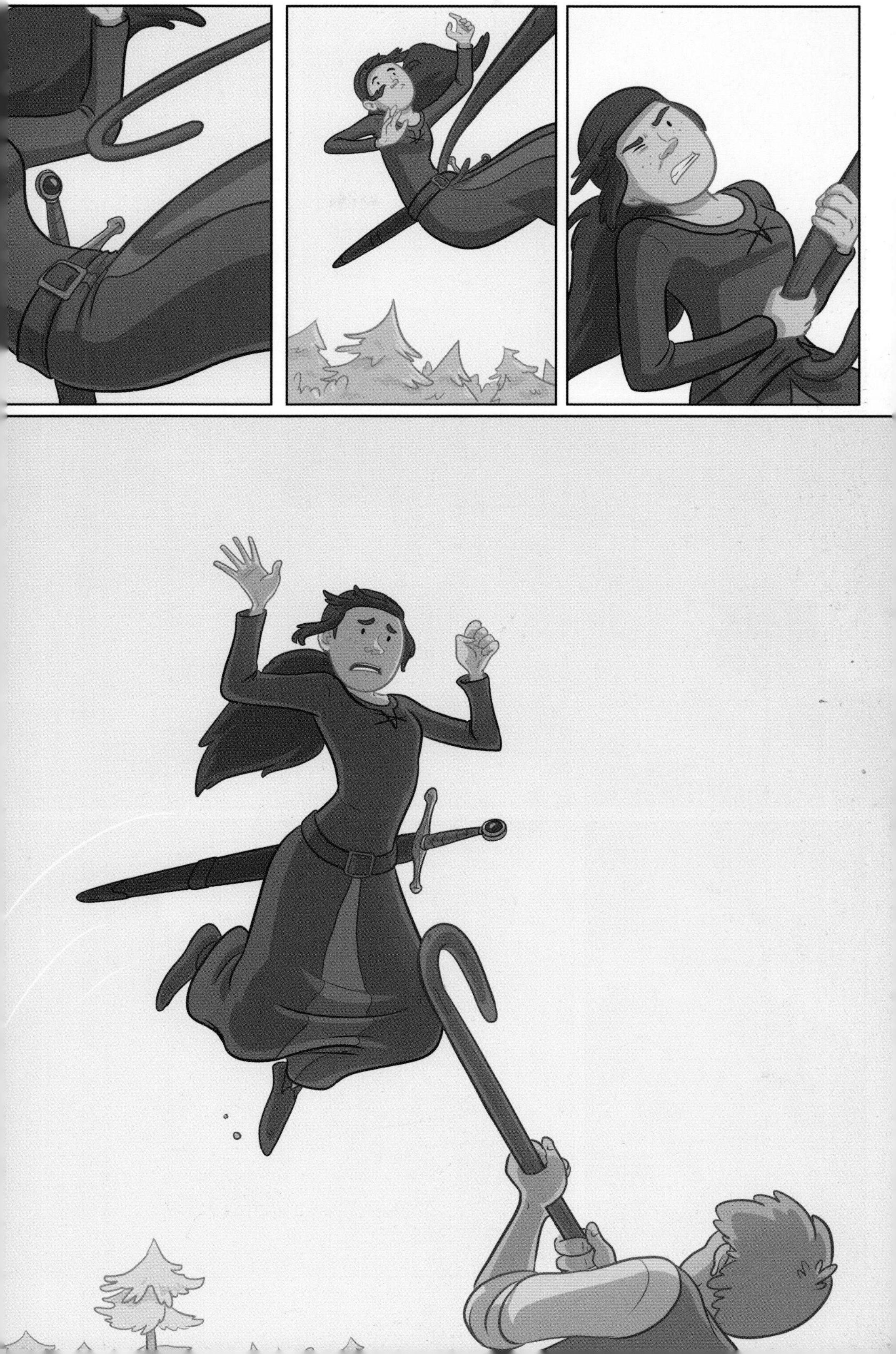

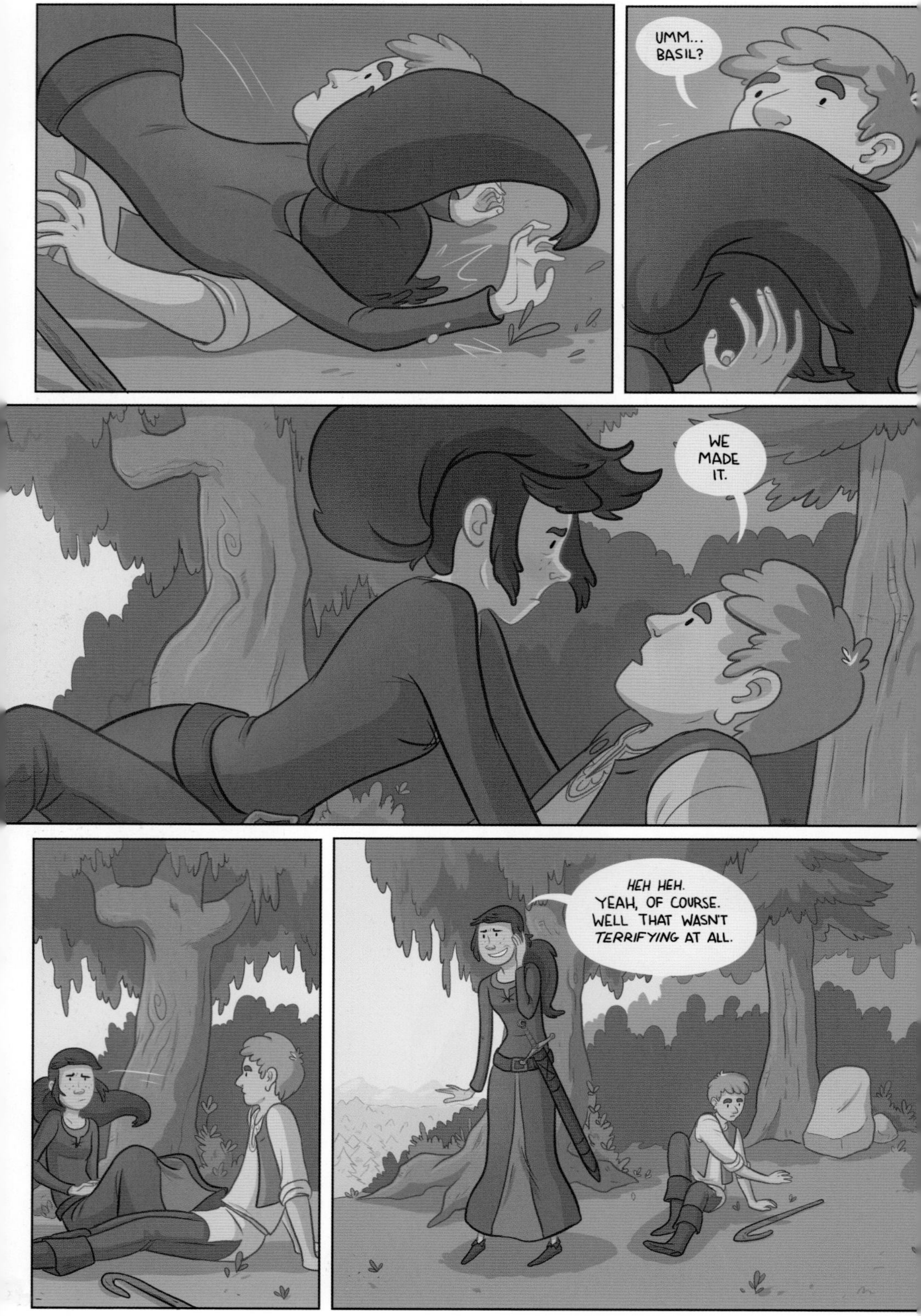
UMM... BASIL?
WE MADE IT.
HEH HEH. YEAH, OF COURSE. WELL THAT WASN'T *TERRIFYING* AT ALL.

THOSE GNOMES ALMOST GOT US *KILLED.*

I DUNNO... I DON'T THINK THIS WAS THE *GNOMES'* FAULT.

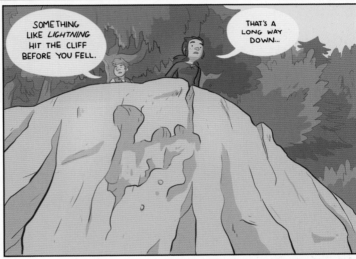

SOMETHING LIKE *LIGHTNING* HIT THE CLIFF BEFORE YOU FELL.

THAT'S A LONG WAY DOWN...

CAME FROM THOSE TREES... AND I ALWAYS THOUGHT IT CAME FROM THE *SKY.*

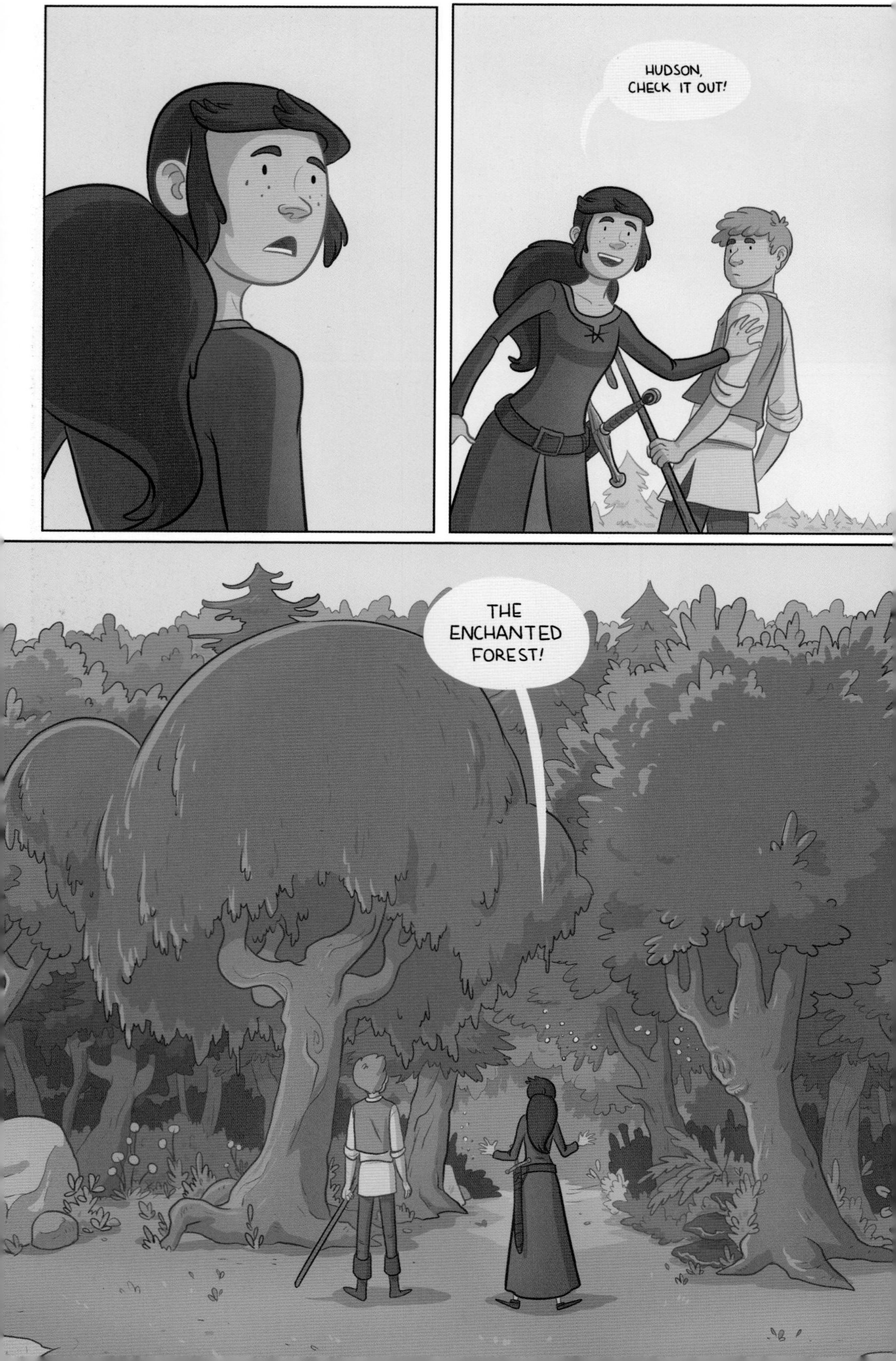
HUDSON, CHECK IT OUT!
THE ENCHANTED FOREST!

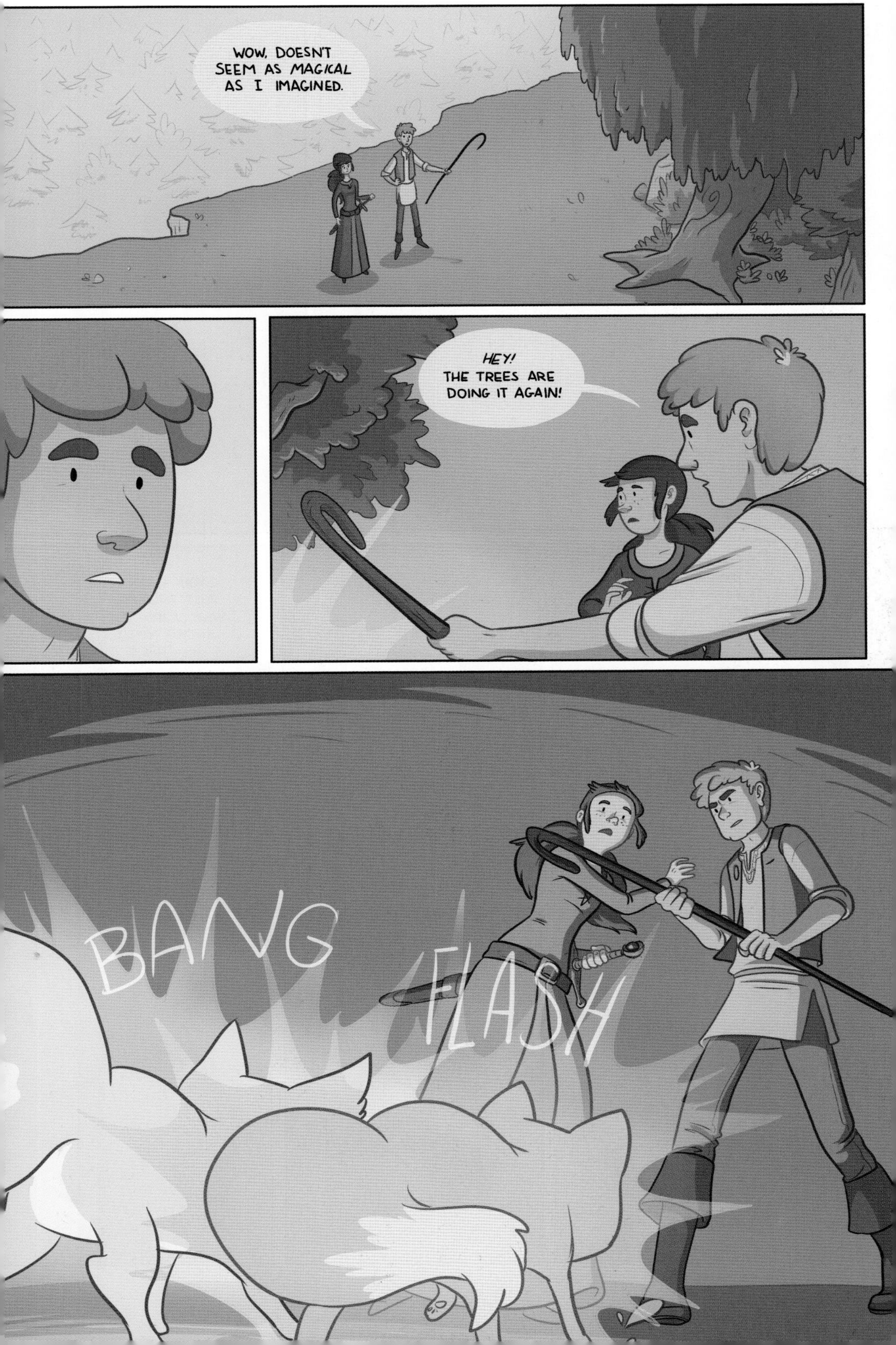
WOW, DOESN'T SEEM AS MAGICAL AS I IMAGINED.
HEY! THE TREES ARE DOING IT AGAIN!
BANG
FLASH

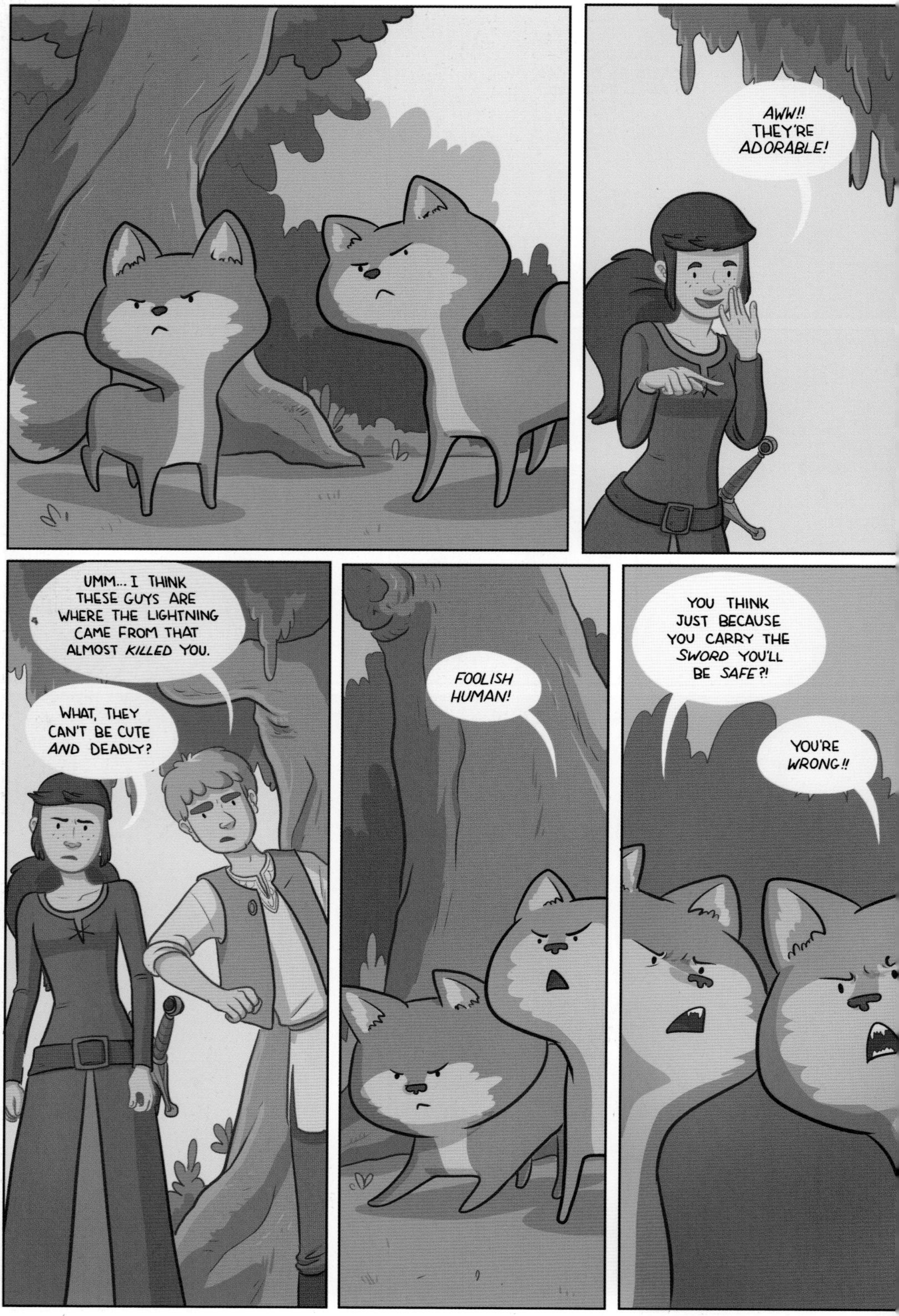
AWW!! THEY'RE ADORABLE!
UMM... I THINK THESE GUYS ARE WHERE THE LIGHTNING CAME FROM THAT ALMOST KILLED YOU.
WHAT, THEY CAN'T BE CUTE AND DEADLY?
FOOLISH HUMAN!
YOU THINK JUST BECAUSE YOU CARRY THE SWORD YOU'LL BE SAFE?!
YOU'RE WRONG!!

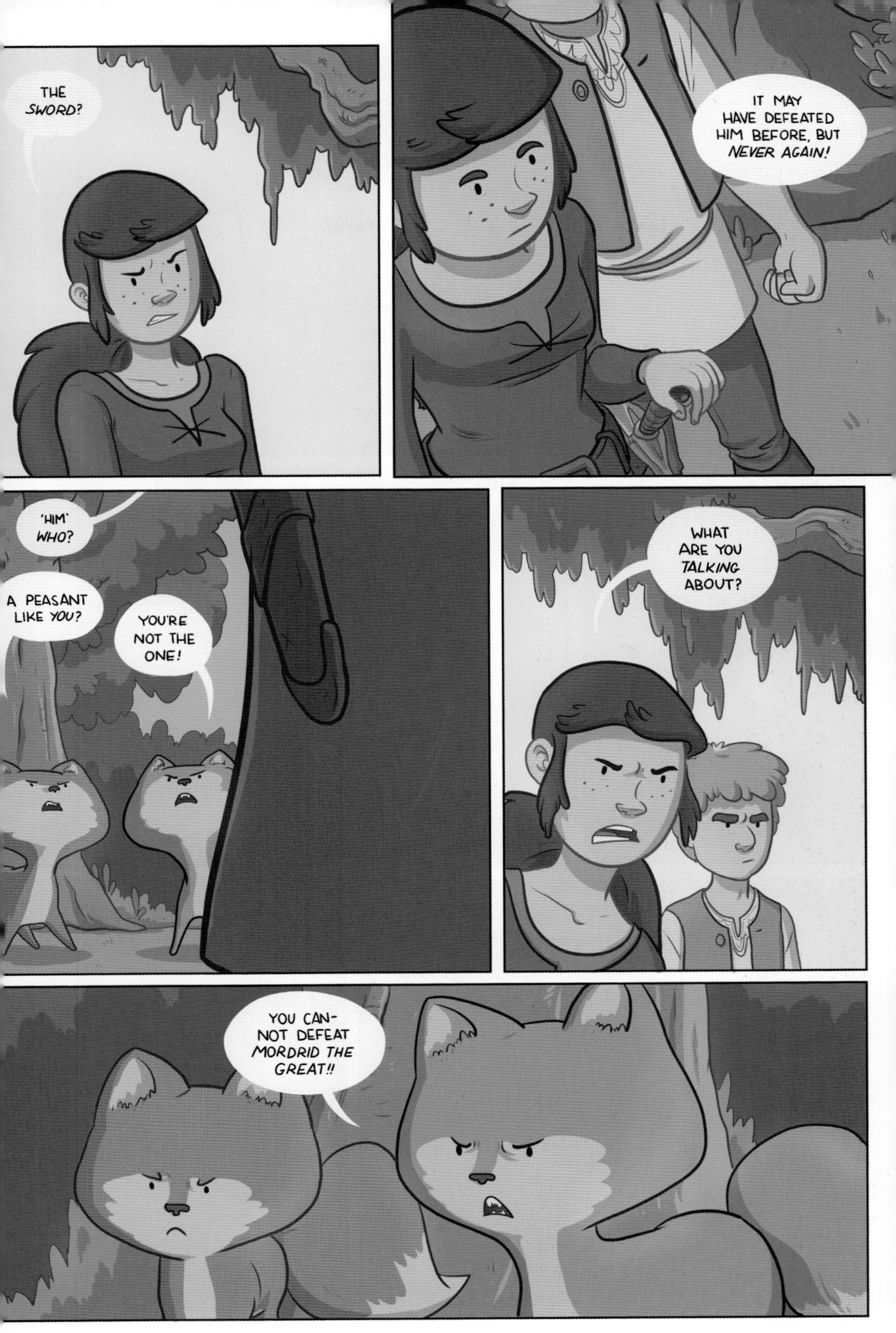
THE SWORD?
IT MAY HAVE DEFEATED HIM BEFORE, BUT NEVER AGAIN!
'HIM' WHO?
A PEASANT LIKE YOU?
YOU'RE NOT THE ONE!
WHAT ARE YOU TALKING ABOUT?
YOU CAN-NOT DEFEAT MORDRID THE GREAT!!

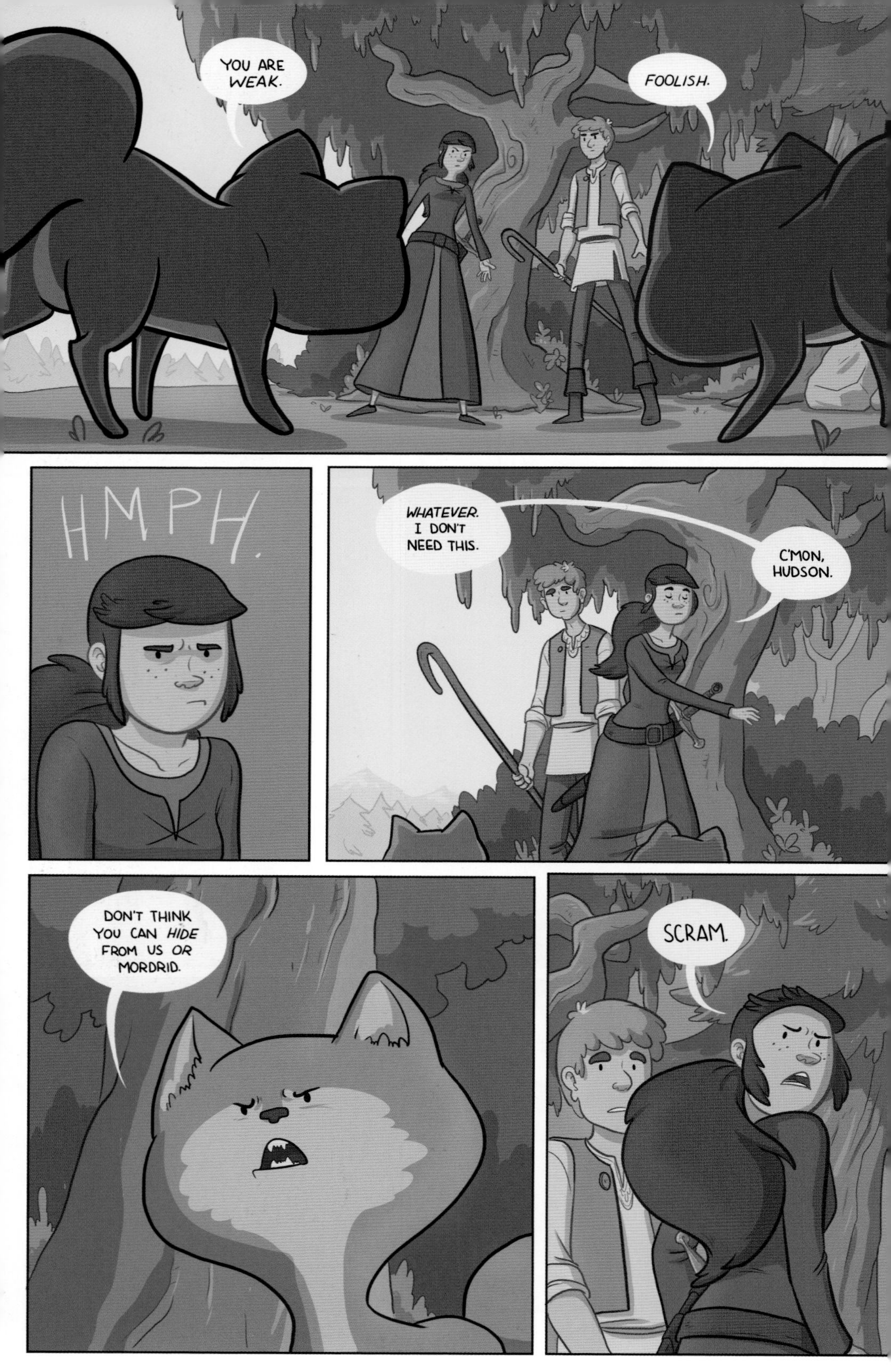
YOU ARE WEAK.
FOOLISH.
HMPH.
WHATEVER. I DON'T NEED THIS.
C'MON, HUDSON.
DON'T THINK YOU CAN *HIDE* FROM US *OR* MORDRID.
SCRAM.

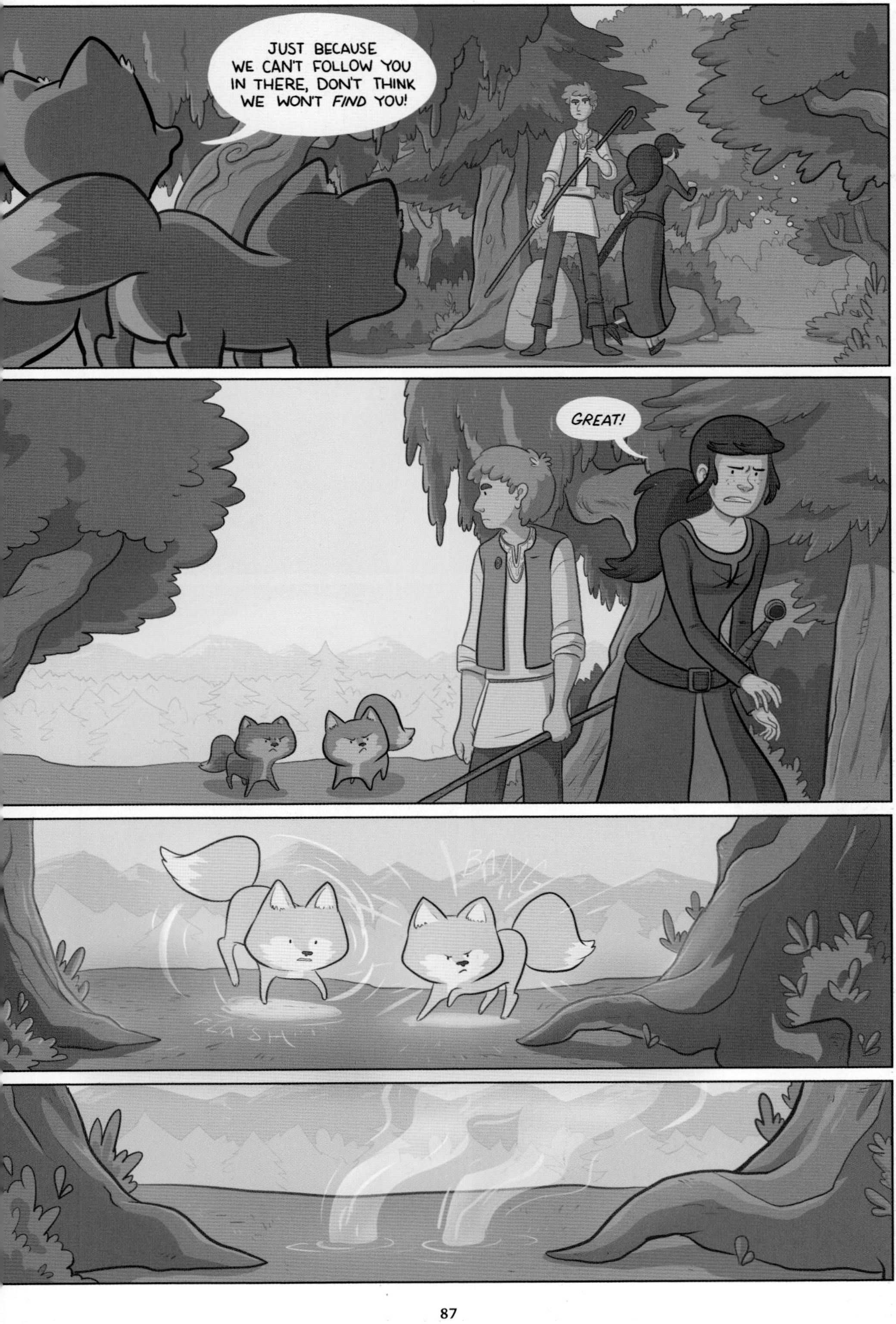
JUST BECAUSE WE CAN'T FOLLOW YOU IN THERE, DON'T THINK WE WON'T *FIND* YOU!
GREAT!
BANG
FLASH

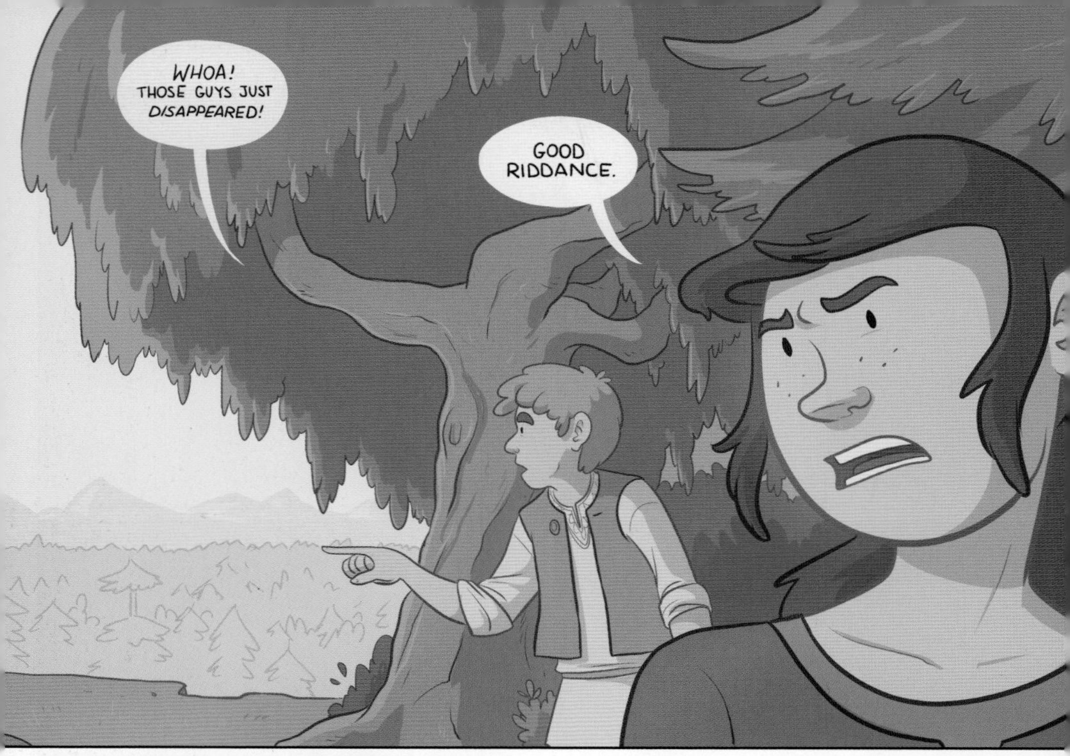
WHOA! THOSE GUYS JUST *DISAPPEARED!*
GOOD RIDDANCE.

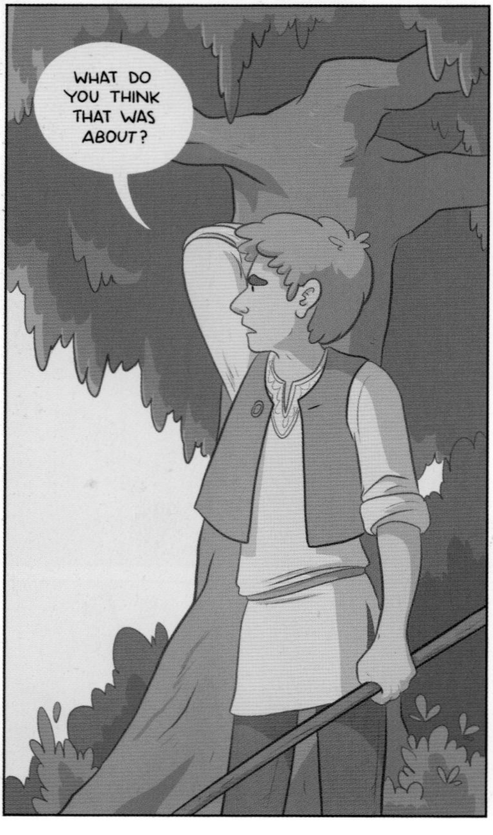
WHAT DO YOU THINK THAT WAS ABOUT?

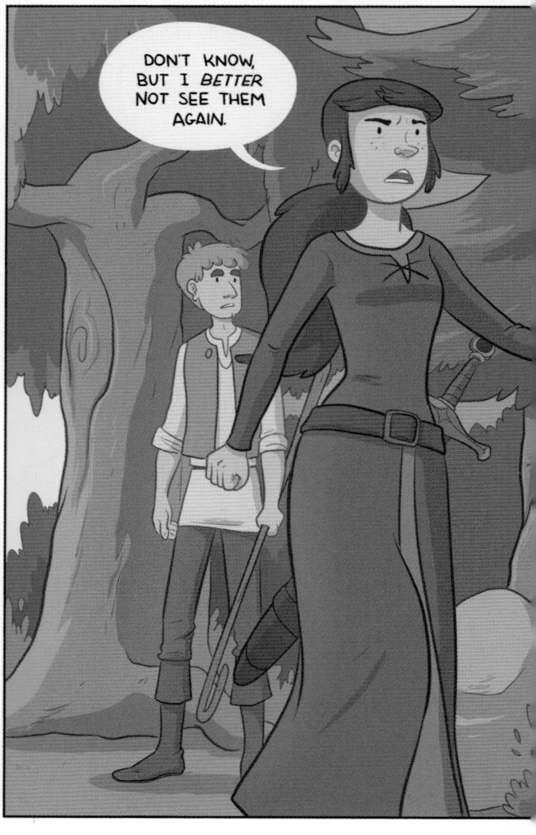
DON'T KNOW, BUT I *BETTER* NOT SEE THEM AGAIN.

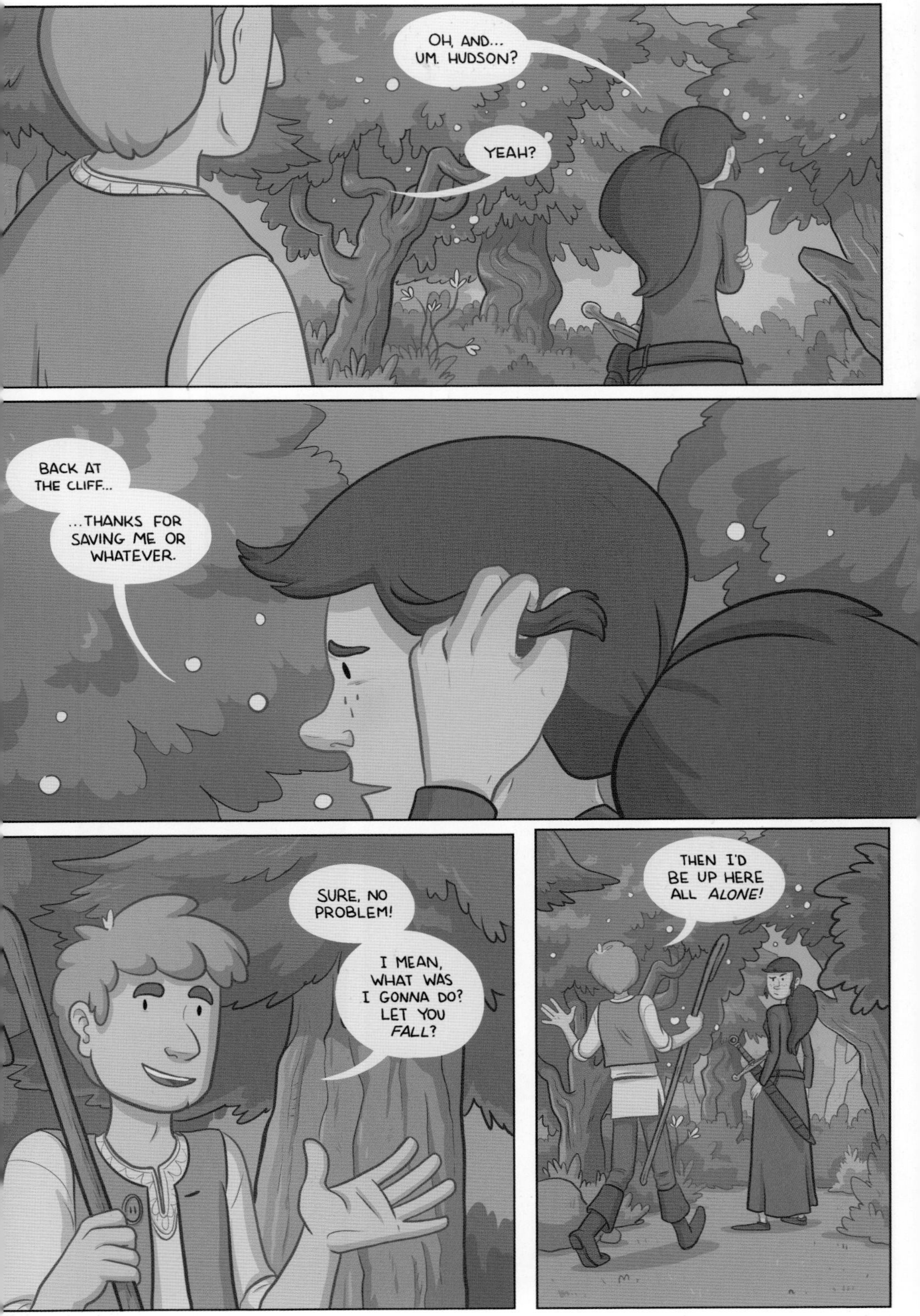
OH, AND... UM. HUDSON?
YEAH?
BACK AT THE CLIFF...
...THANKS FOR SAVING ME OR WHATEVER.
SURE, NO PROBLEM!
I MEAN, WHAT WAS I GONNA DO? LET YOU *FALL*?
THEN I'D BE UP HERE ALL *ALONE*!

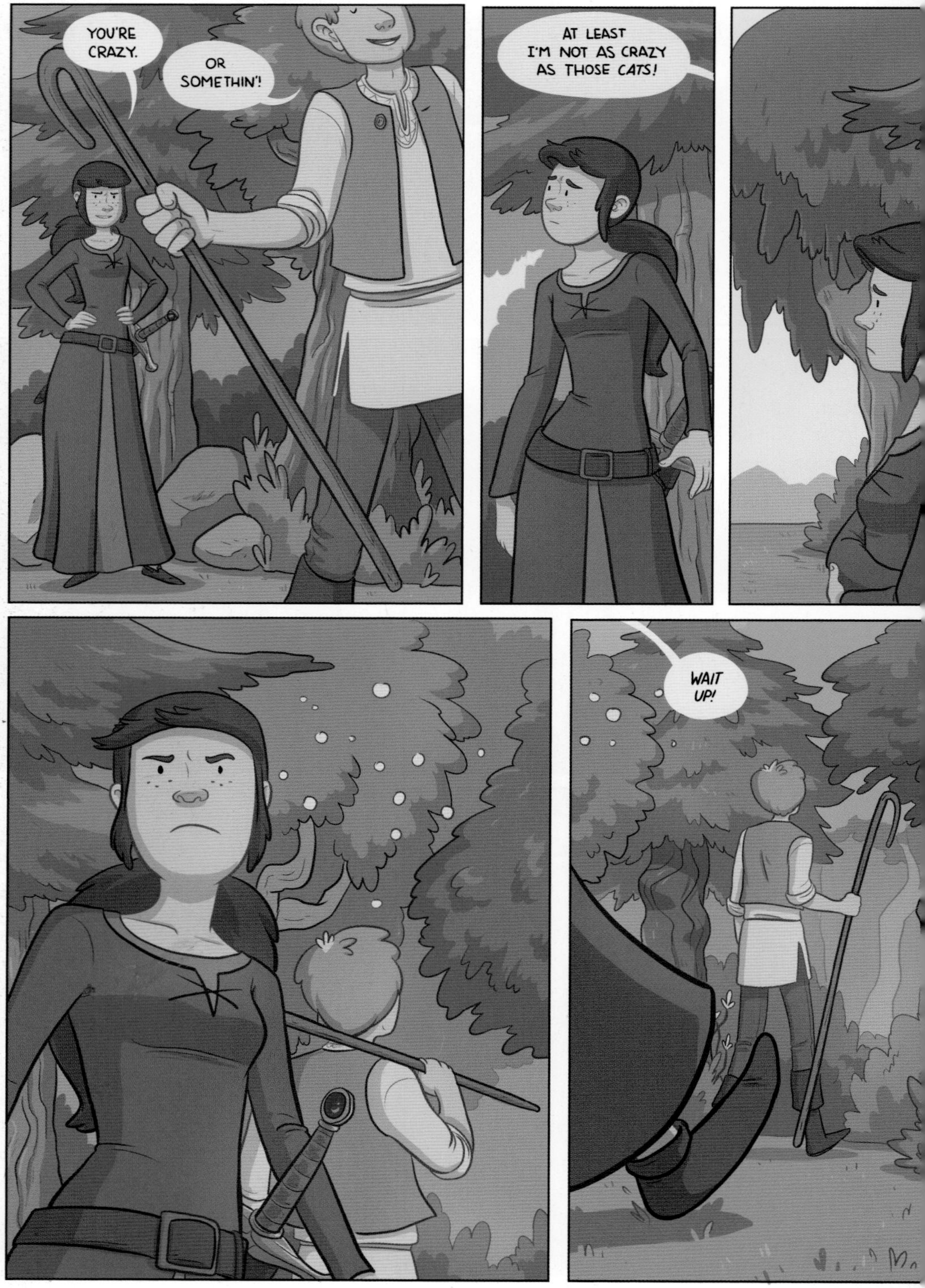
YOU'RE CRAZY.
OR SOMETHIN'!
AT LEAST I'M NOT AS CRAZY AS THOSE *CATS*!
WAIT UP!

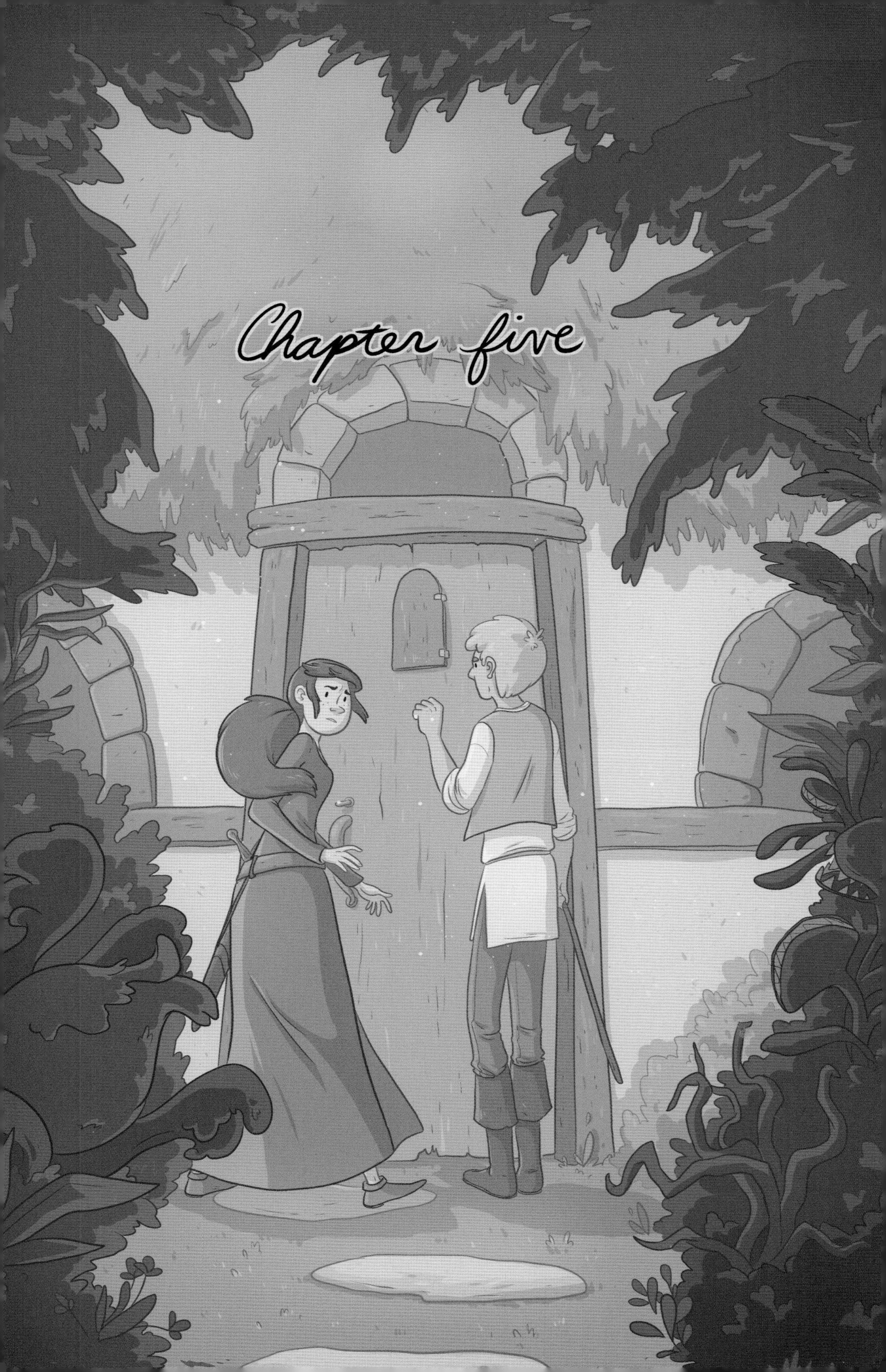
Chapter five

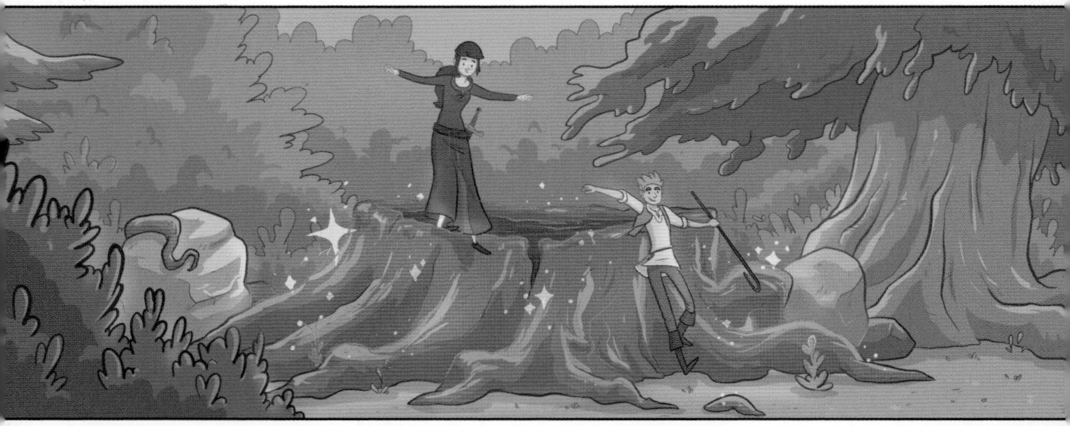

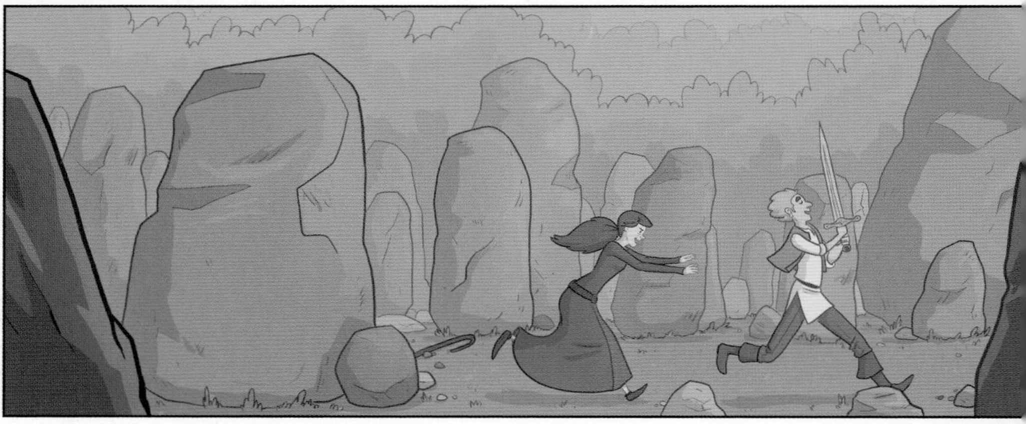

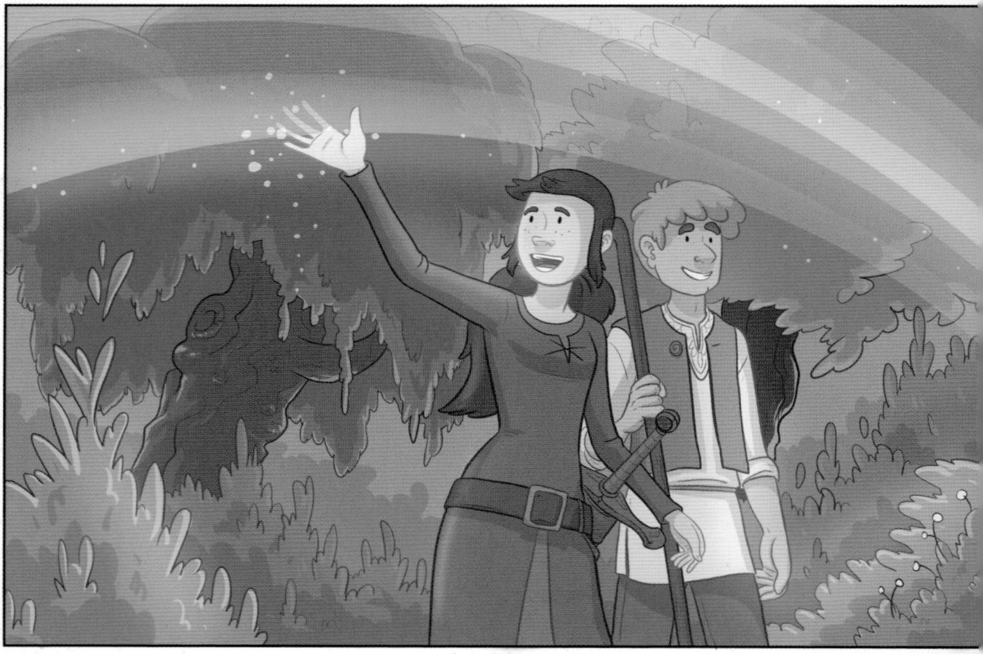

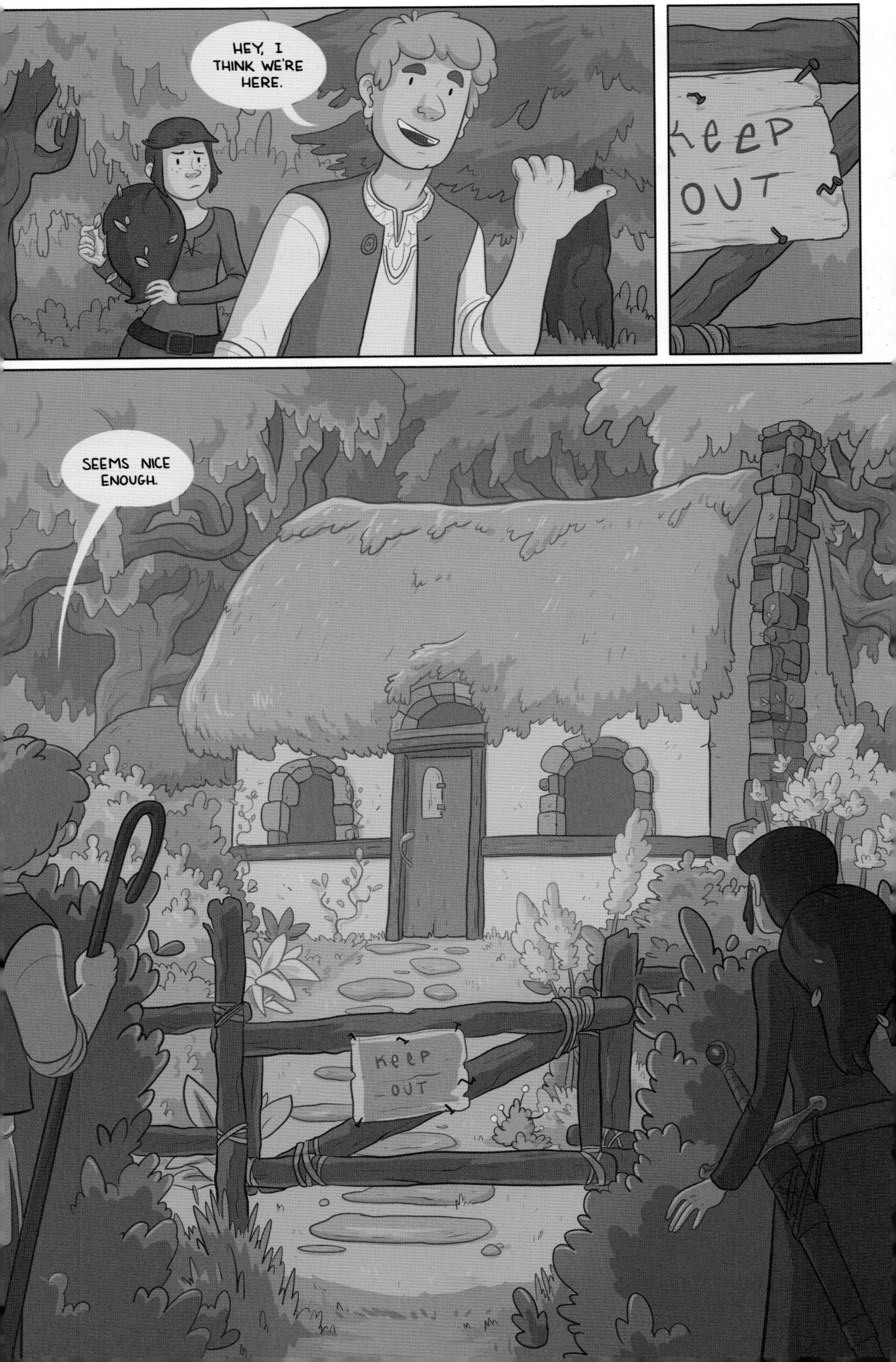
HEY, I THINK WE'RE HERE.
KEEP OUT
SEEMS NICE ENOUGH.
KEEP OUT

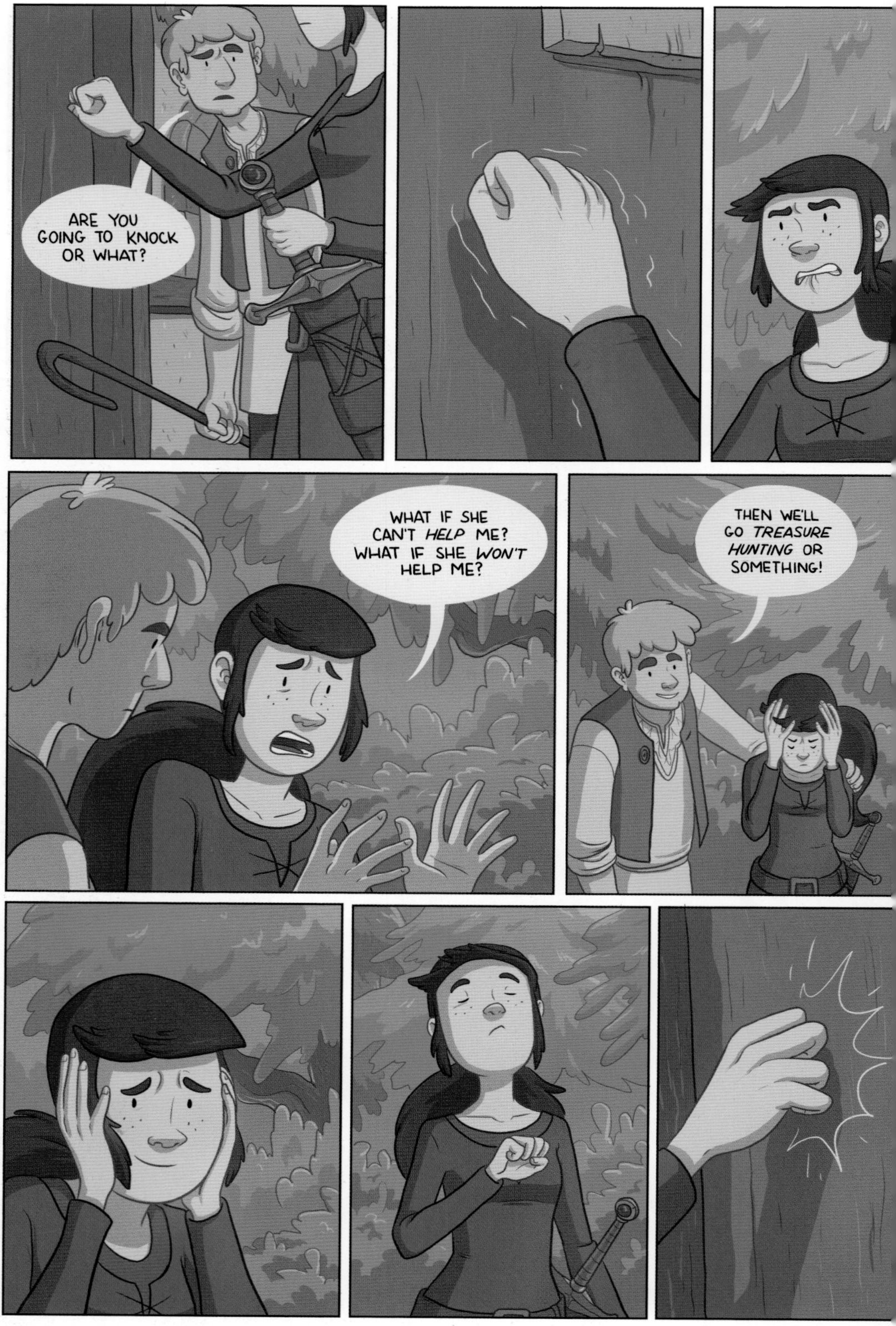
ARE YOU GOING TO KNOCK OR WHAT?
WHAT IF SHE CAN'T *HELP* ME? WHAT IF SHE *WON'T* HELP ME?
THEN WE'LL GO *TREASURE HUNTING* OR SOMETHING!

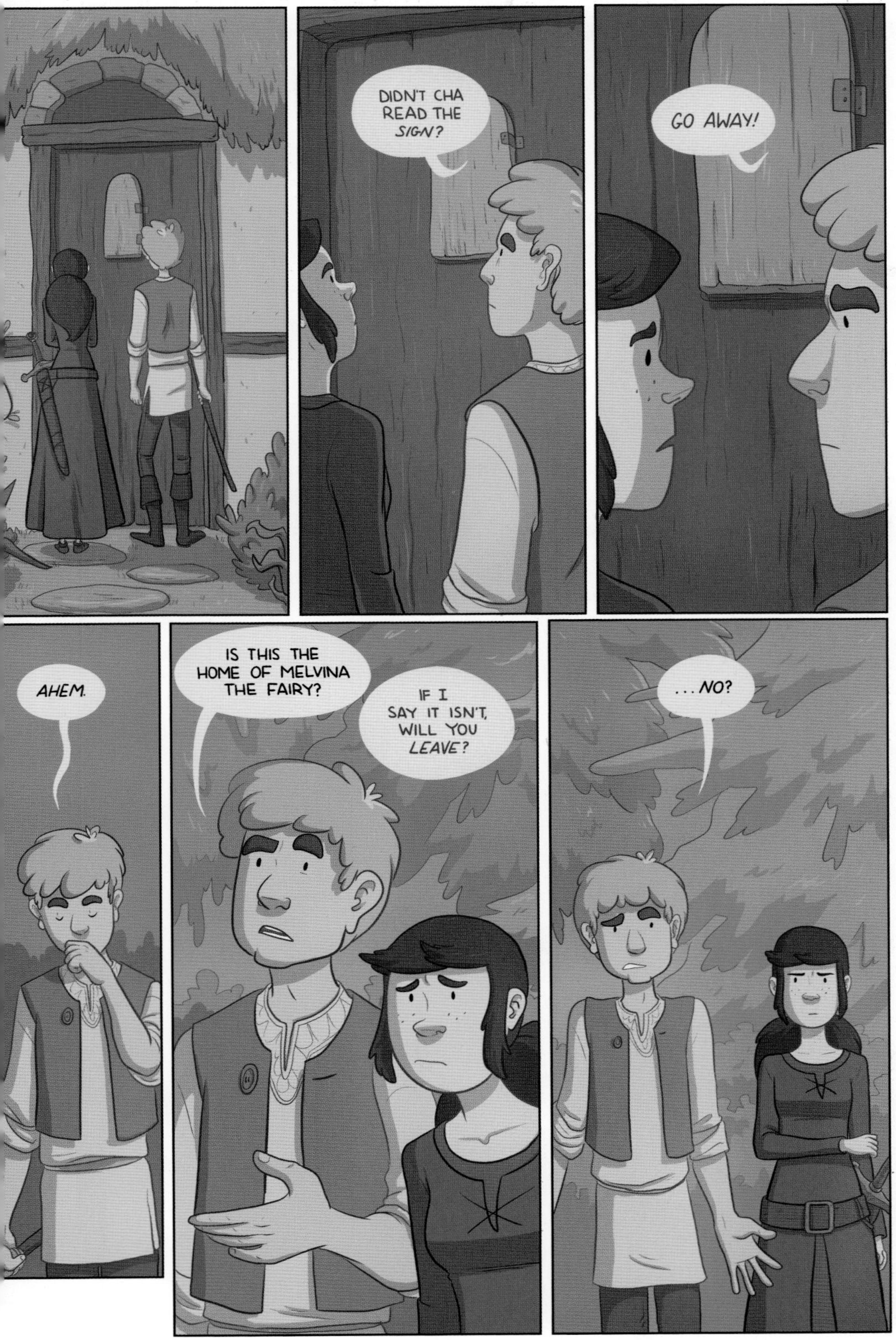
DIDN'T CHA READ THE SIGN?
GO AWAY!
AHEM.
IS THIS THE HOME OF MELVINA THE FAIRY?
IF I SAY IT ISN'T, WILL YOU LEAVE?
...NO?

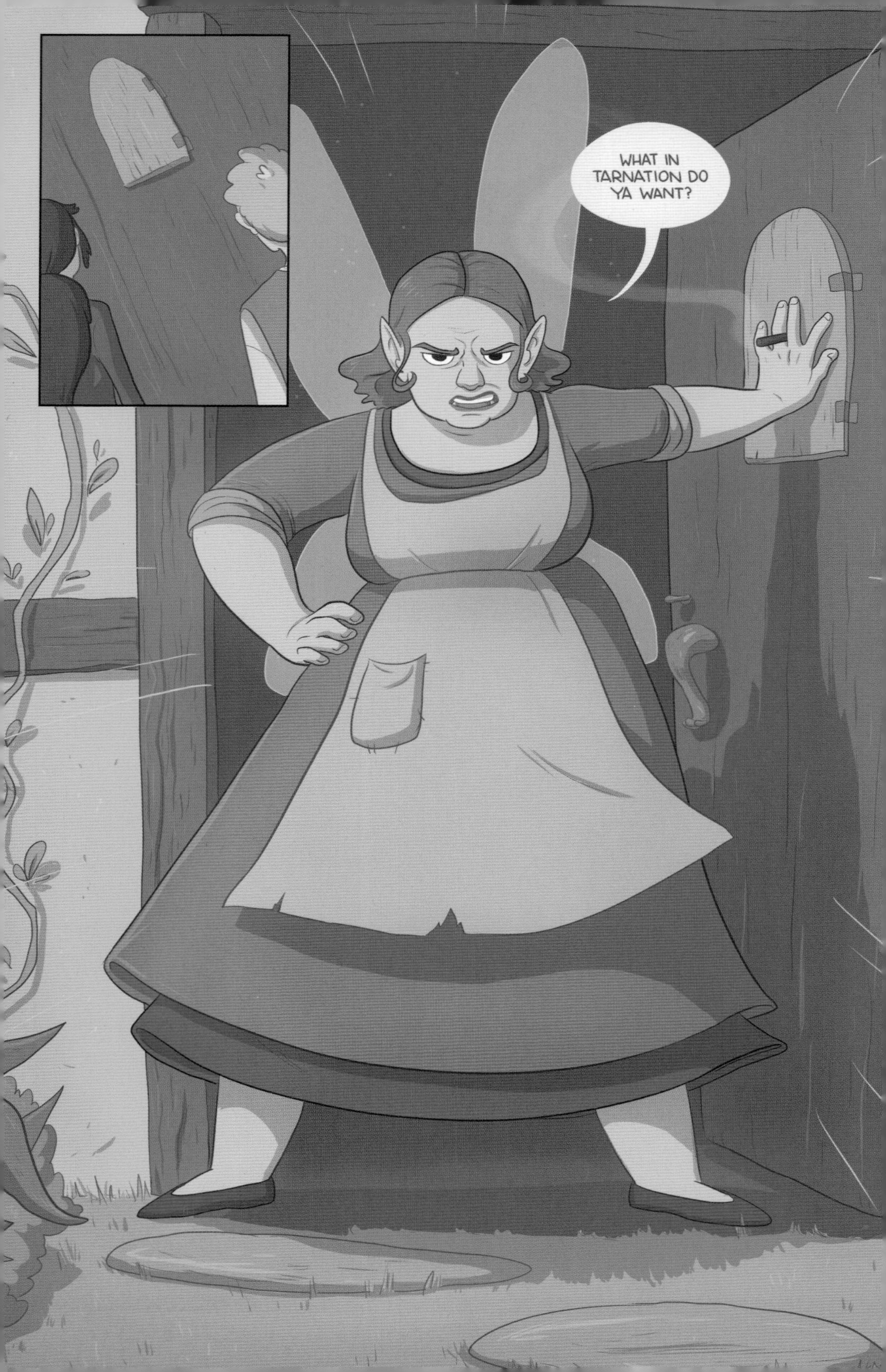
WHAT IN TARNATION DO YA WANT?

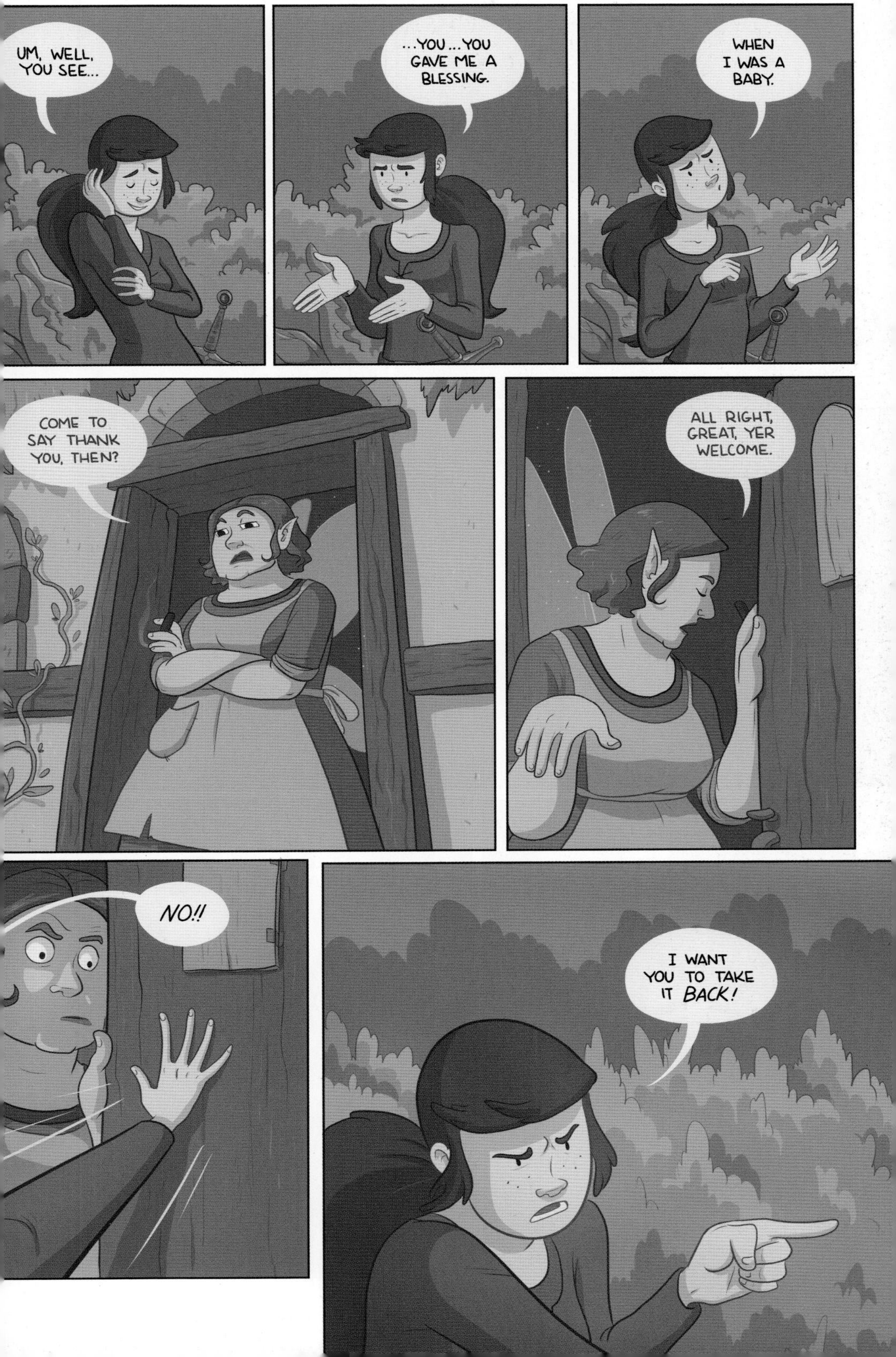
UM, WELL, YOU SEE...
...YOU...YOU GAVE ME A BLESSING.
WHEN I WAS A BABY.
COME TO SAY THANK YOU, THEN?
ALL RIGHT, GREAT, YER WELCOME.
NO!!
I WANT YOU TO TAKE IT *BACK!*

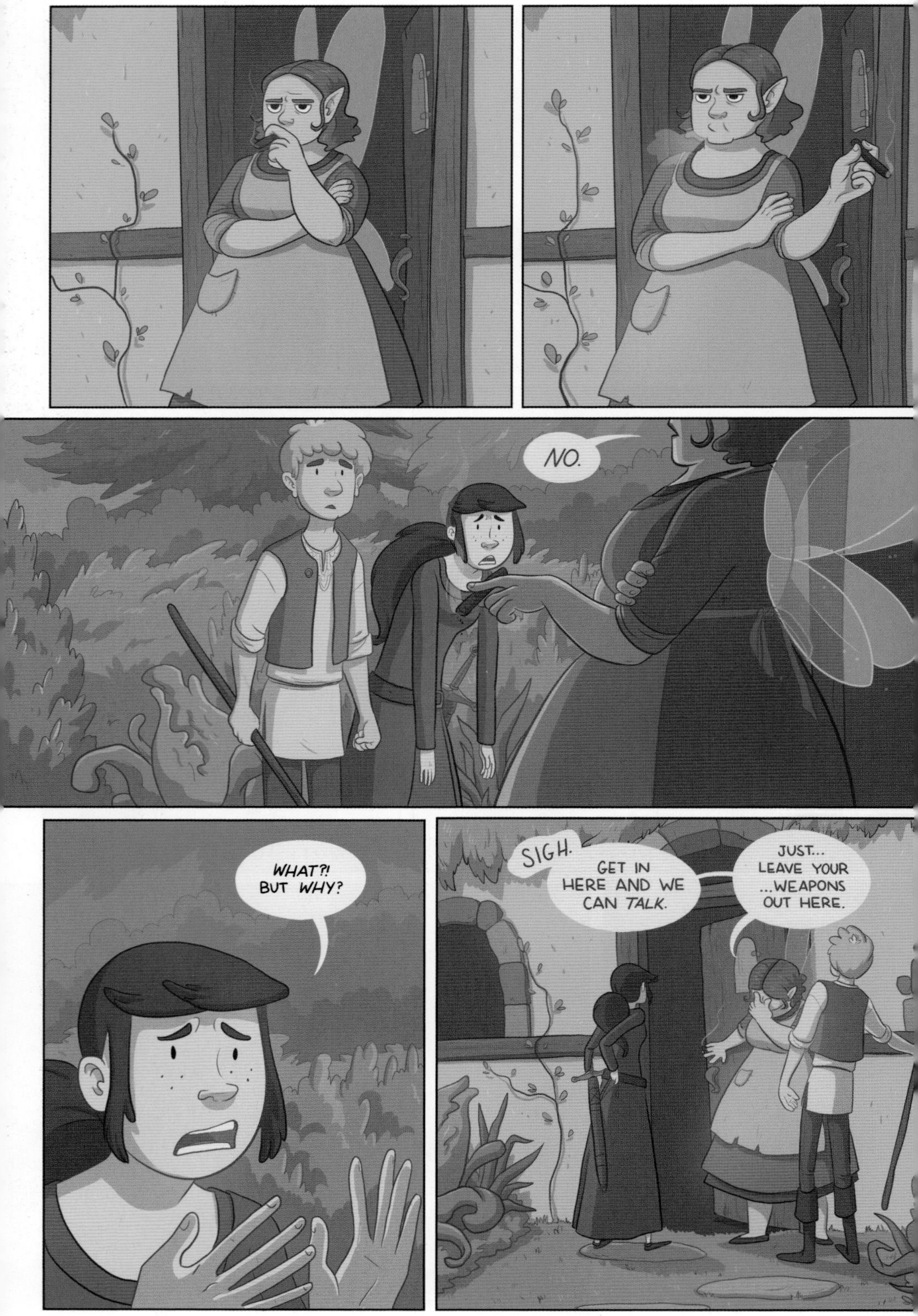
NO.
WHAT?! BUT WHY?
SIGH.
GET IN HERE AND WE CAN TALK.
JUST... LEAVE YOUR ...WEAPONS OUT HERE.

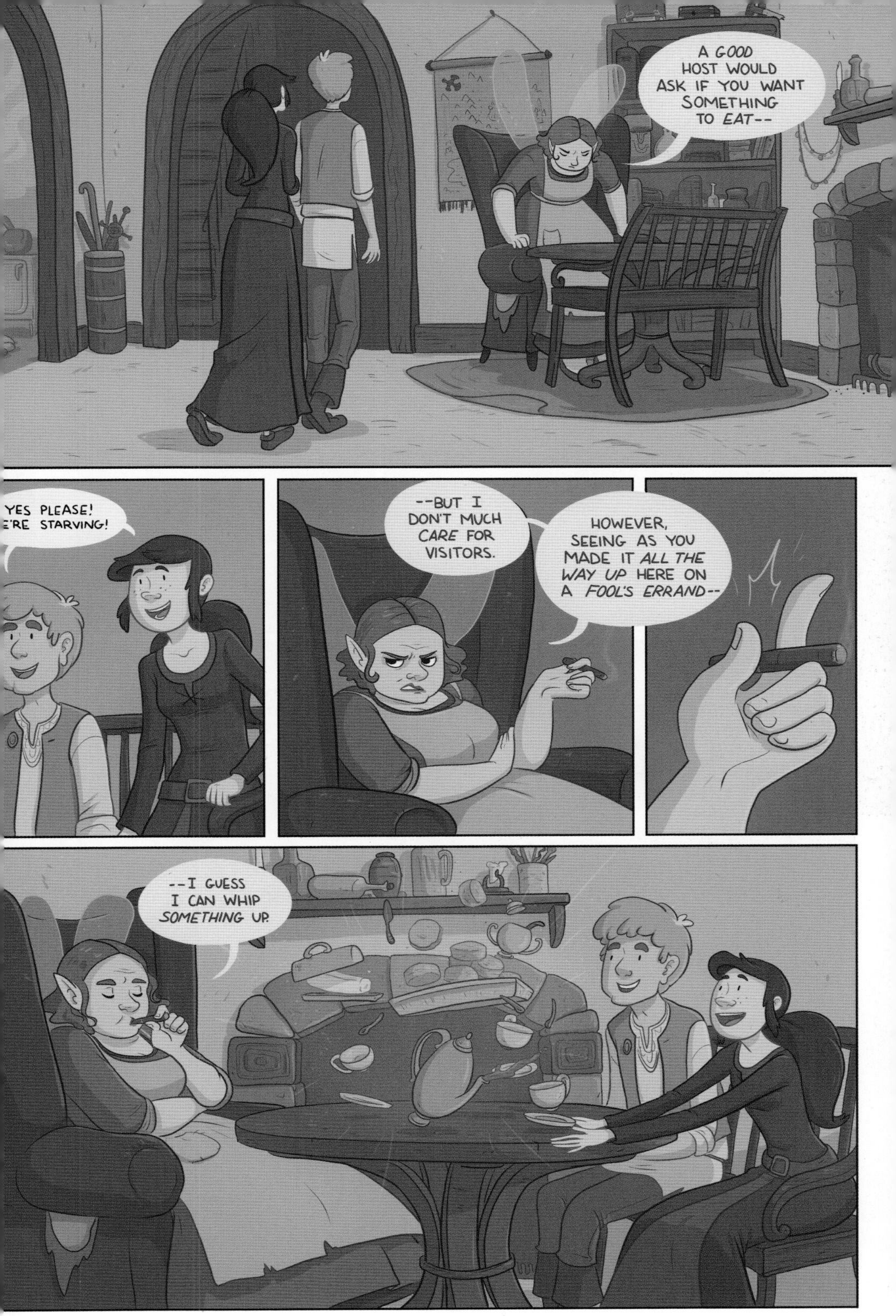
A GOOD HOST WOULD ASK IF YOU WANT SOMETHING TO EAT--
YES PLEASE! E'RE STARVING!
--BUT I DON'T MUCH CARE FOR VISITORS.
HOWEVER, SEEING AS YOU MADE IT ALL THE WAY UP HERE ON A FOOL'S ERRAND--
--I GUESS I CAN WHIP SOMETHING UP.

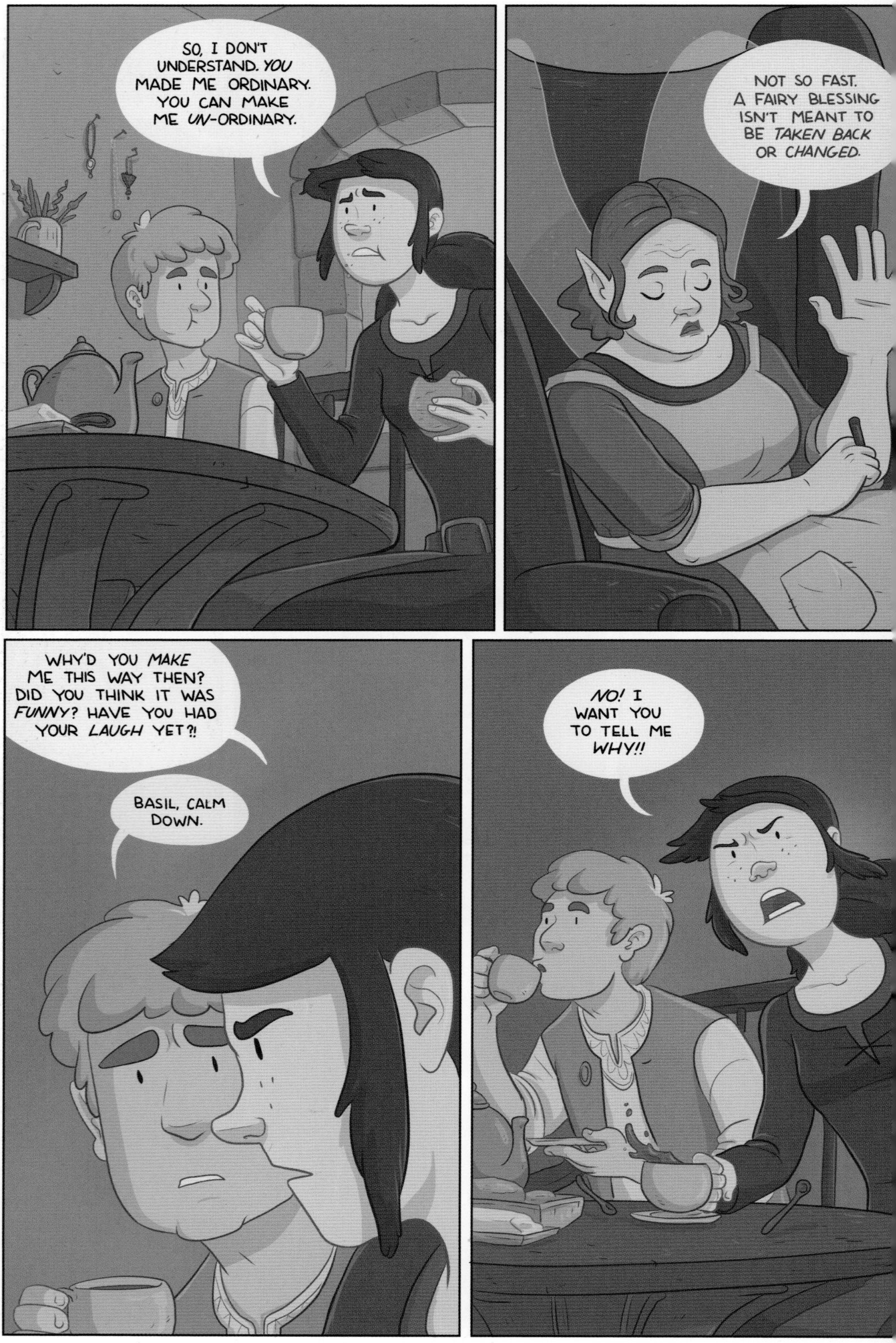
SO, I DON'T UNDERSTAND. YOU MADE ME ORDINARY. YOU CAN MAKE ME UN-ORDINARY.
NOT SO FAST. A FAIRY BLESSING ISN'T MEANT TO BE TAKEN BACK OR CHANGED.
WHY'D YOU MAKE ME THIS WAY THEN? DID YOU THINK IT WAS FUNNY? HAVE YOU HAD YOUR LAUGH YET?!
BASIL, CALM DOWN.
NO! I WANT YOU TO TELL ME WHY!!

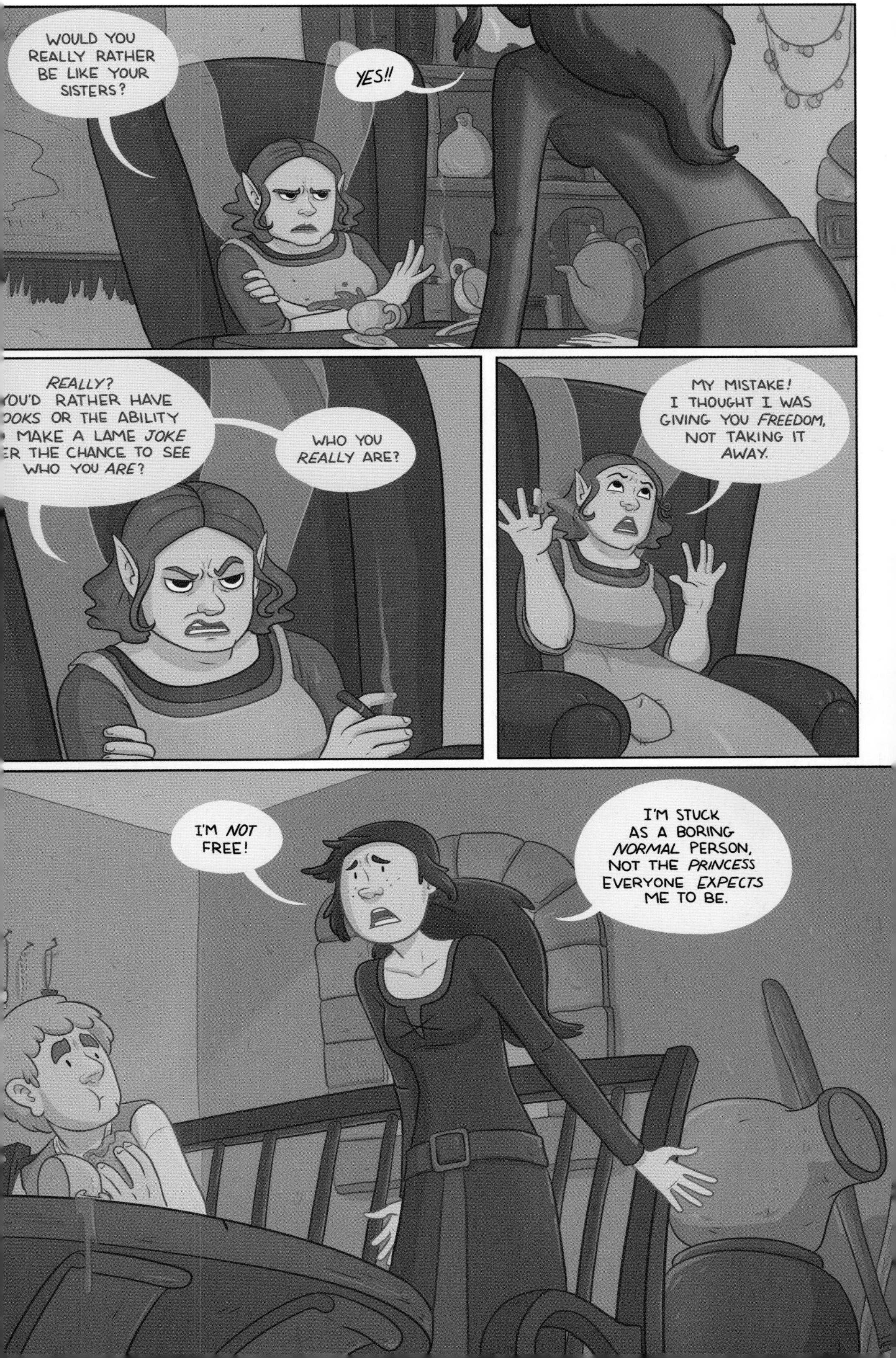
WOULD YOU REALLY RATHER BE LIKE YOUR SISTERS?
YES!!
REALLY? YOU'D RATHER HAVE OOKS OR THE ABILITY MAKE A LAME JOKE ER THE CHANCE TO SEE WHO YOU ARE?
WHO YOU REALLY ARE?
MY MISTAKE! I THOUGHT I WAS GIVING YOU FREEDOM, NOT TAKING IT AWAY.
I'M NOT FREE!
I'M STUCK AS A BORING NORMAL PERSON, NOT THE PRINCESS EVERYONE EXPECTS ME TO BE.

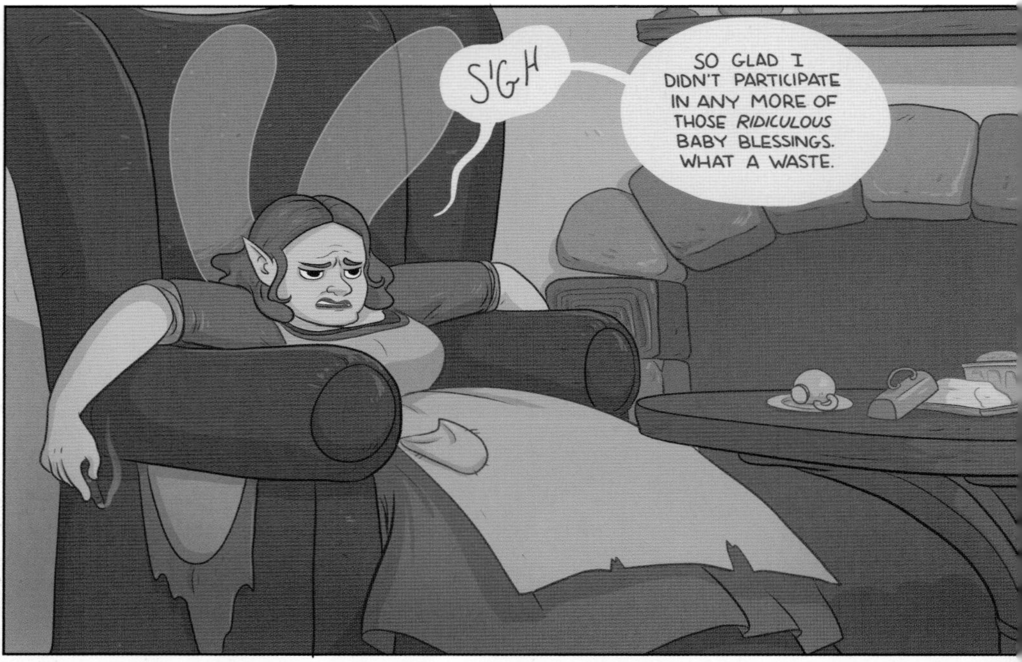
SIGH
SO GLAD I DIDN'T PARTICIPATE IN ANY MORE OF THOSE *RIDICULOUS* BABY BLESSINGS. WHAT A WASTE.

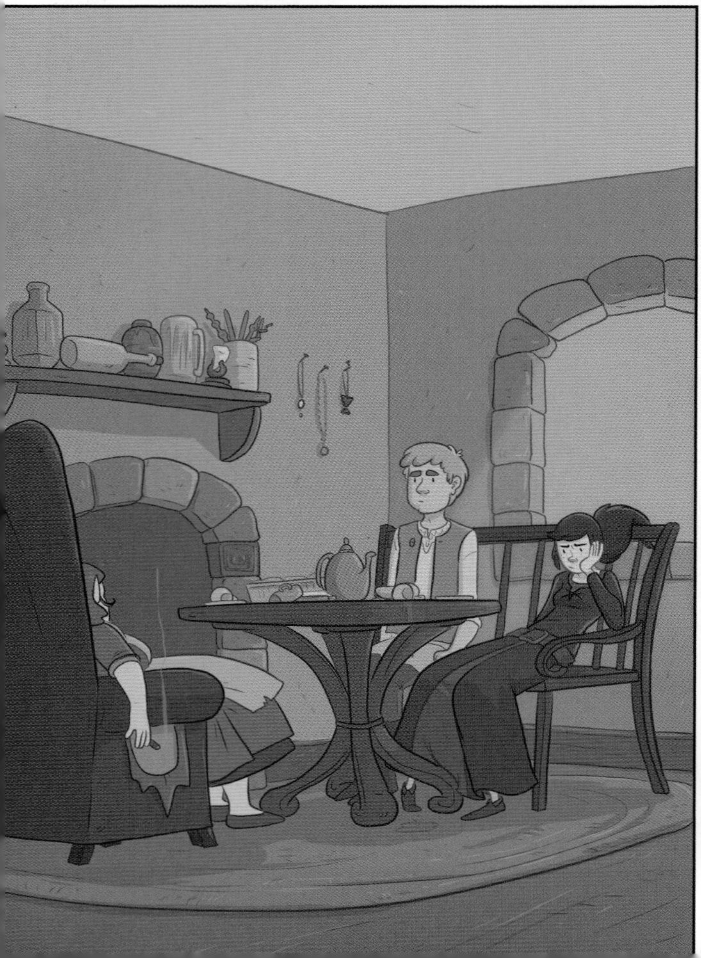

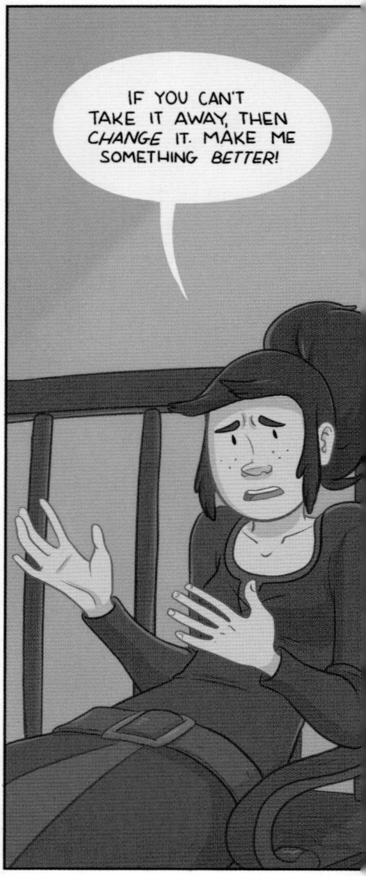
IF YOU CAN'T TAKE IT AWAY, THEN *CHANGE* IT. MAKE ME SOMETHING *BETTER*!

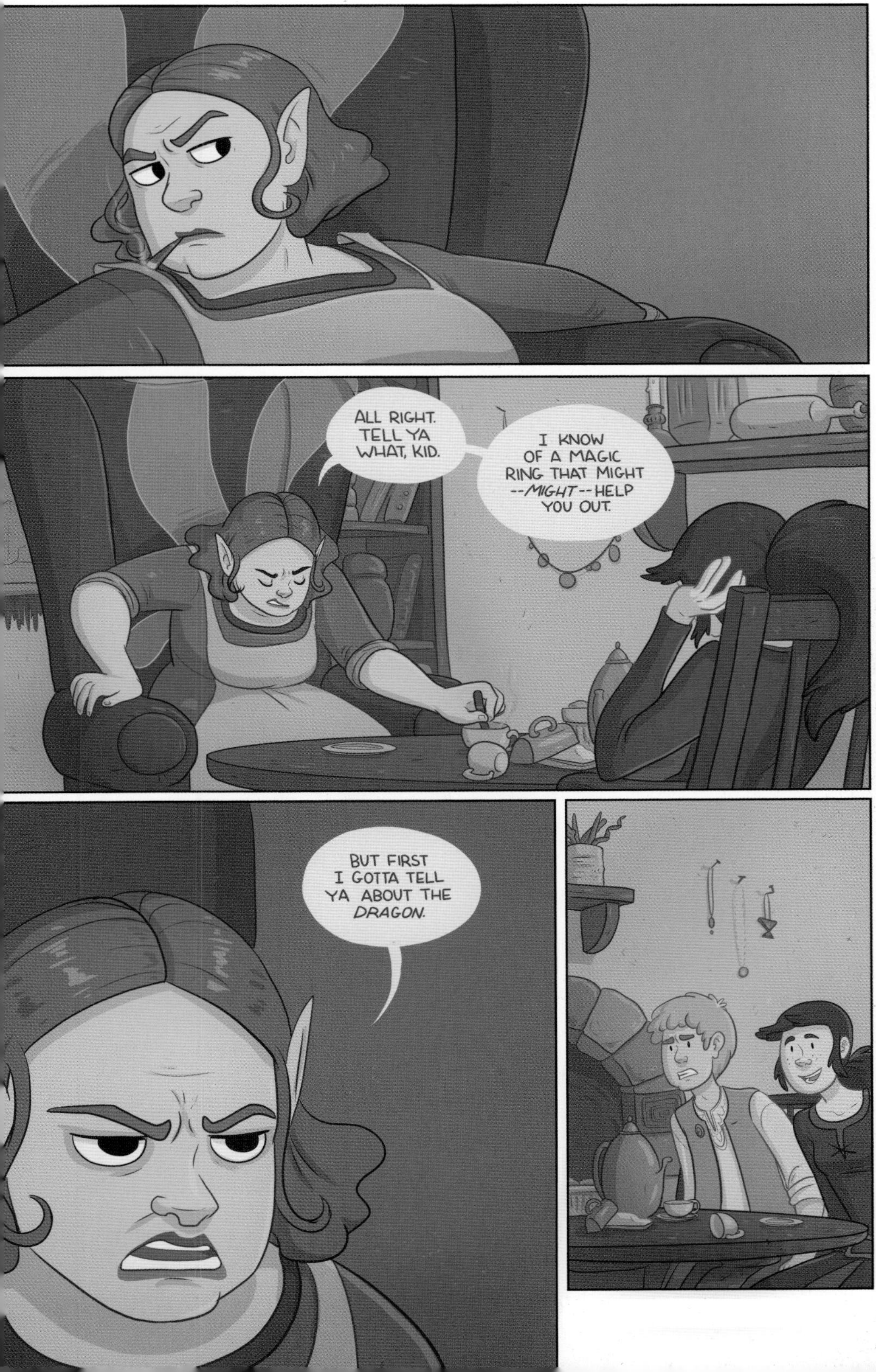
ALL RIGHT. TELL YA WHAT, KID.
I KNOW OF A MAGIC RING THAT MIGHT --*MIGHT*-- HELP YOU OUT.
BUT FIRST I GOTTA TELL YA ABOUT THE *DRAGON*.

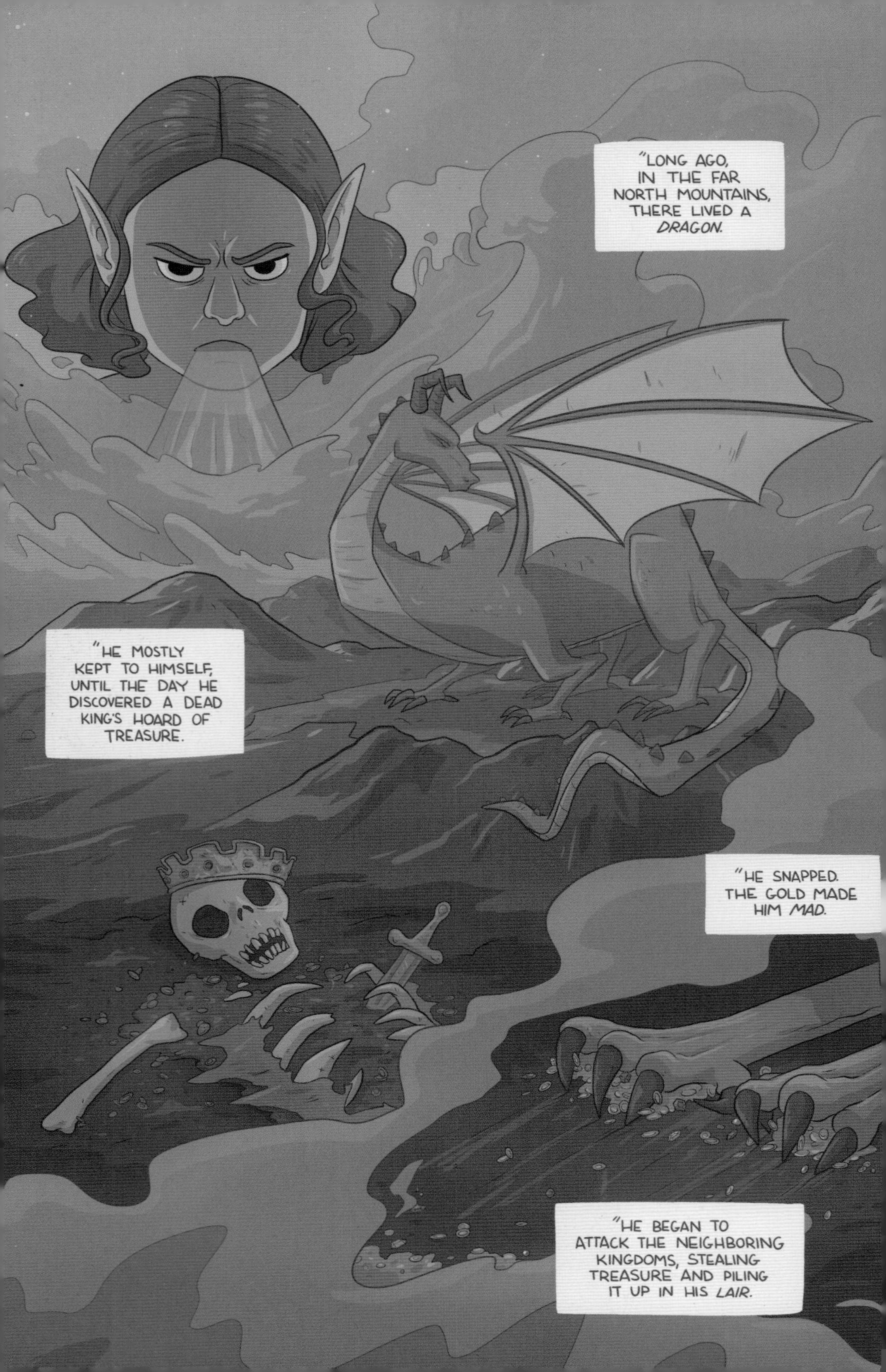
"LONG AGO, IN THE FAR NORTH MOUNTAINS, THERE LIVED A *DRAGON*.
"HE MOSTLY KEPT TO HIMSELF, UNTIL THE DAY HE DISCOVERED A DEAD KING'S HOARD OF TREASURE.
"HE SNAPPED. THE GOLD MADE HIM *MAD*.
"HE BEGAN TO ATTACK THE NEIGHBORING KINGDOMS, STEALING TREASURE AND PILING IT UP IN HIS *LAIR*.

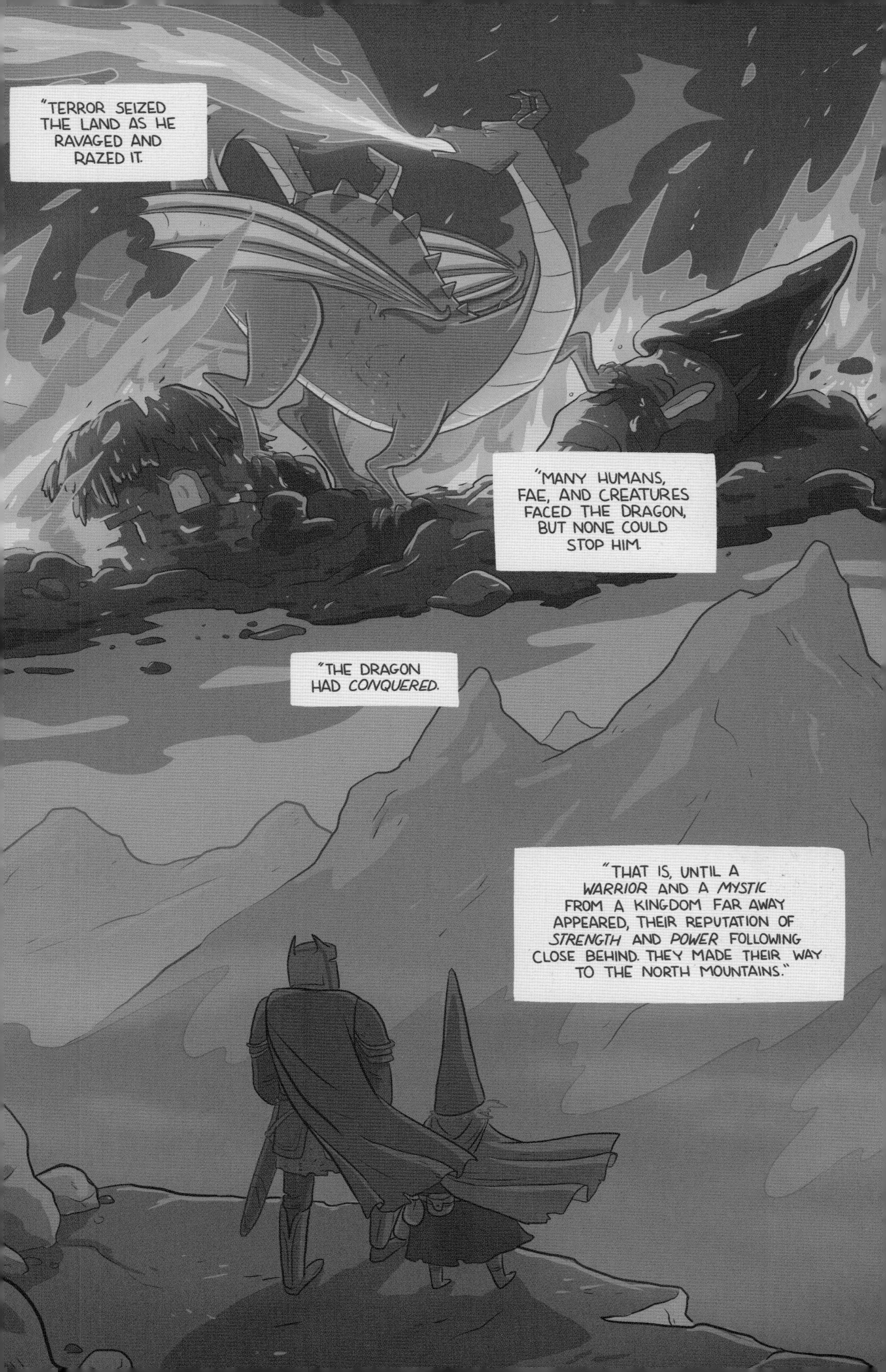
"TERROR SEIZED THE LAND AS HE RAVAGED AND RAZED IT.
"MANY HUMANS, FAE, AND CREATURES FACED THE DRAGON, BUT NONE COULD STOP HIM.
"THE DRAGON HAD *CONQUERED*.
"THAT IS, UNTIL A *WARRIOR* AND A *MYSTIC* FROM A KINGDOM FAR AWAY APPEARED, THEIR REPUTATION OF *STRENGTH* AND *POWER* FOLLOWING CLOSE BEHIND. THEY MADE THEIR WAY TO THE NORTH MOUNTAINS."

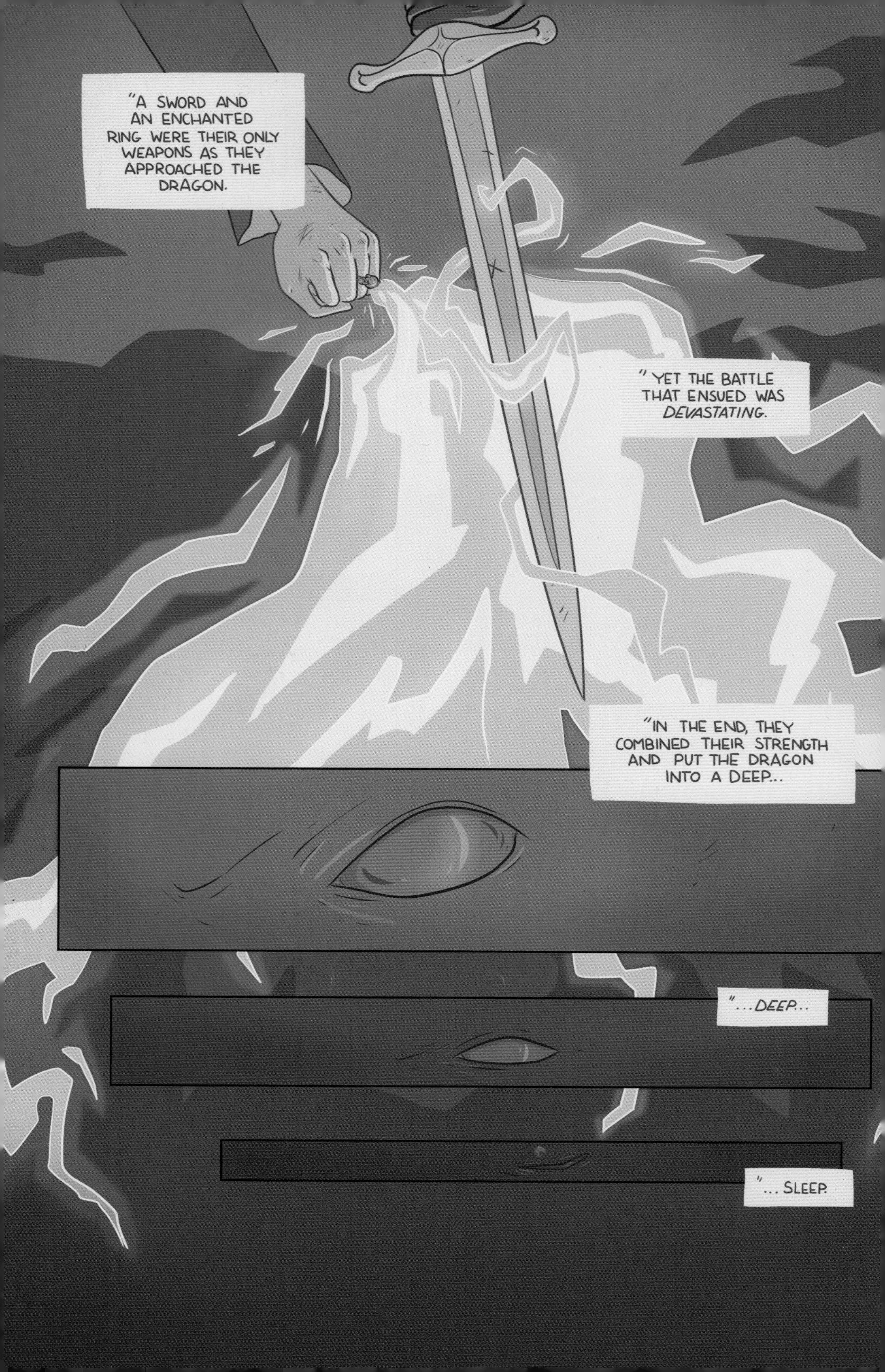
"A SWORD AND AN ENCHANTED RING WERE THEIR ONLY WEAPONS AS THEY APPROACHED THE DRAGON.
"YET THE BATTLE THAT ENSUED WAS *DEVASTATING*.
"IN THE END, THEY COMBINED THEIR STRENGTH AND PUT THE DRAGON INTO A DEEP...
"...*DEEP*...
"... SLEEP.

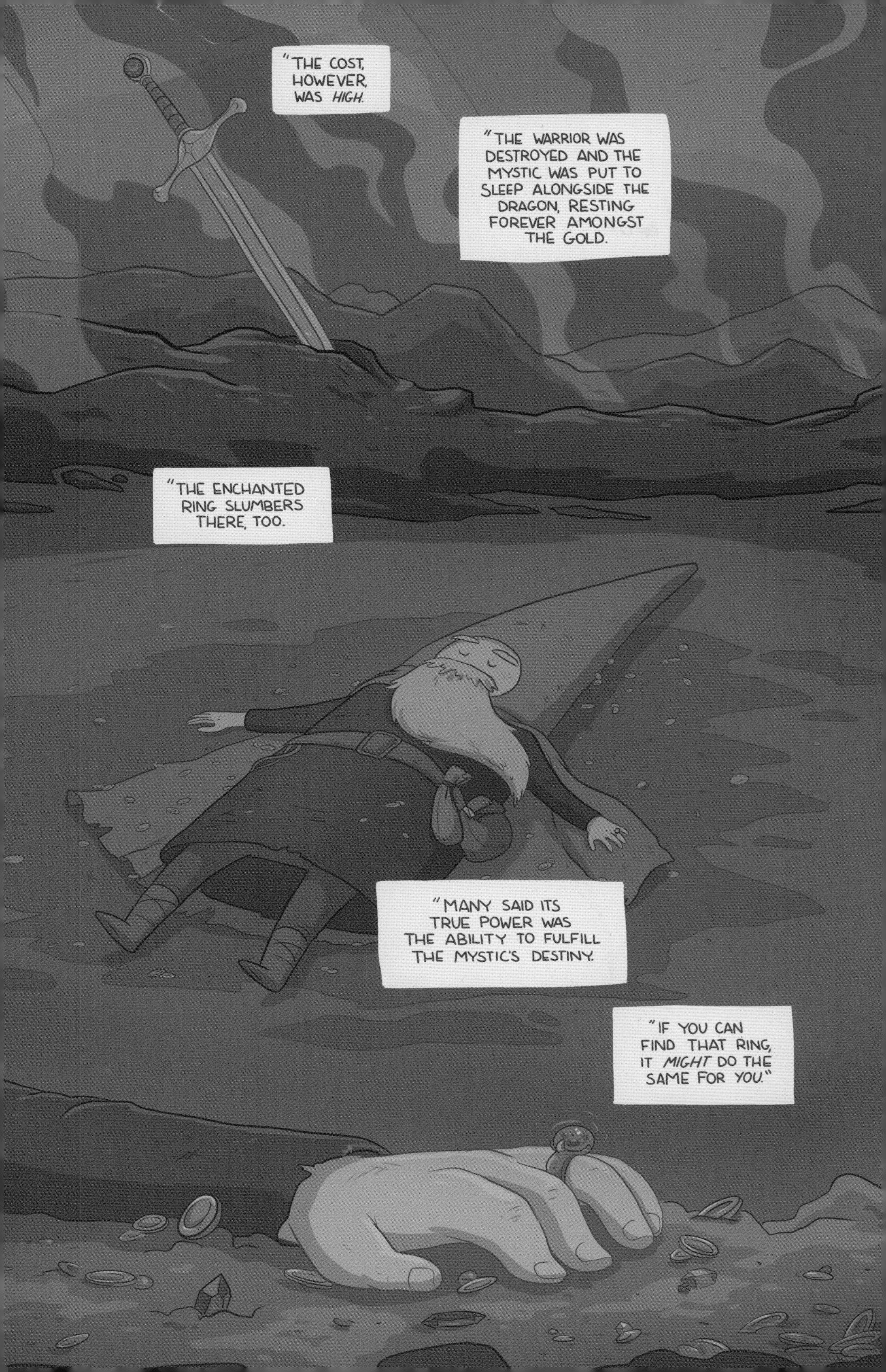
"THE COST, HOWEVER, WAS *HIGH*.
"THE WARRIOR WAS DESTROYED AND THE MYSTIC WAS PUT TO SLEEP ALONGSIDE THE DRAGON, RESTING FOREVER AMONGST THE GOLD.
"THE ENCHANTED RING SLUMBERS THERE, TOO.
"MANY SAID ITS TRUE POWER WAS THE ABILITY TO FULFILL THE MYSTIC'S DESTINY.
"IF YOU CAN FIND THAT RING, IT *MIGHT* DO THE SAME FOR *YOU*."

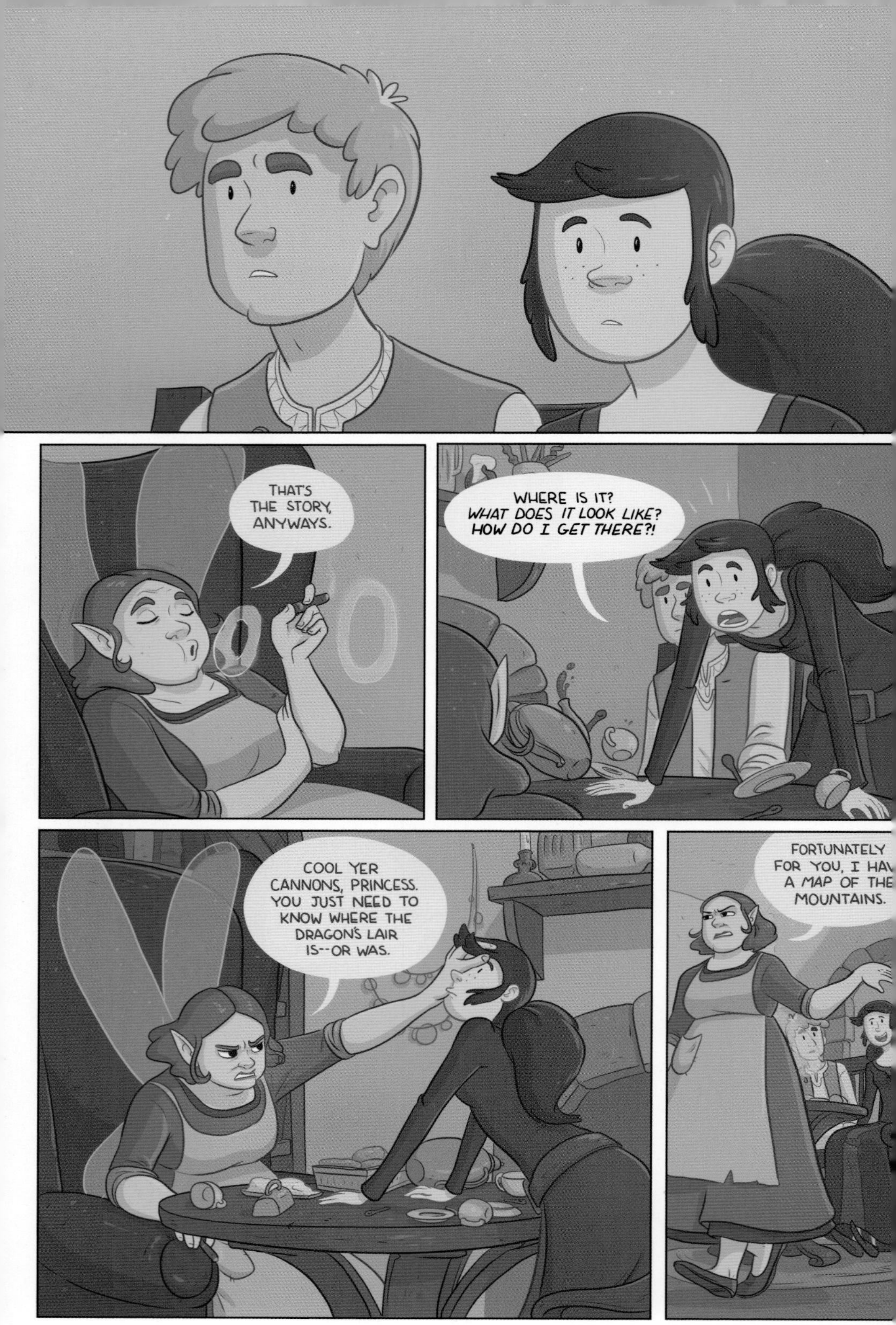
THAT'S THE STORY, ANYWAYS.
WHERE IS IT? WHAT DOES IT LOOK LIKE? HOW DO I GET THERE?!
COOL YER CANNONS, PRINCESS. YOU JUST NEED TO KNOW WHERE THE DRAGON'S LAIR IS--OR WAS.
FORTUNATELY FOR YOU, I HAV A MAP OF THE MOUNTAINS.

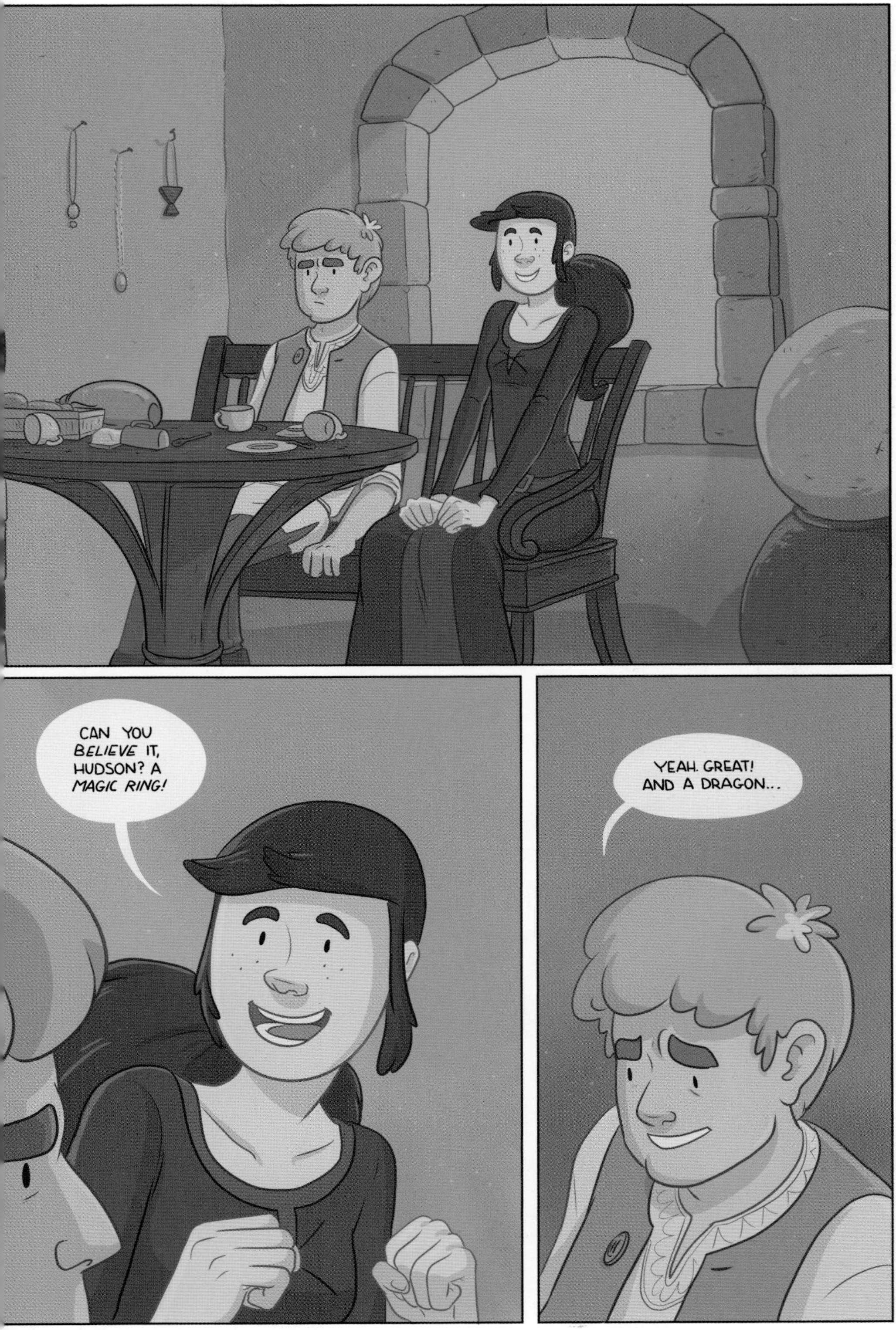
CAN YOU *BELIEVE* IT, HUDSON? A *MAGIC RING!*
YEAH. GREAT! AND A DRAGON...

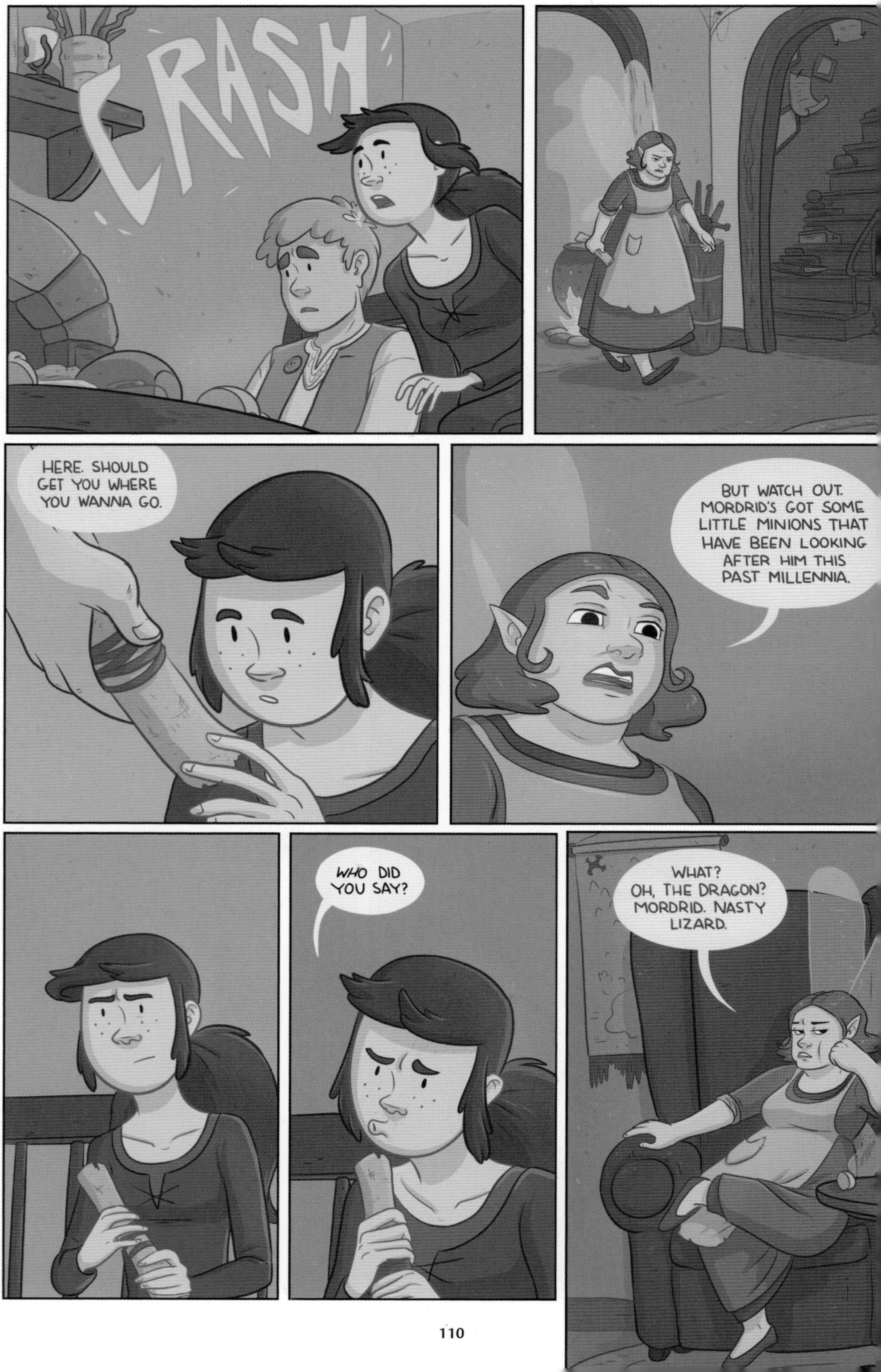
CRASH
HERE. SHOULD GET YOU WHERE YOU WANNA GO.
BUT WATCH OUT. MORDRID'S GOT SOME LITTLE MINIONS THAT HAVE BEEN LOOKING AFTER HIM THIS PAST MILLENNIA.
WHO DID YOU SAY?
WHAT? OH, THE DRAGON? MORDRID. NASTY LIZARD.

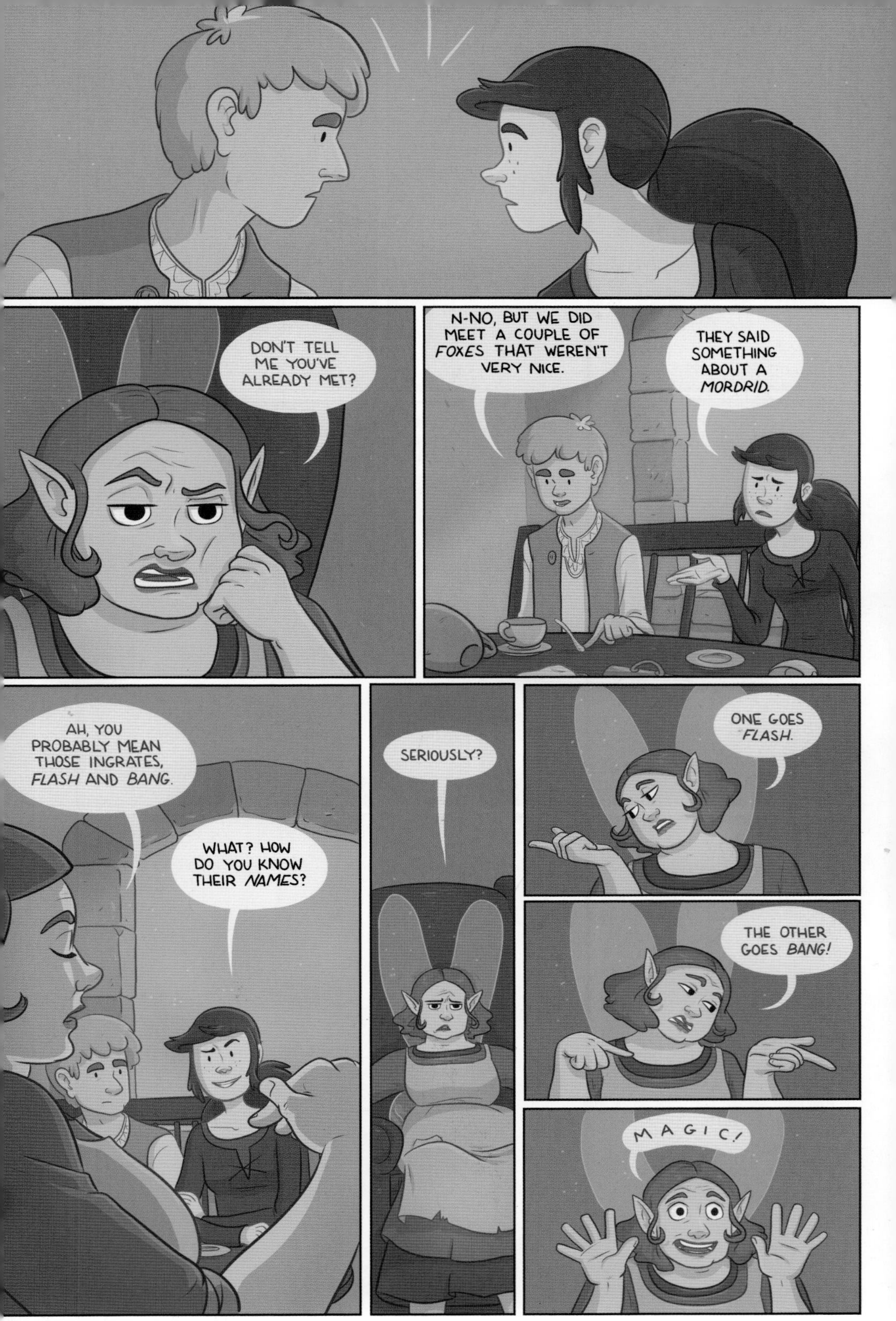
DON'T TELL ME YOU'VE ALREADY MET?
N-NO, BUT WE DID MEET A COUPLE OF *FOXES* THAT WEREN'T VERY NICE.
THEY SAID SOMETHING ABOUT A *MORDRID.*
AH, YOU PROBABLY MEAN THOSE INGRATES, *FLASH* AND *BANG.*
WHAT? HOW DO YOU KNOW THEIR *NAMES*?
SERIOUSLY?
ONE GOES *FLASH.*
THE OTHER GOES *BANG!*
M A G I C!

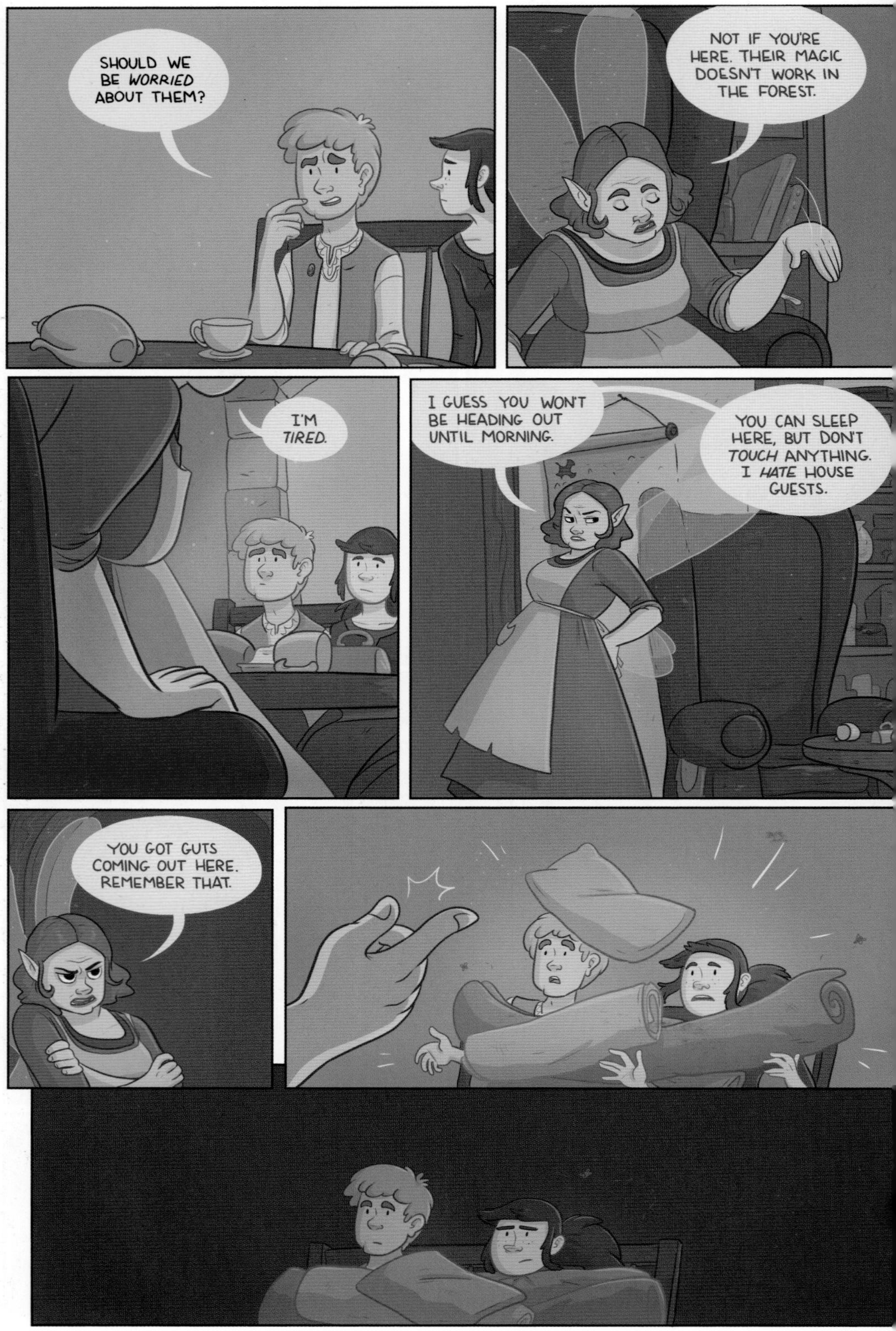
SHOULD WE BE WORRIED ABOUT THEM?
NOT IF YOU'RE HERE. THEIR MAGIC DOESN'T WORK IN THE FOREST.
I'M TIRED.
I GUESS YOU WON'T BE HEADING OUT UNTIL MORNING.
YOU CAN SLEEP HERE, BUT DON'T TOUCH ANYTHING. I HATE HOUSE GUESTS.
YOU GOT GUTS COMING OUT HERE. REMEMBER THAT.

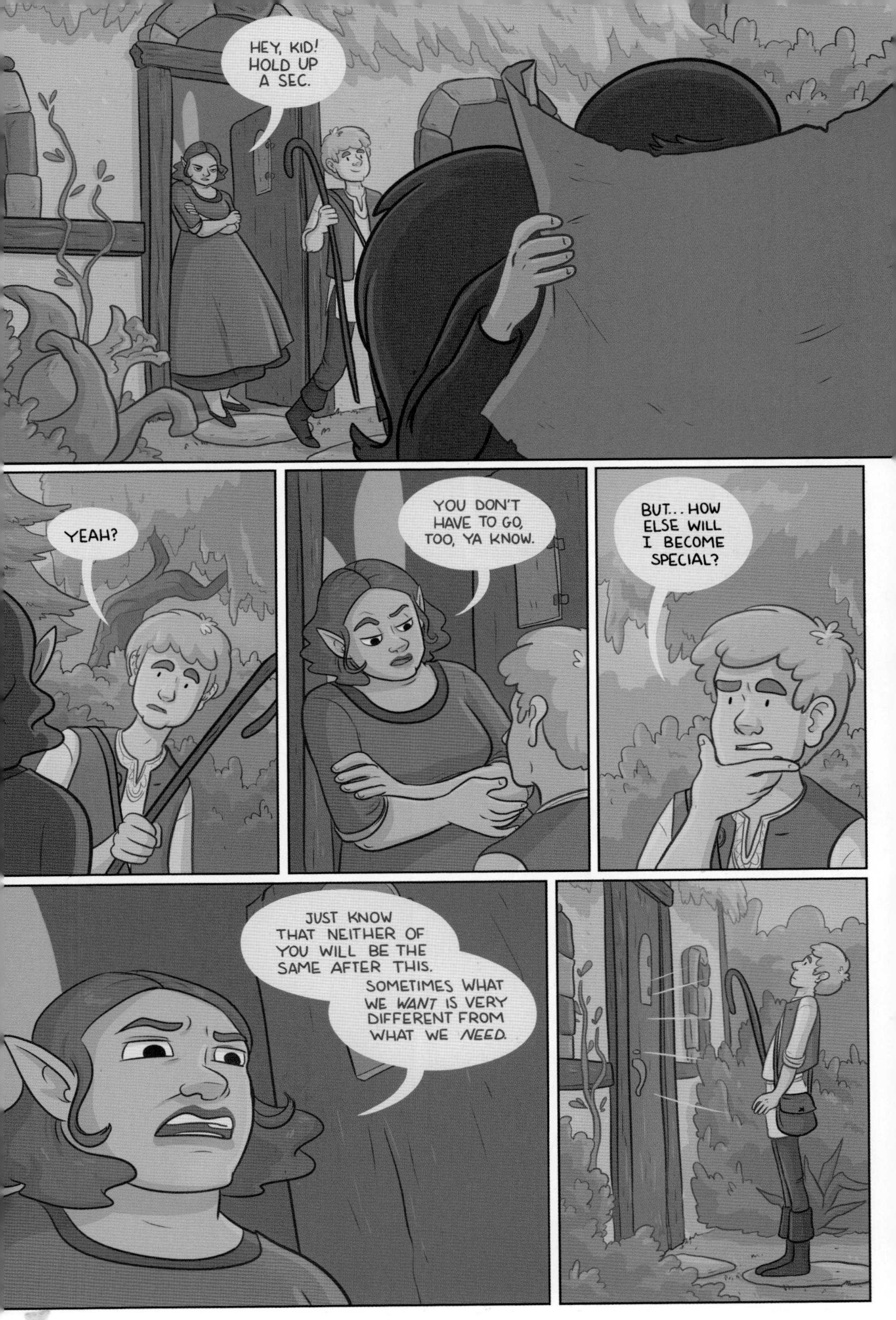
HEY, KID! HOLD UP A SEC.
YEAH?
YOU DON'T HAVE TO GO, TOO, YA KNOW.
BUT... HOW ELSE WILL I BECOME SPECIAL?
JUST KNOW THAT NEITHER OF YOU WILL BE THE SAME AFTER THIS.
SOMETIMES WHAT WE *WANT* IS VERY DIFFERENT FROM WHAT WE *NEED*.

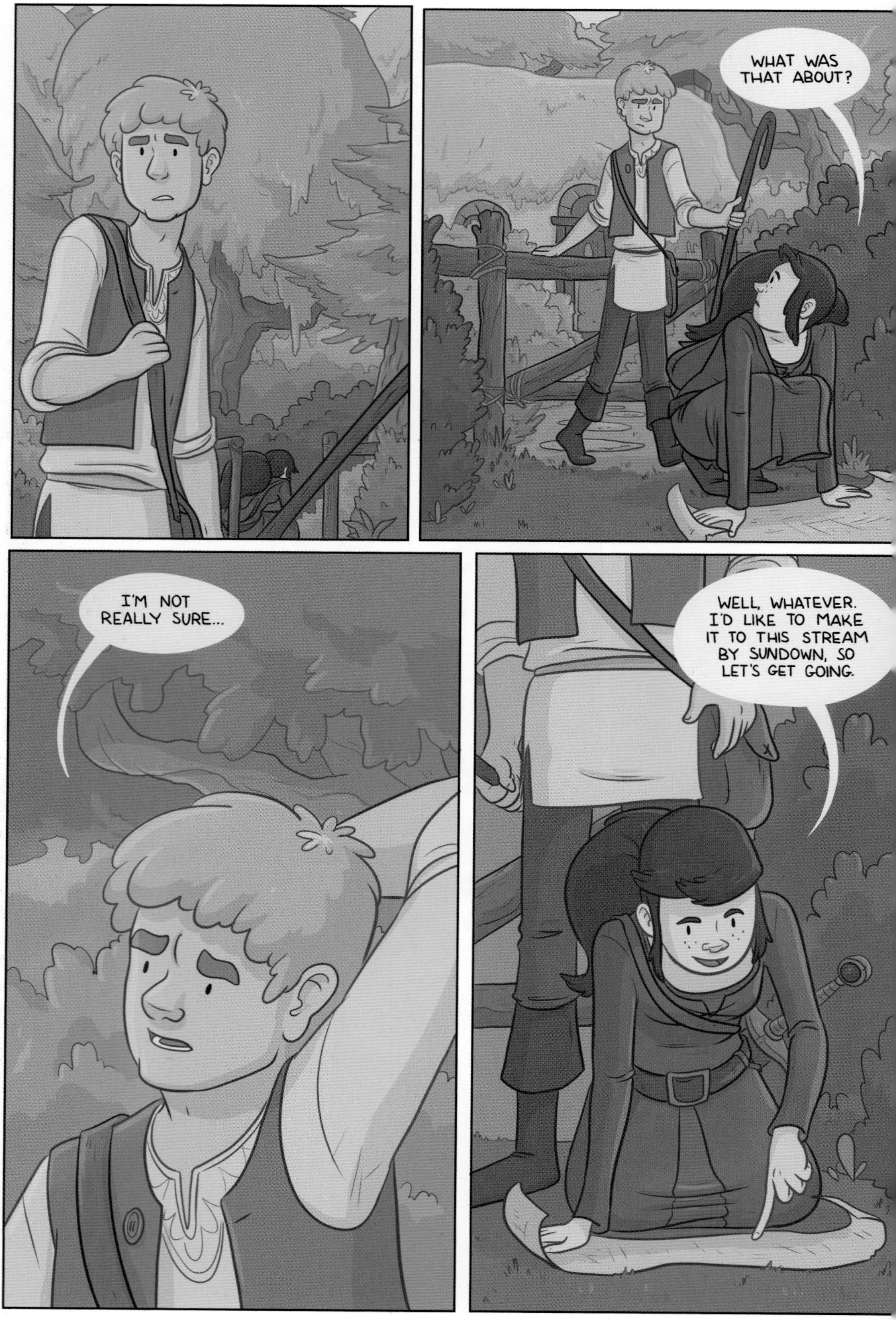
WHAT WAS THAT ABOUT?
I'M NOT REALLY SURE...
WELL, WHATEVER. I'D LIKE TO MAKE IT TO THIS STREAM BY SUNDOWN, SO LET'S GET GOING.

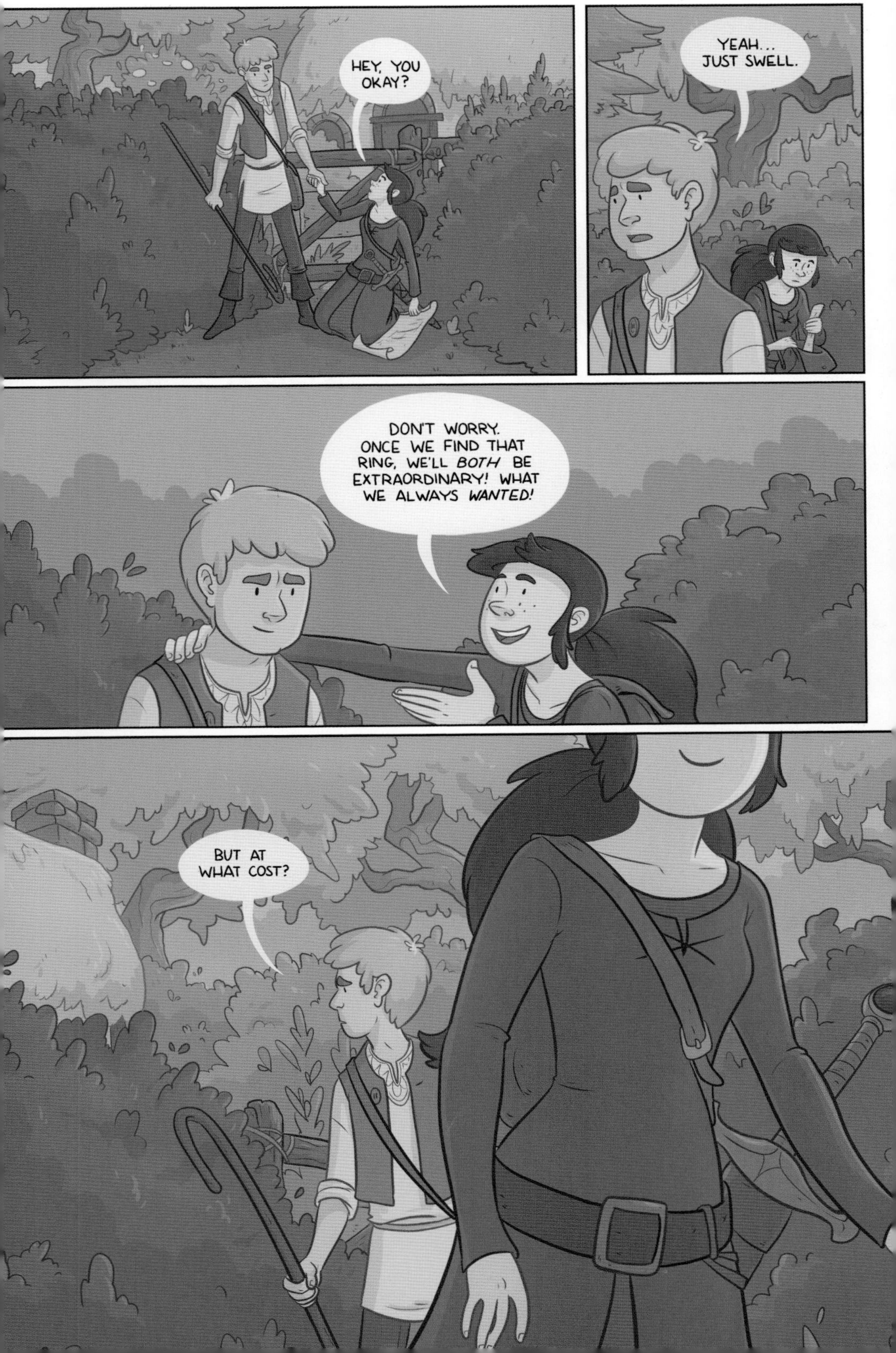
HEY, YOU OKAY?
YEAH... JUST SWELL.
DON'T WORRY. ONCE WE FIND THAT RING, WE'LL *BOTH* BE EXTRAORDINARY! WHAT WE ALWAYS *WANTED*!
BUT AT WHAT COST?

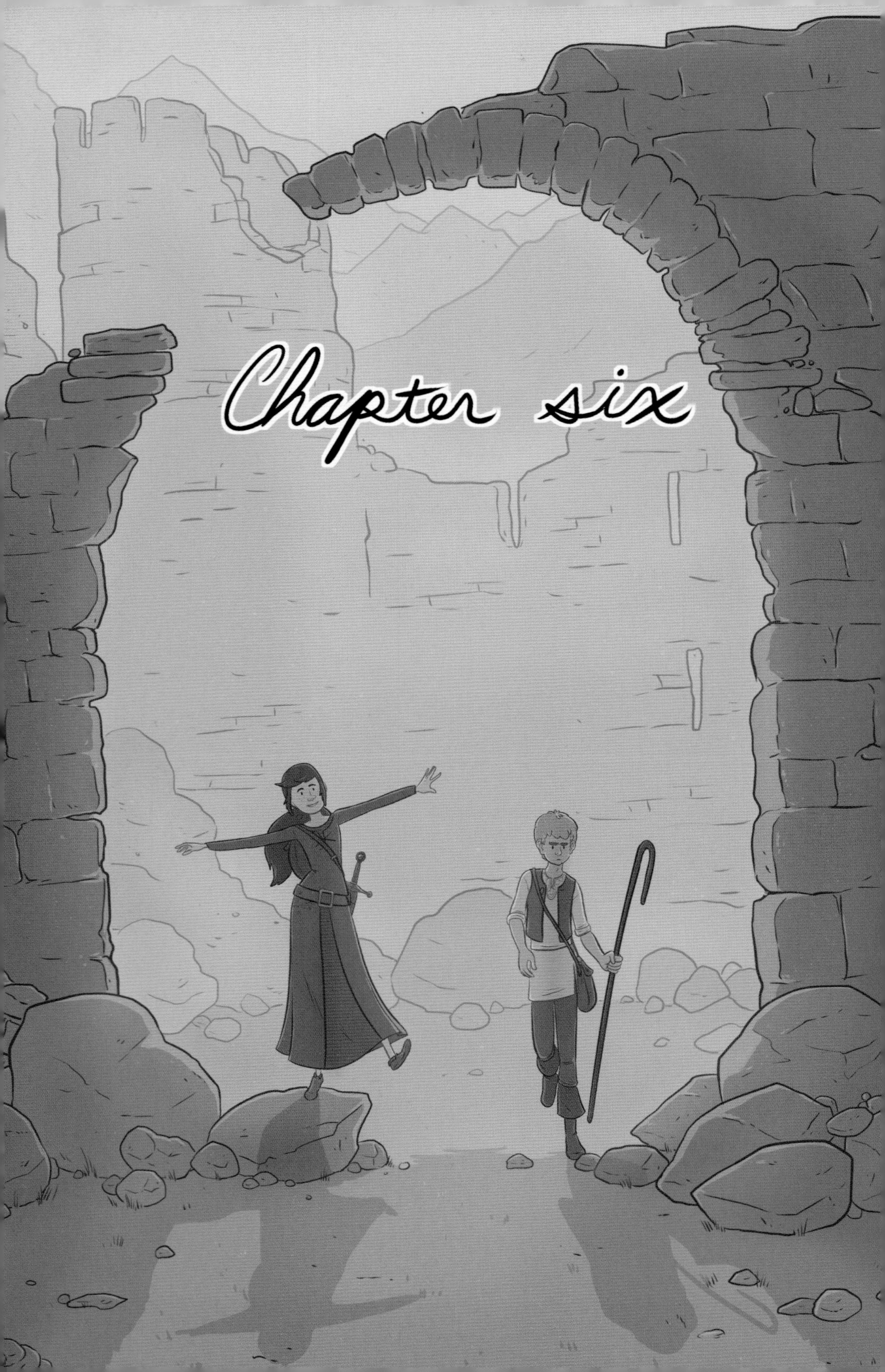
Chapter six

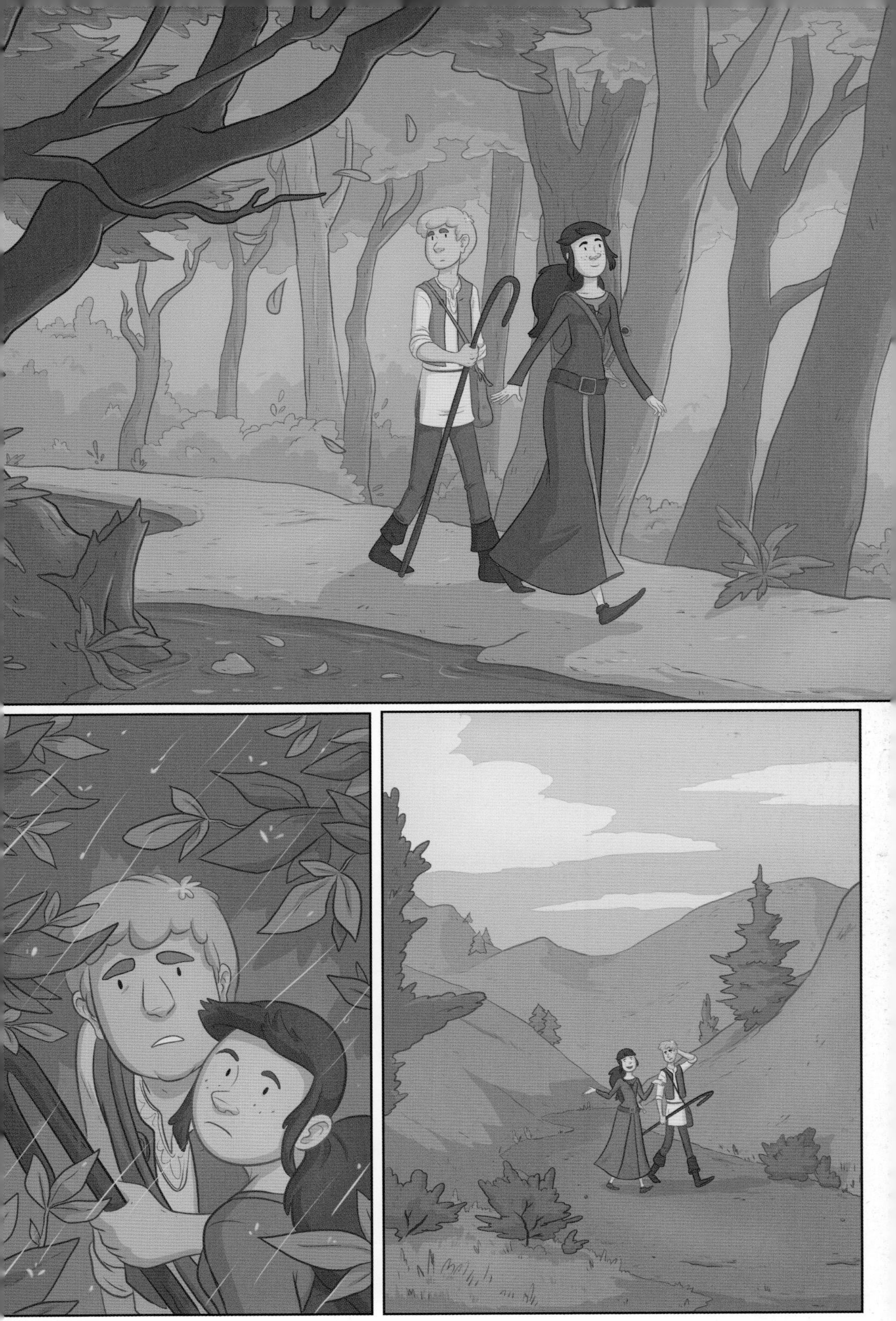

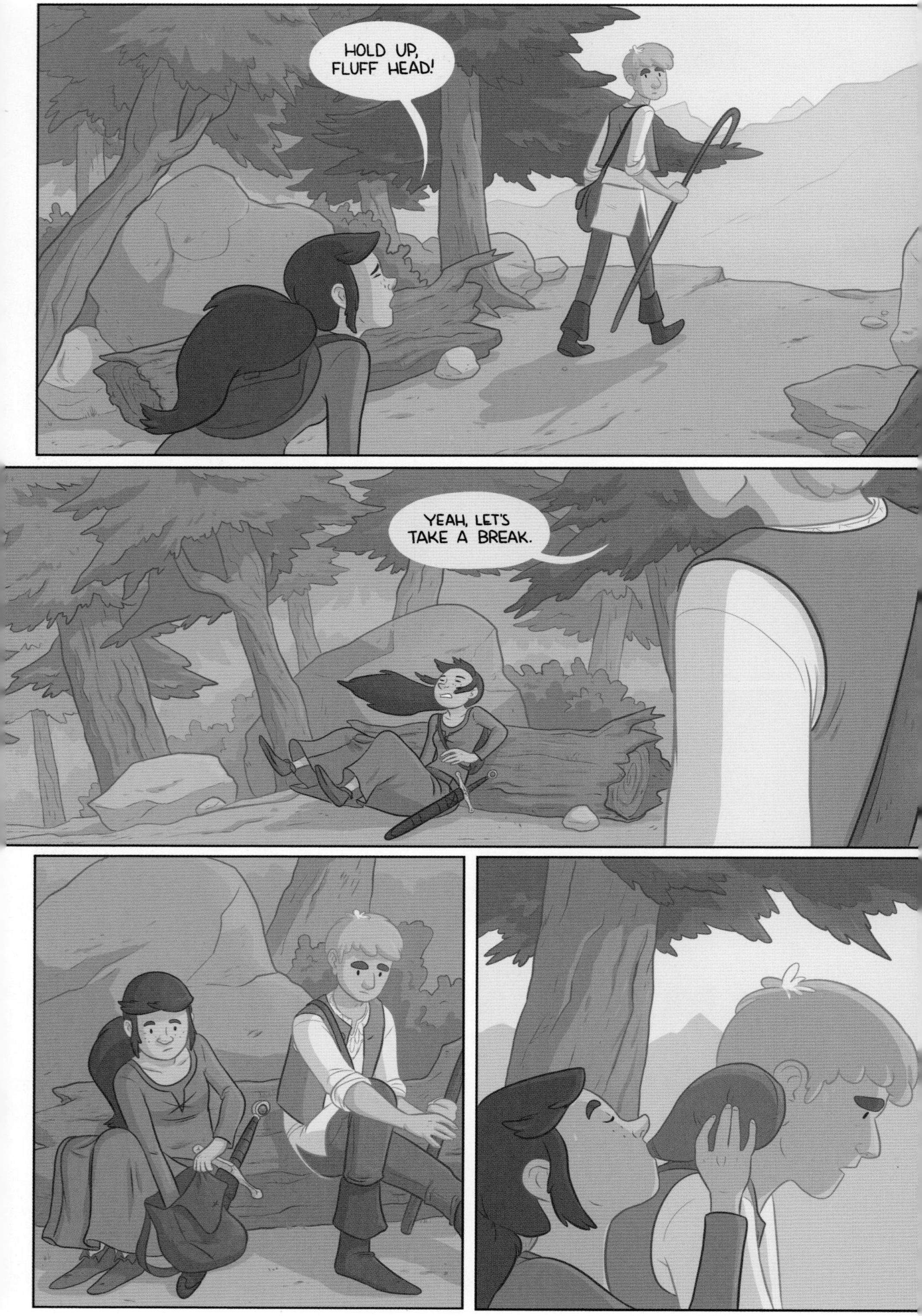
HOLD UP, FLUFF HEAD!
YEAH, LET'S TAKE A BREAK.

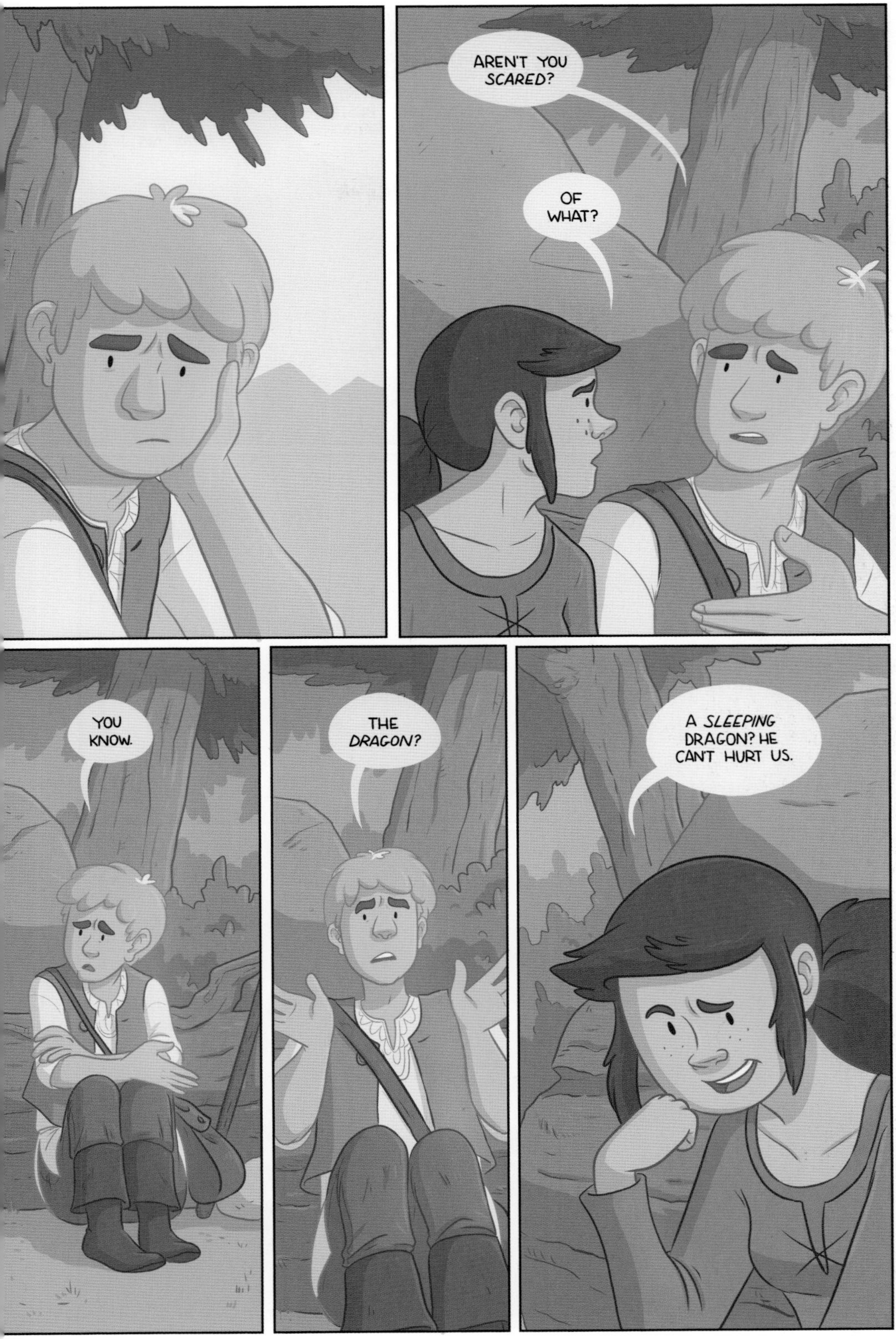
AREN'T YOU *SCARED*?
OF WHAT?
YOU KNOW.
THE *DRAGON*?
A *SLEEPING* DRAGON? HE CAN'T HURT US.

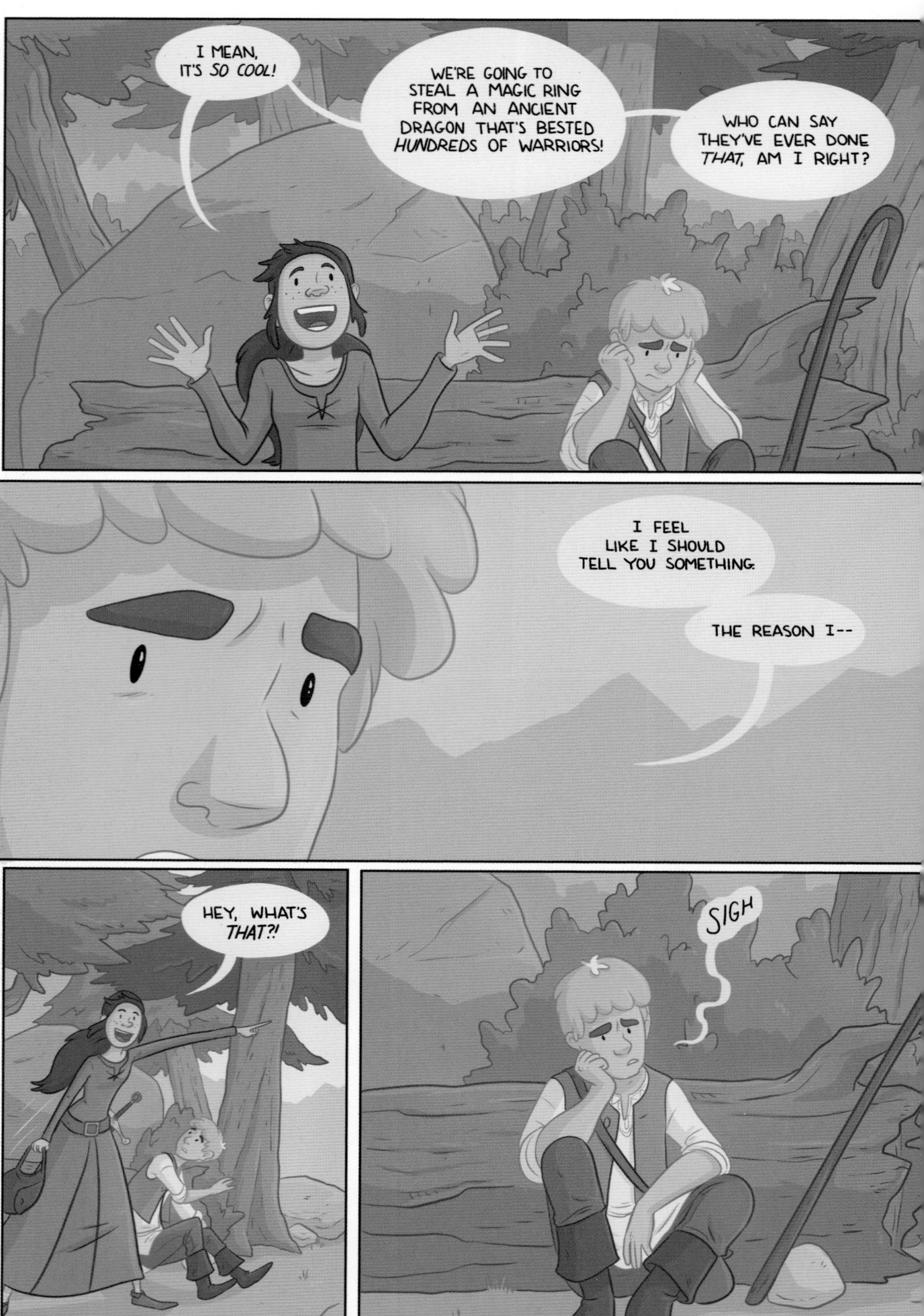
I MEAN, IT'S *SO COOL!*
WE'RE GOING TO STEAL A MAGIC RING FROM AN ANCIENT DRAGON THAT'S BESTED *HUNDREDS* OF WARRIORS!
WHO CAN SAY THEY'VE EVER DONE *THAT*, AM I RIGHT?
I FEEL LIKE I SHOULD TELL YOU SOMETHING.
THE REASON I--
HEY, WHAT'S *THAT?!*
SIGH

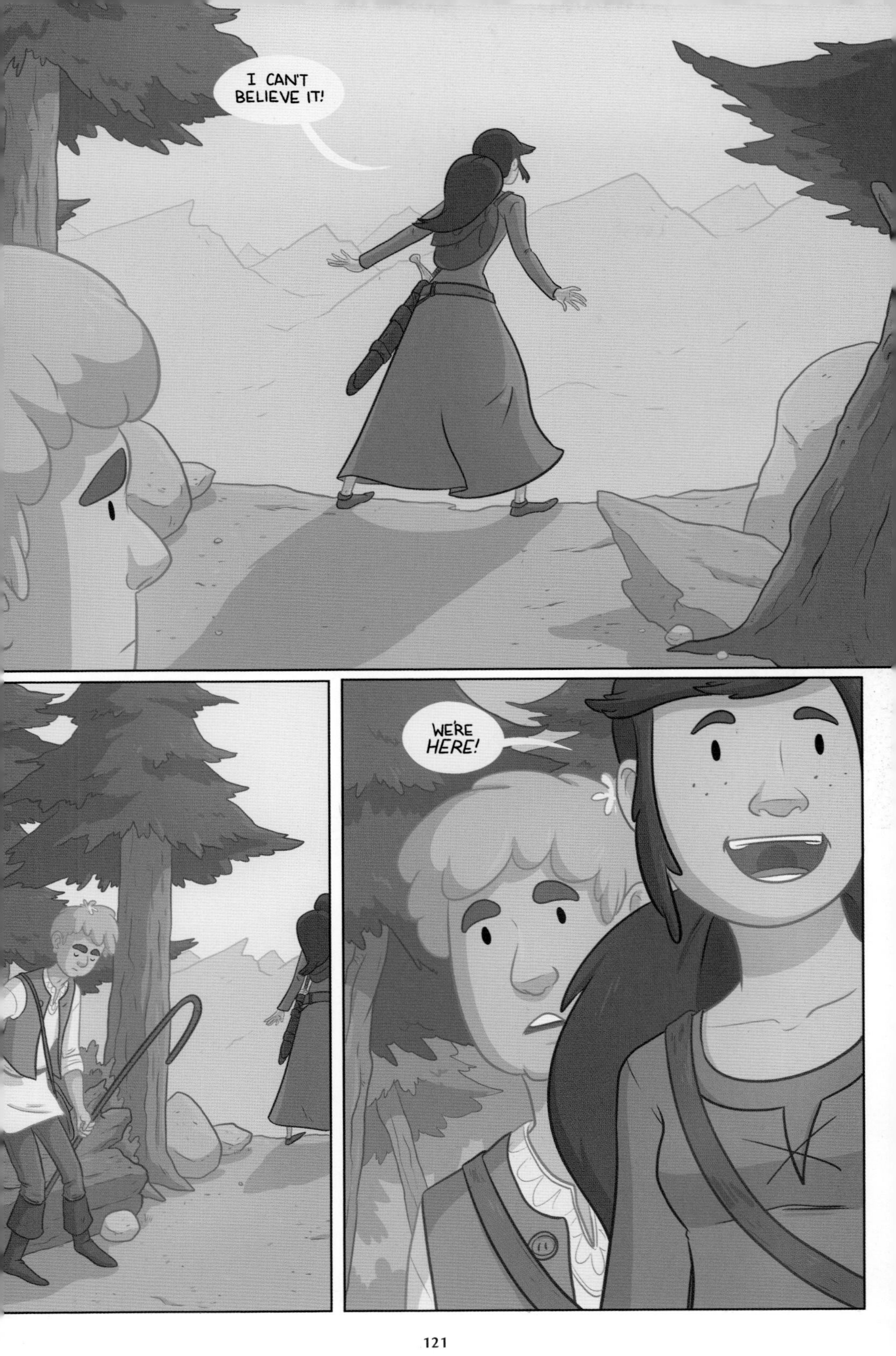
I CAN'T BELIEVE IT!
WE'RE HERE!

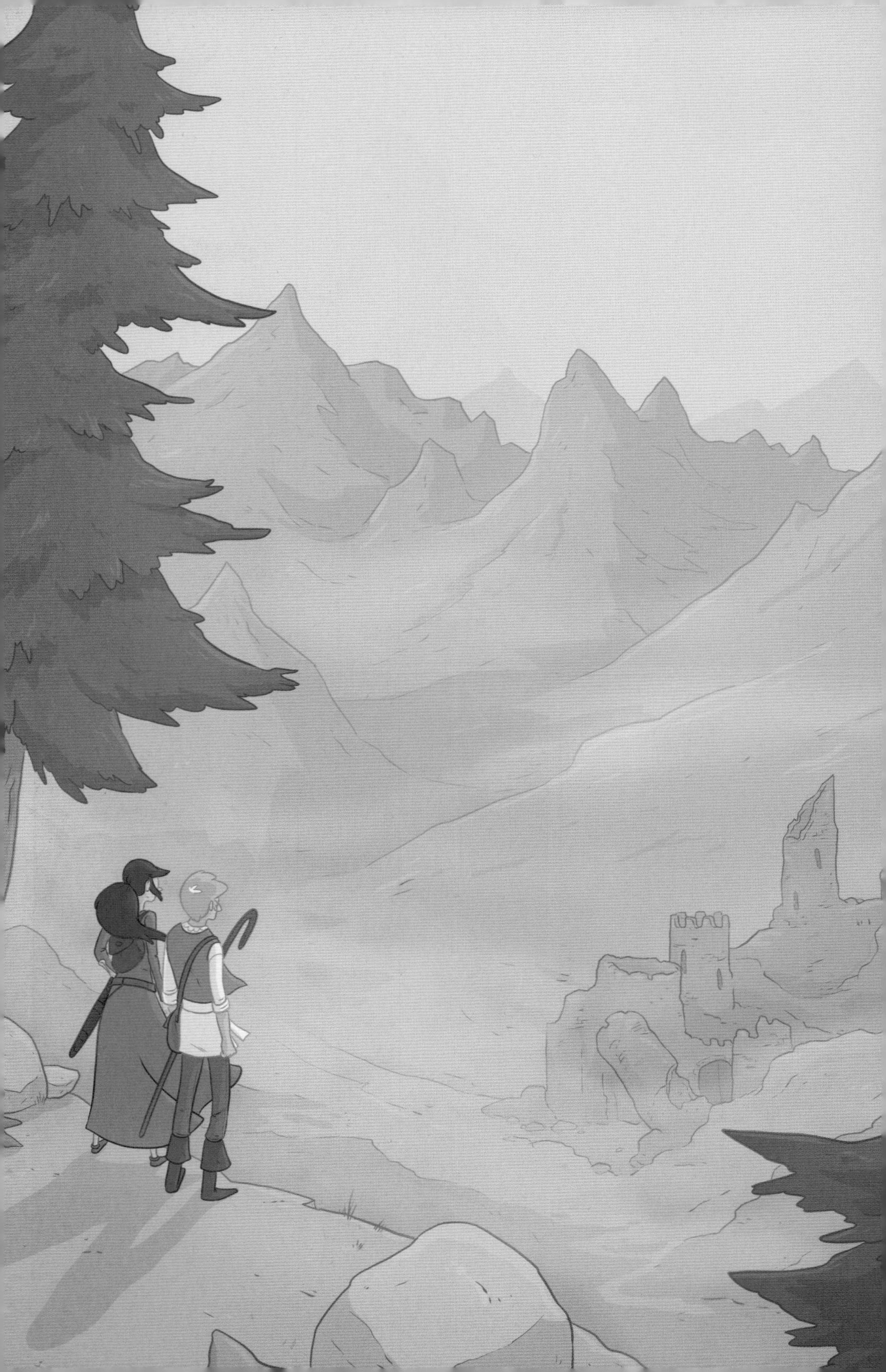

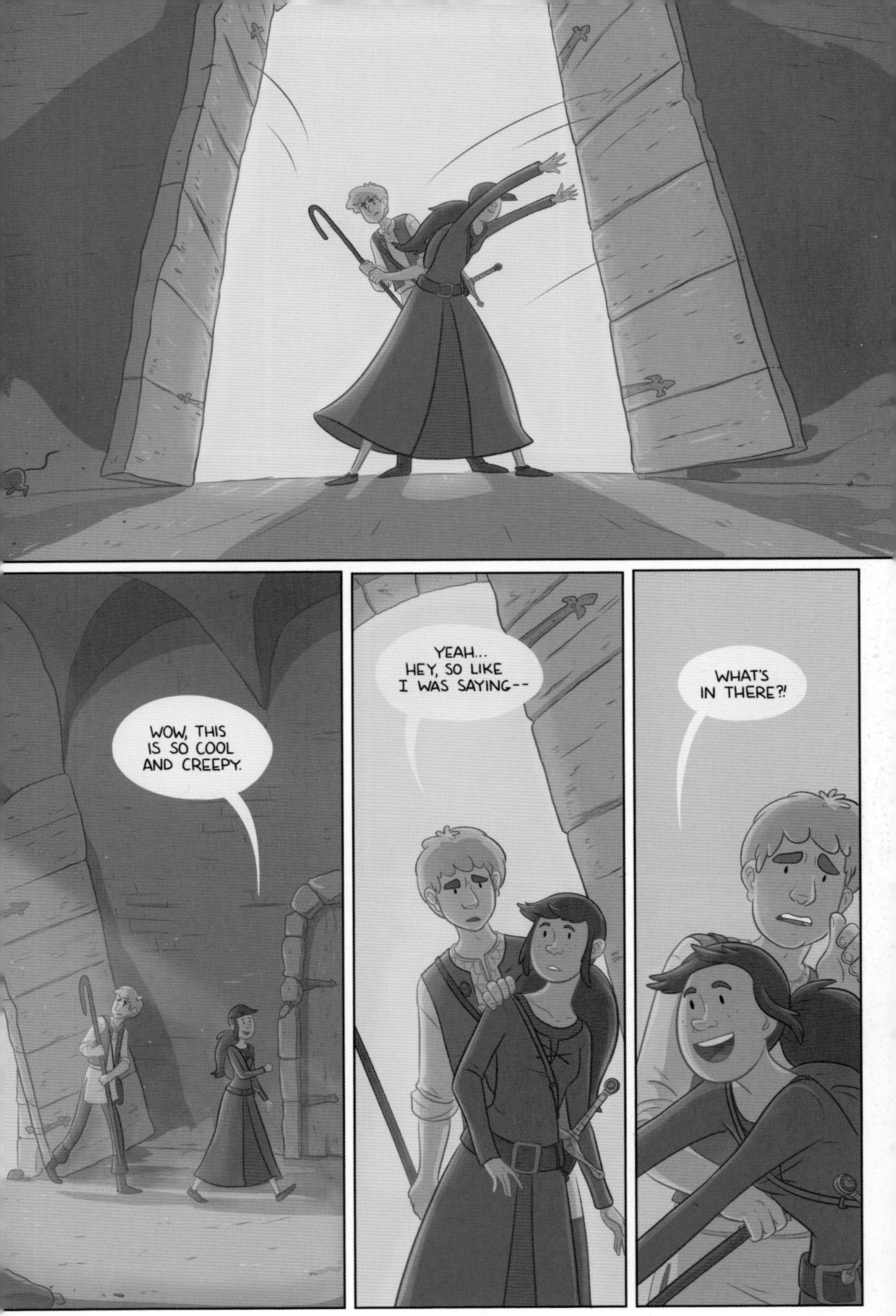
WOW, THIS IS SO COOL AND CREEPY.
YEAH... HEY, SO LIKE I WAS SAYING--
WHAT'S IN THERE?!

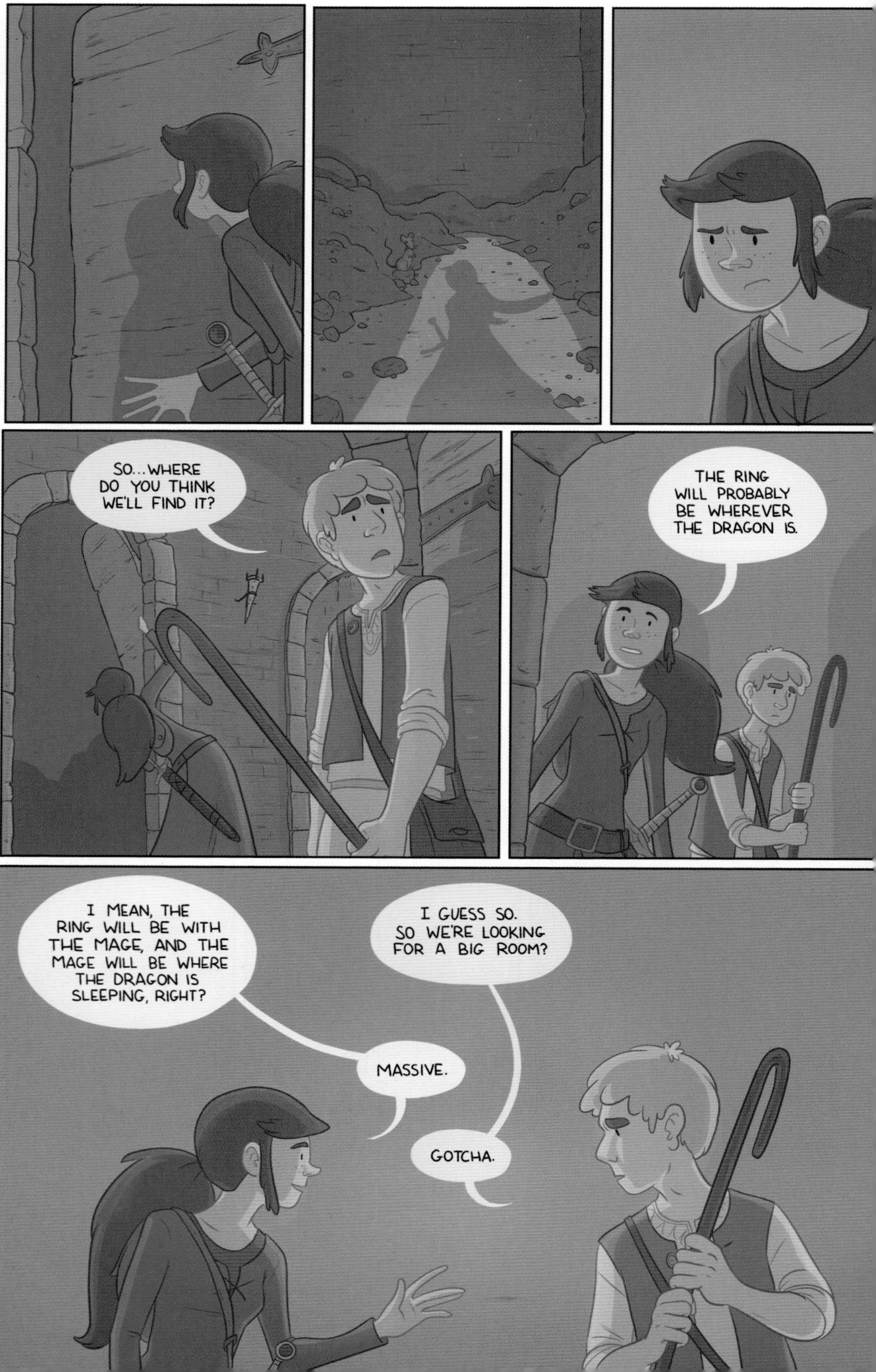
SO...WHERE DO YOU THINK WE'LL FIND IT?
THE RING WILL PROBABLY BE WHEREVER THE DRAGON IS.
I MEAN, THE RING WILL BE WITH THE MAGE, AND THE MAGE WILL BE WHERE THE DRAGON IS SLEEPING, RIGHT?
I GUESS SO. SO WE'RE LOOKING FOR A BIG ROOM?
MASSIVE.
GOTCHA.

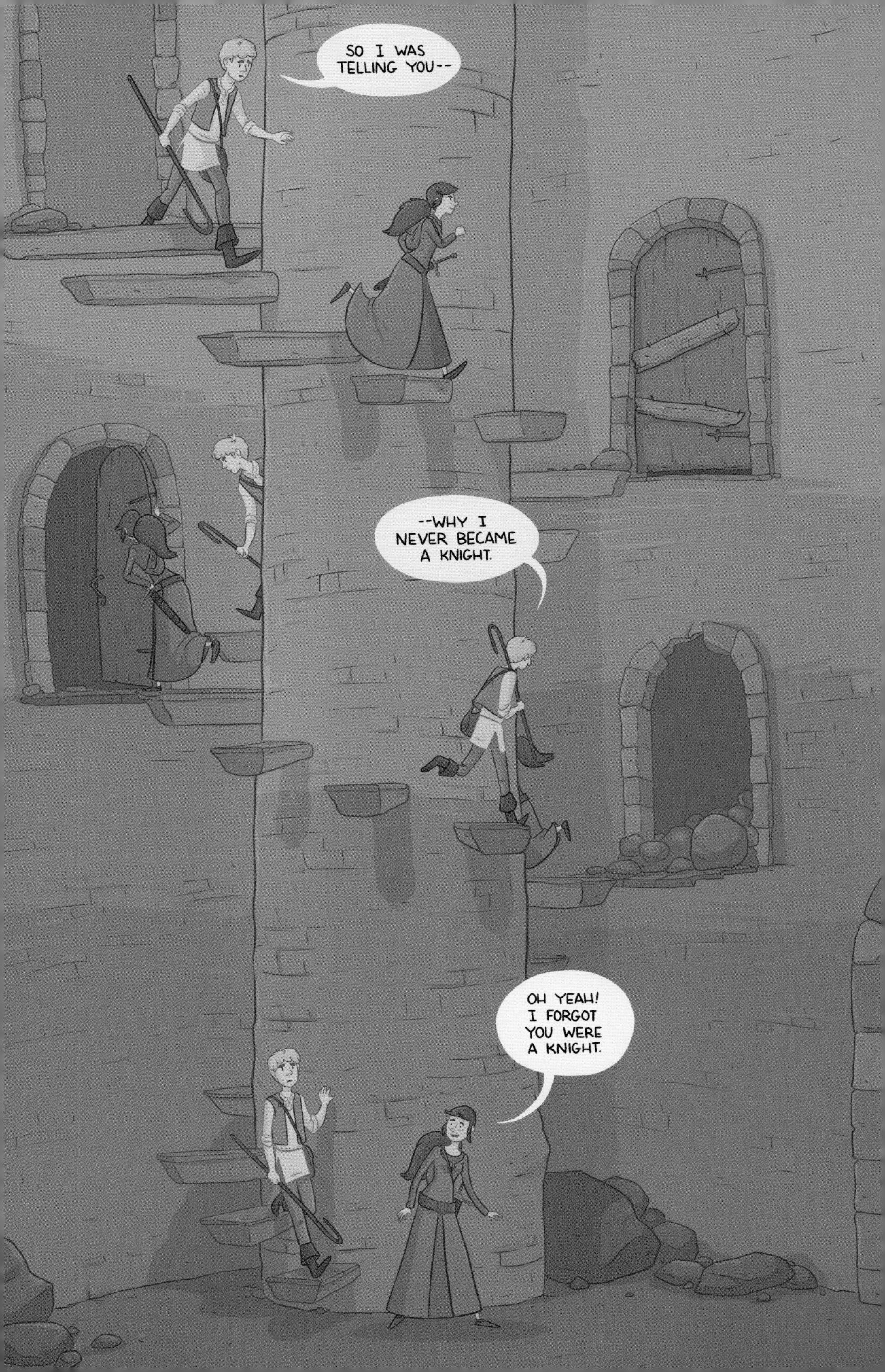
SO I WAS TELLING YOU--
--WHY I NEVER BECAME A KNIGHT.
OH YEAH! I FORGOT YOU WERE A KNIGHT.

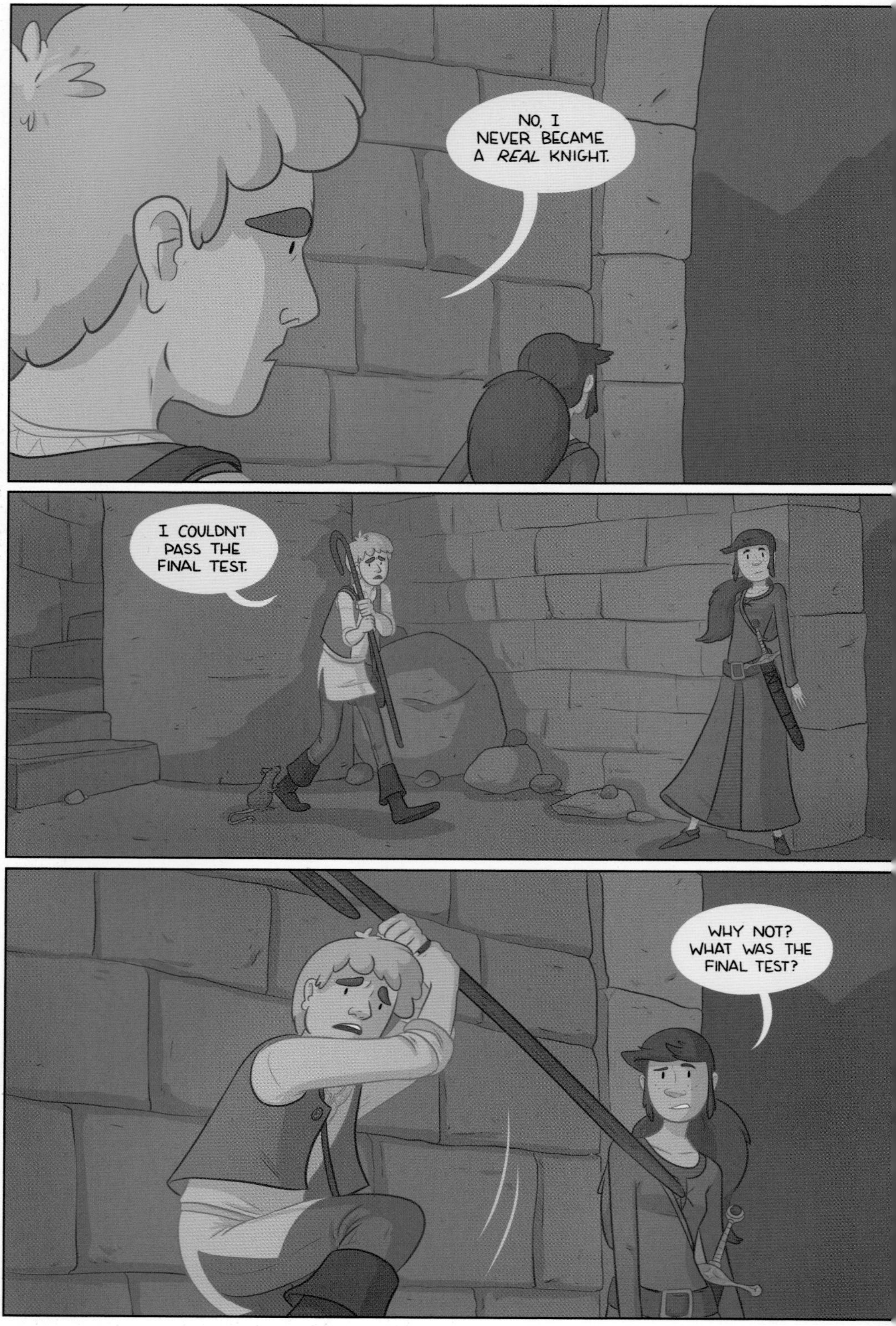
NO, I NEVER BECAME A *REAL* KNIGHT.
I COULDN'T PASS THE FINAL TEST.
WHY NOT? WHAT WAS THE FINAL TEST?

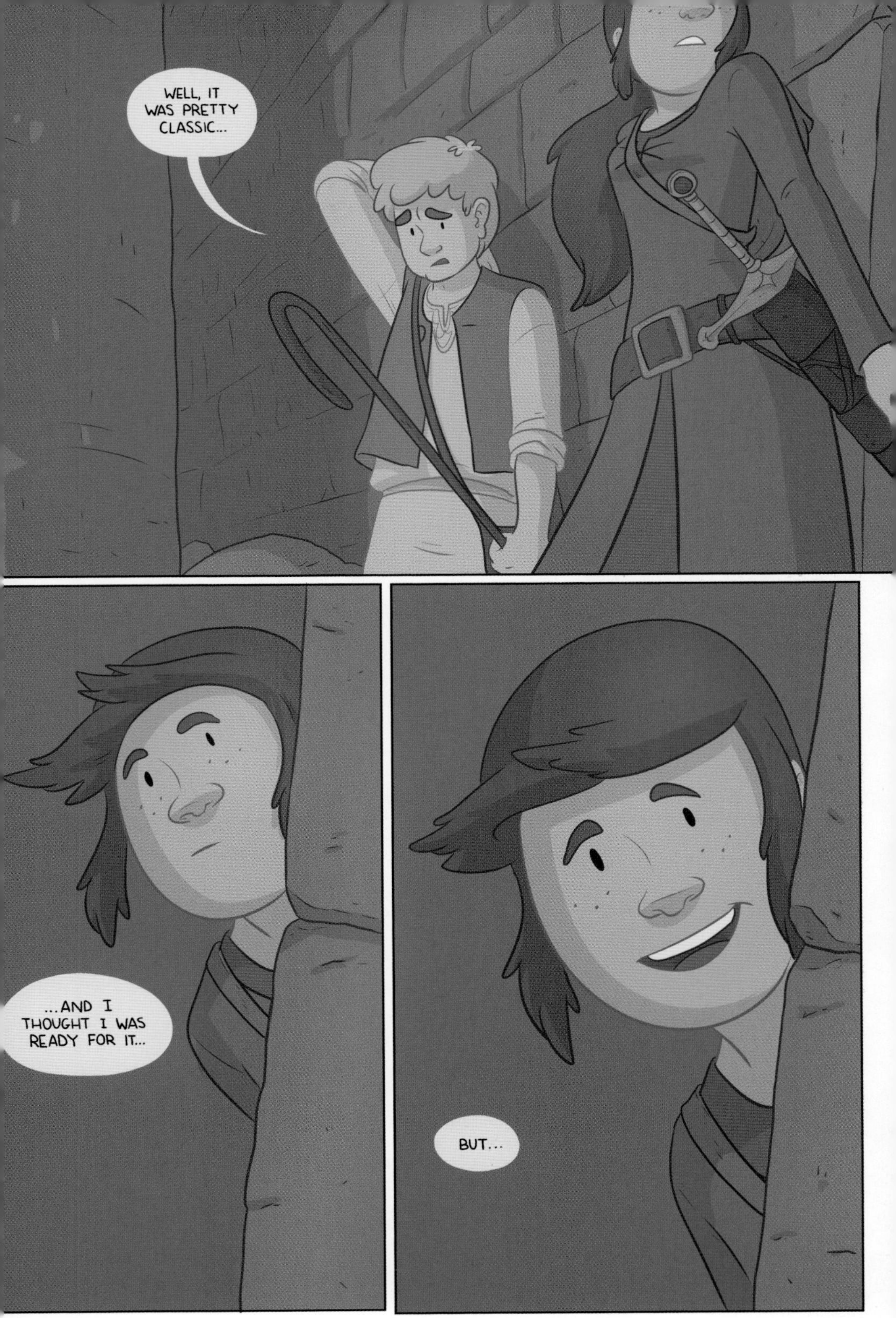
WELL, IT WAS PRETTY CLASSIC...
...AND I THOUGHT I WAS READY FOR IT...
BUT...

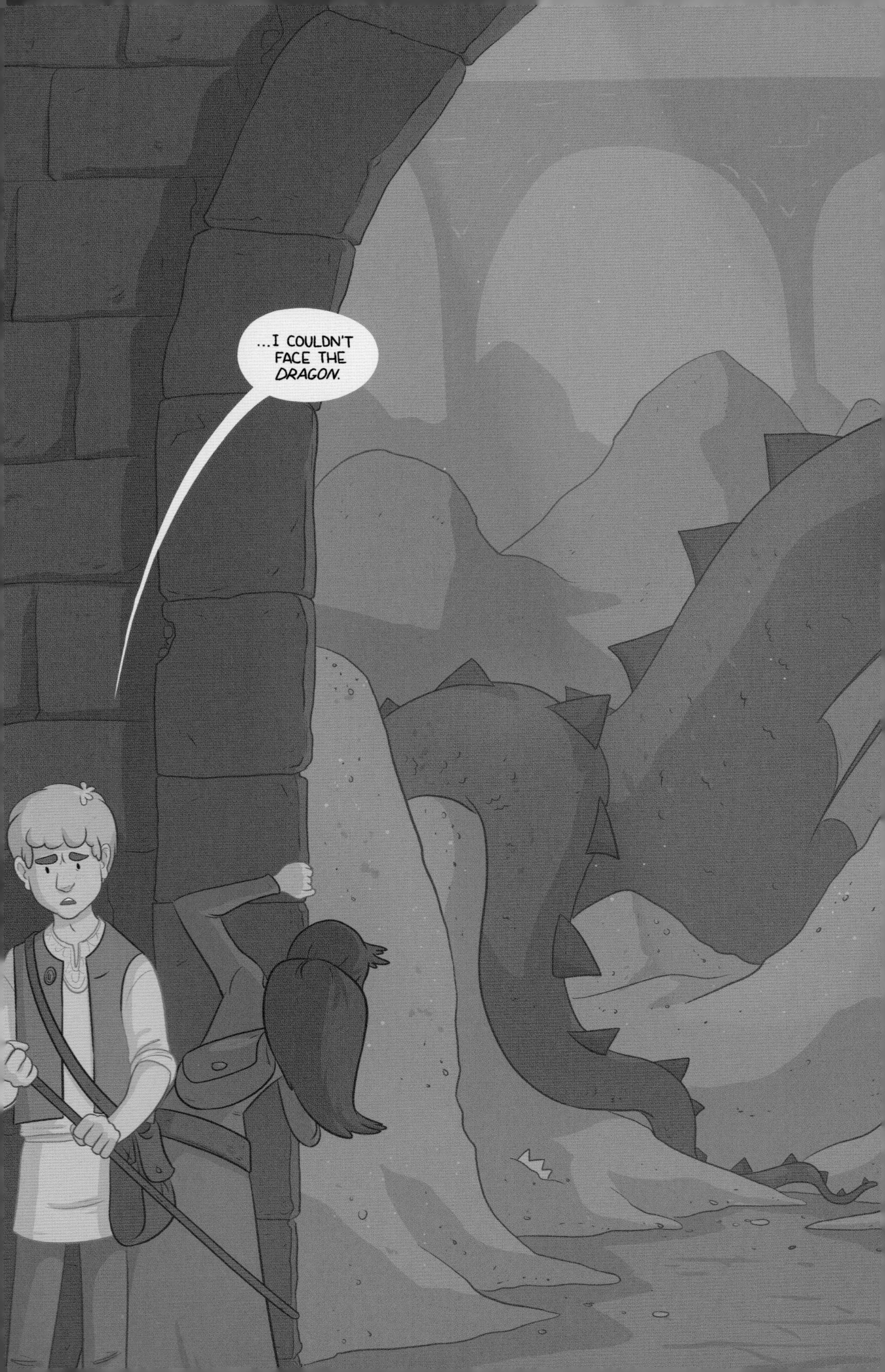
...I COULDN'T FACE THE *DRAGON*.

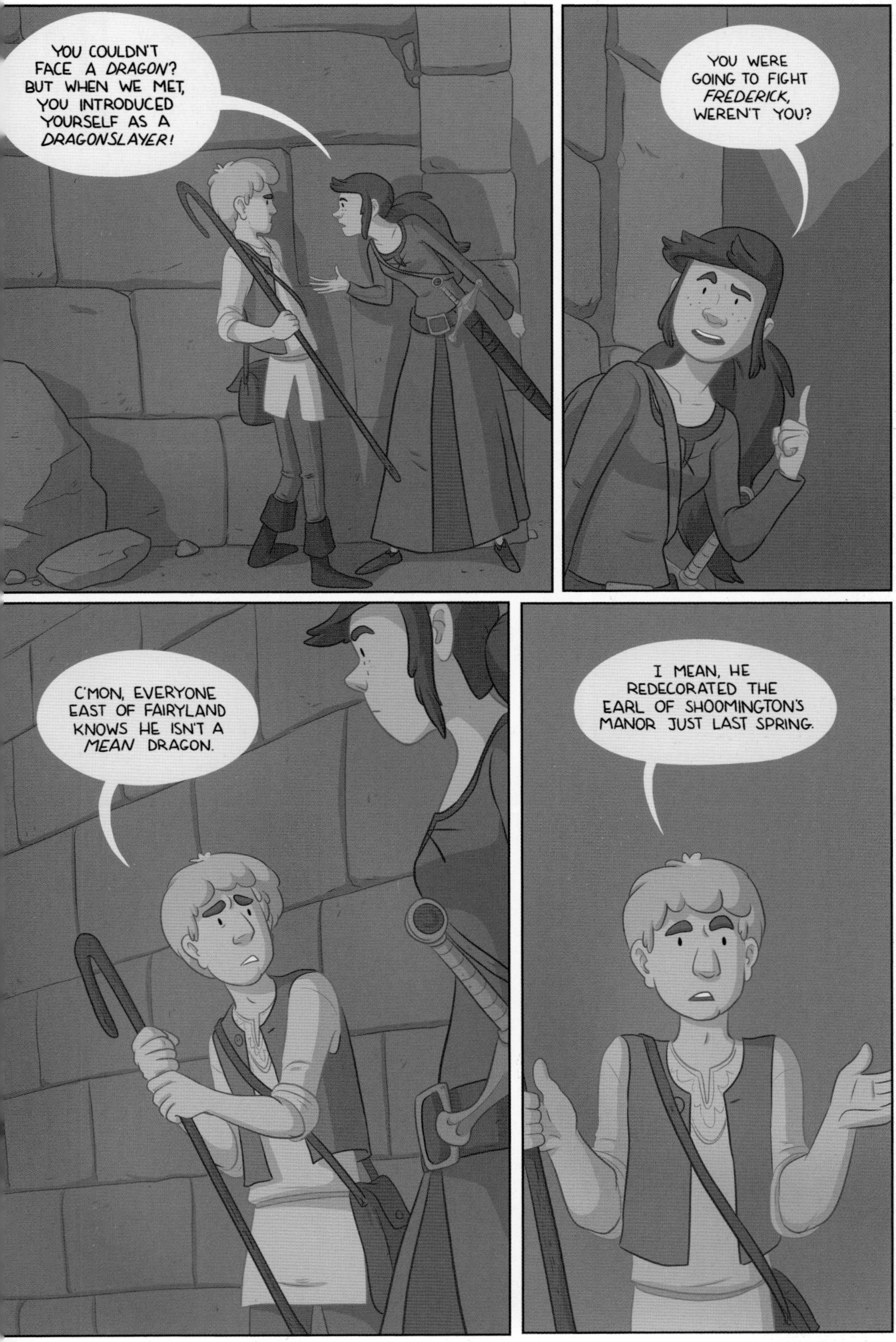
YOU COULDN'T FACE A *DRAGON*? BUT WHEN WE MET, YOU INTRODUCED YOURSELF AS A *DRAGONSLAYER*!
YOU WERE GOING TO FIGHT *FREDERICK*, WEREN'T YOU?
C'MON, EVERYONE EAST OF FAIRYLAND KNOWS HE ISN'T A *MEAN* DRAGON.
I MEAN, HE REDECORATED THE EARL OF SHOOMINGTON'S MANOR JUST LAST SPRING.

SO LET ME GET THIS STRAIGHT.

YOU'RE AFRAID OF FACING A DRAGON, BUT YOU WERE GOING TO MAKE IT *LOOK* LIKE YOU HAD RESCUED ME FROM FREDERICK?

I CAN RESPECT THAT.

NOW YOU KNOW *PLEASE* DON'T MA ME GO IN THERE

I'VE GOT IT FROM HERE.

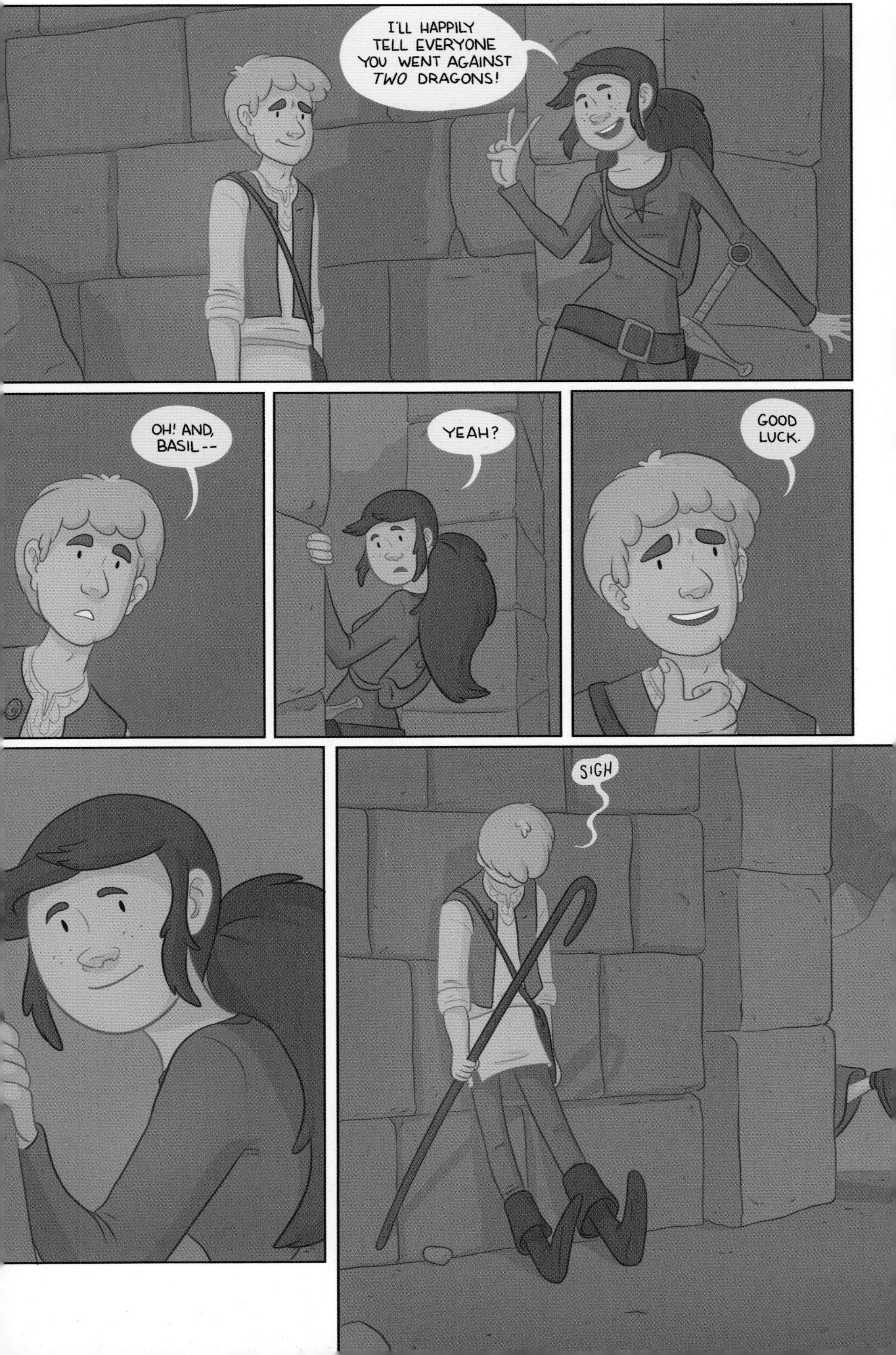
I'LL HAPPILY TELL EVERYONE YOU WENT AGAINST *TWO* DRAGONS!
OH! AND, BASIL--
YEAH?
GOOD LUCK.
SIGH

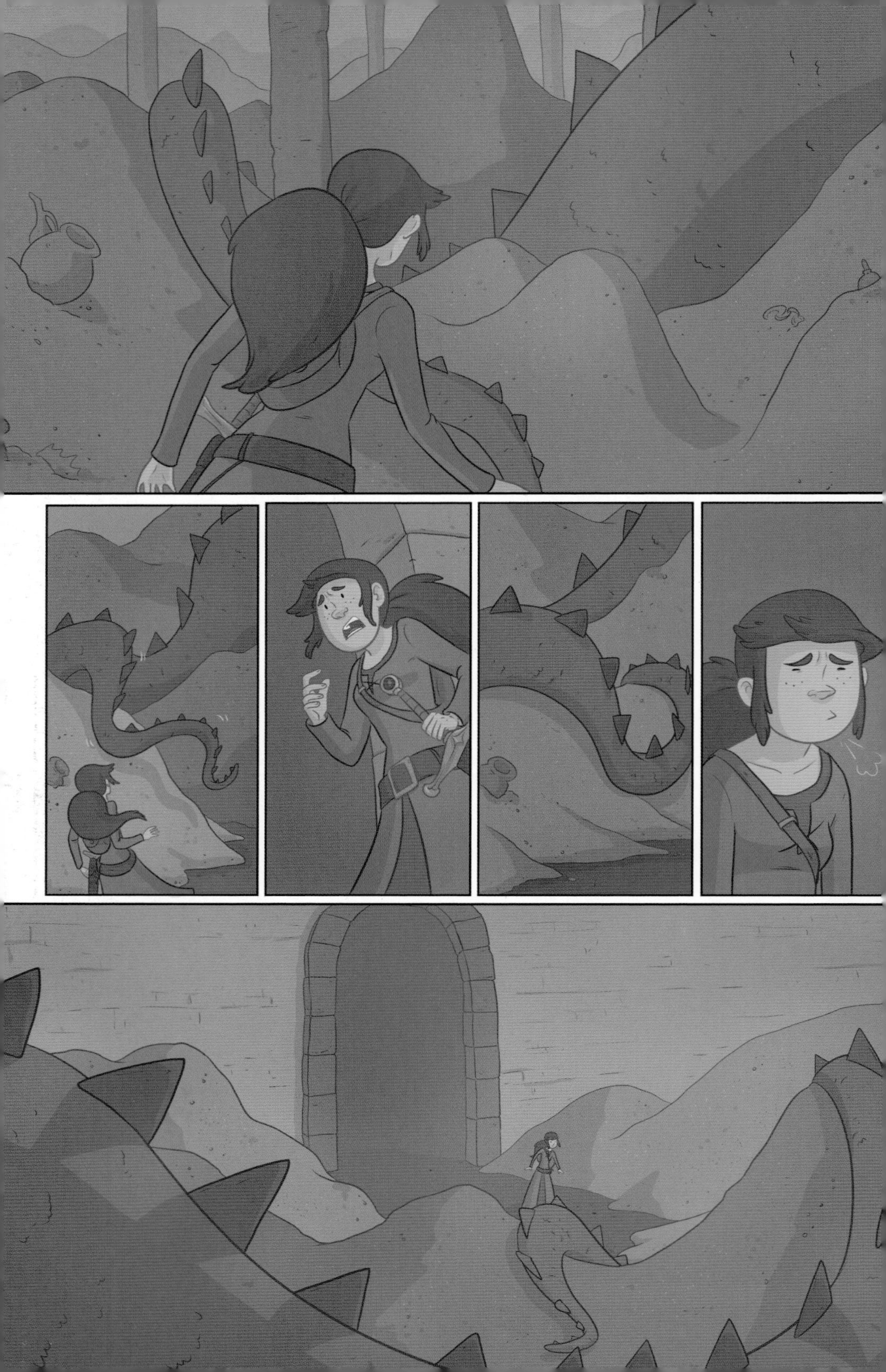

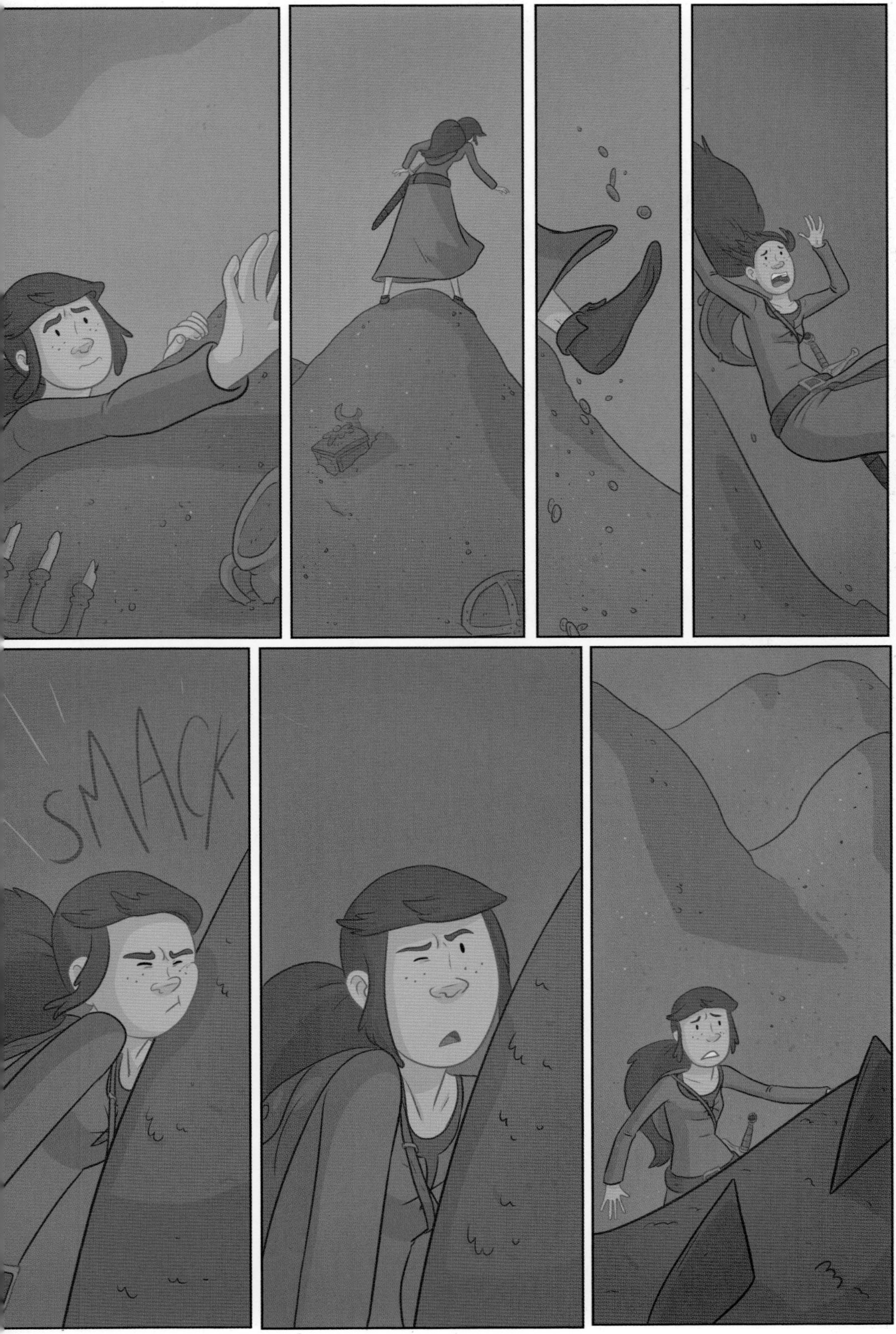
SMACK

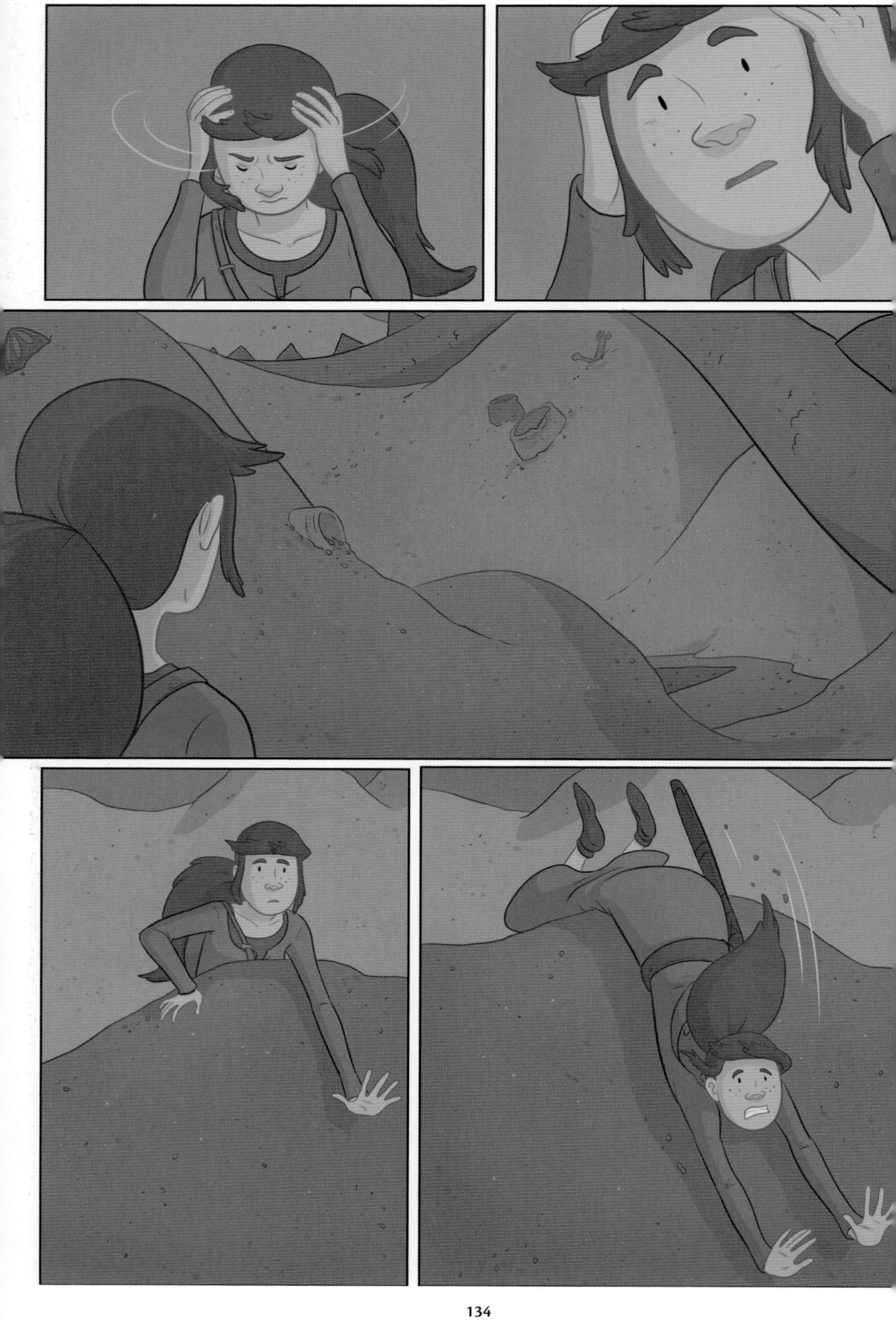

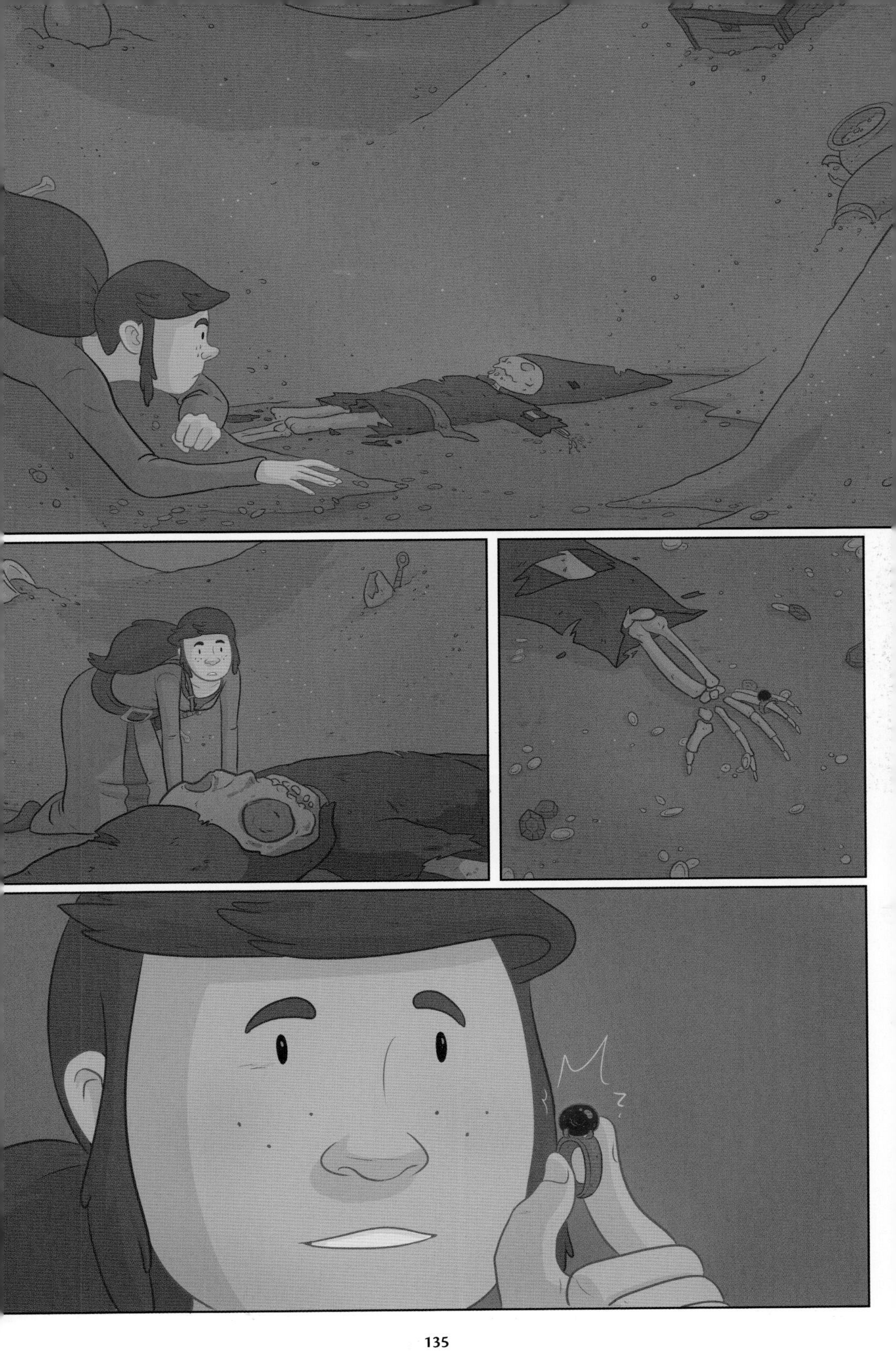

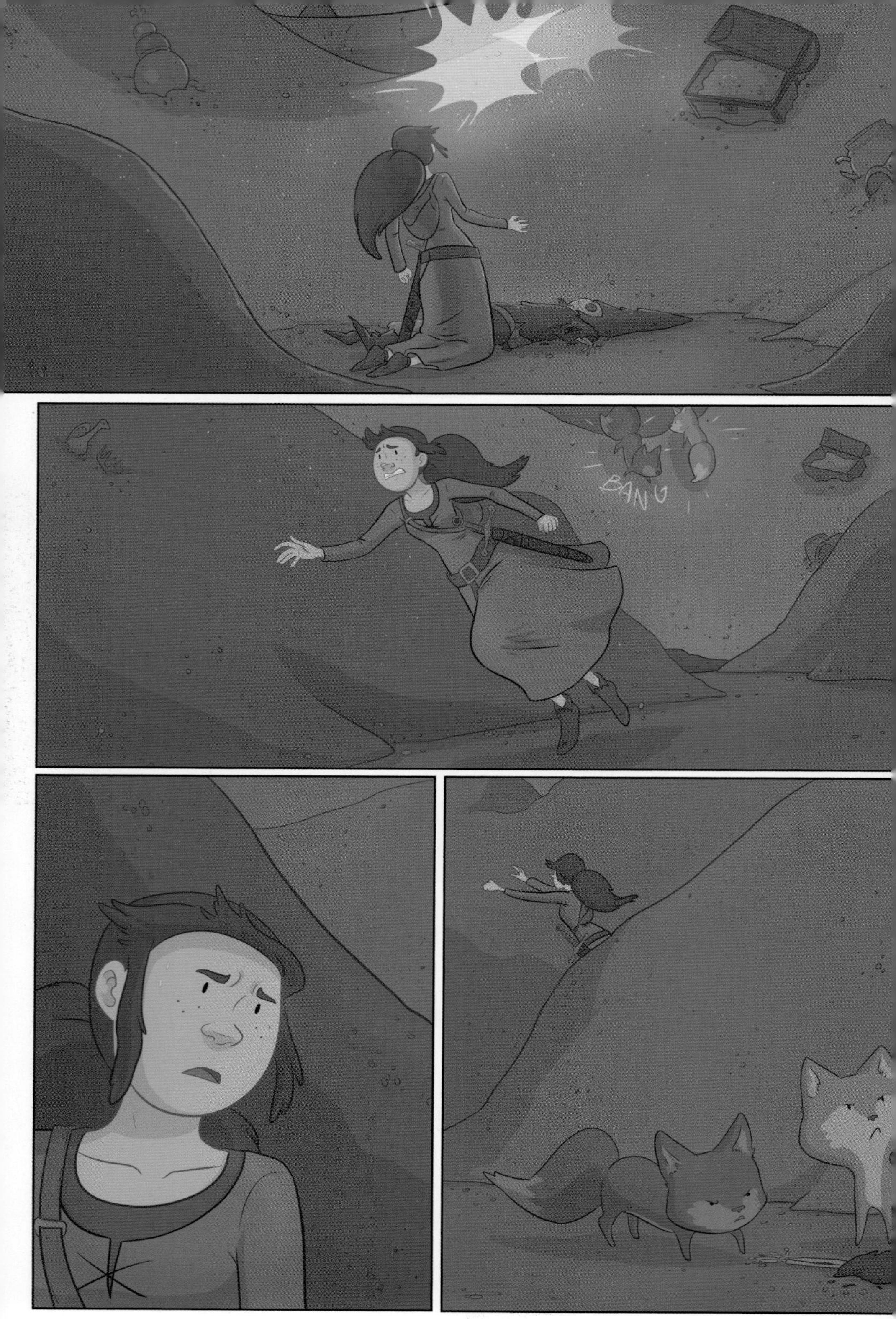
BANG

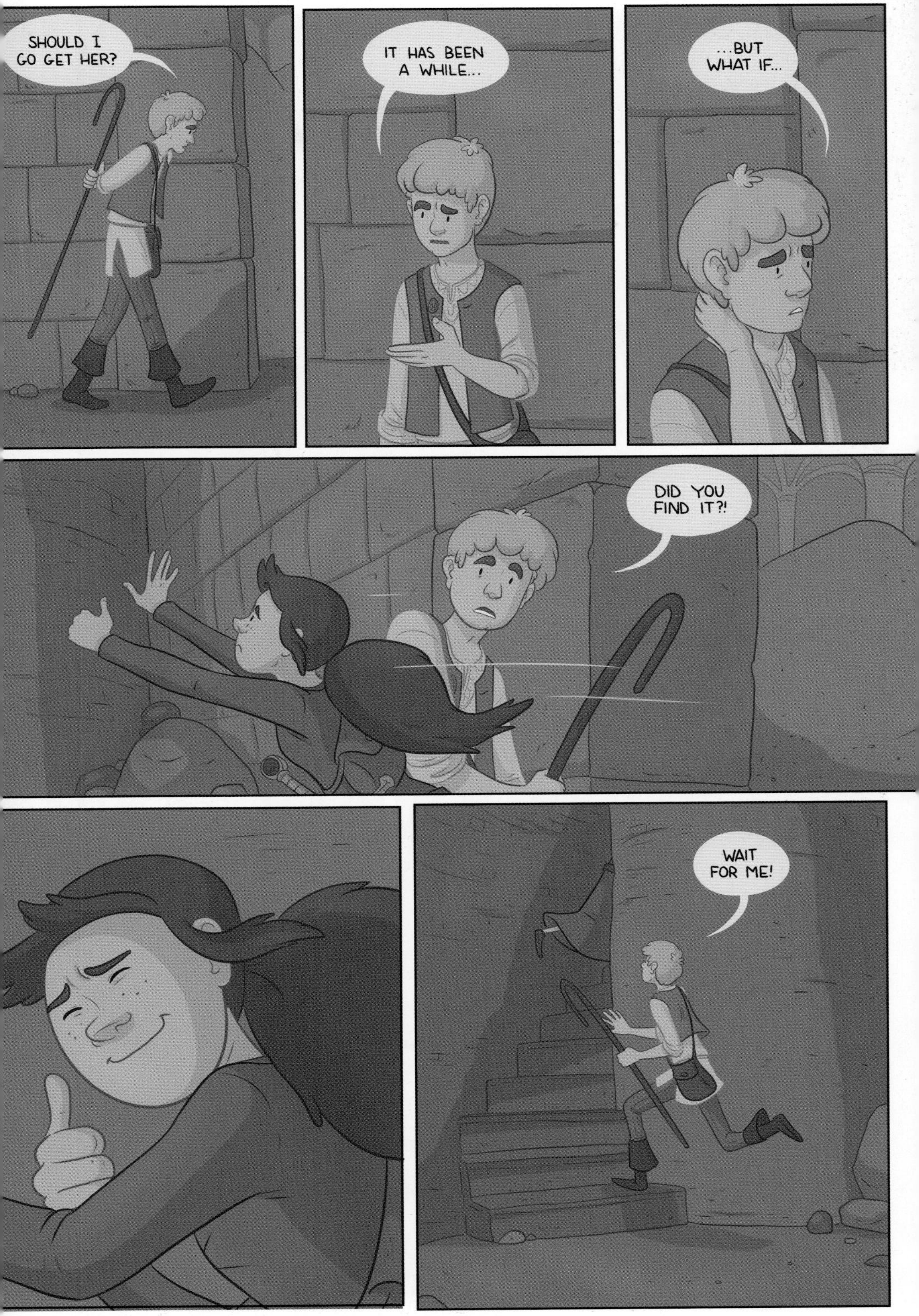
SHOULD I GO GET HER?
IT HAS BEEN A WHILE...
...BUT WHAT IF...
DID YOU FIND IT?!
WAIT FOR ME!

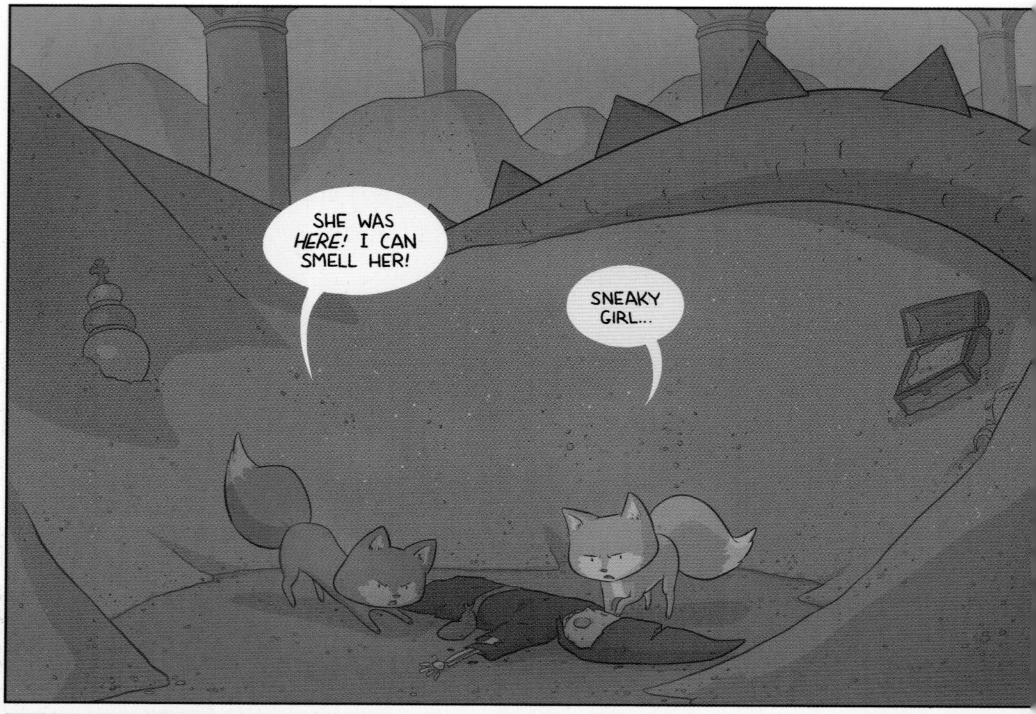
SHE WAS *HERE!* I CAN SMELL HER!
SNEAKY GIRL...

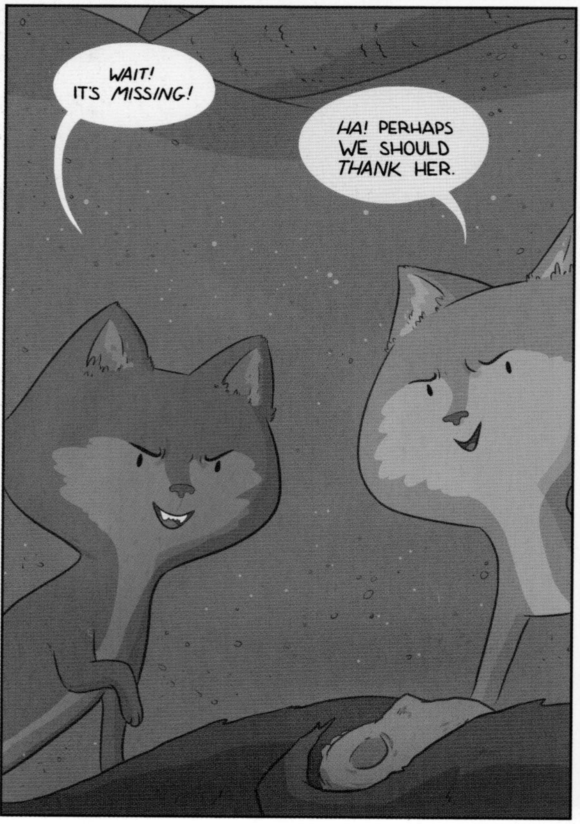
WAIT! IT'S *MISSING!*
HA! PERHAPS WE SHOULD *THANK* HER.

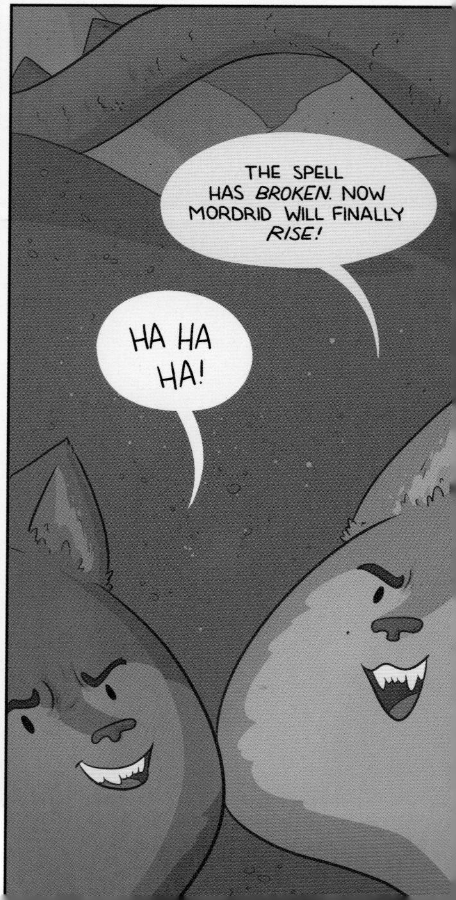
THE SPELL HAS *BROKEN.* NOW MORDRID WILL FINALLY *RISE!*
HA HA HA!

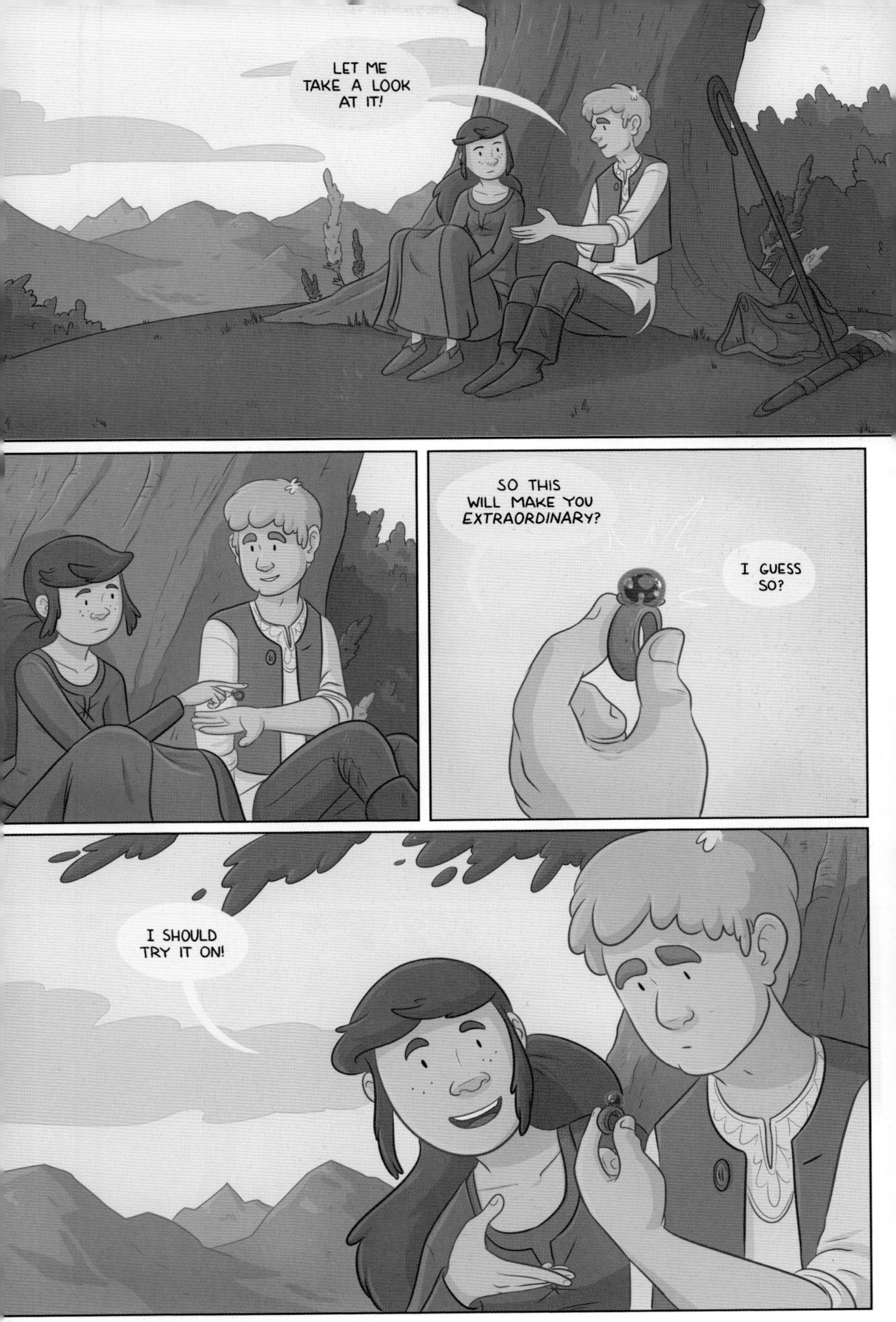
LET ME TAKE A LOOK AT IT!
SO THIS WILL MAKE YOU *EXTRAORDINARY*?
I GUESS SO?
I SHOULD TRY IT ON!

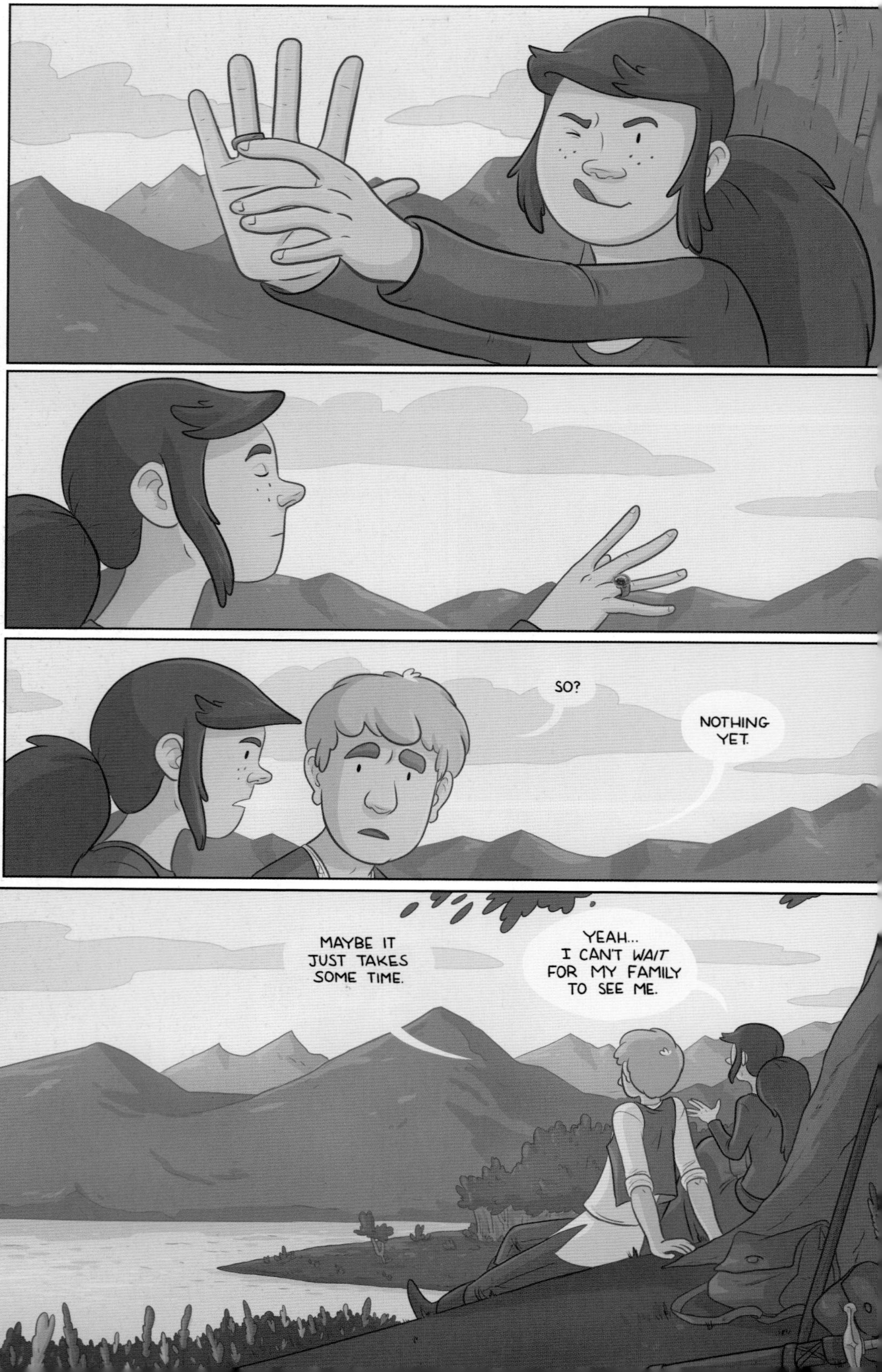
SO?
NOTHING YET.
MAYBE IT JUST TAKES SOME TIME.
YEAH... I CAN'T *WAIT* FOR MY FAMILY TO SEE ME.

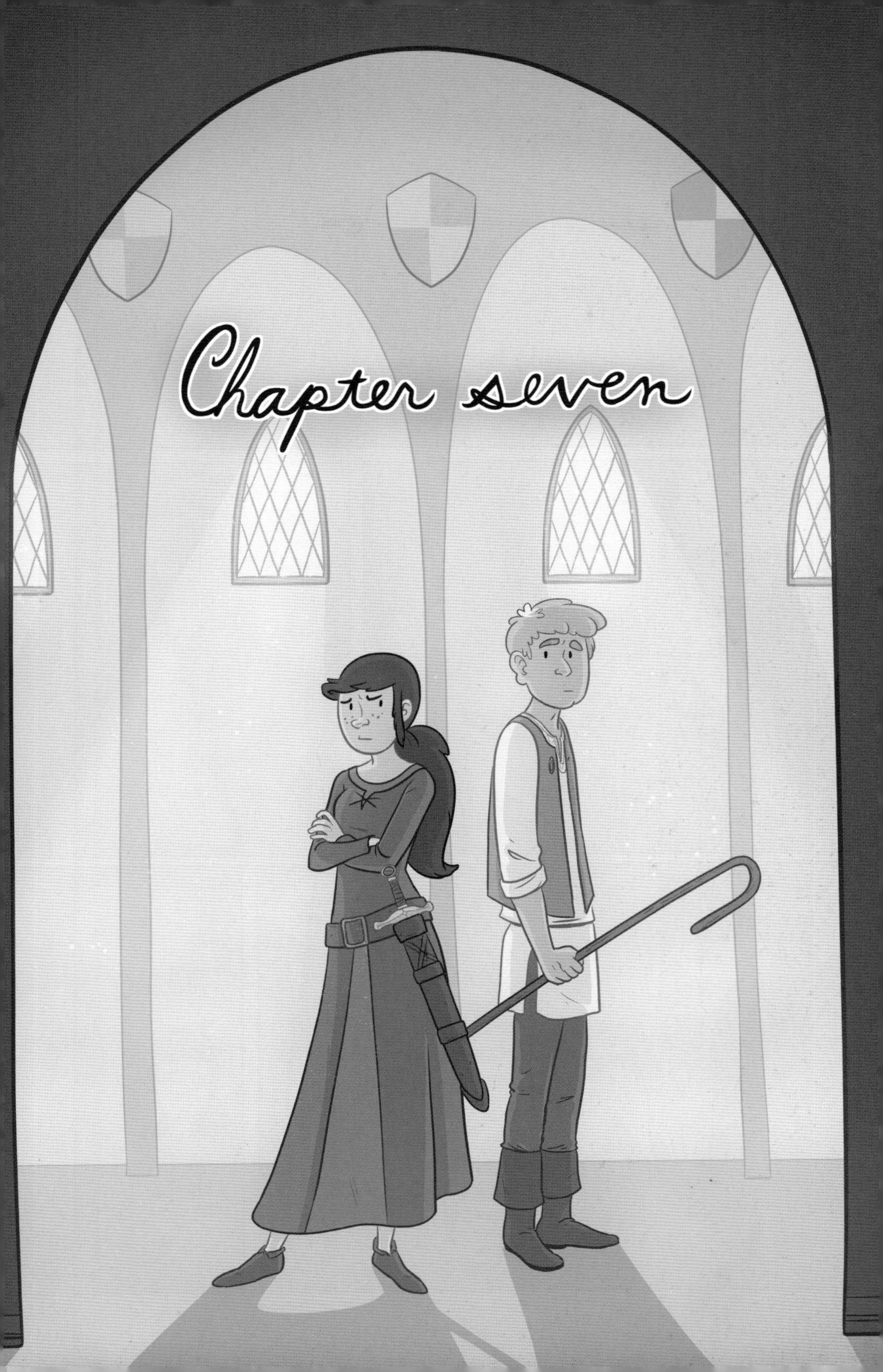
Chapter seven

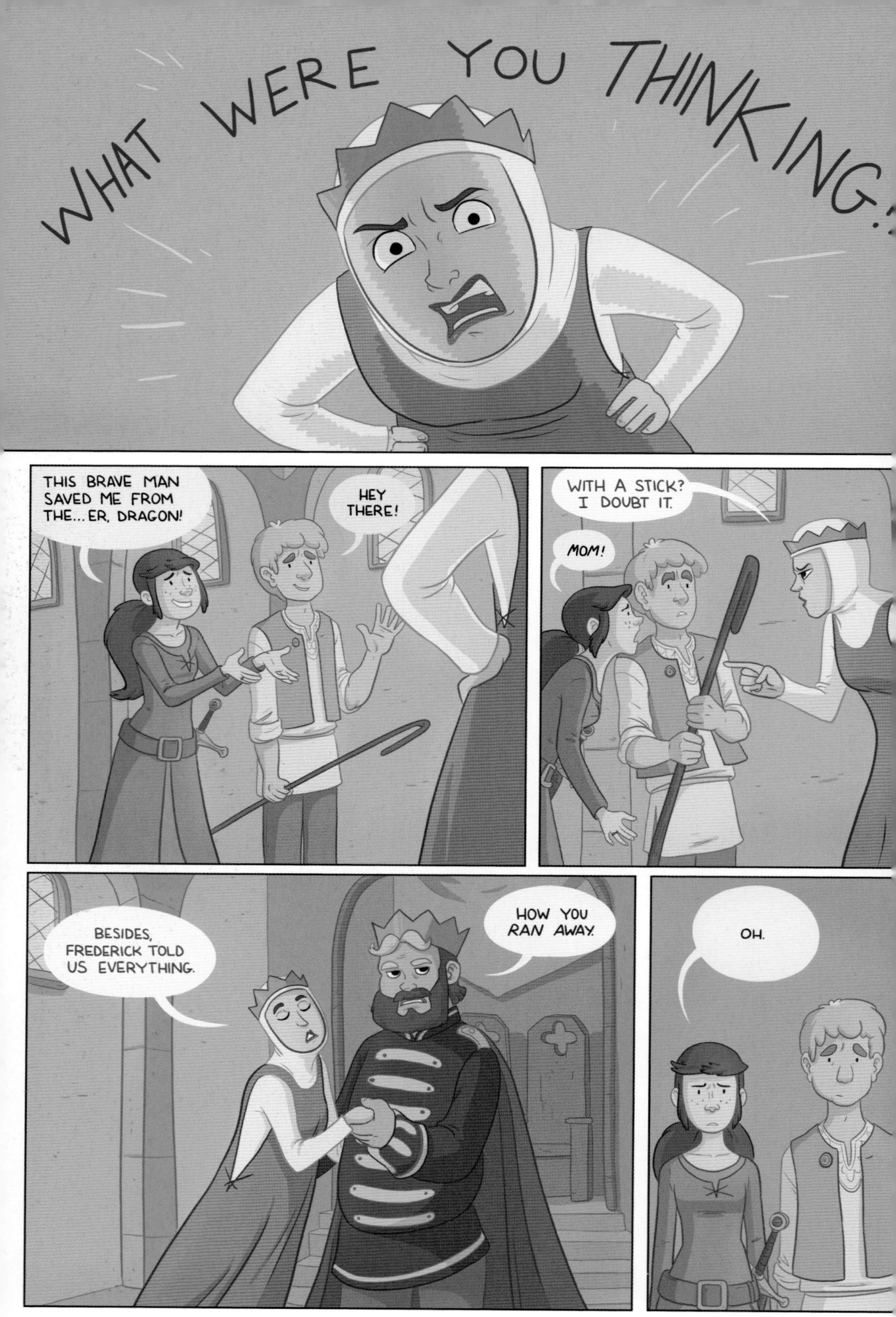
WHAT WERE YOU THINKING!?
THIS BRAVE MAN SAVED ME FROM THE... ER, DRAGON!
HEY THERE!
WITH A STICK? I DOUBT IT.
MOM!
BESIDES, FREDERICK TOLD US EVERYTHING.
HOW YOU RAN AWAY.
OH.

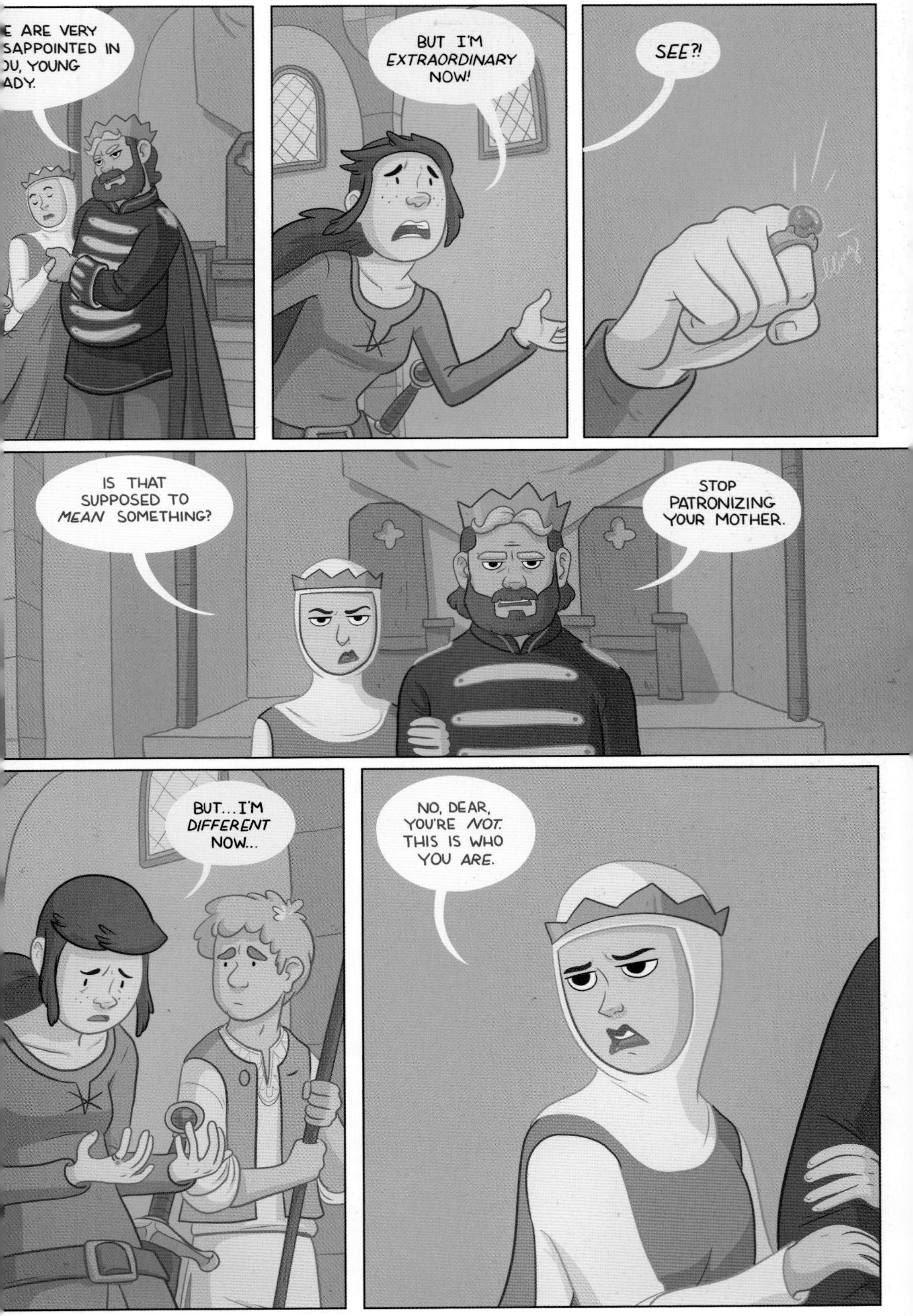
E ARE VERY
SAPPOINTED IN
OU, YOUNG
ADY.
BUT I'M *EXTRAORDINARY* NOW!
SEE?!
IS THAT SUPPOSED TO *MEAN* SOMETHING?
STOP PATRONIZING YOUR MOTHER.
BUT...I'M *DIFFERENT* NOW...
NO, DEAR, YOU'RE *NOT.* THIS IS WHO YOU *ARE.*

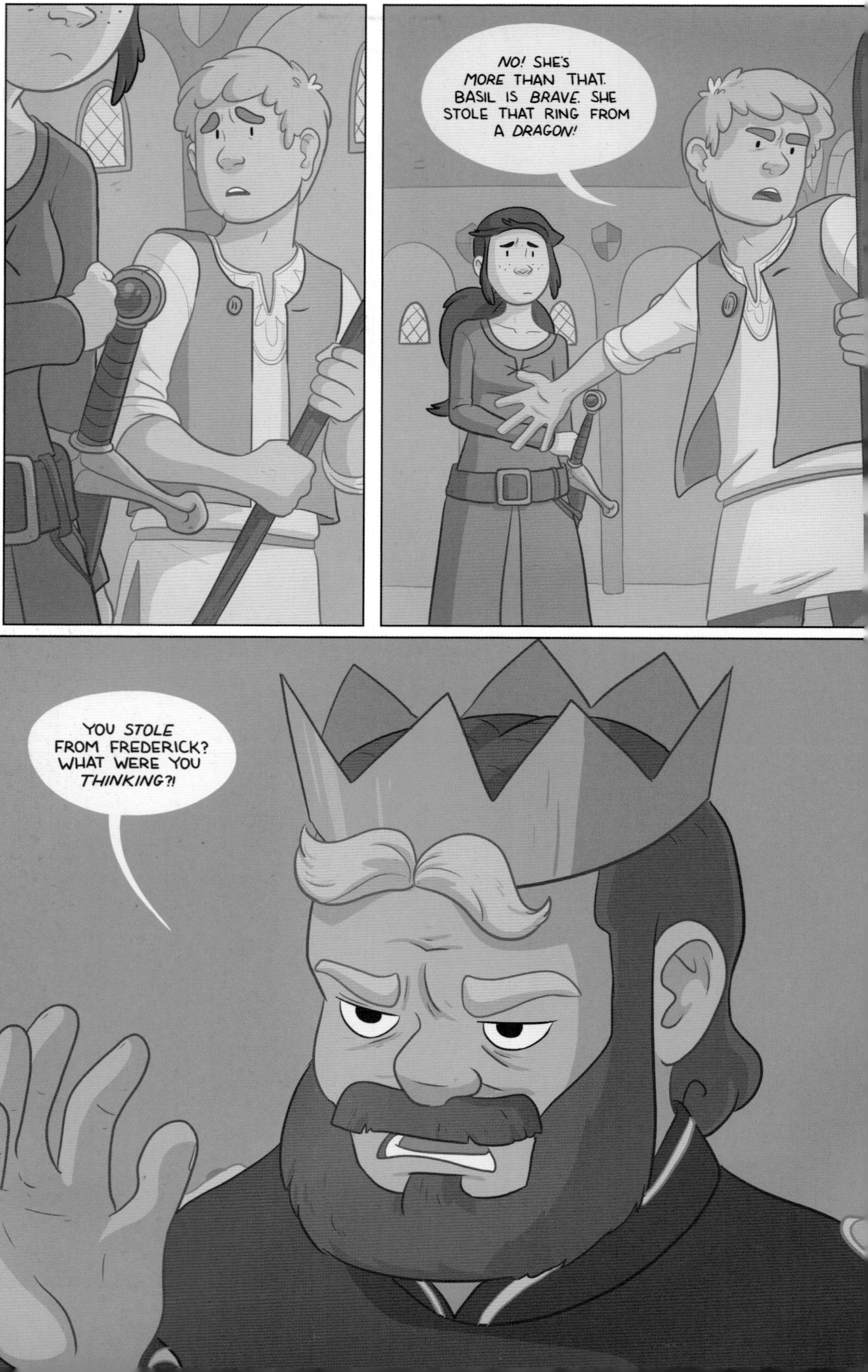
NO! SHE'S MORE THAN THAT. BASIL IS BRAVE. SHE STOLE THAT RING FROM A DRAGON!
YOU STOLE FROM FREDERICK? WHAT WERE YOU THINKING?!

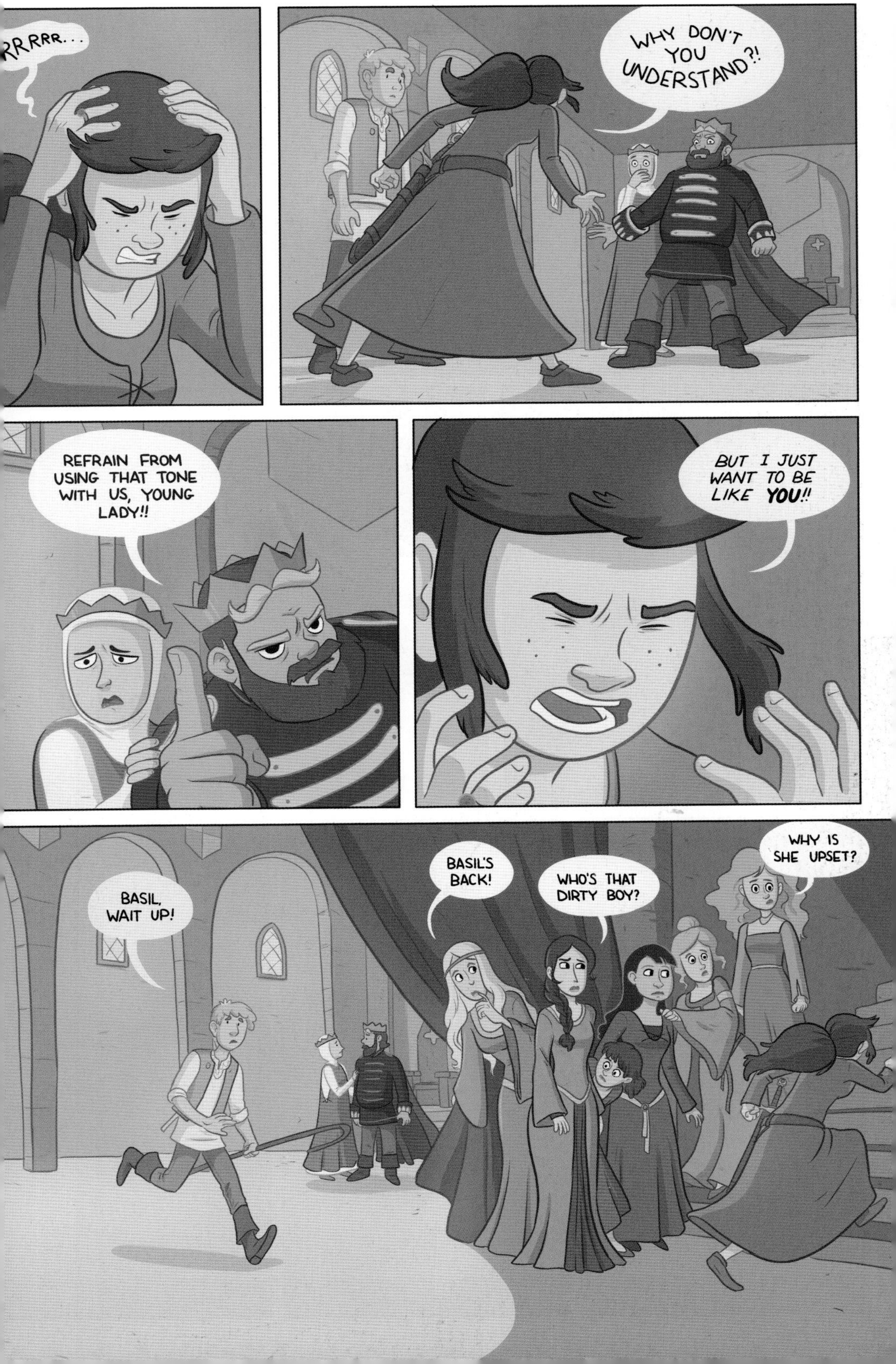
RRRRR...
WHY DON'T YOU UNDERSTAND?!
REFRAIN FROM USING THAT TONE WITH US, YOUNG LADY!!
BUT I JUST WANT TO BE LIKE **YOU**!!
BASIL, WAIT UP!
BASIL'S BACK!
WHO'S THAT DIRTY BOY?
WHY IS SHE UPSET?

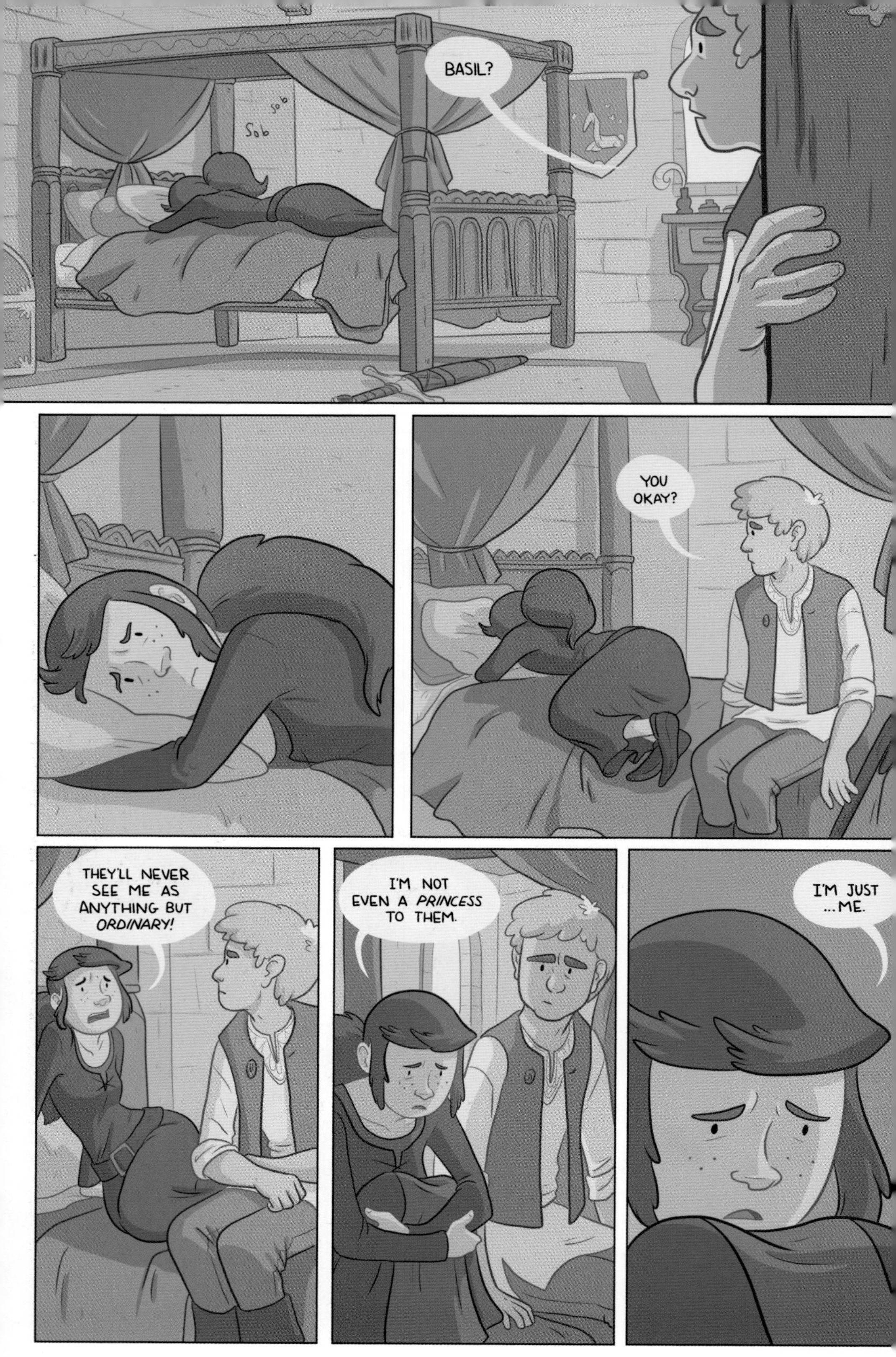
Sob
sob
BASIL?
YOU OKAY?
THEY'LL NEVER SEE ME AS ANYTHING BUT *ORDINARY!*
I'M NOT EVEN A *PRINCESS* TO THEM.
I'M JUST ...ME.

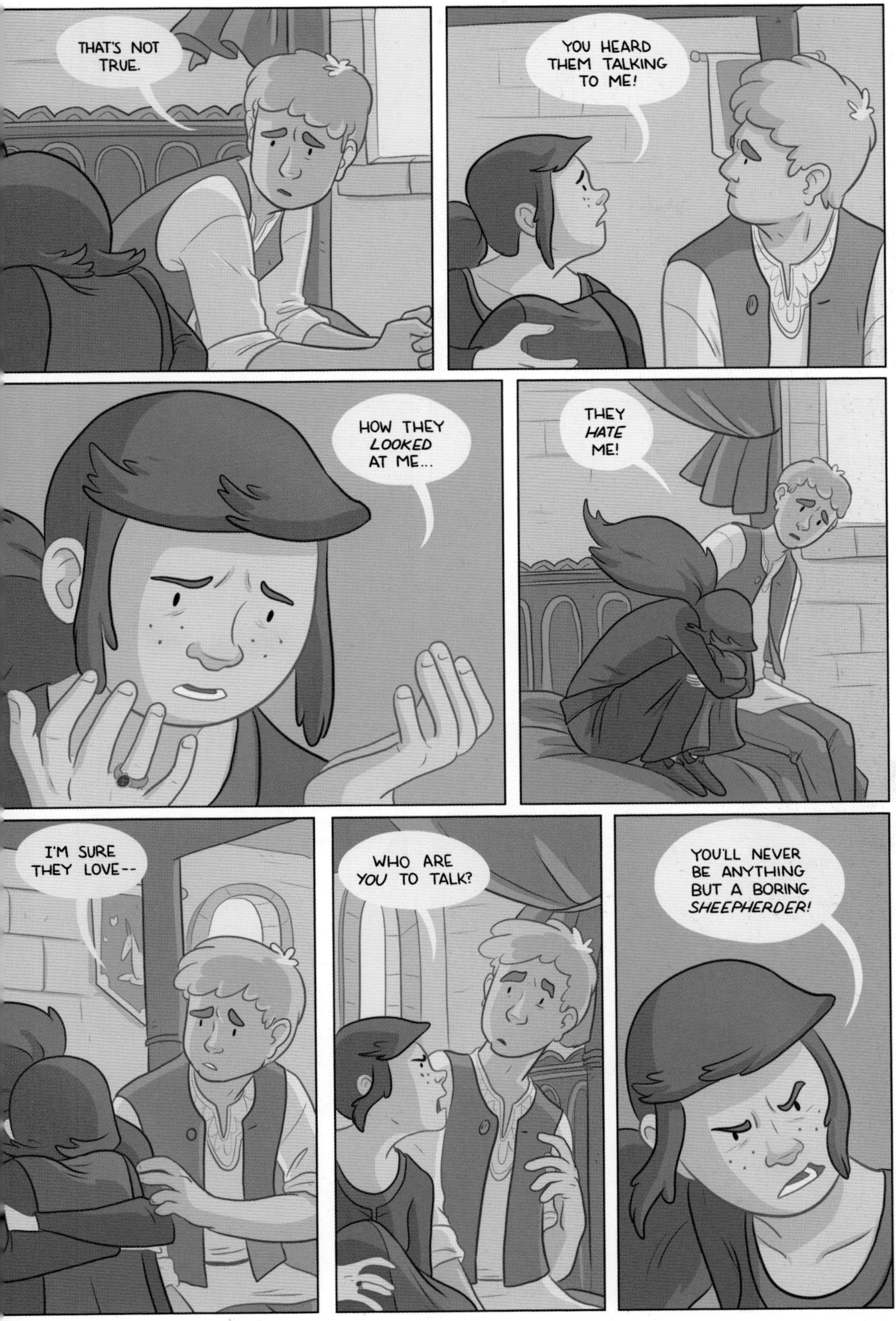
THAT'S NOT TRUE.
YOU HEARD THEM TALKING TO ME!
HOW THEY *LOOKED* AT ME...
THEY *HATE* ME!
I'M SURE THEY LOVE--
WHO ARE *YOU* TO TALK?
YOU'LL NEVER BE ANYTHING BUT A BORING *SHEEPHERDER*!

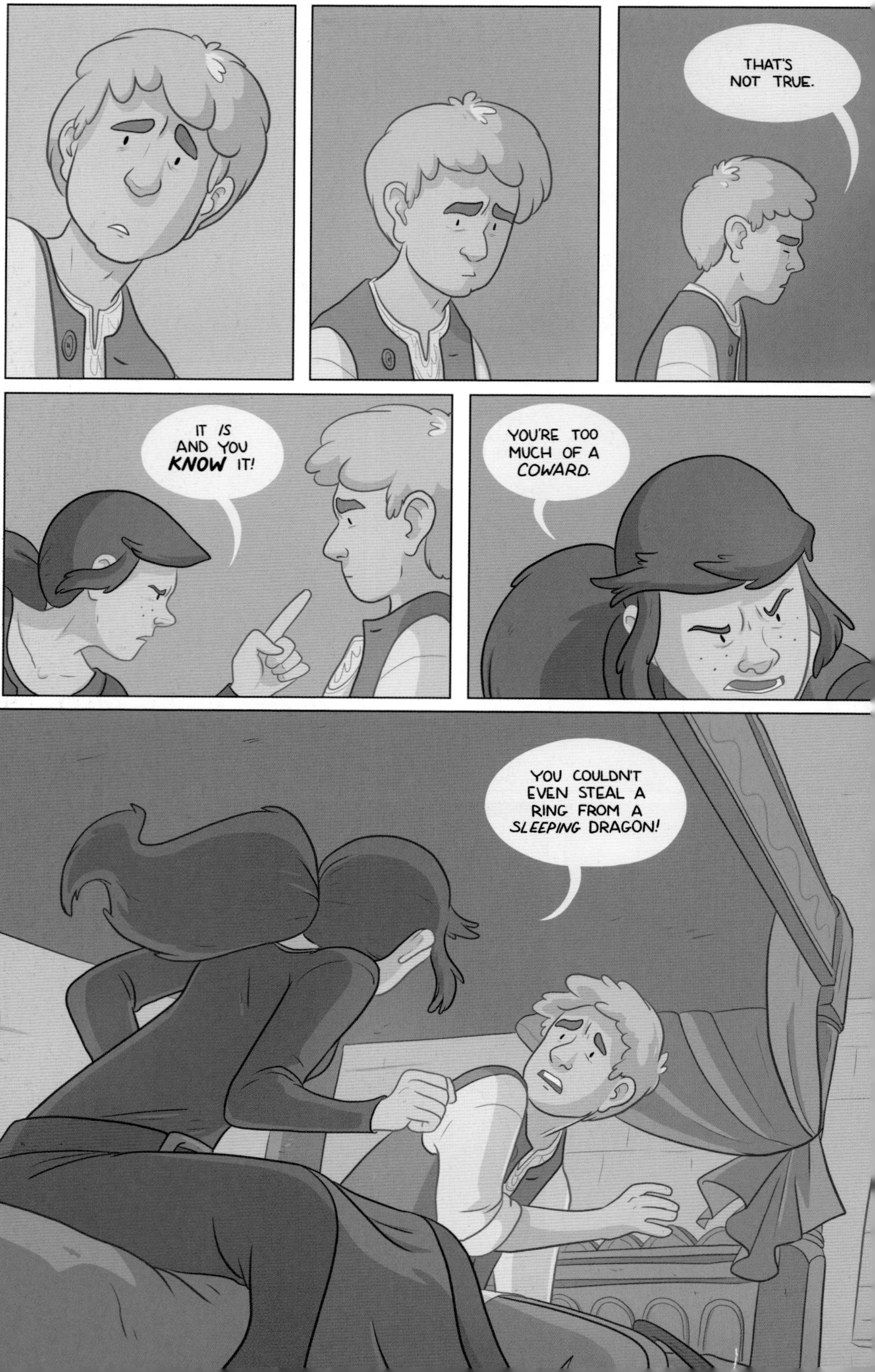
THAT'S NOT TRUE.
IT *IS* AND YOU ***KNOW*** IT!
YOU'RE TOO MUCH OF A *COWARD.*
YOU COULDN'T EVEN STEAL A RING FROM A *SLEEPING* DRAGON!

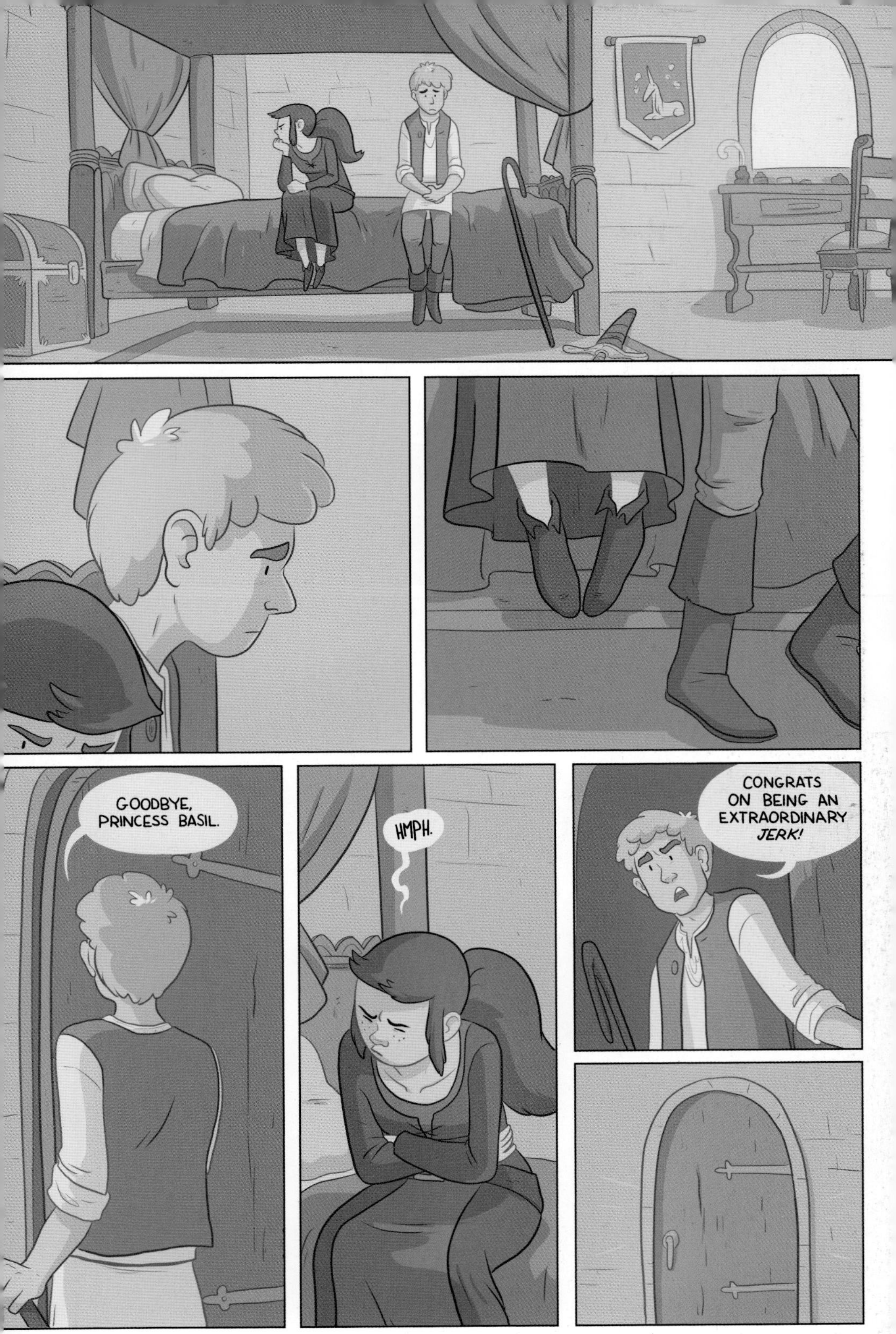
GOODBYE, PRINCESS BASIL.
HMPH.
CONGRATS ON BEING AN EXTRAORDINARY *JERK!*

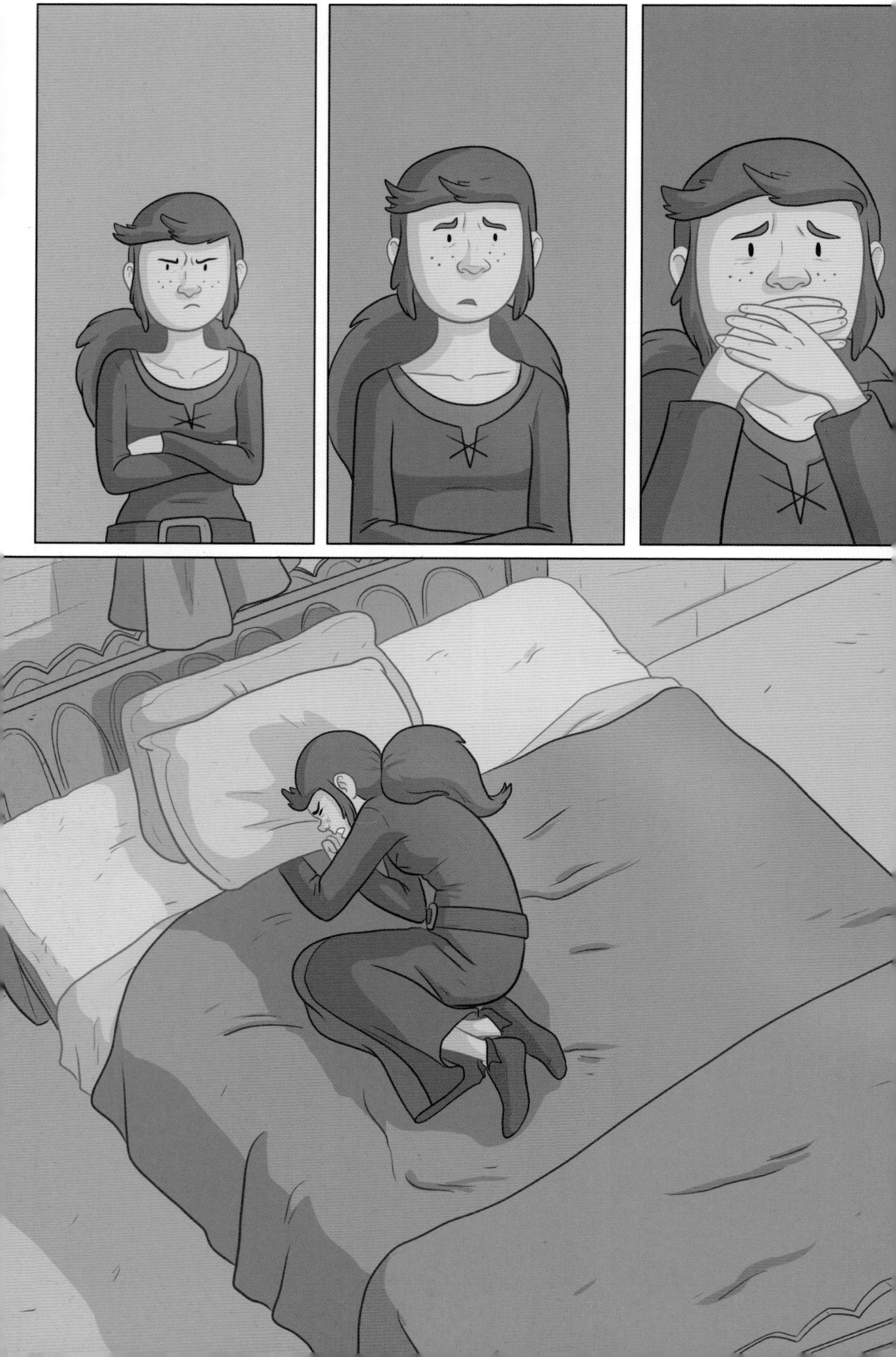

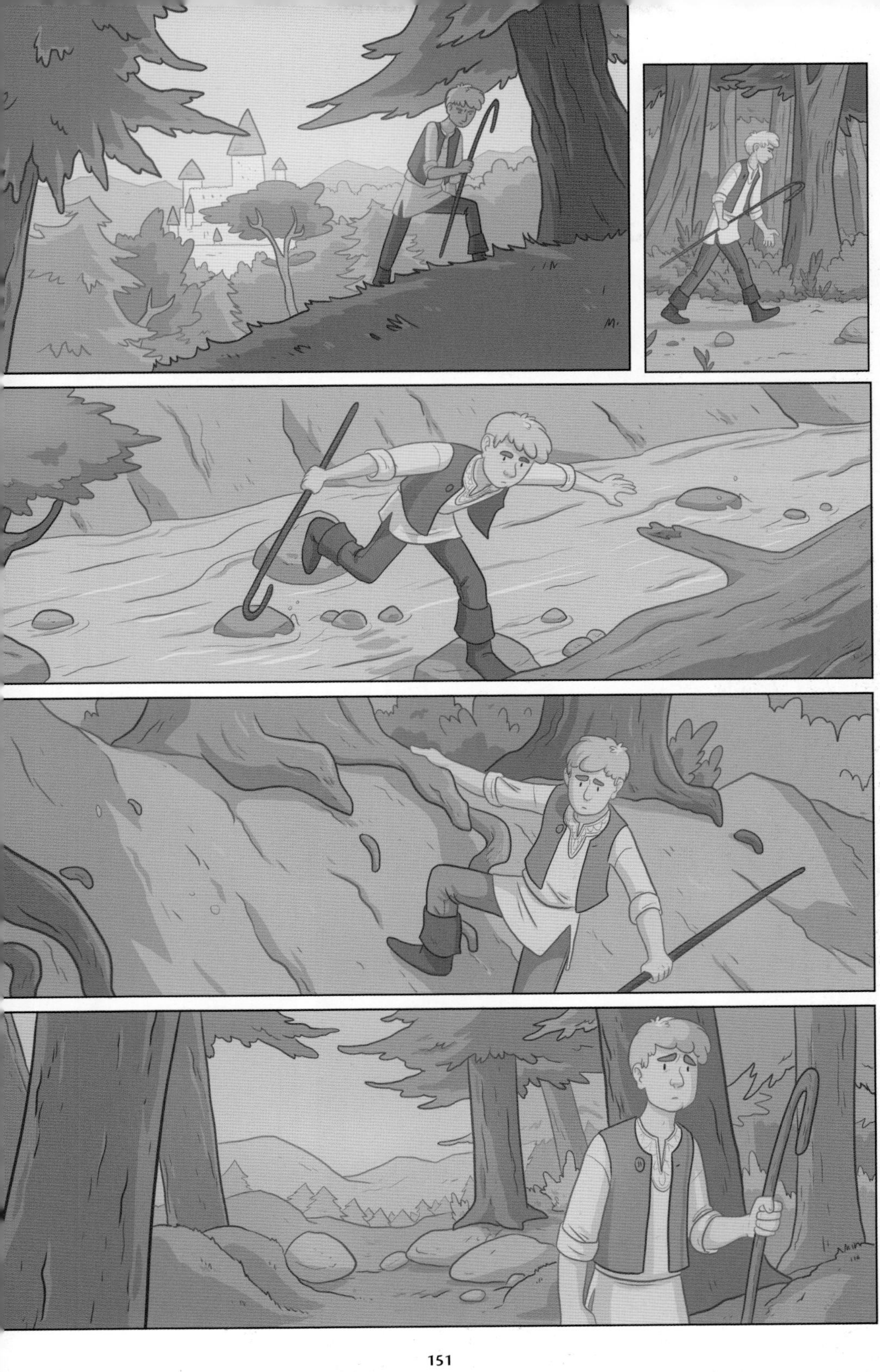

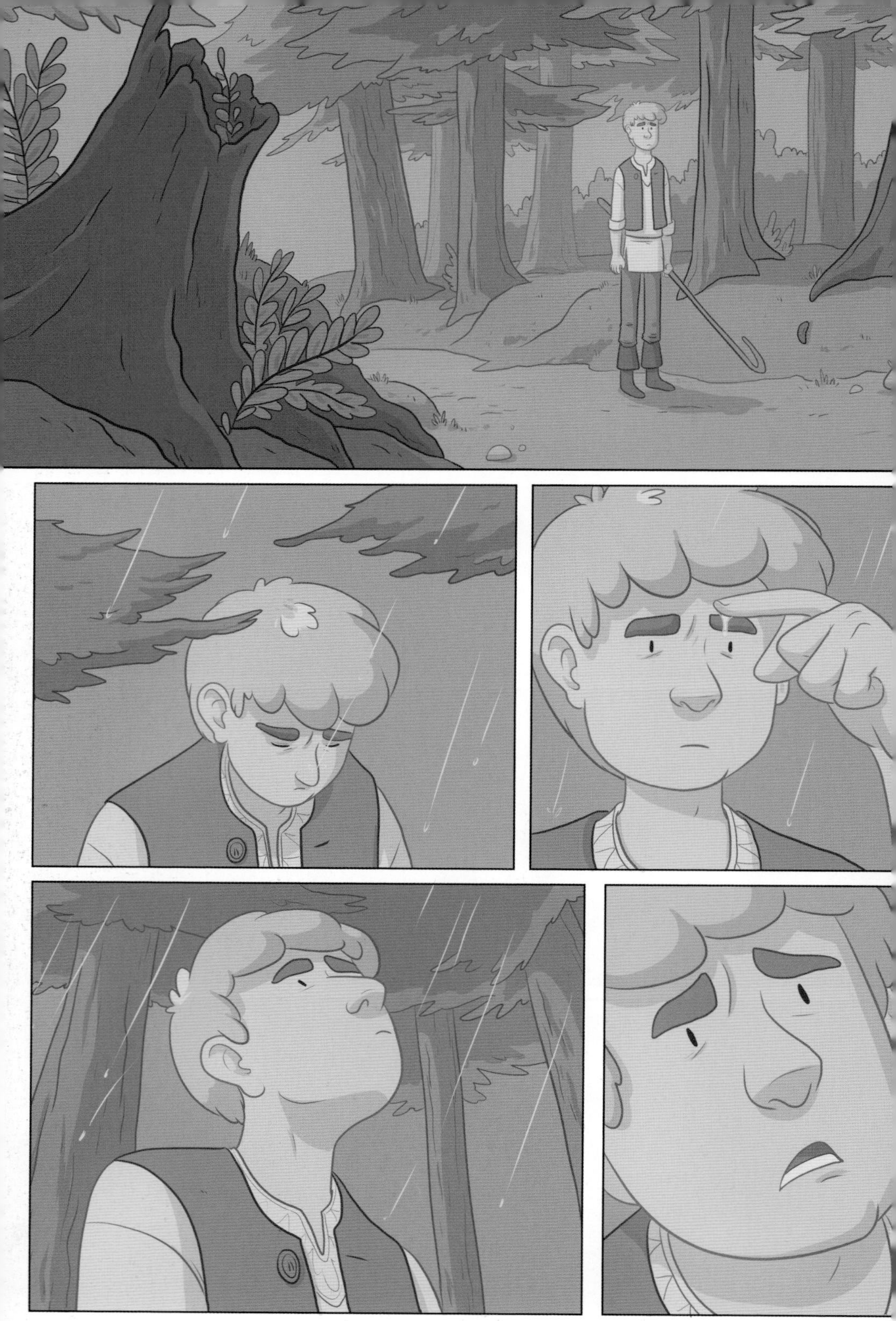

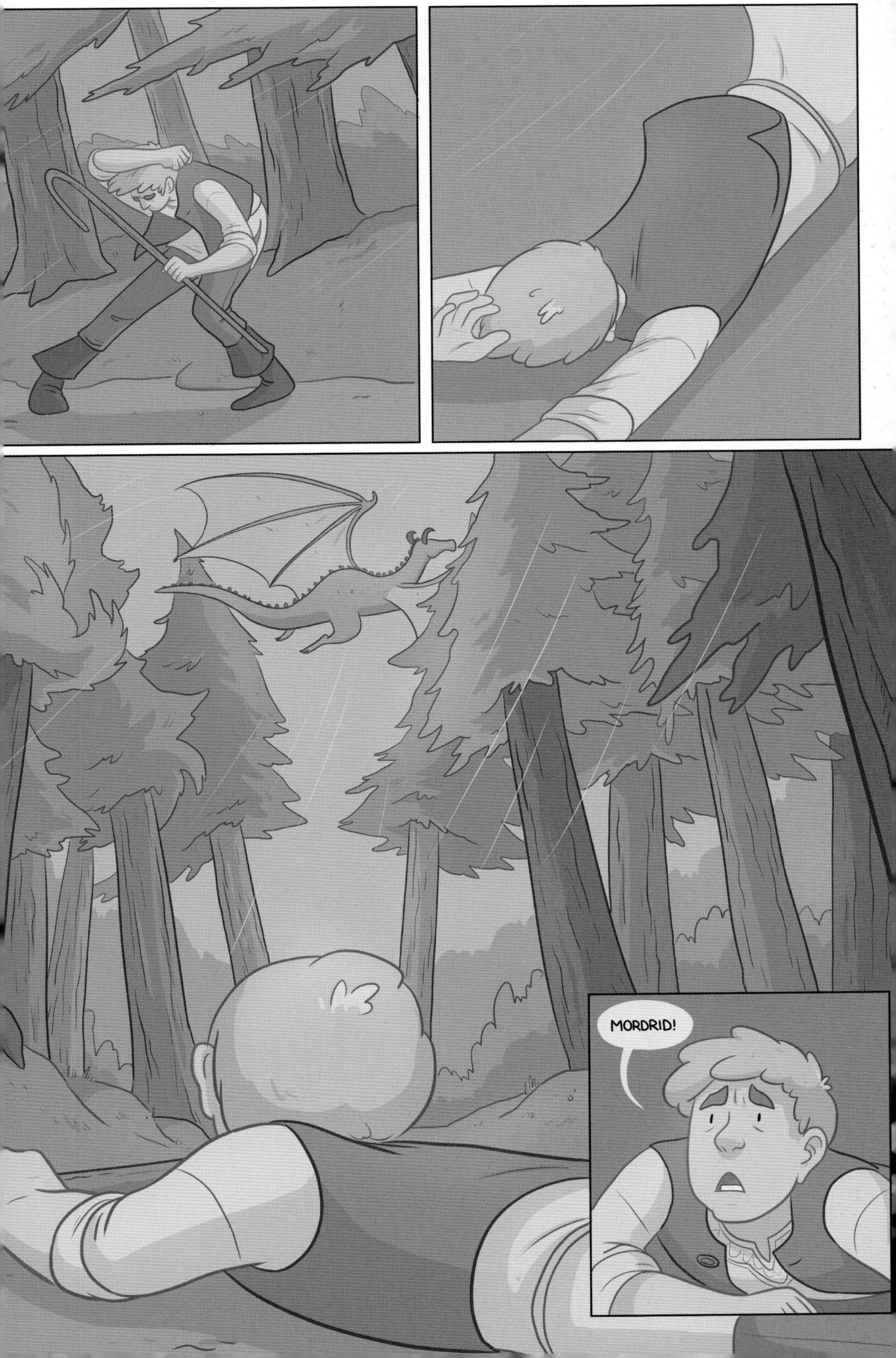
MORDRID!

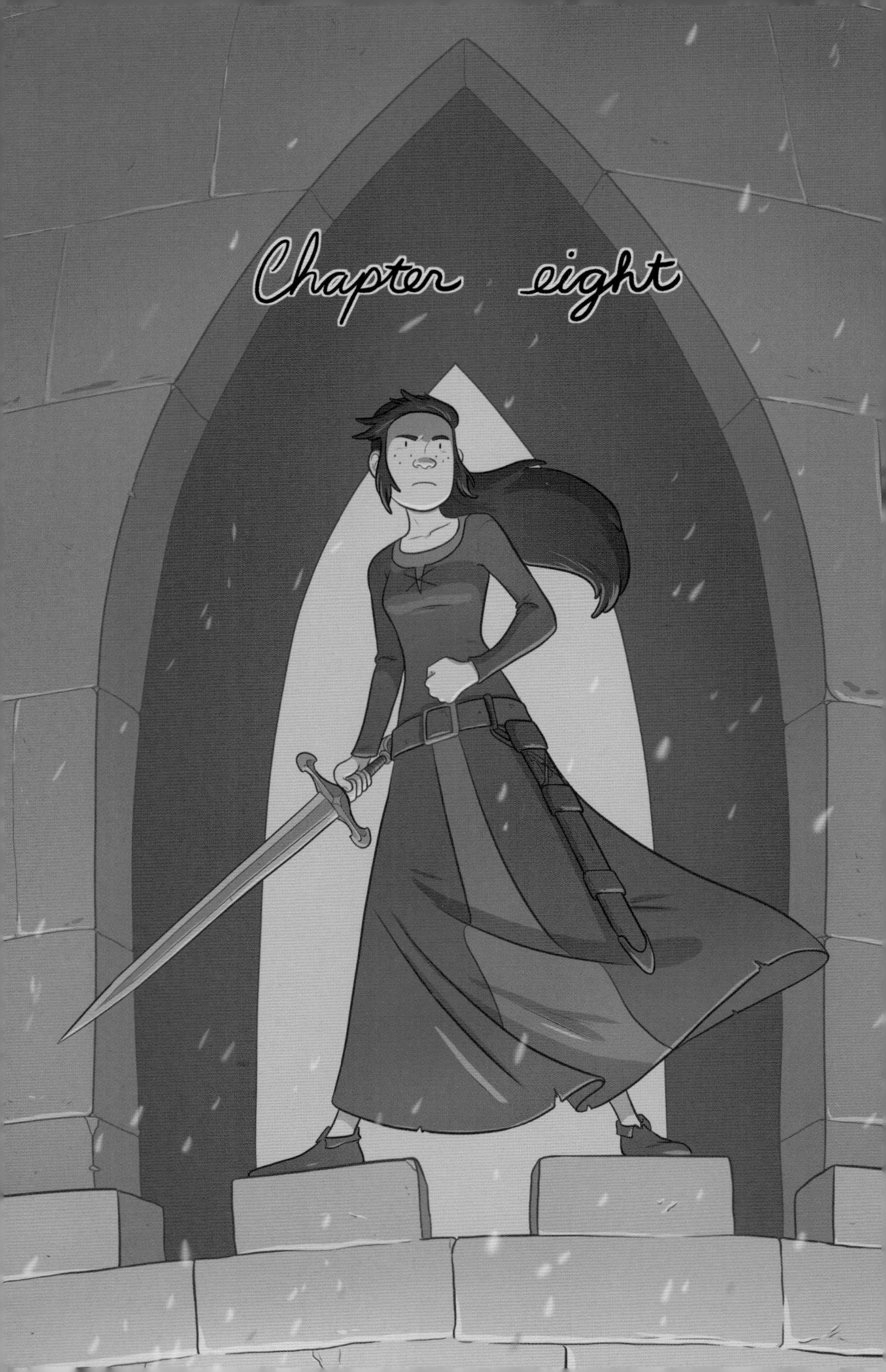
Chapter eight

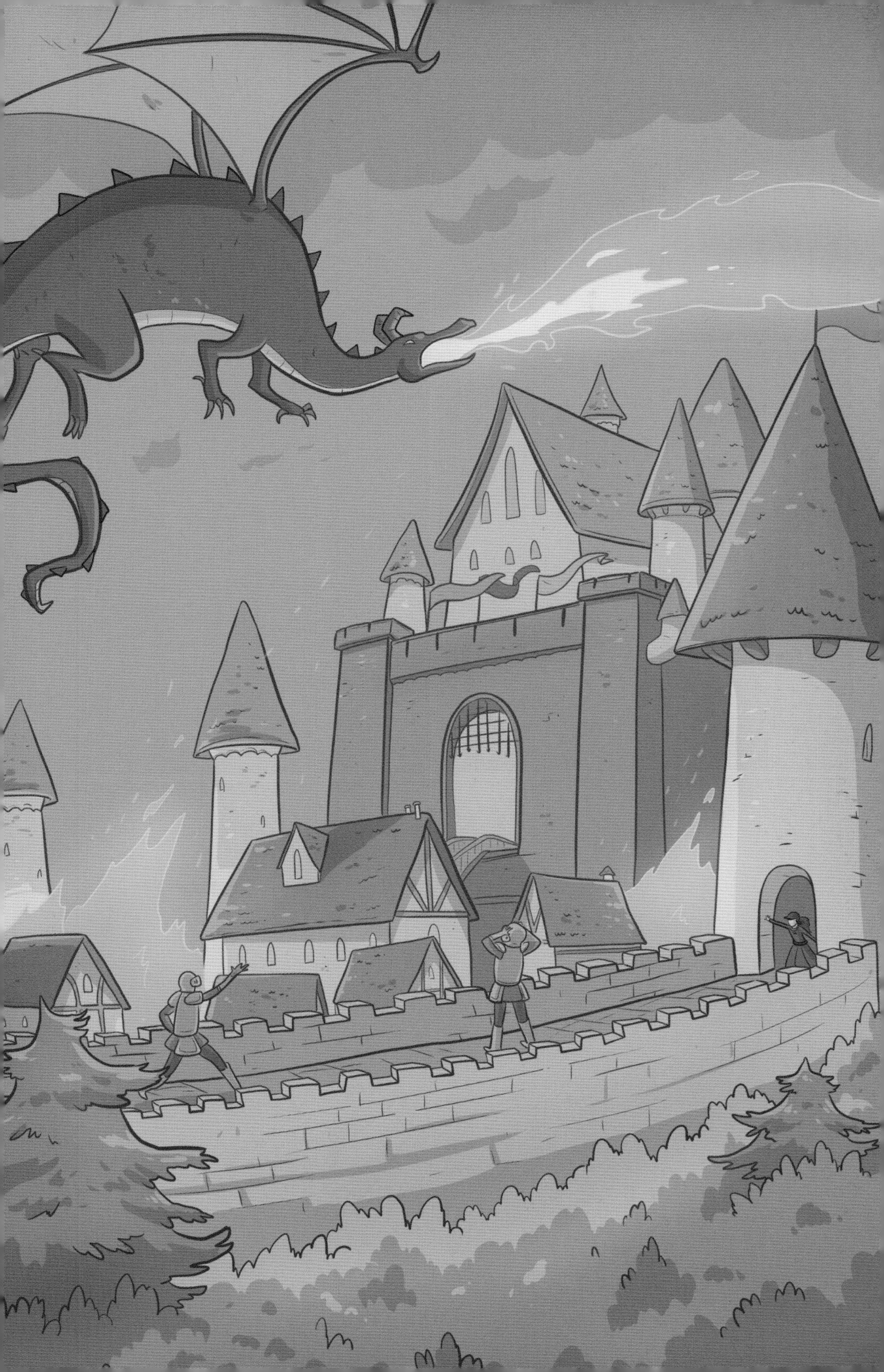

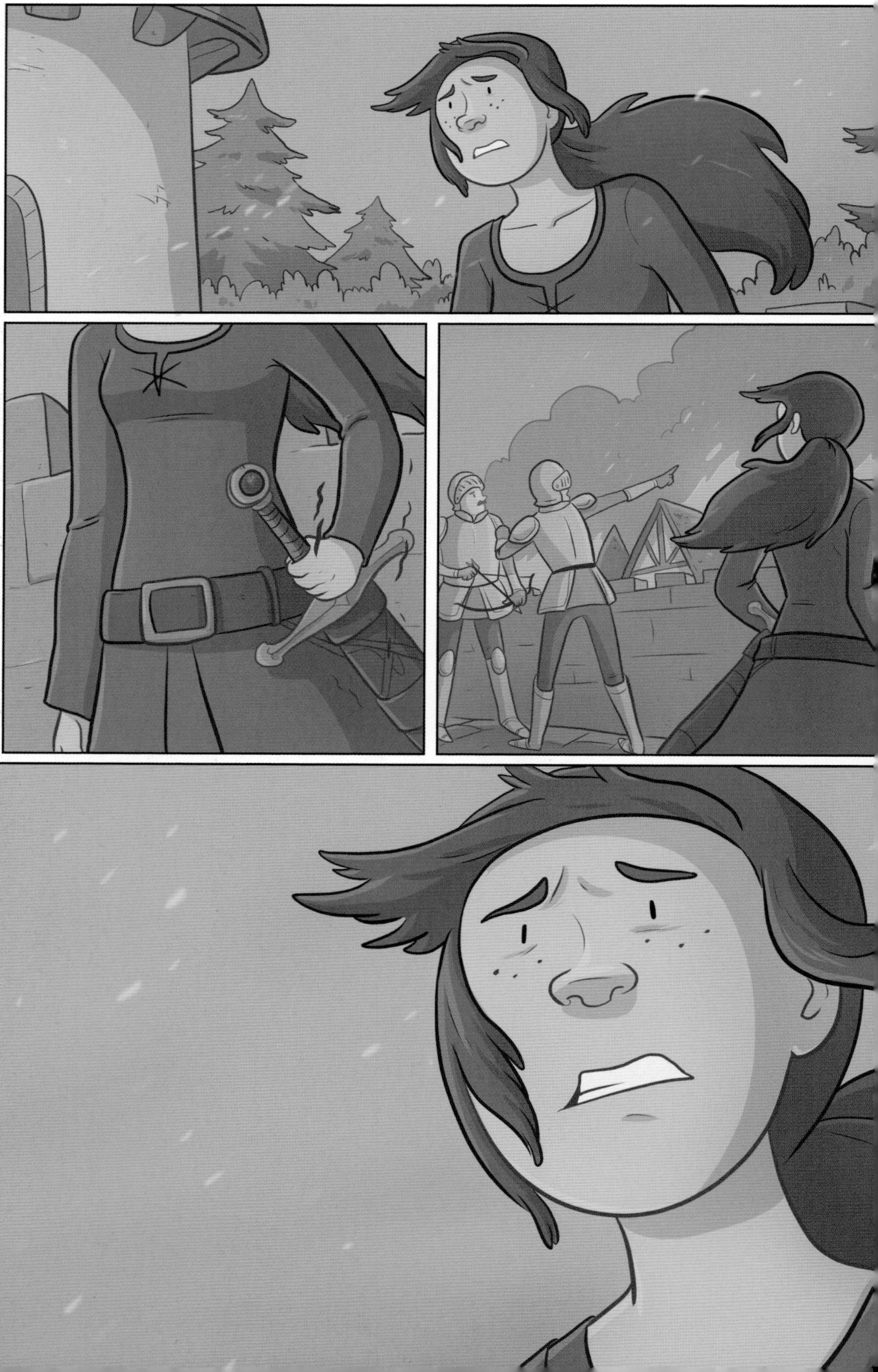

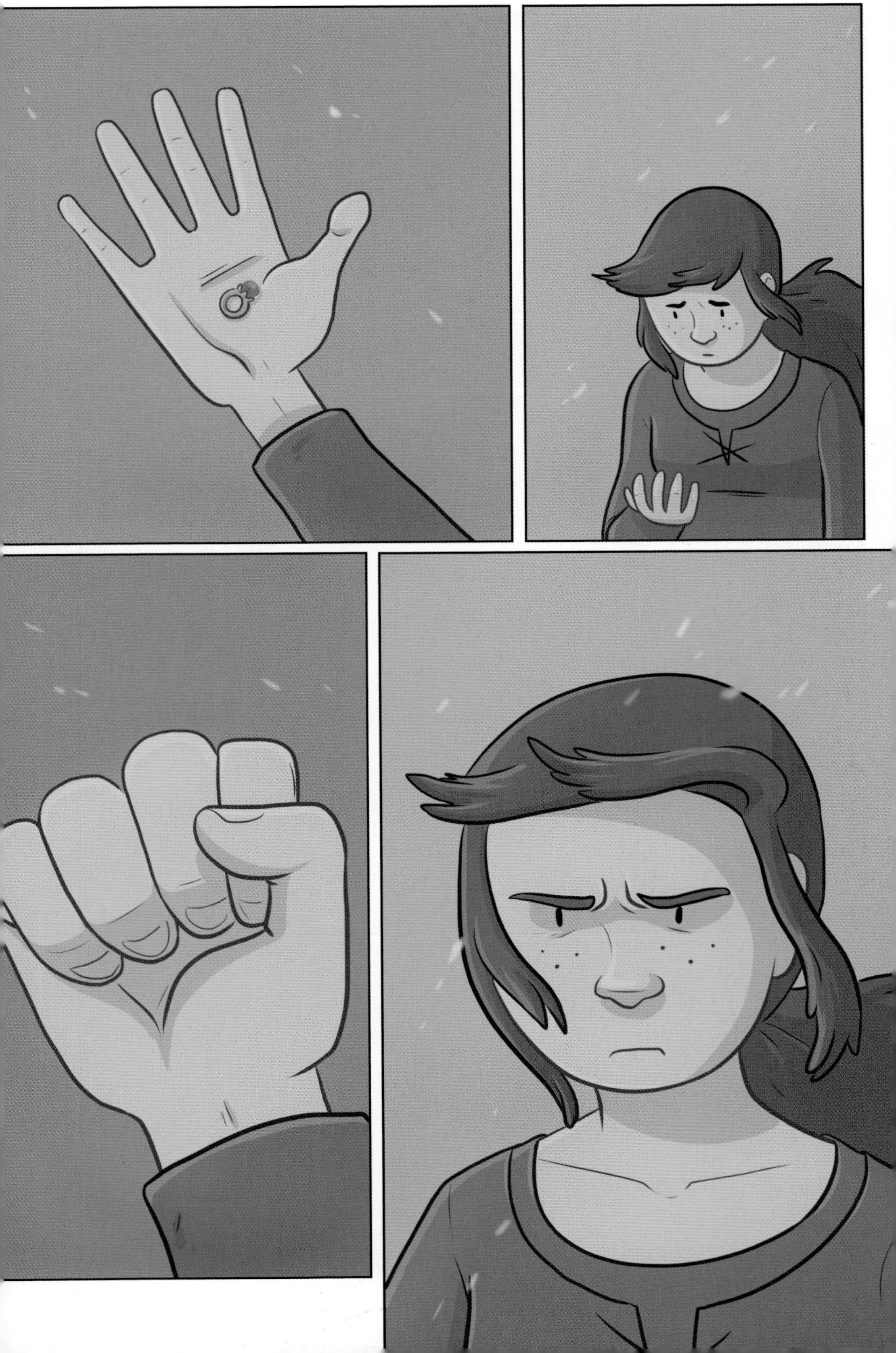

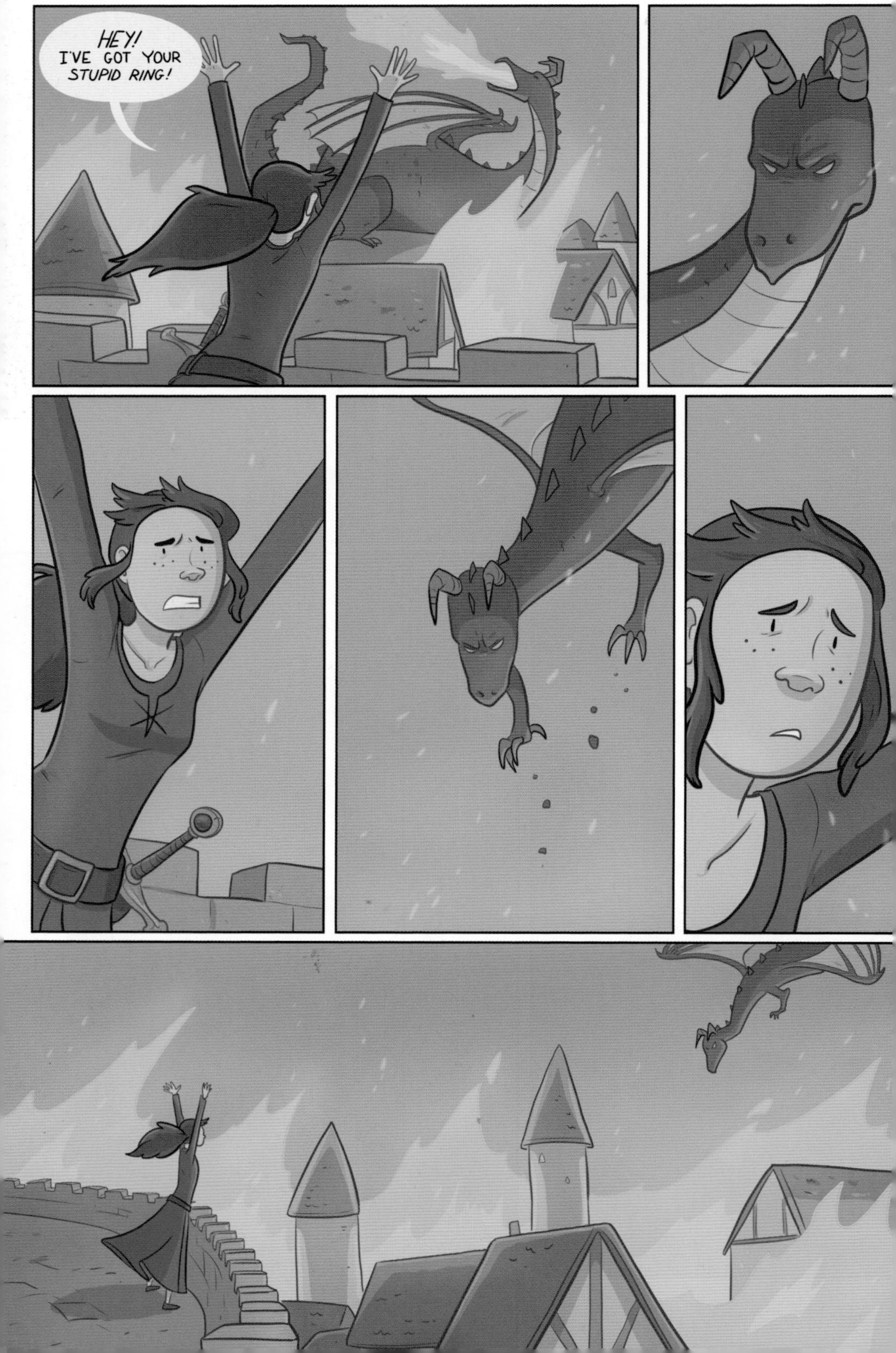
HEY! I'VE GOT YOUR STUPID RING!

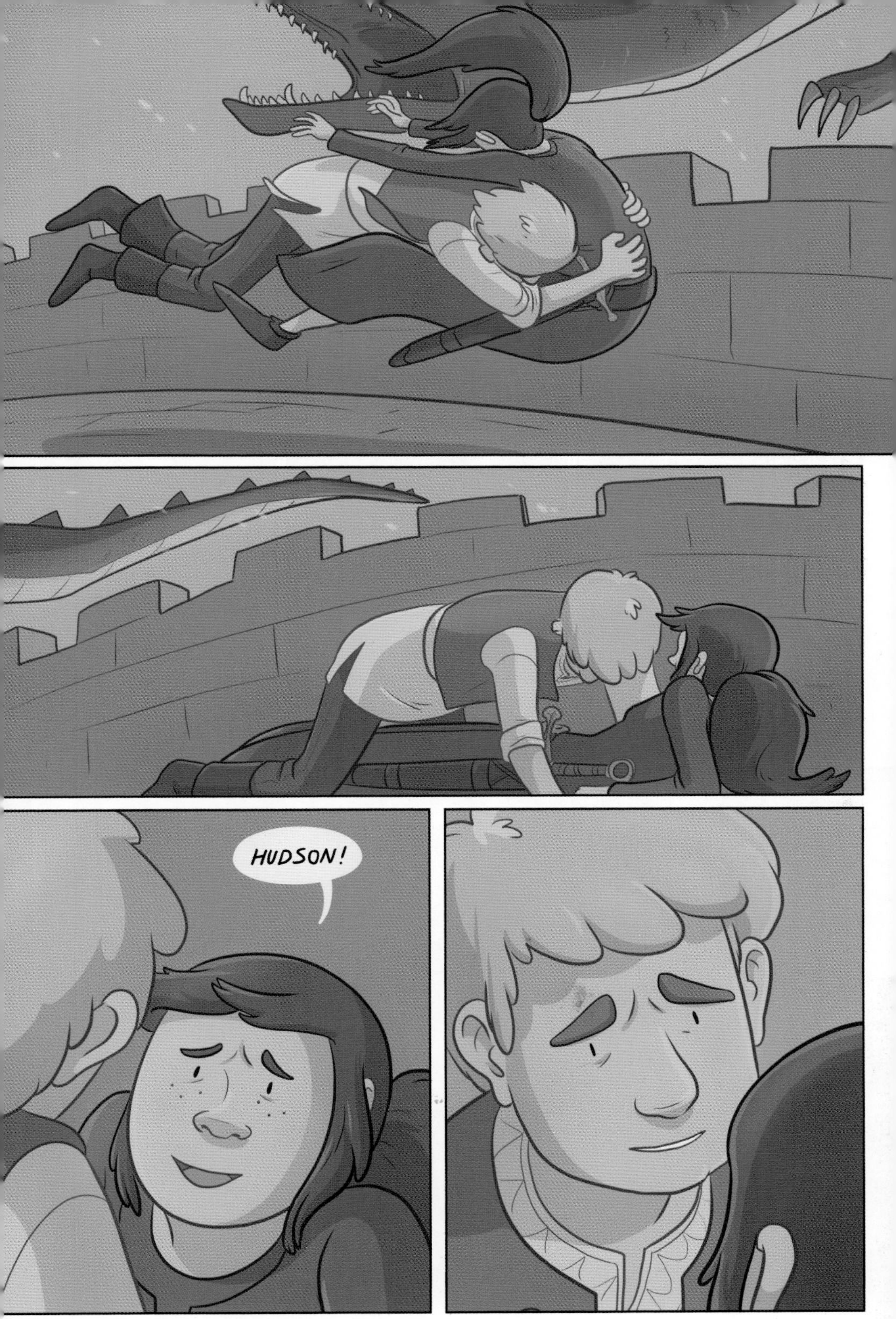
HUDSON!

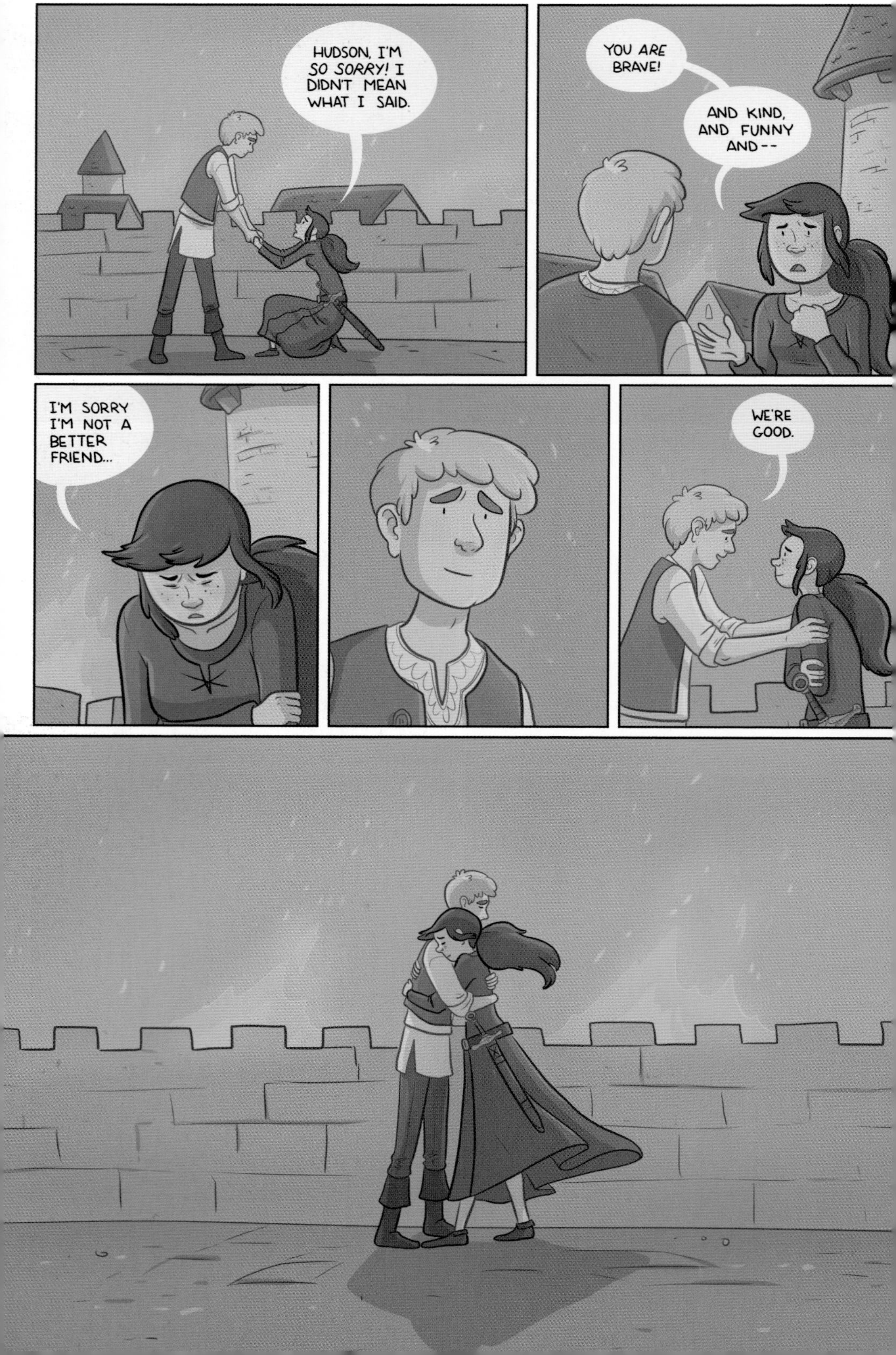
HUDSON, I'M SO SORRY! I DIDN'T MEAN WHAT I SAID.
YOU ARE BRAVE!
AND KIND, AND FUNNY AND--
I'M SORRY I'M NOT A BETTER FRIEND...
WE'RE GOOD.

READY TO TACKLE THIS BEAST?

BUT *HOW*? HUNDREDS OF *REAL WARRIORS* COULDN'T!

MAYBE HE'S STILL SLEEPY?

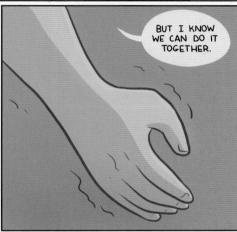

BUT I KNOW WE CAN DO IT TOGETHER.

TOGETHER.

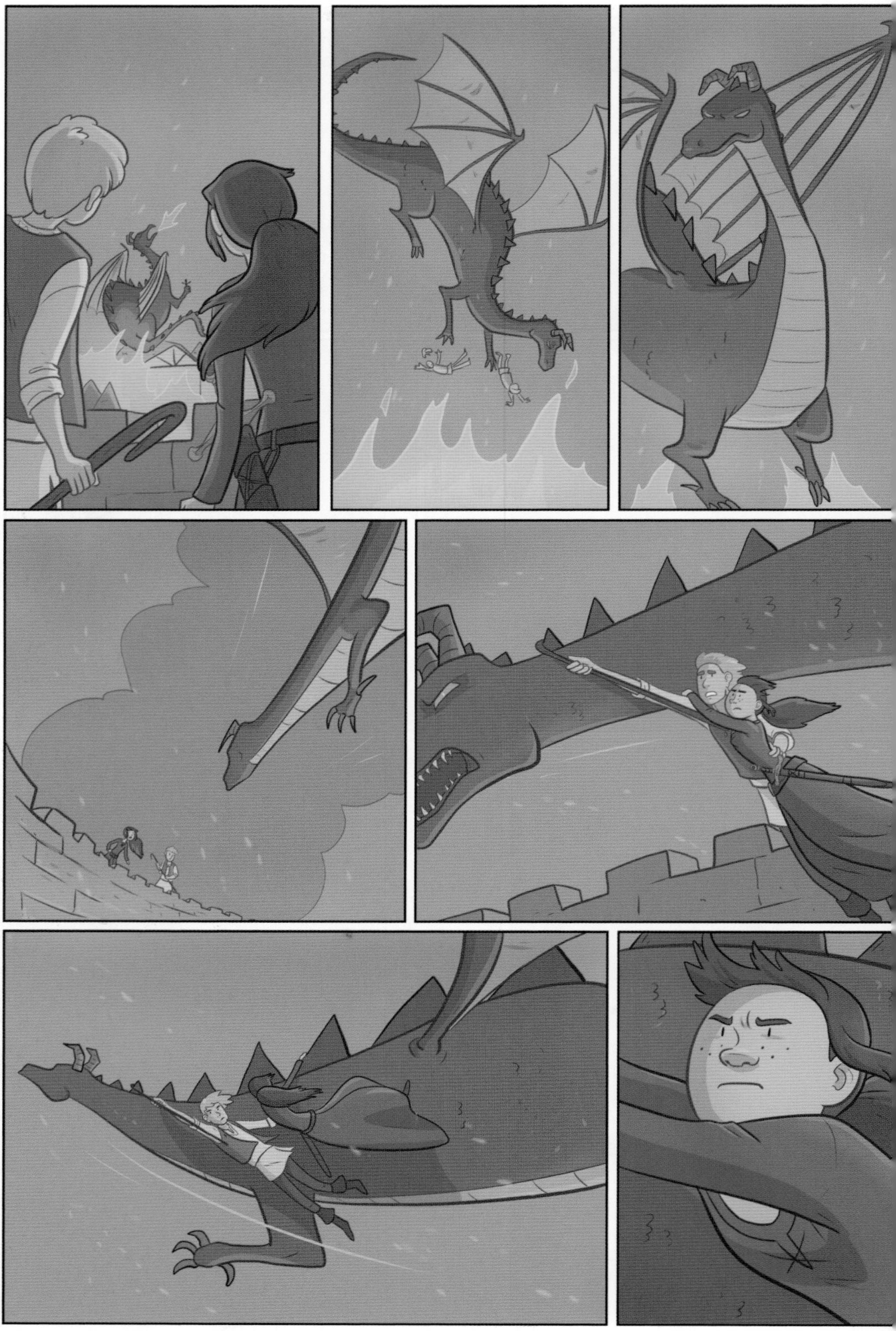

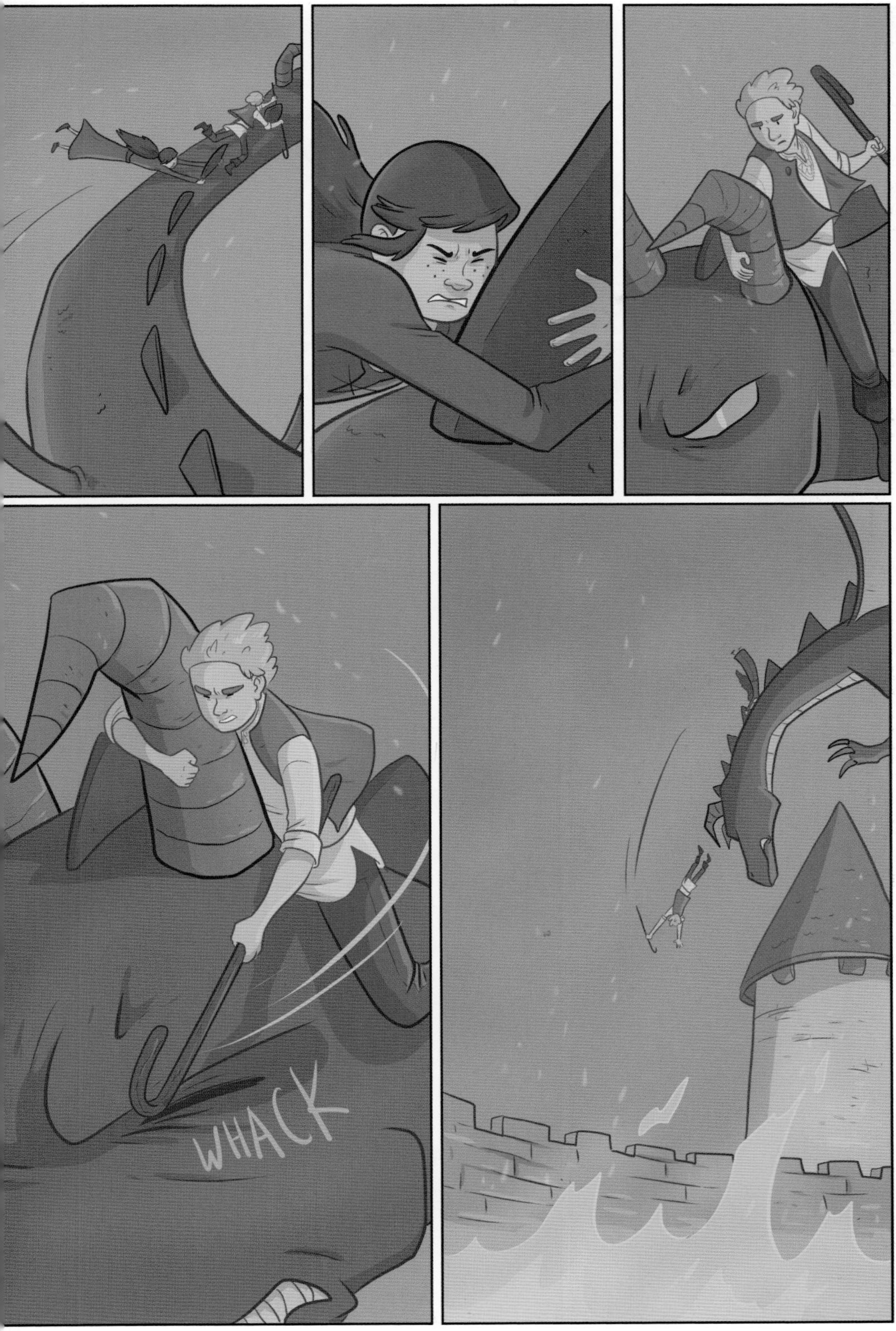
WHACK

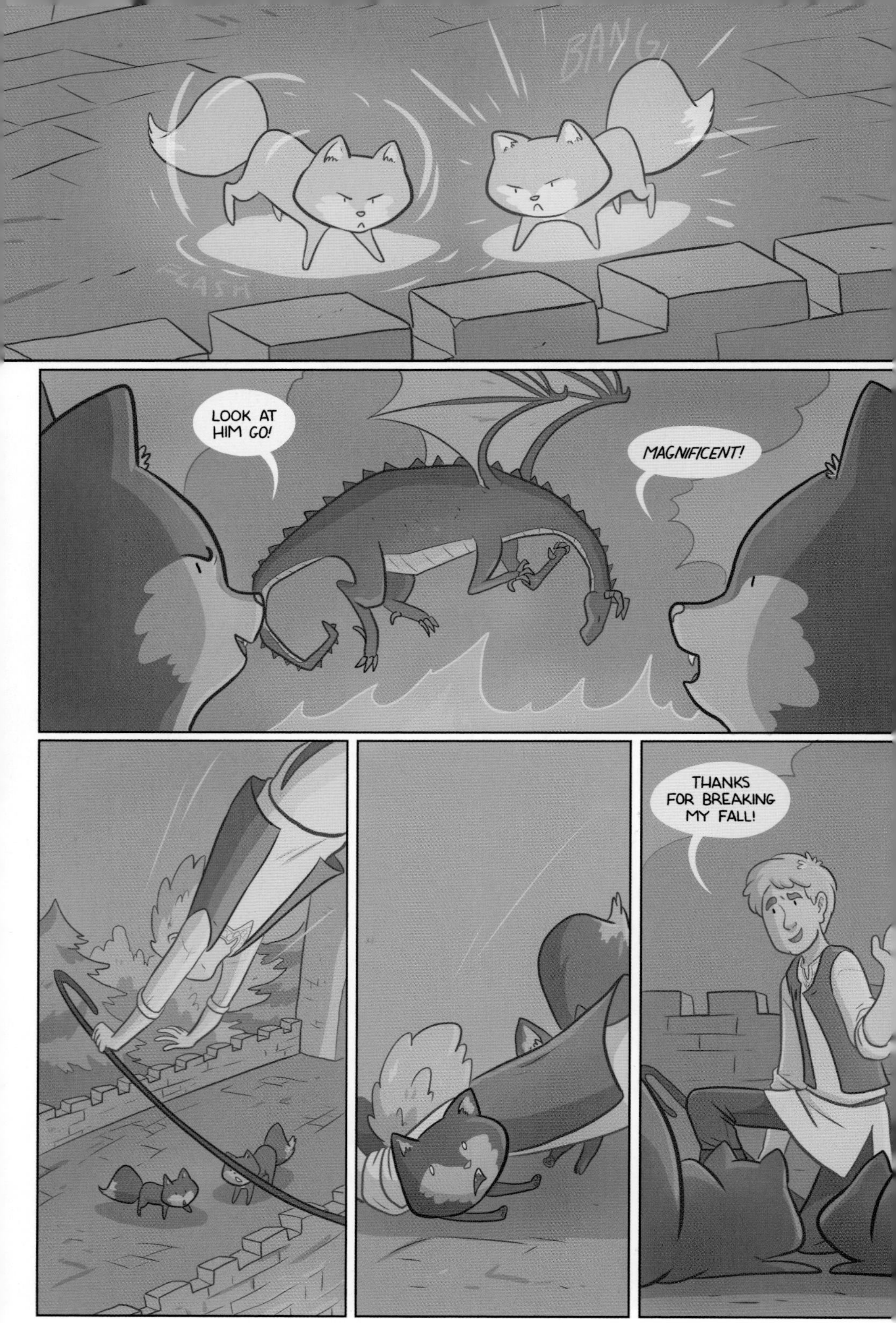
BANG
FLASH
LOOK AT HIM GO!
MAGNIFICENT!
THANKS FOR BREAKING MY FALL!

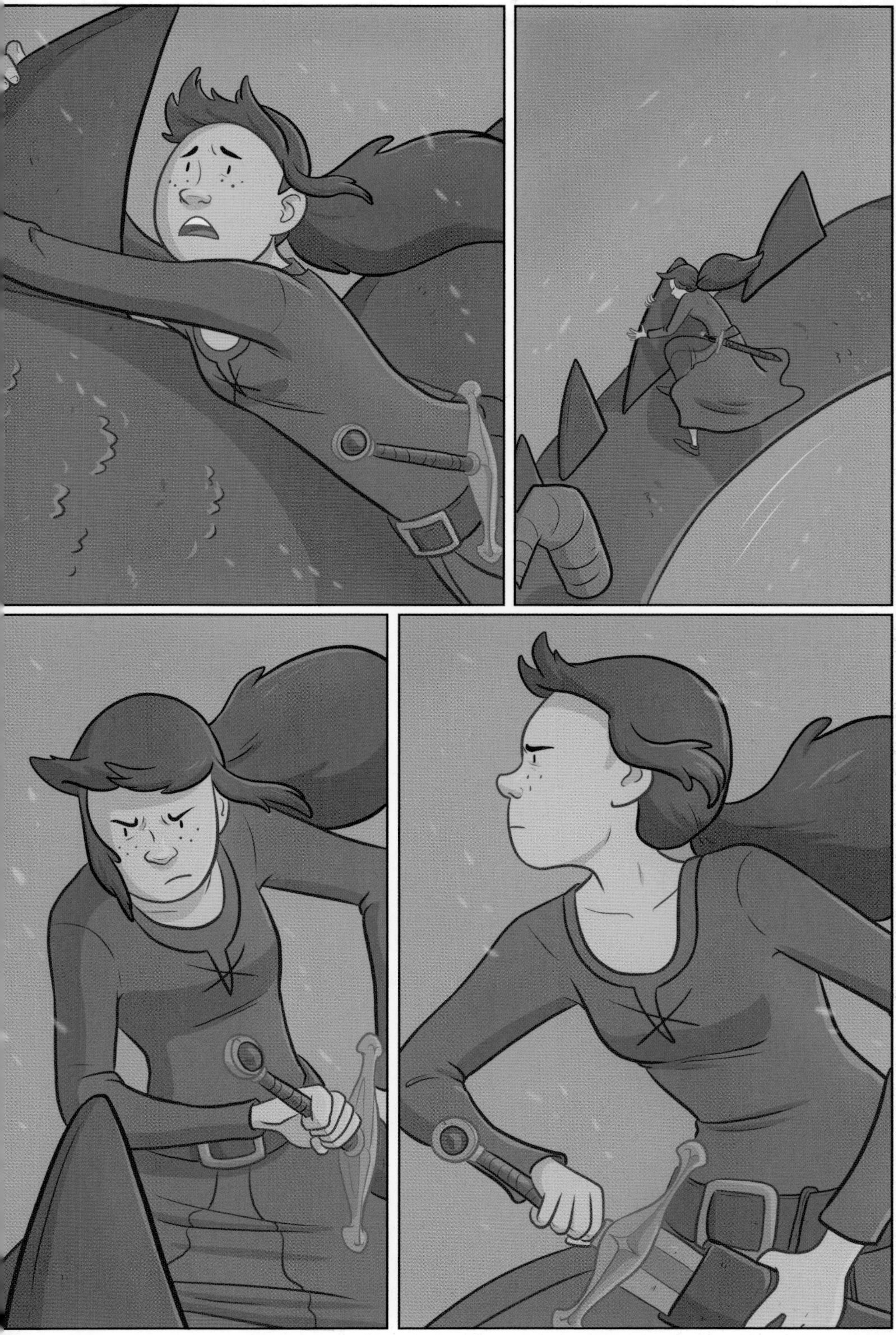

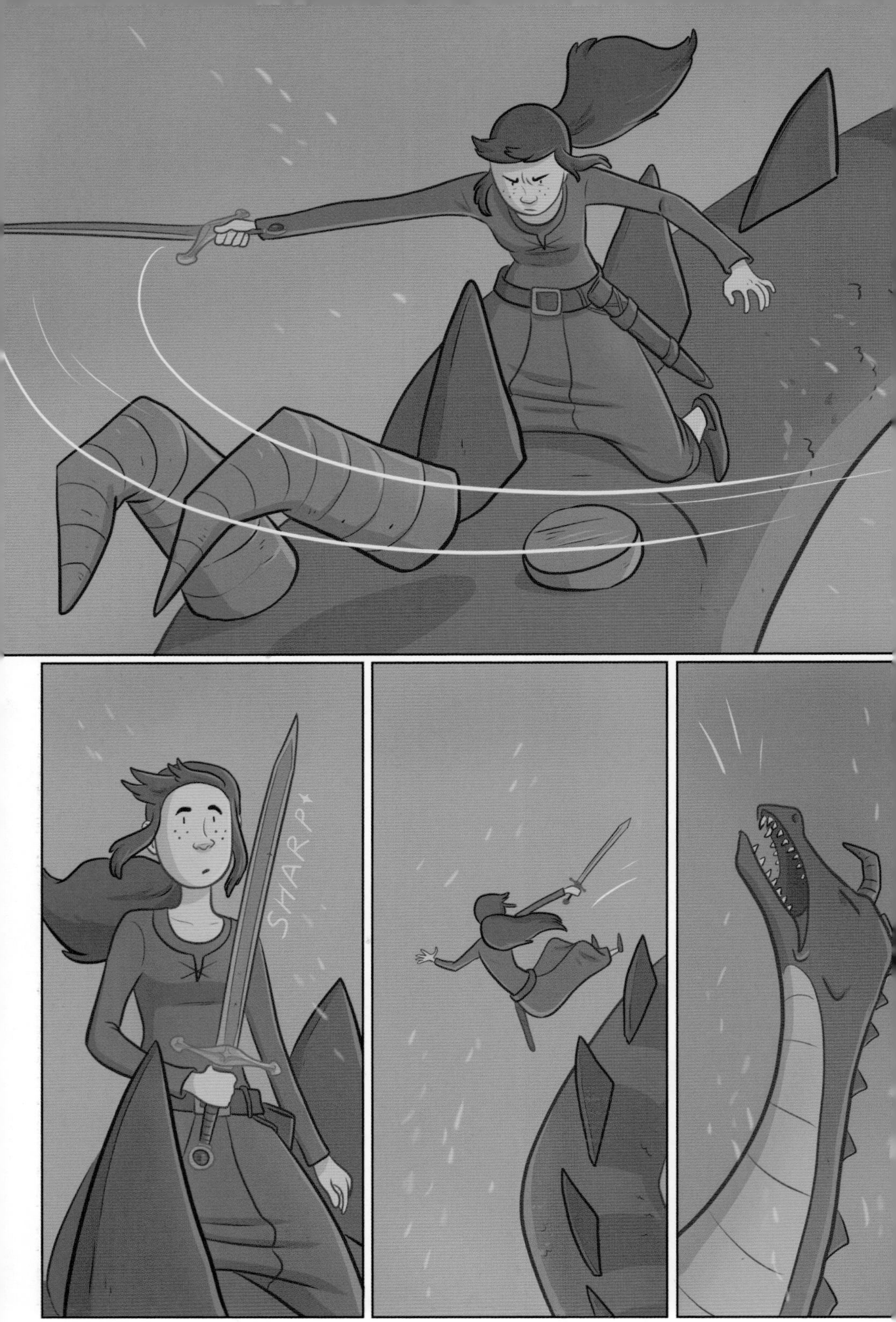
SHARP

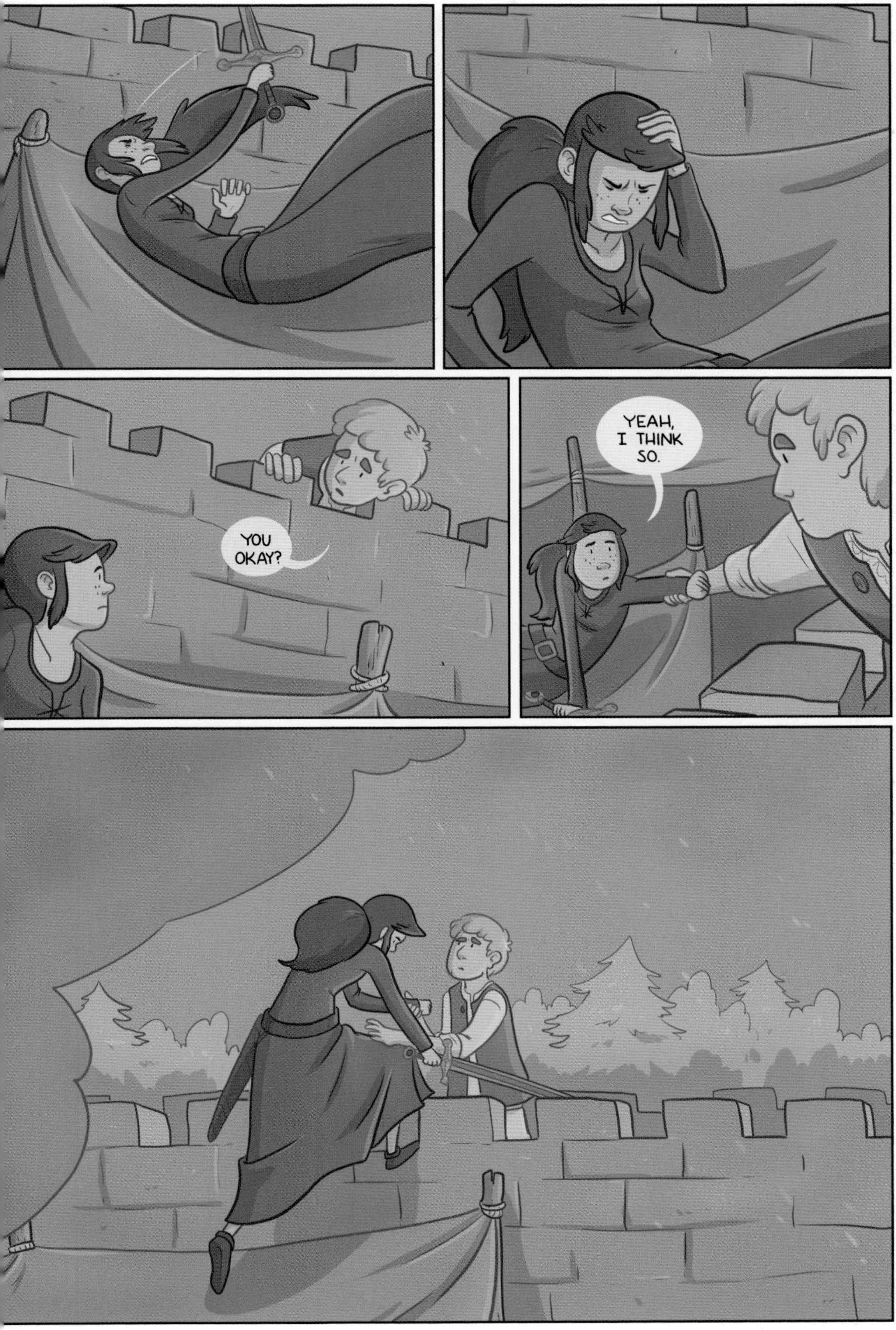
YOU OKAY?
YEAH, I THINK SO.

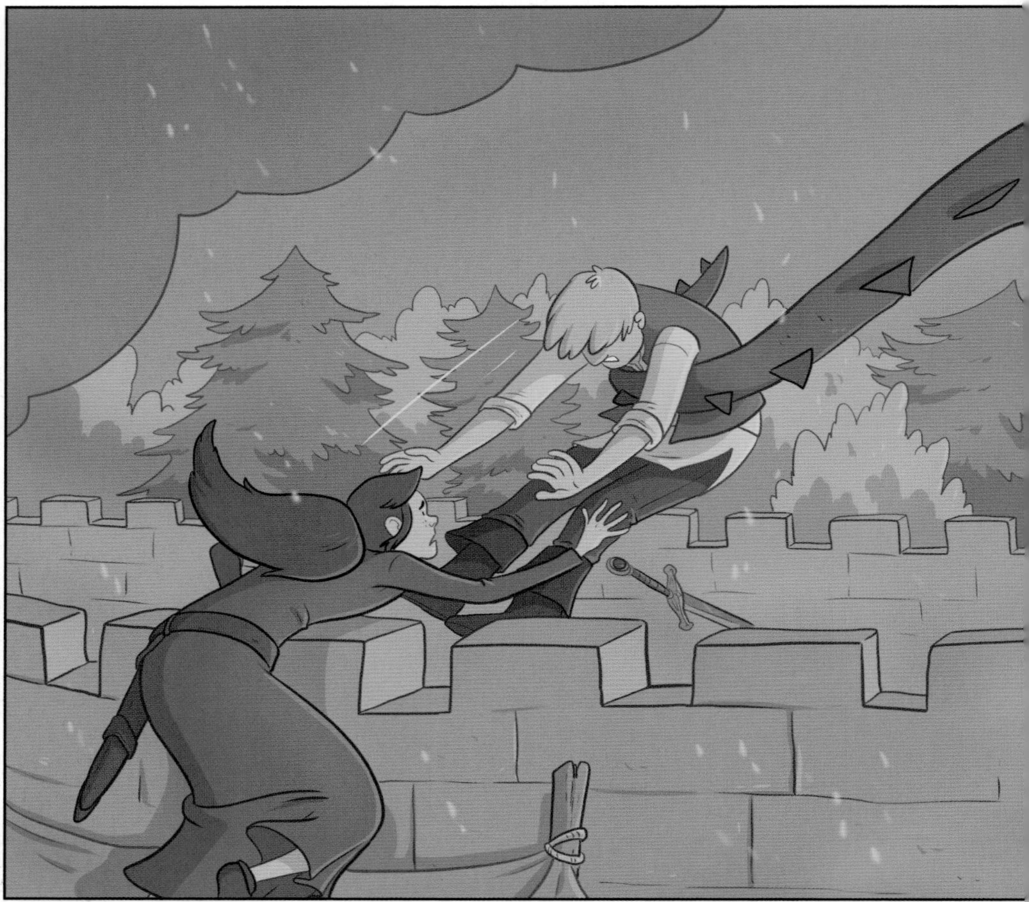

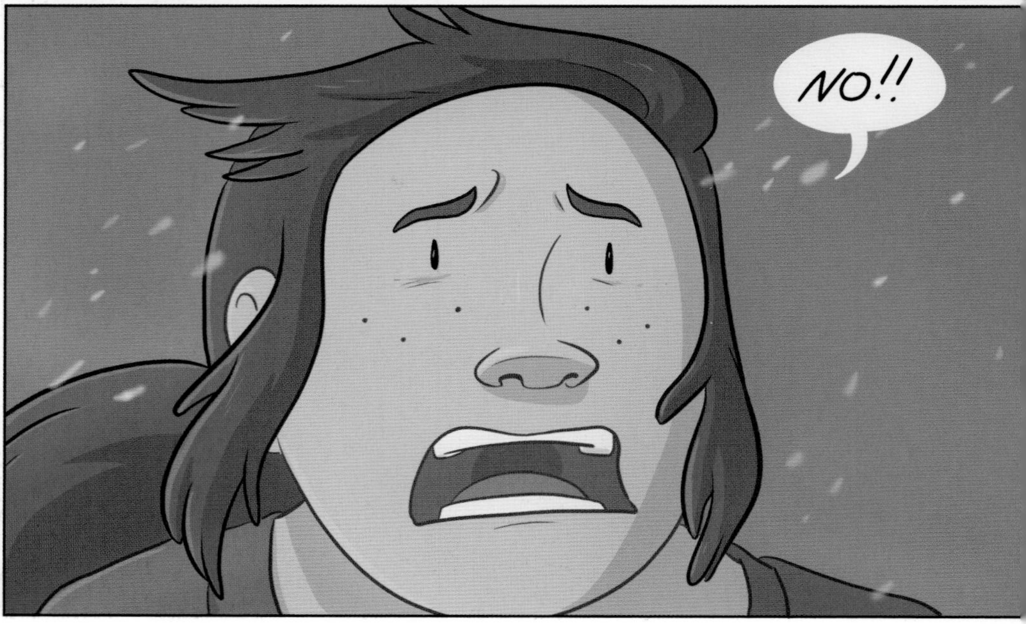
NO!!

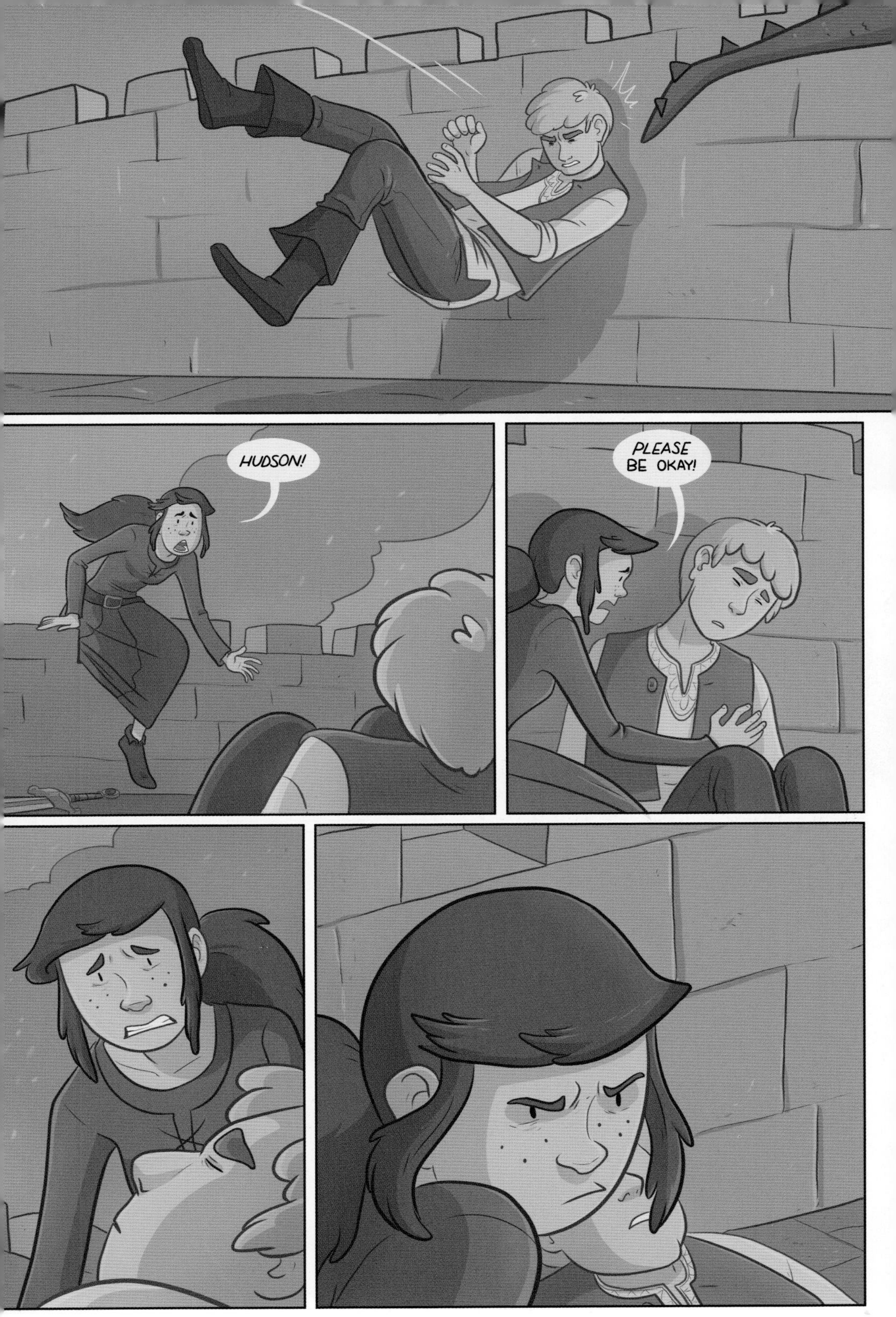
HUDSON!
PLEASE BE OKAY!

HEY MORDRID!

I'M NOT FINISHED WITH YOU!

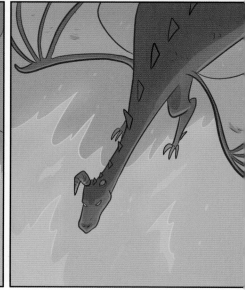

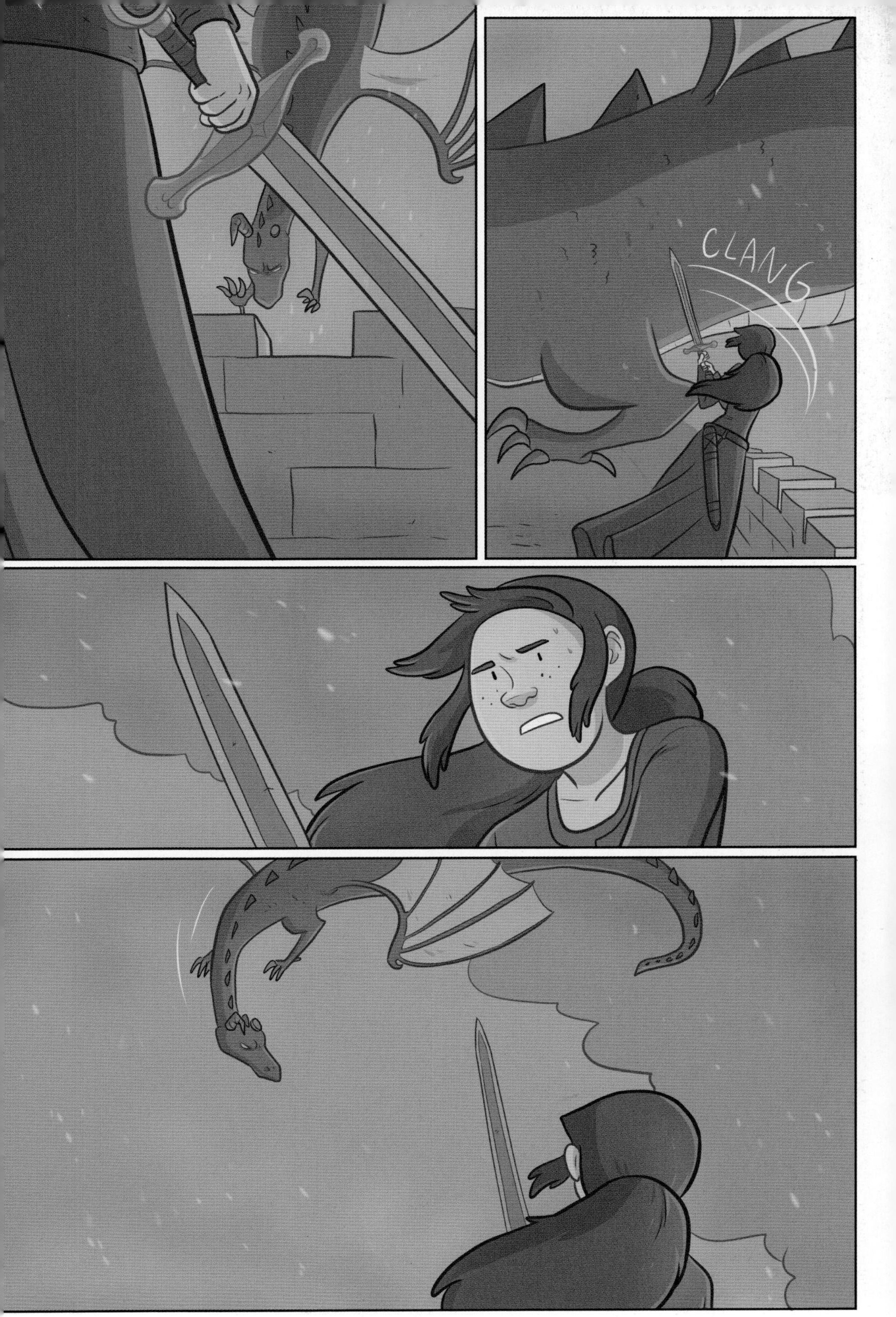
CLANG

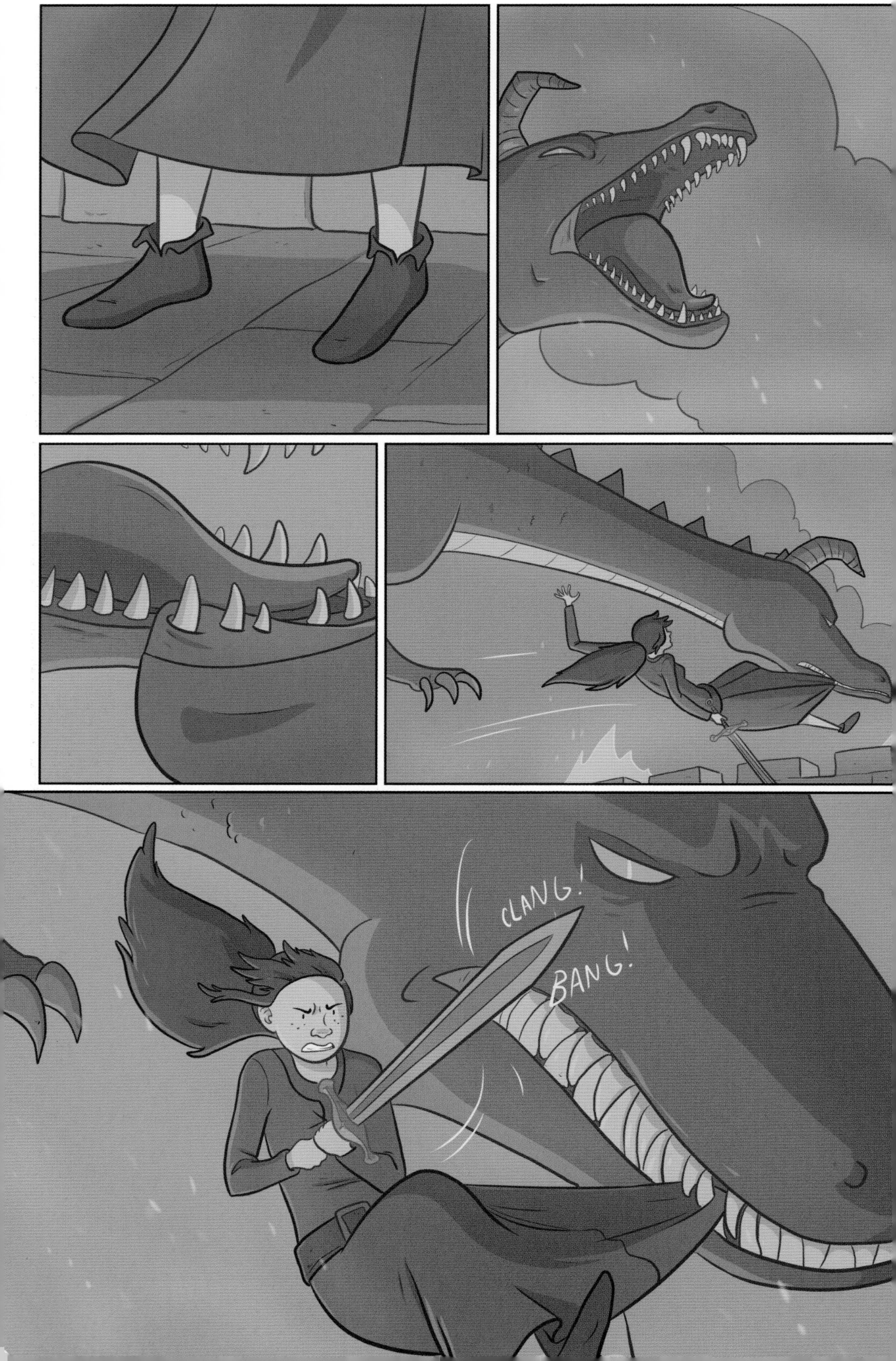
CLANG!
BANG!

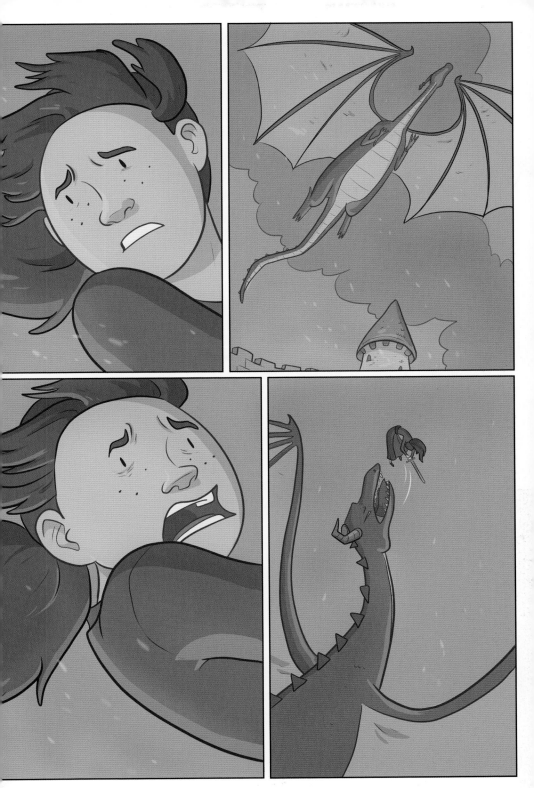

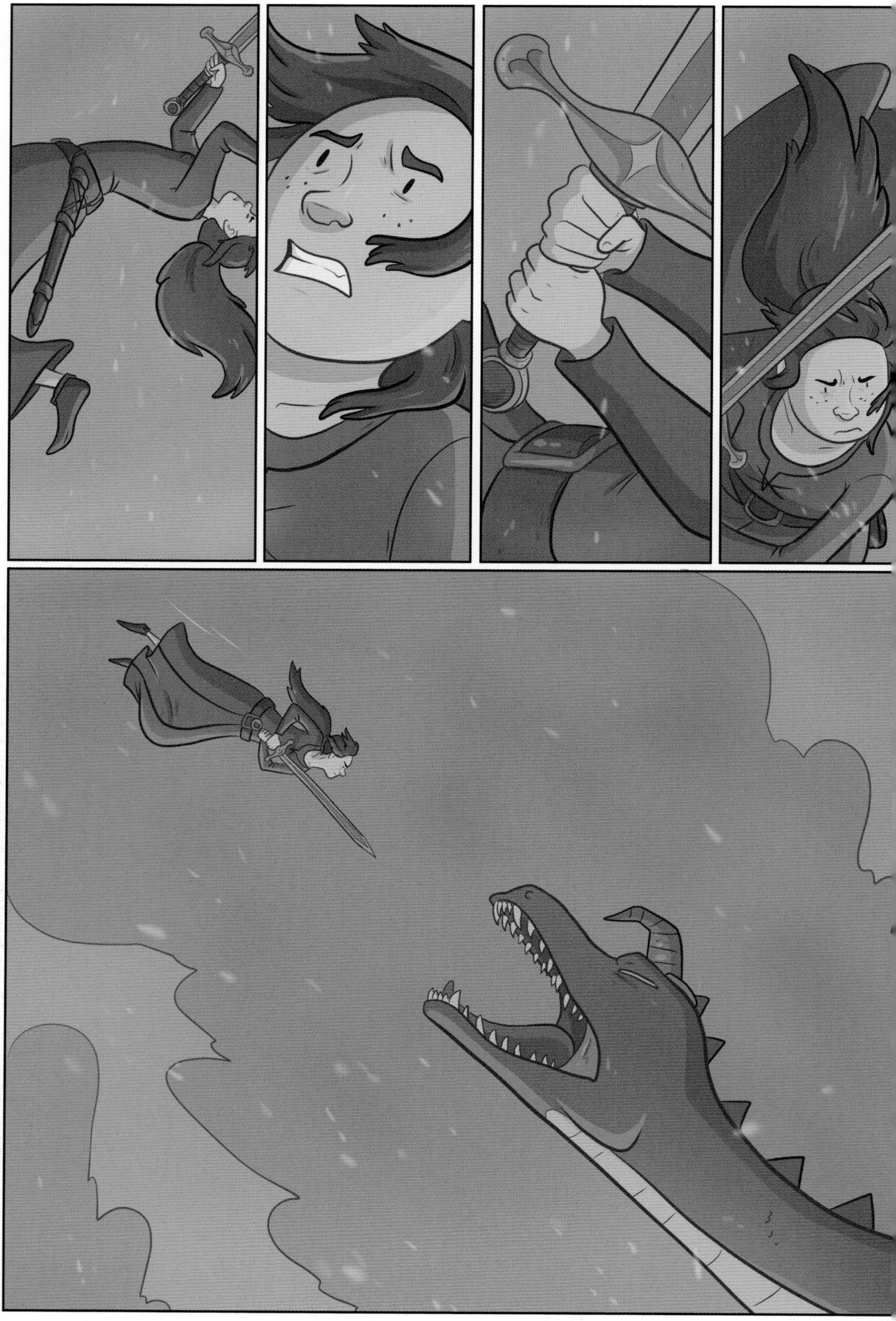

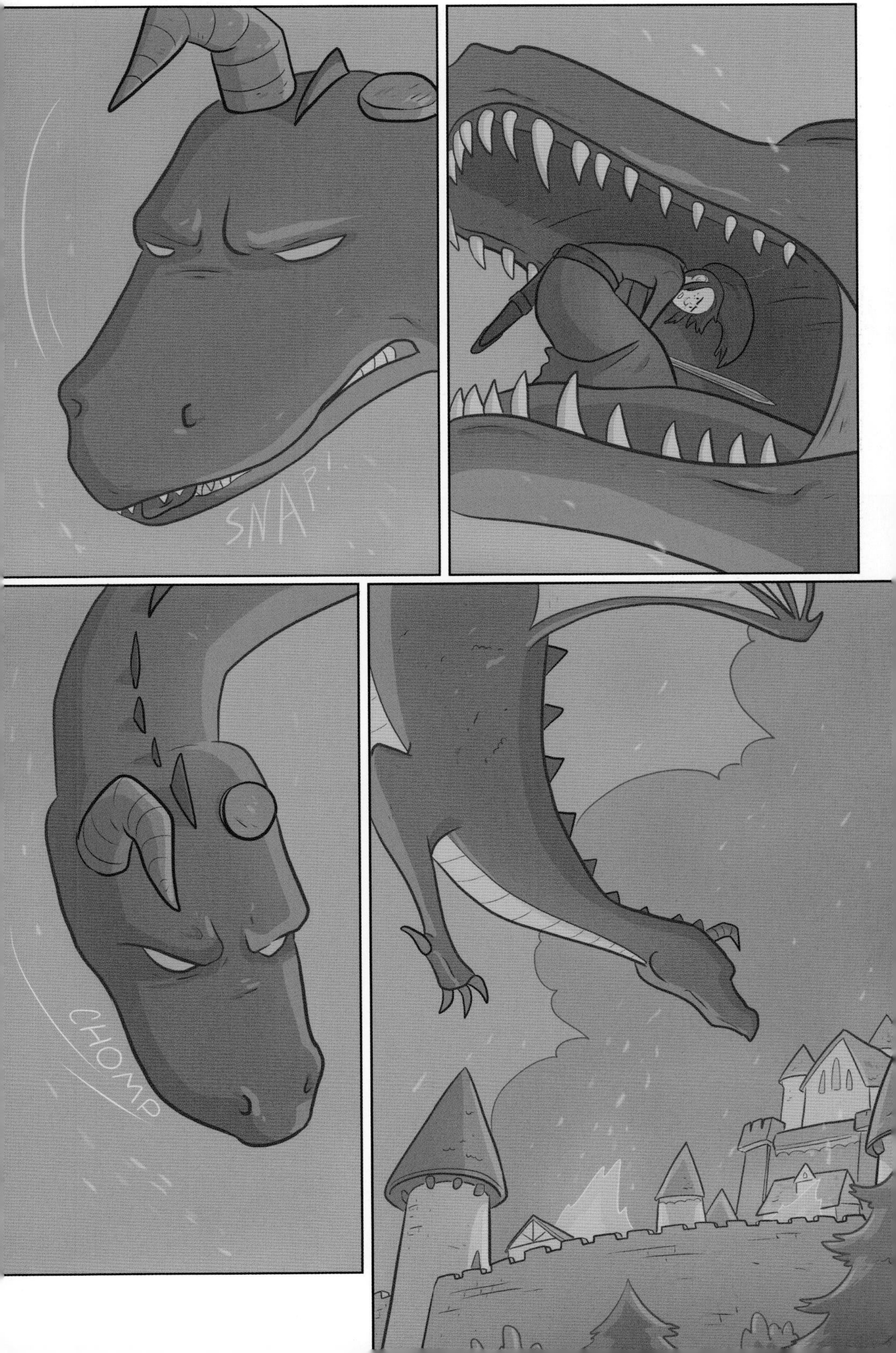
SNAP!
CHOMP

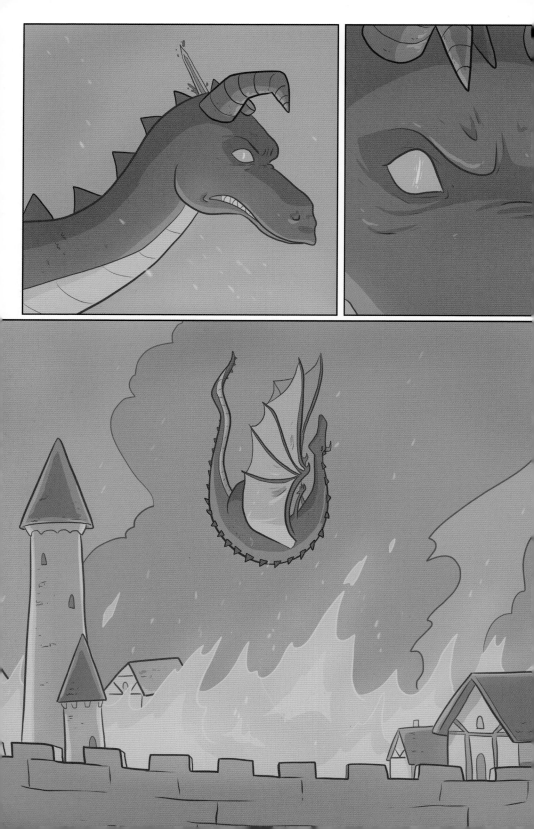

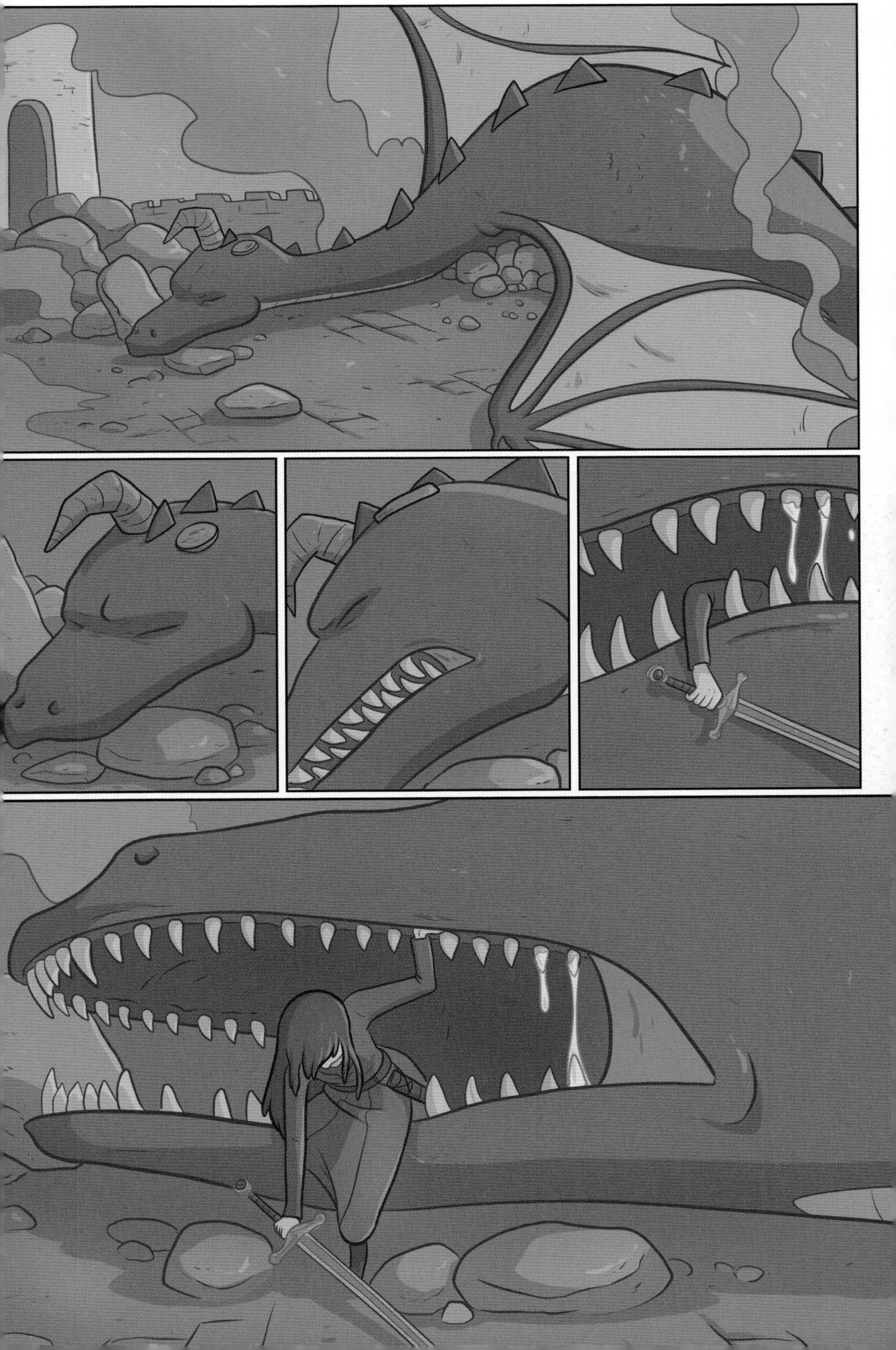

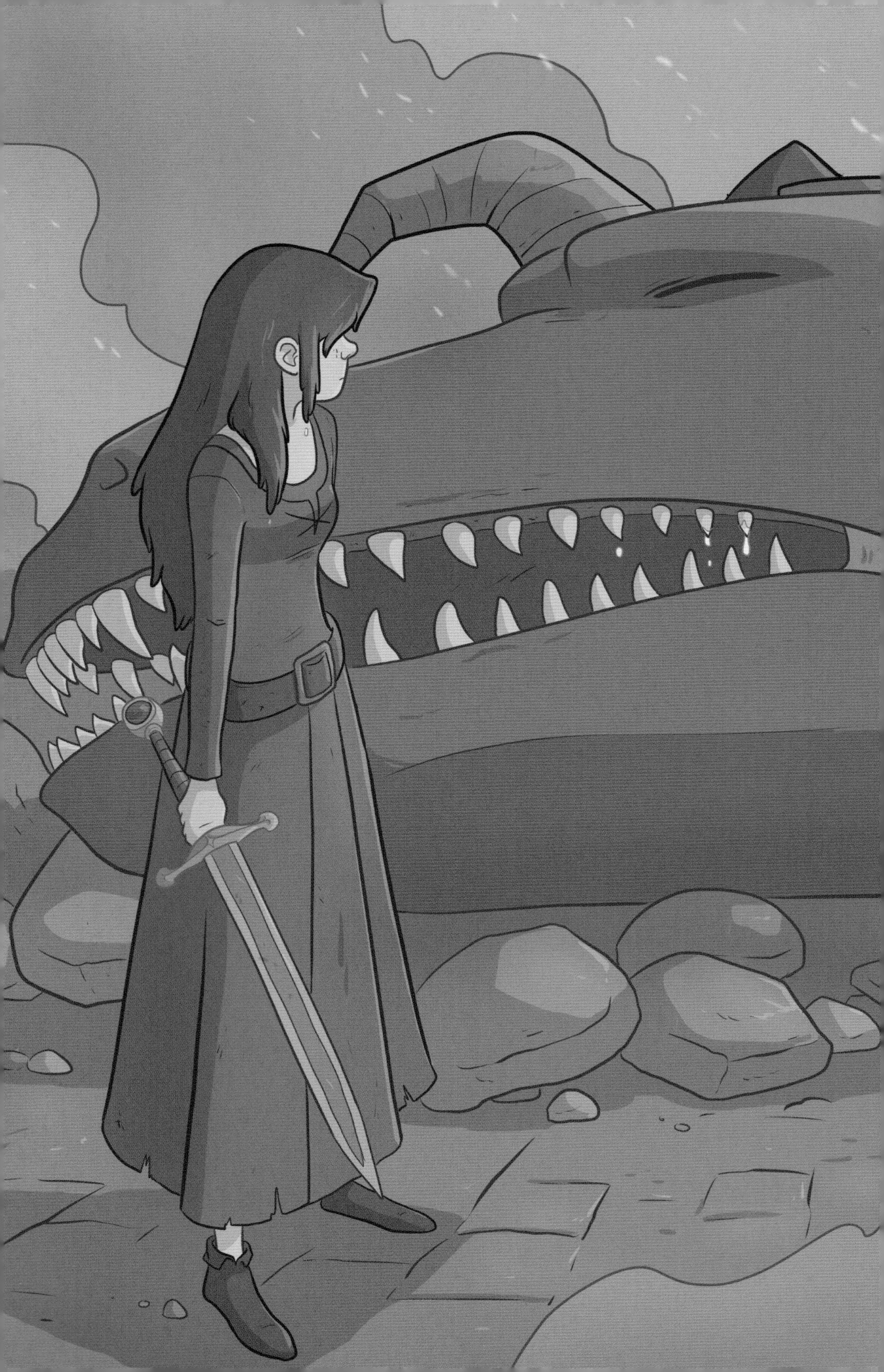

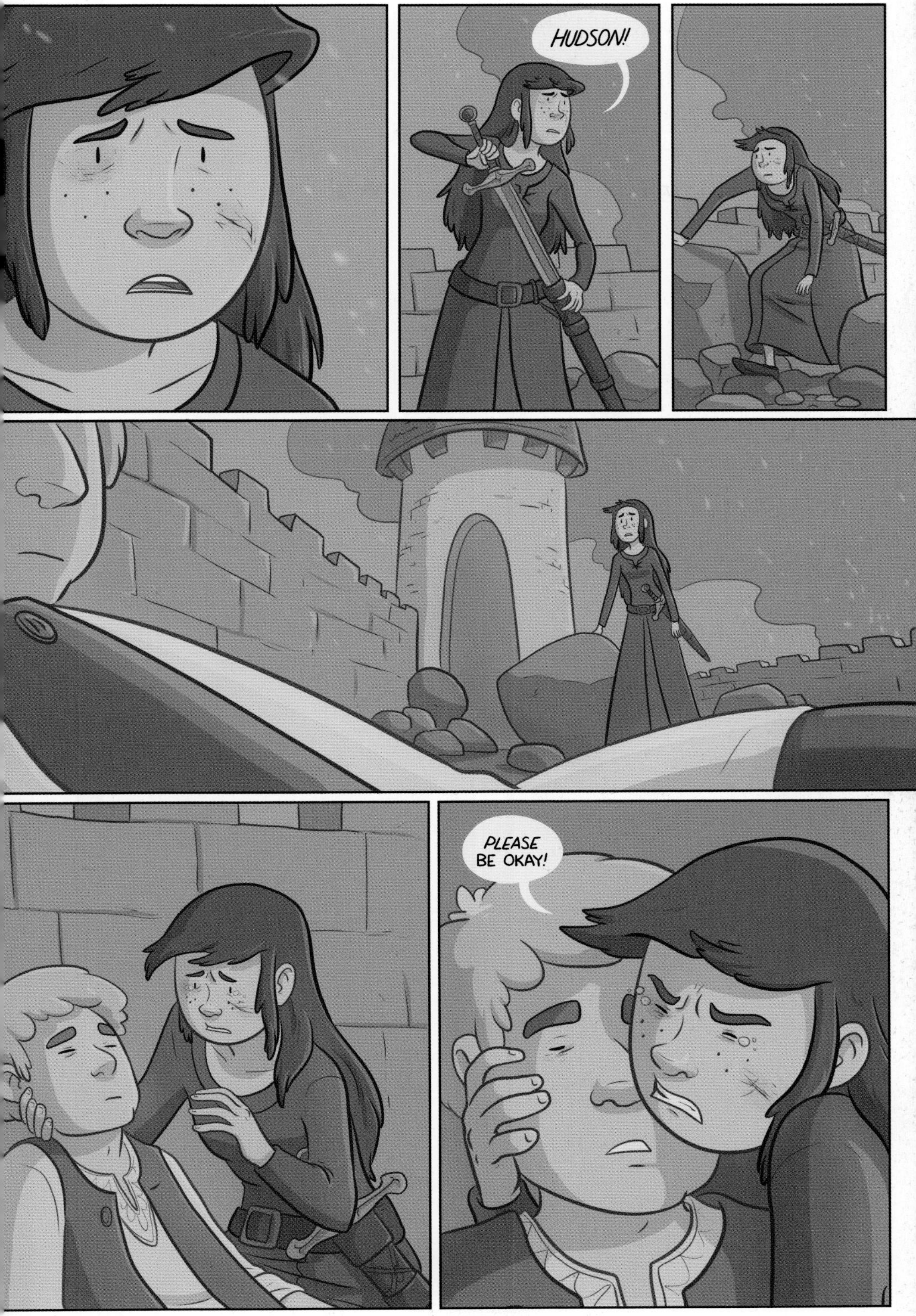
HUDSON!
PLEASE BE OKAY!

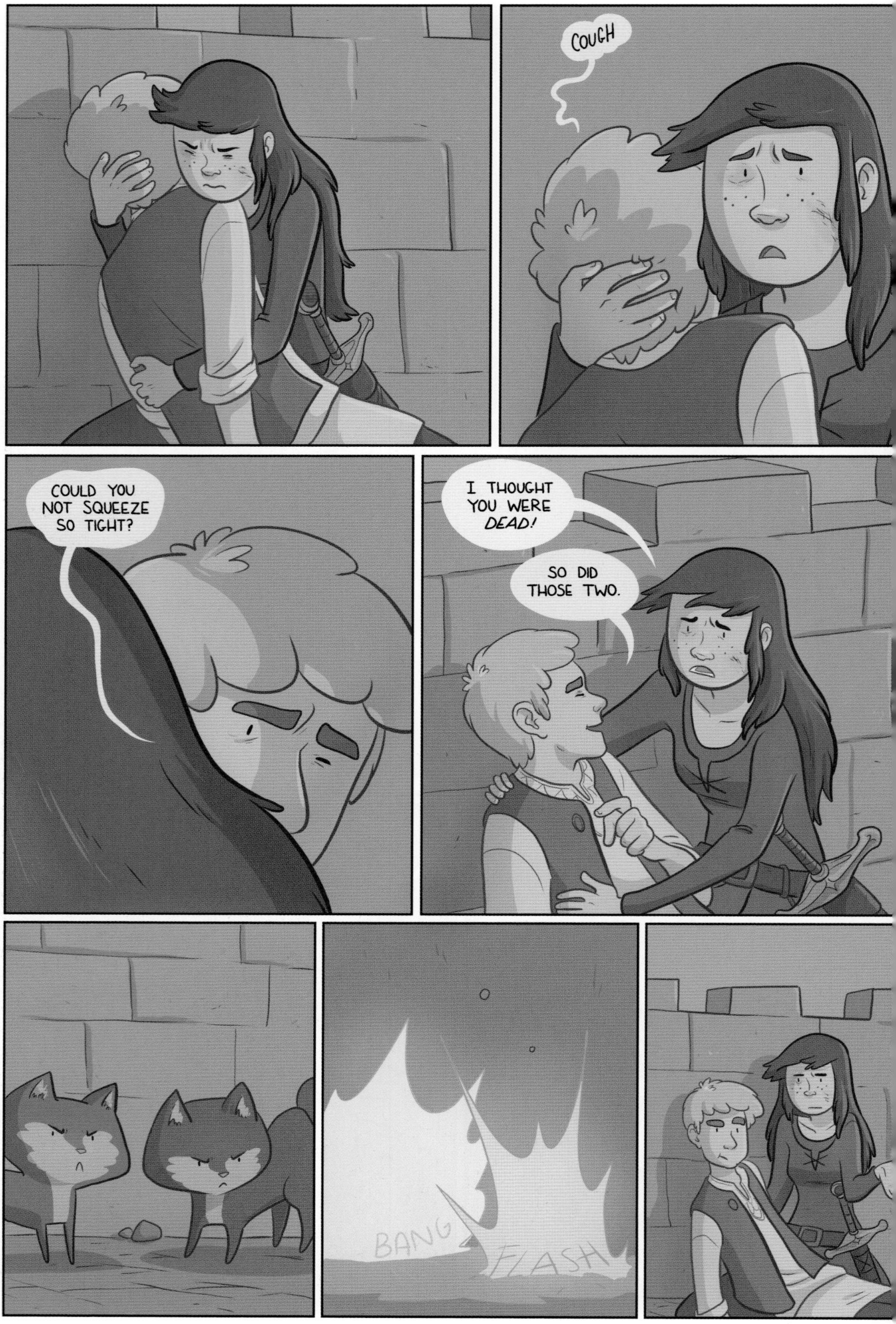
COUGH
COULD YOU NOT SQUEEZE SO TIGHT?
I THOUGHT YOU WERE *DEAD!*
SO DID THOSE TWO.
BANG
FLASH

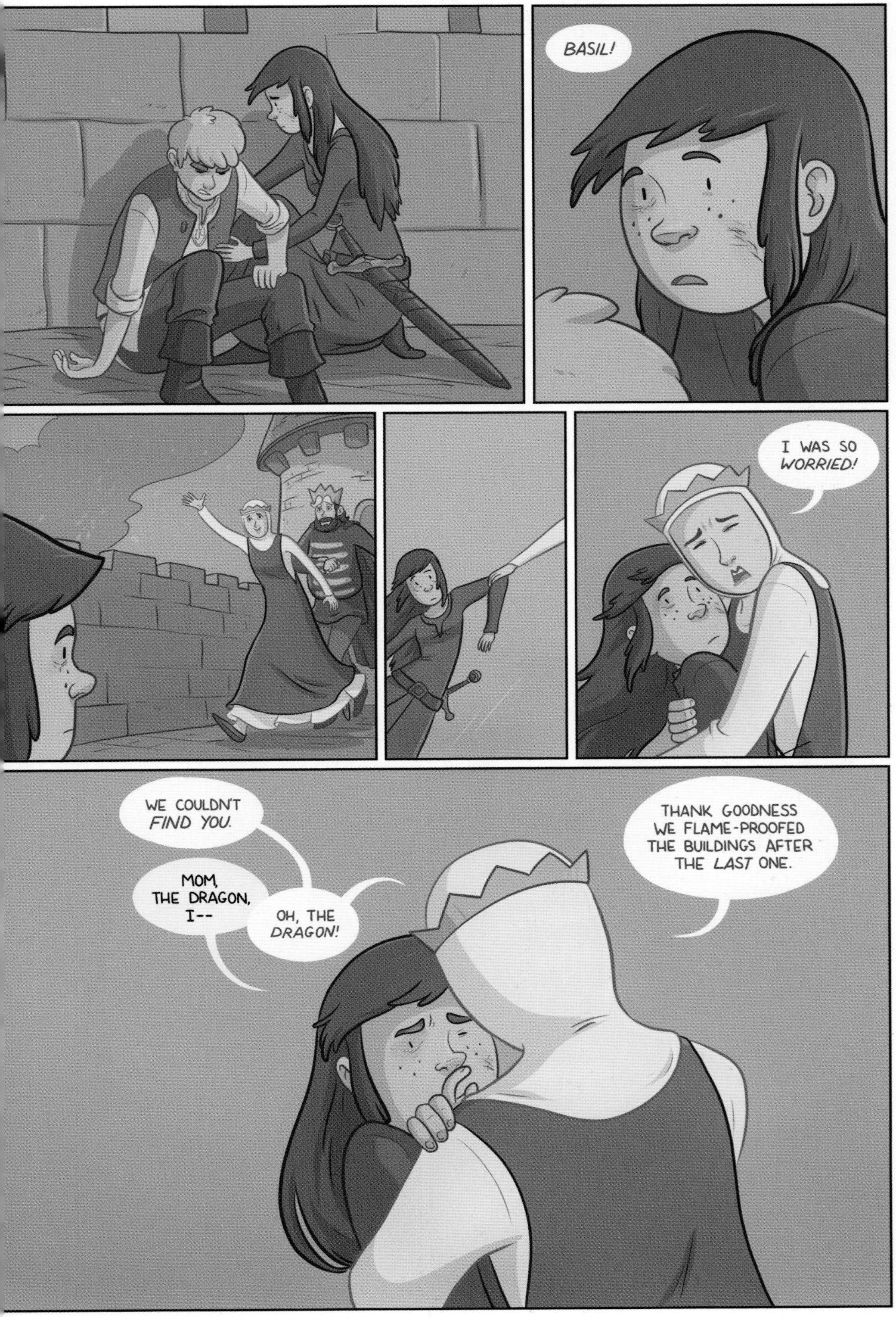
BASIL!
I WAS SO *WORRIED!*
WE COULDN'T *FIND YOU.*
MOM, THE DRAGON, I--
OH, THE *DRAGON!*
THANK GOODNESS WE FLAME-PROOFED THE BUILDINGS AFTER THE *LAST* ONE.

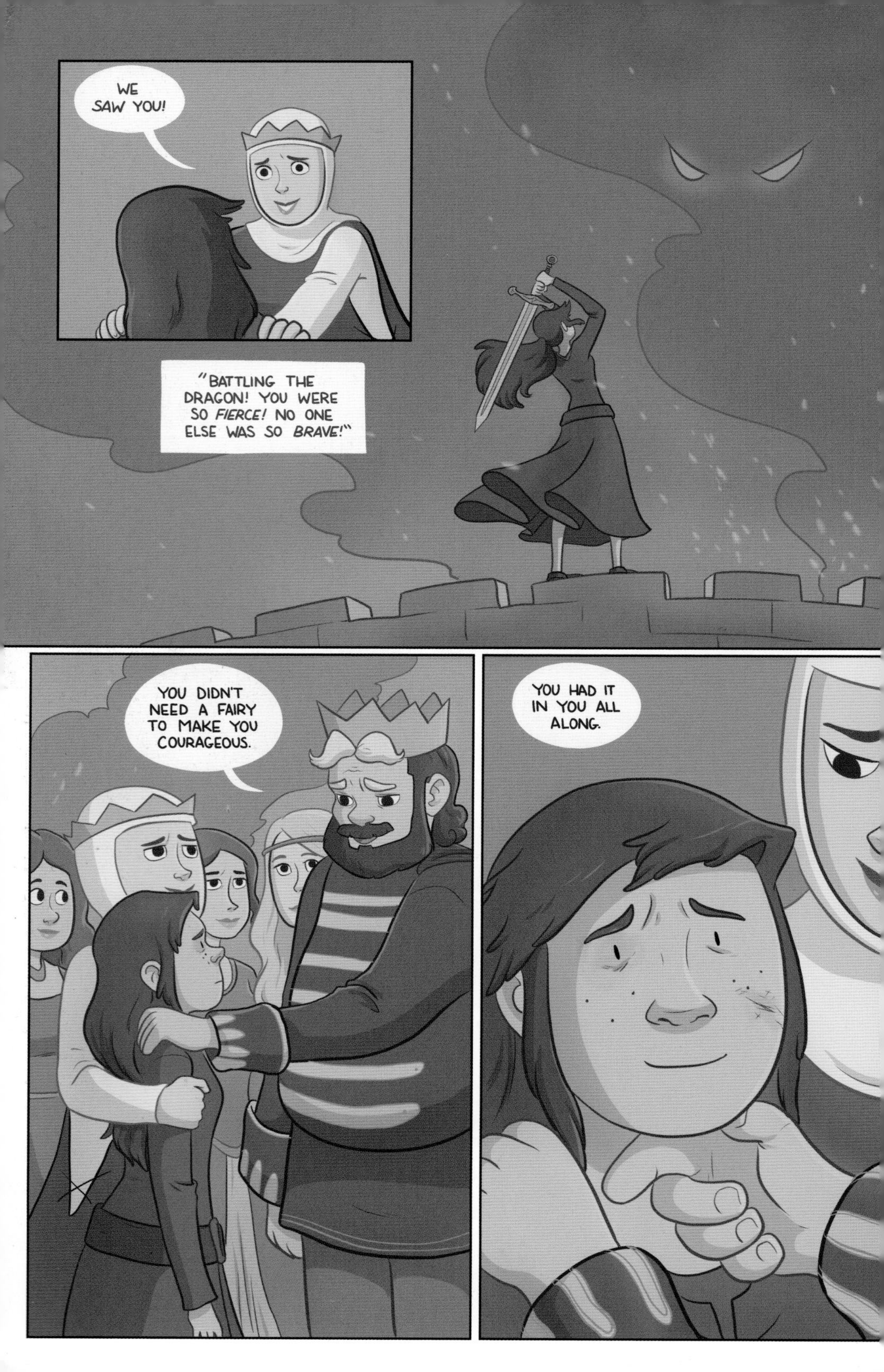
WE SAW YOU!
"BATTLING THE DRAGON! YOU WERE SO *FIERCE!* NO ONE ELSE WAS SO *BRAVE!*"
YOU DIDN'T NEED A FAIRY TO MAKE YOU COURAGEOUS.
YOU HAD IT IN YOU ALL ALONG.

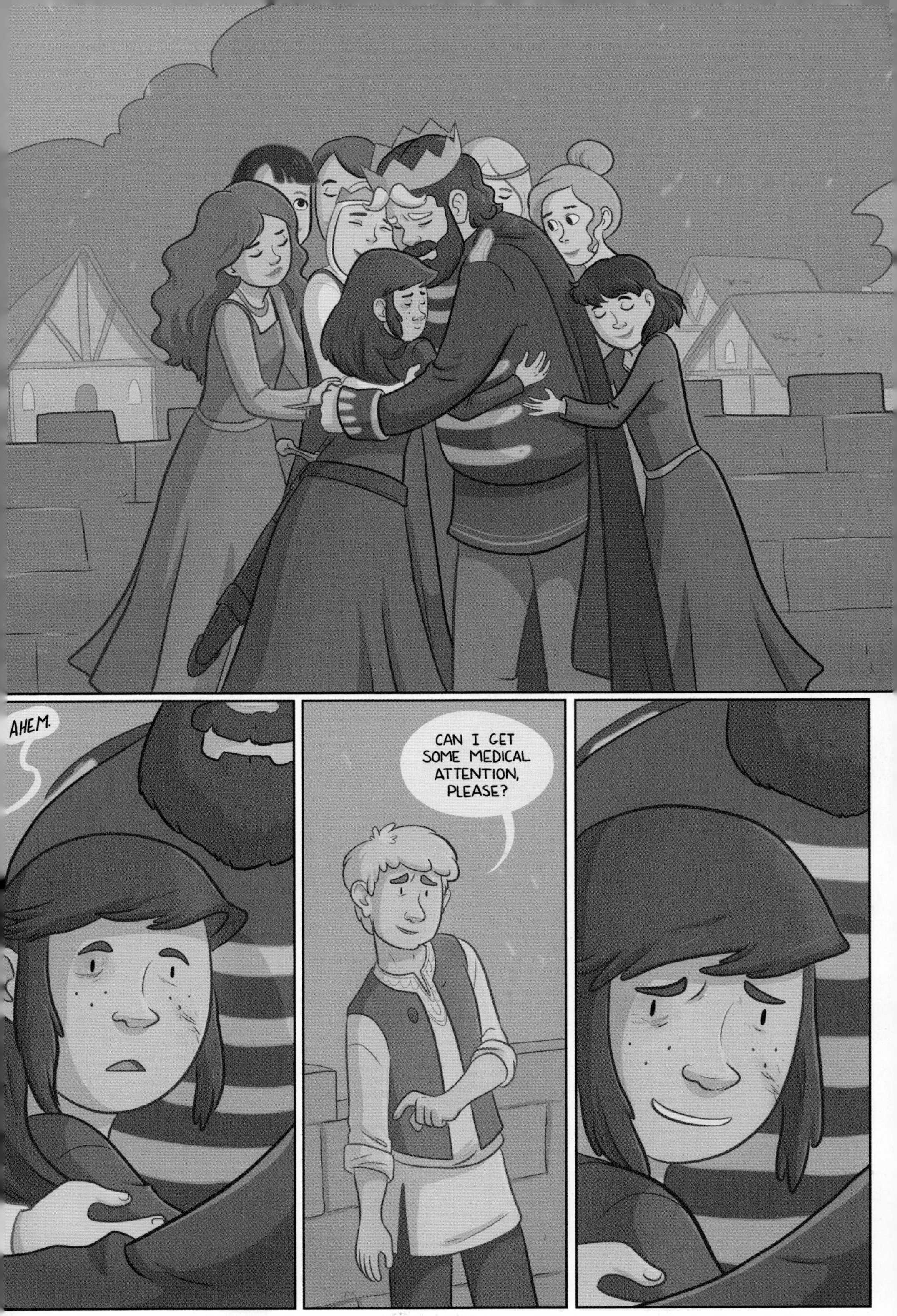
AHEM.
CAN I GET SOME MEDICAL ATTENTION, PLEASE?

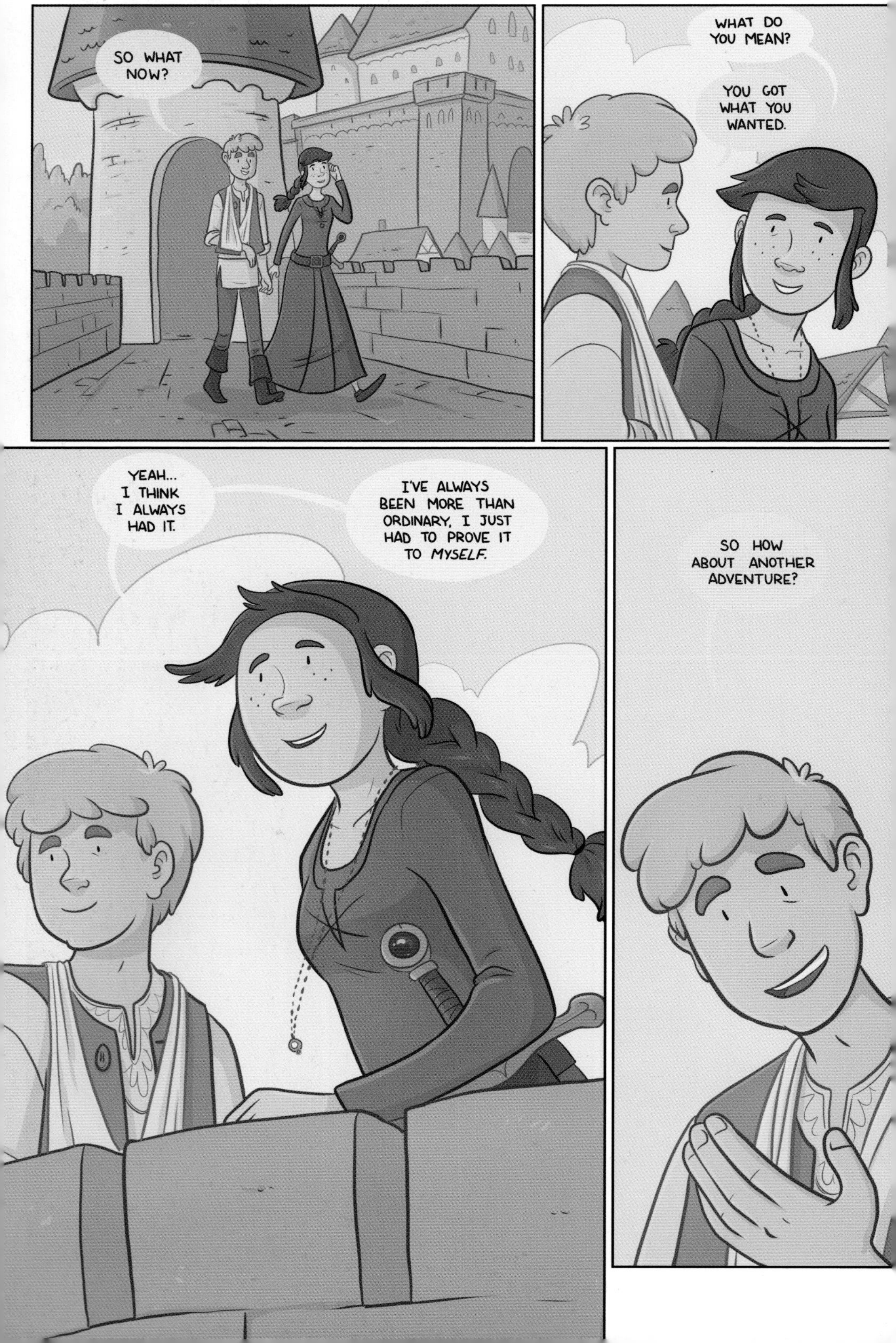
SO WHAT NOW?
WHAT DO YOU MEAN?
YOU GOT WHAT YOU WANTED.
YEAH... I THINK I ALWAYS HAD IT.
I'VE ALWAYS BEEN MORE THAN ORDINARY, I JUST HAD TO PROVE IT TO *MYSELF*.
SO HOW ABOUT ANOTHER ADVENTURE?

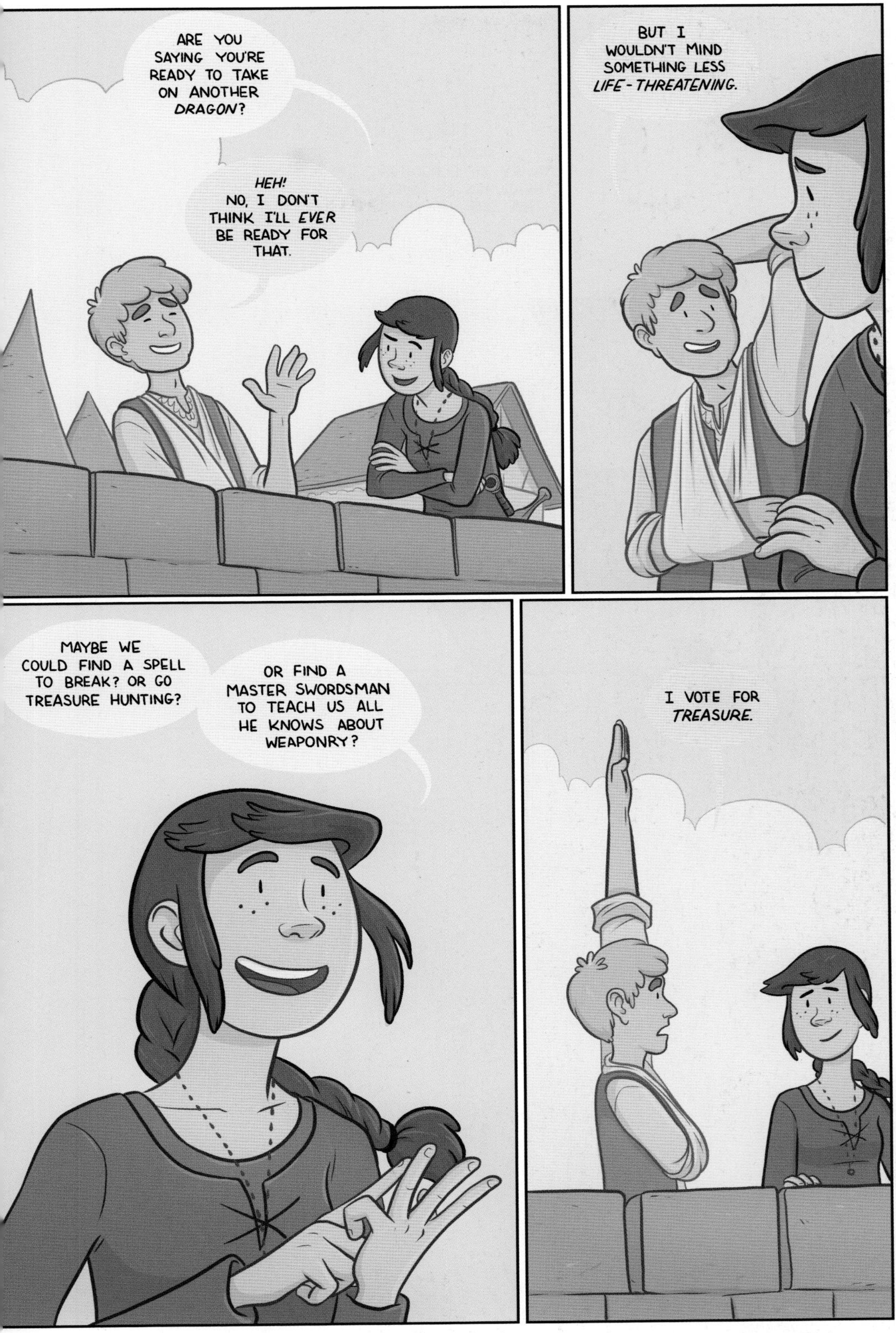
ARE YOU SAYING YOU'RE READY TO TAKE ON ANOTHER *DRAGON*?
HEH! NO, I DON'T THINK I'LL *EVER* BE READY FOR THAT.
BUT I WOULDN'T MIND SOMETHING LESS *LIFE-THREATENING*.
MAYBE WE COULD FIND A SPELL TO BREAK? OR GO TREASURE HUNTING?
OR FIND A MASTER SWORDSMAN TO TEACH US ALL HE KNOWS ABOUT WEAPONRY?
I VOTE FOR *TREASURE*.

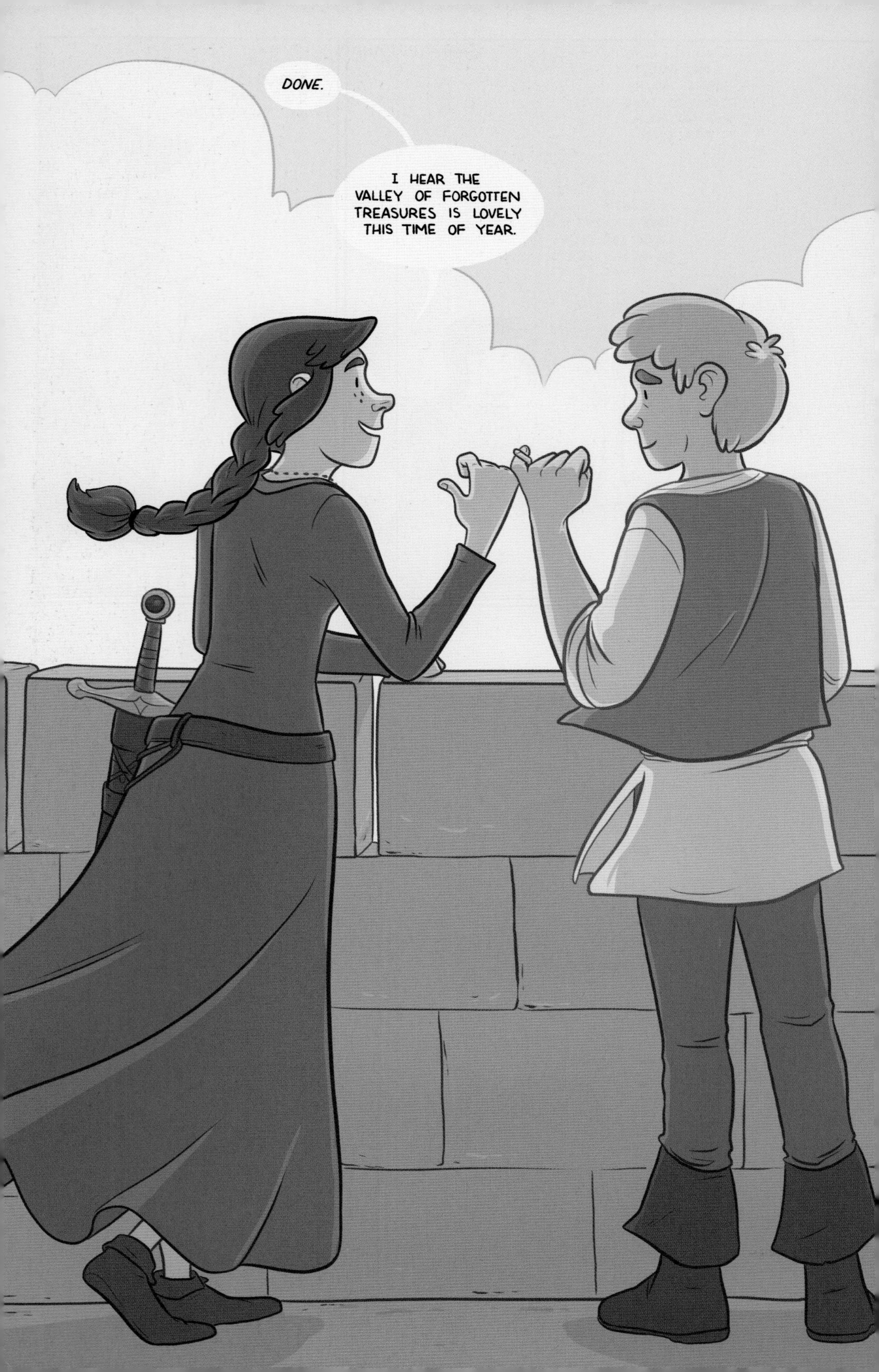
DONE.
I HEAR THE VALLEY OF FORGOTTEN TREASURES IS LOVELY THIS TIME OF YEAR.

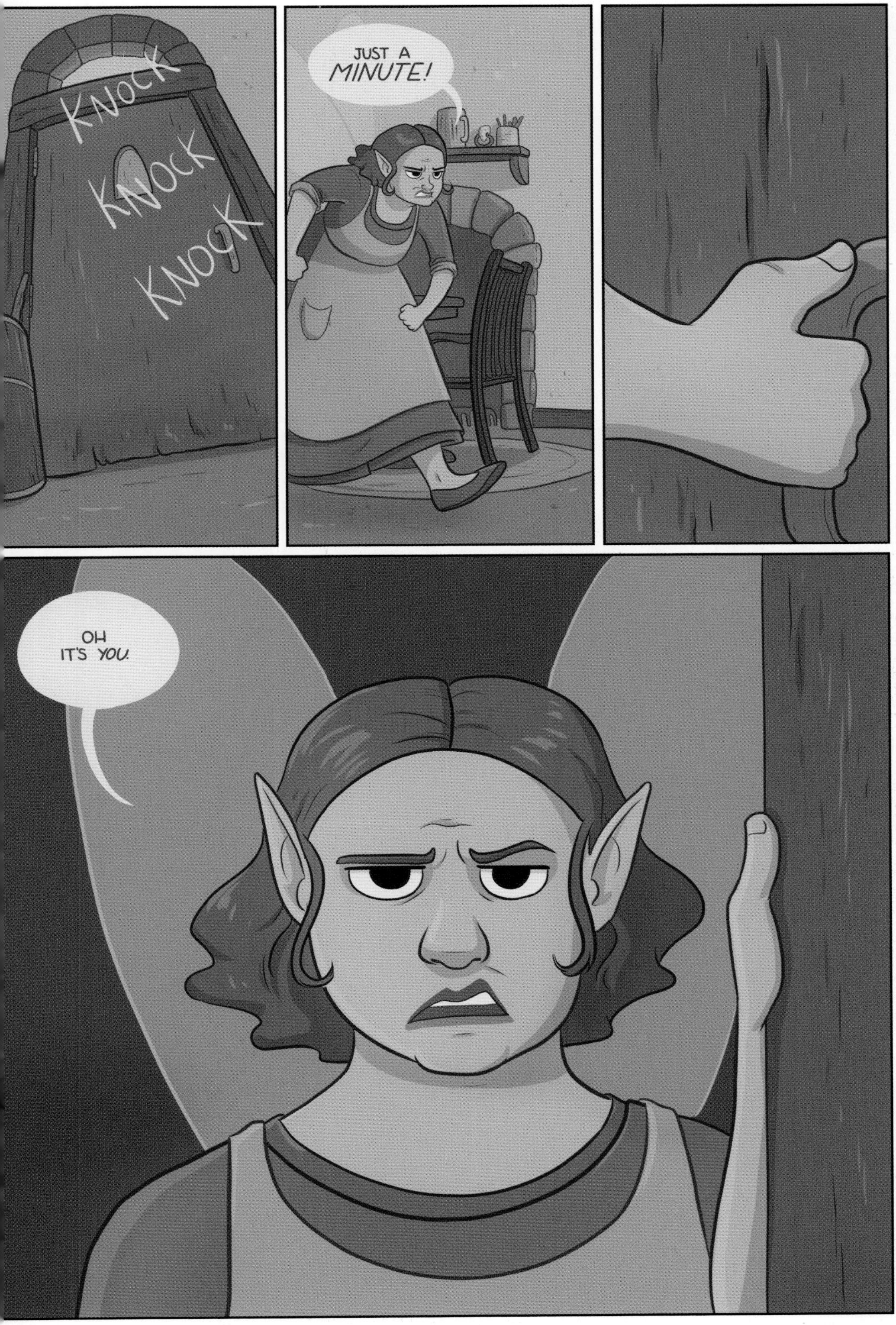
KNOCK
KNOCK
KNOCK
JUST A MINUTE!
OH IT'S YOU.

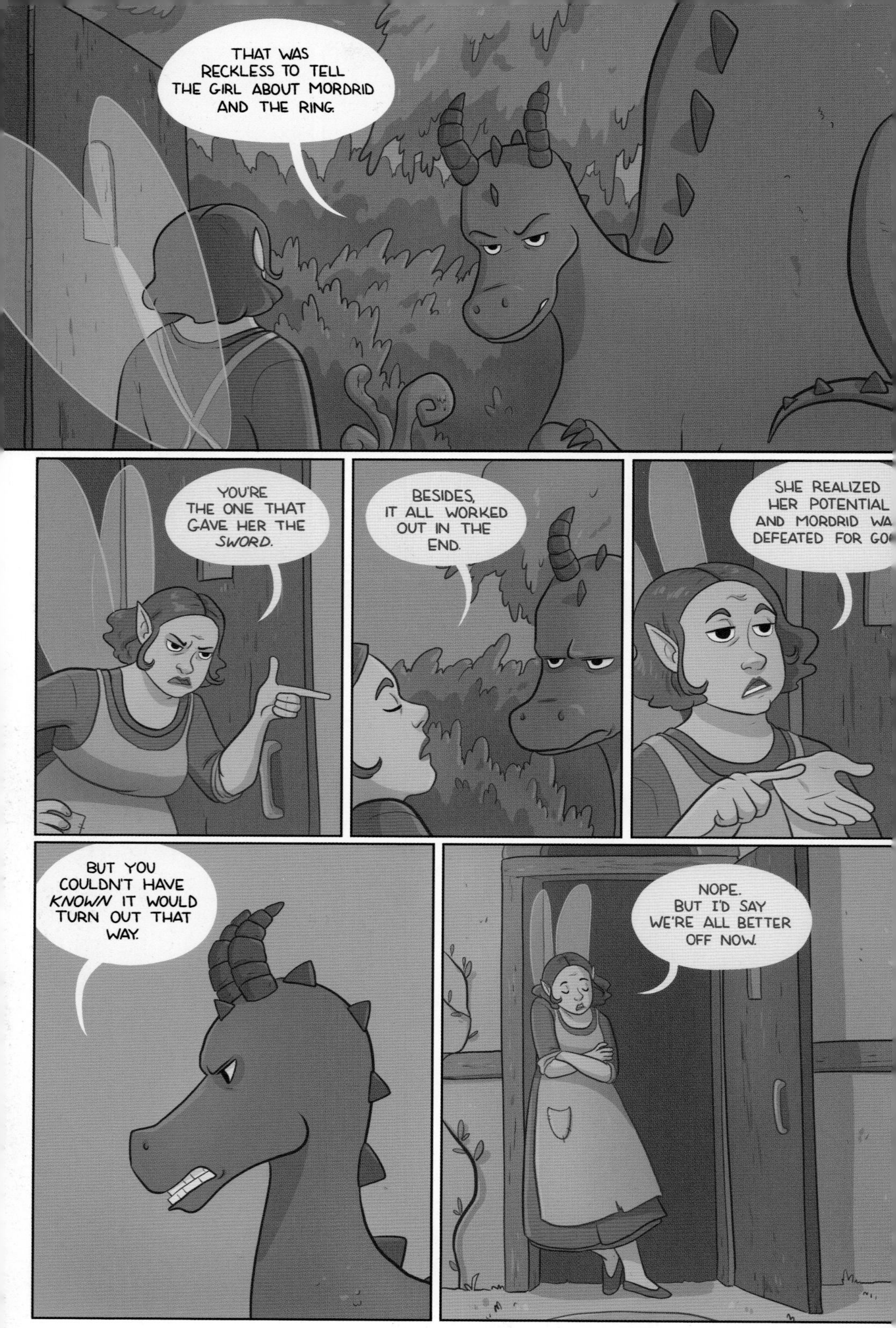
THAT WAS RECKLESS TO TELL THE GIRL ABOUT MORDRID AND THE RING.
YOU'RE THE ONE THAT GAVE HER THE *SWORD*.
BESIDES, IT ALL WORKED OUT IN THE END.
SHE REALIZED HER POTENTIAL AND MORDRID WA DEFEATED FOR GO
BUT YOU COULDN'T HAVE *KNOWN* IT WOULD TURN OUT THAT WAY.
NOPE. BUT I'D SAY WE'RE ALL BETTER OFF NOW.

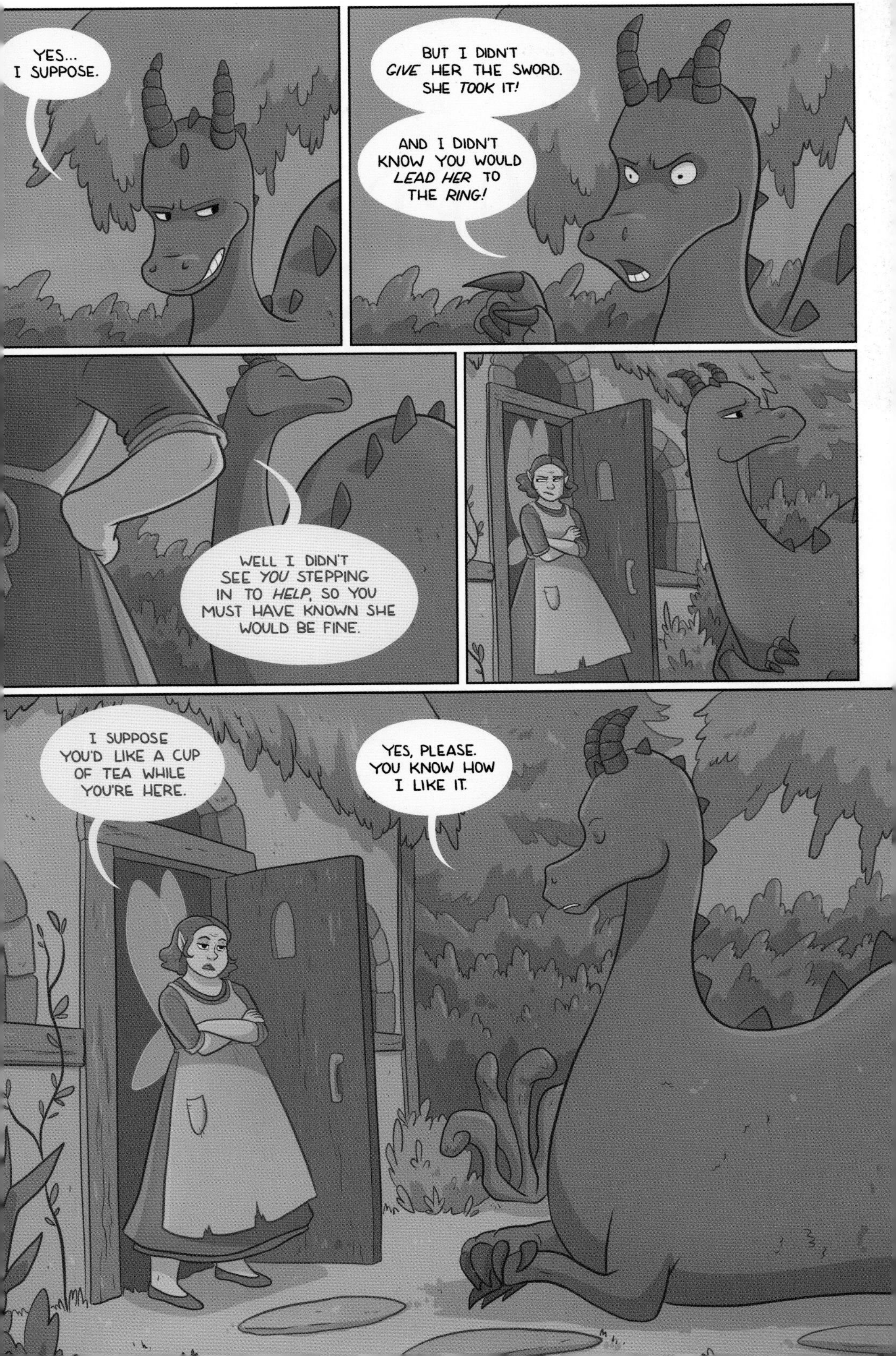
YES... I SUPPOSE.
BUT I DIDN'T *GIVE* HER THE SWORD. SHE *TOOK* IT!
AND I DIDN'T KNOW YOU WOULD *LEAD HER* TO THE *RING!*
WELL I DIDN'T SEE *YOU* STEPPING IN TO *HELP*, SO YOU MUST HAVE KNOWN SHE WOULD BE FINE.
I SUPPOSE YOU'D LIKE A CUP OF TEA WHILE YOU'RE HERE.
YES, PLEASE. YOU KNOW HOW I LIKE IT.

AN EXTRAORDINARY SKETCHBOOK

PROCESS ART AND NOTES BY CASSIE ANDERSON

ORIGIN STORIES

This project originally began as a four-page assignment in college. As it continued to develop, it turned into a pitch for an animated series, which heavily influenced the first iteration as a webcomic. My intent was to capture the nostalgia of watching a princess movie, something I tried to achieve through shapes, design, and color.

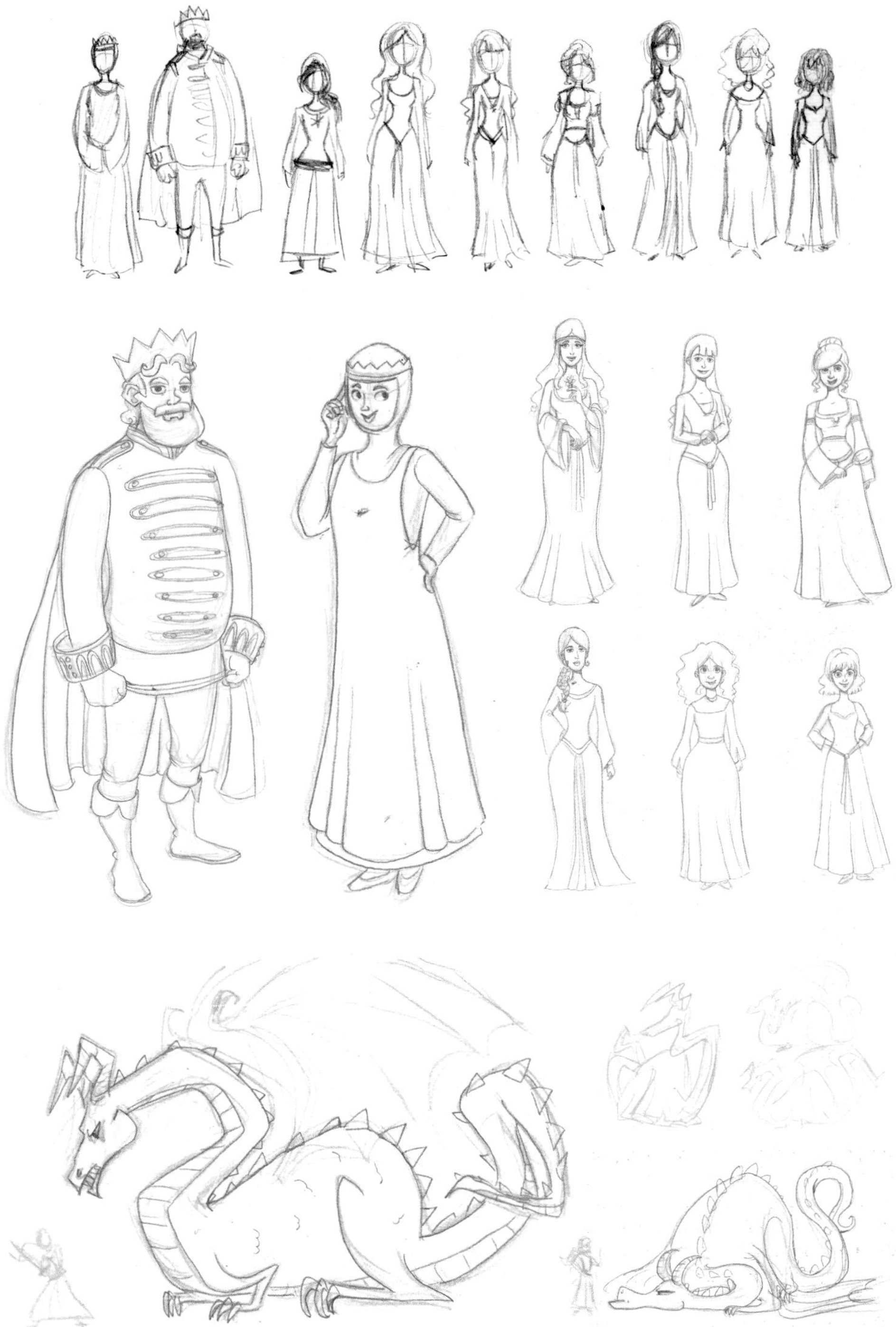

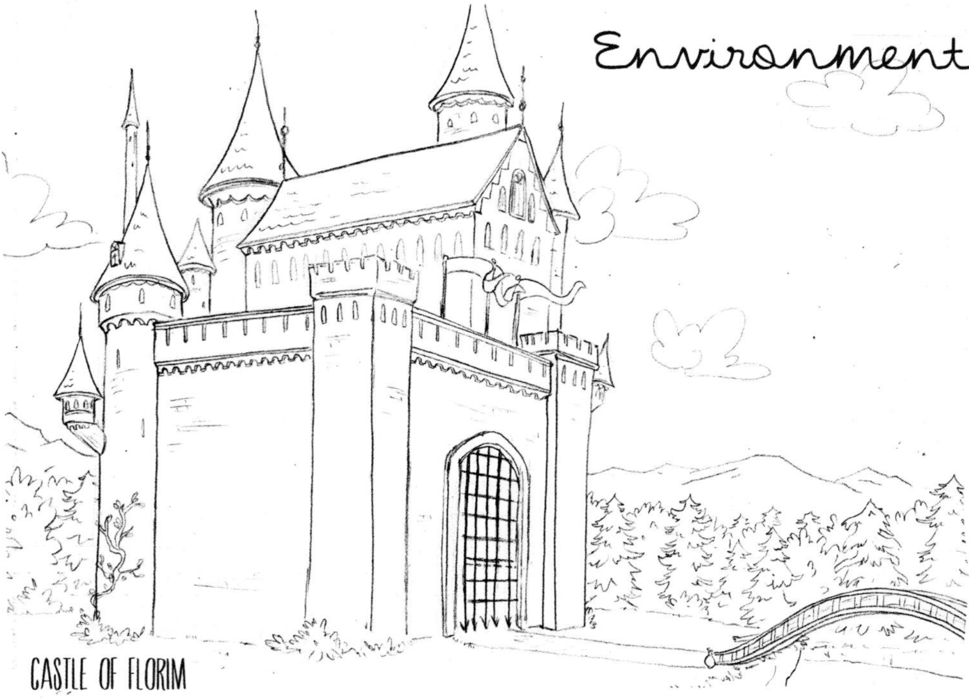

CASTLE OF FLORIM

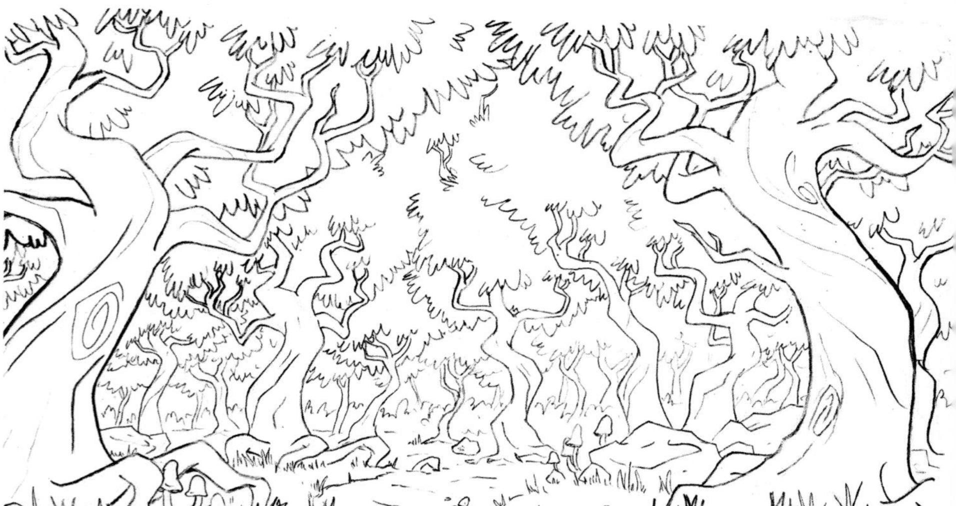

ENCHANTED FOREST

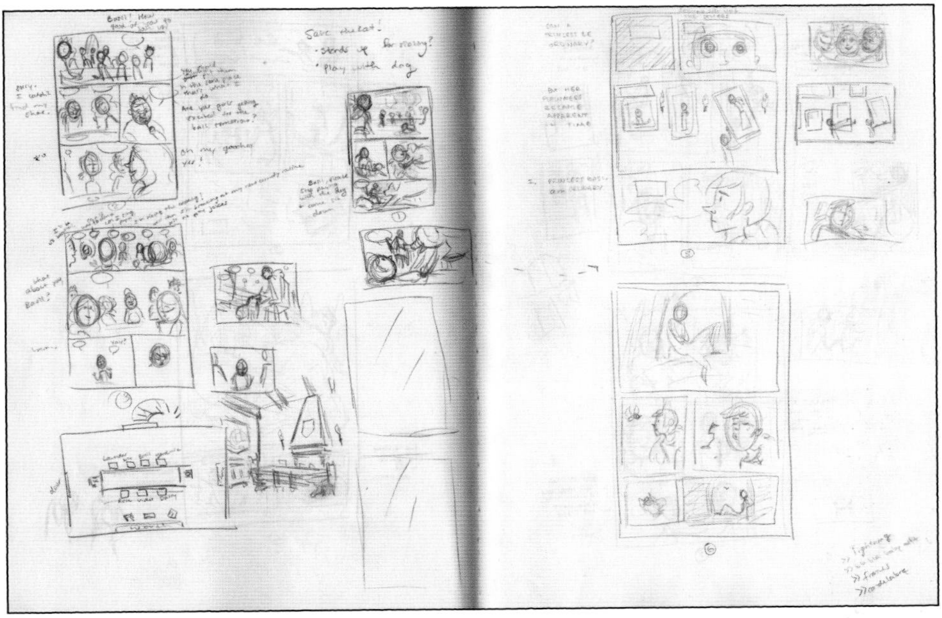

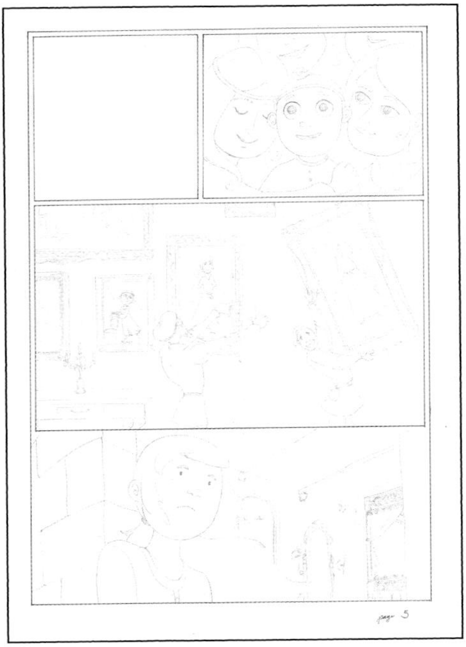
page 5

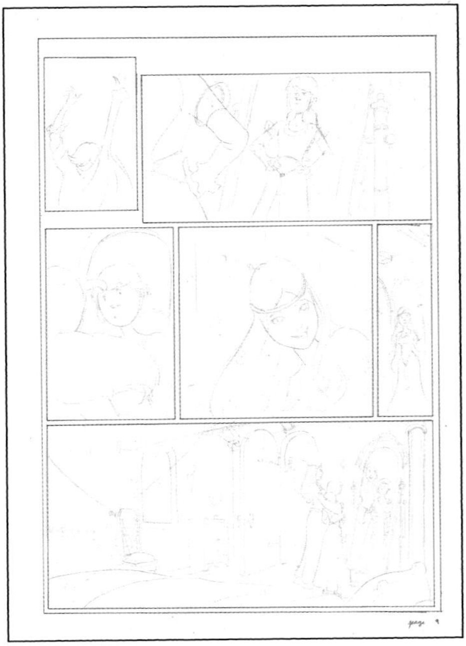
page 9

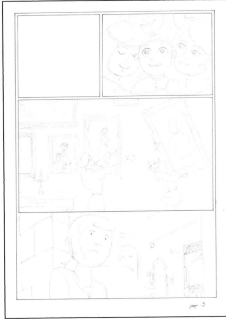

SKETCHES AND PENCILS

I filled a whole sketchbook with designs and thumbnails for this story. Instead of a formal comic script, I wrote a detailed outline, broke it into chapters, then scripted and created layouts simultaneously. Once I settled on layouts I was happy with for an entire chapter, I sketched it out on a much larger piece of paper to be inked later on the computer.

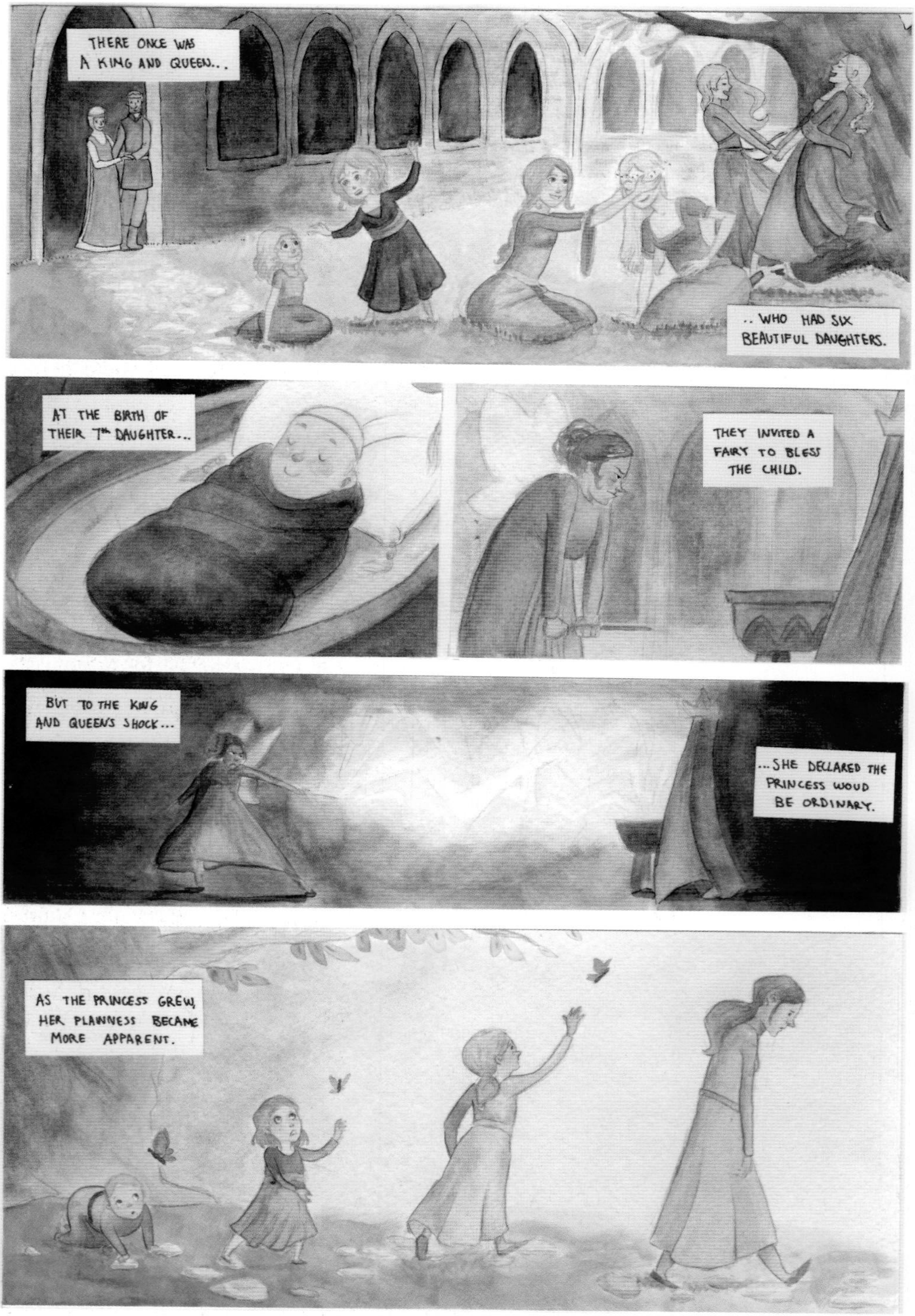
THERE ONCE WAS A KING AND QUEEN...
.. WHO HAD SIX BEAUTIFUL DAUGHTERS.
AT THE BIRTH OF THEIR 7TH DAUGHTER...
THEY INVITED A FAIRY TO BLESS THE CHILD.
BUT TO THE KING AND QUEENS SHOCK...
...SHE DECLARED THE PRINCESS WOUD BE ORDINARY.
AS THE PRINCESS GREW, HER PLAINNESS BECAME MORE APPARENT.

These are the original four pages from college. They were created using watercolors, ink, acrylic, and colored pencil. While I ended up going in a very different stylistic direction, these pages set the tone for the rest of the story.

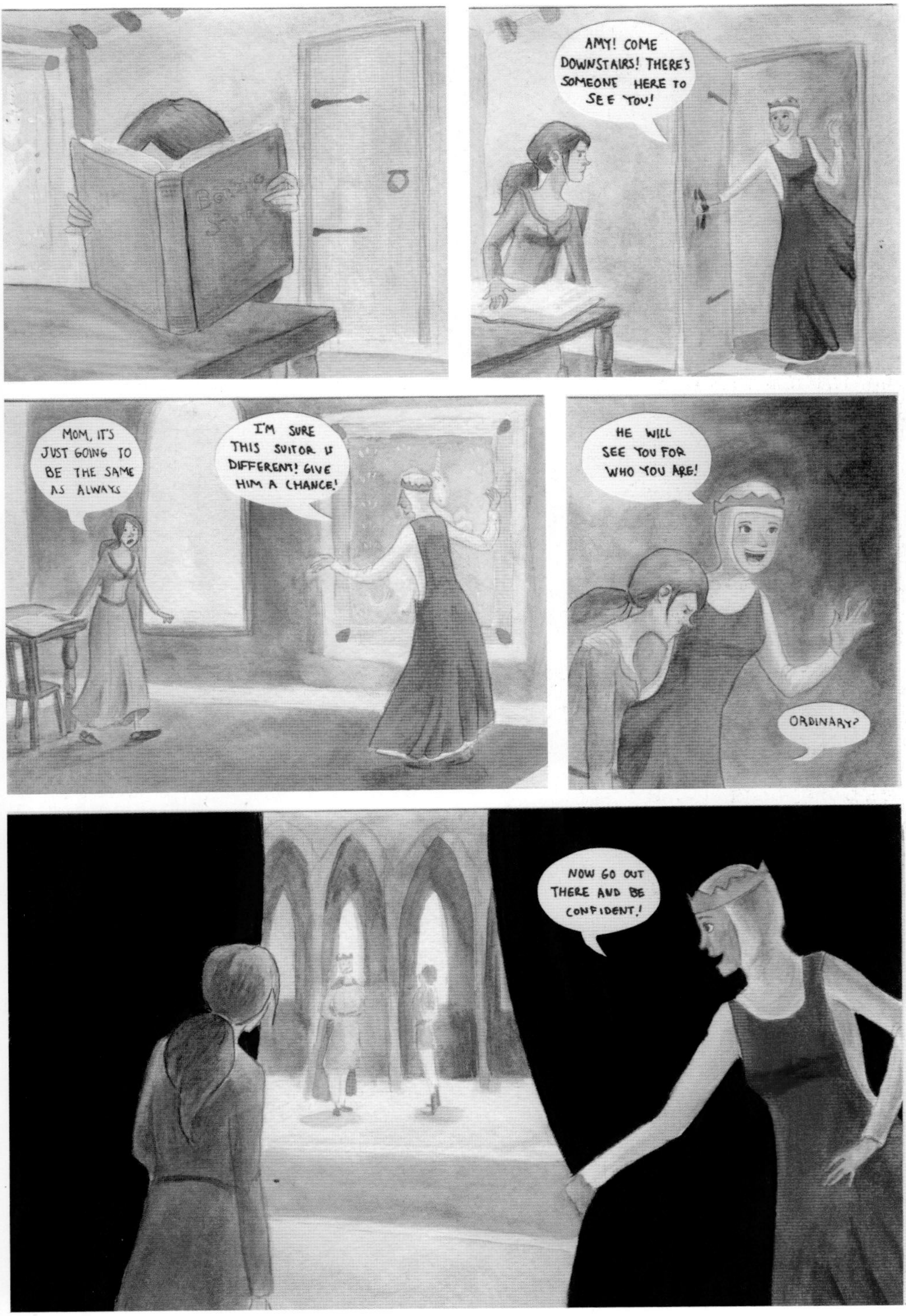
AMY! COME DOWNSTAIRS! THERE'S SOMEONE HERE TO SEE YOU!
MOM, IT'S JUST GOING TO BE THE SAME AS ALWAYS
I'M SURE THIS SUITOR IS DIFFERENT! GIVE HIM A CHANCE!
HE WILL SEE YOU FOR WHO YOU ARE!
ORDINARY?
NOW GO OUT THERE AND BE CONFIDENT!

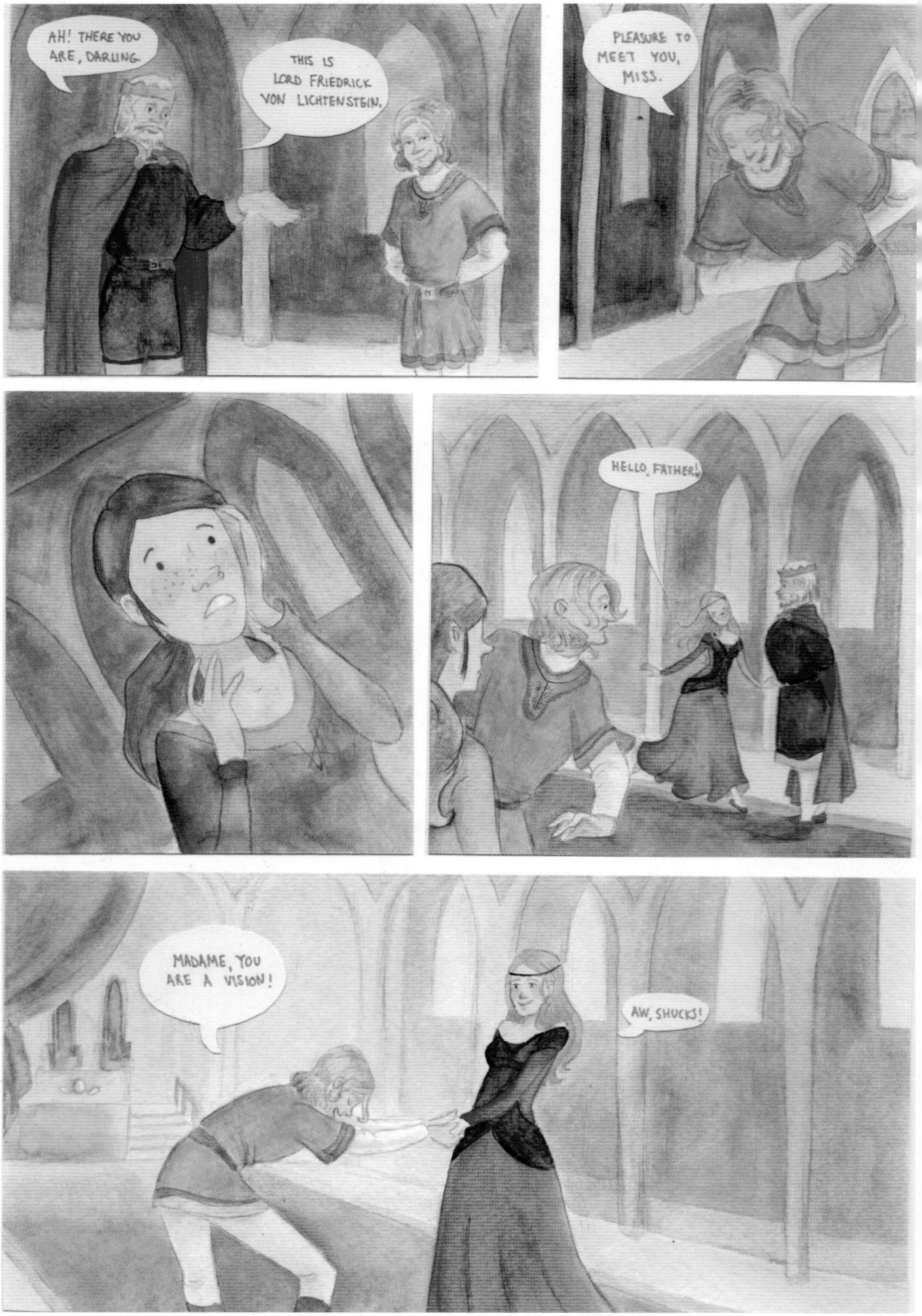
AH! THERE YOU ARE, DARLING.
THIS IS LORD FRIEDRICK VON LICHTENSTEIN.
PLEASURE TO MEET YOU, MISS.
HELLO, FATHER!
MADAME, YOU ARE A VISION!
AW, SHUCKS!

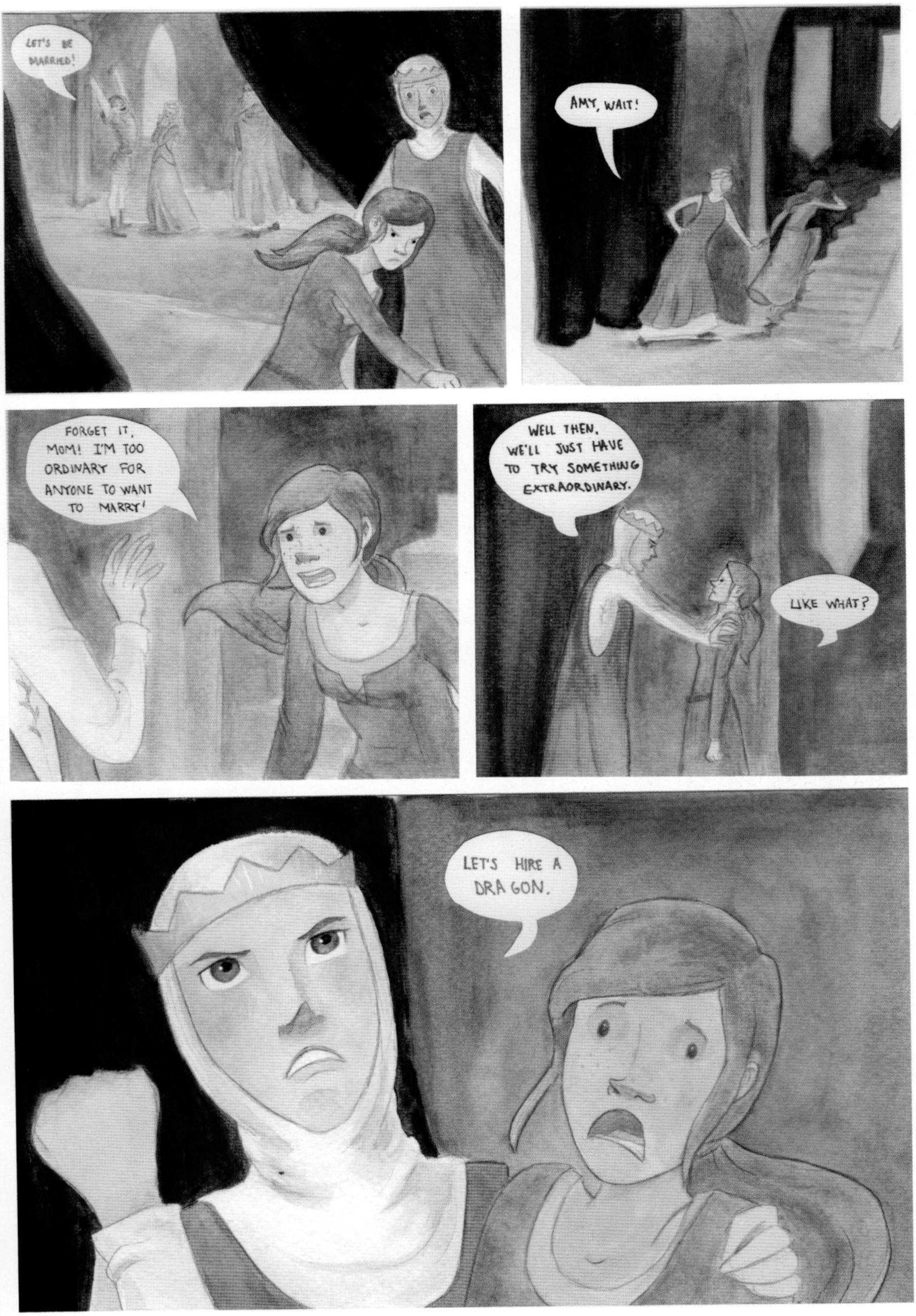
LET'S BE MARRIED!
AMY, WAIT!
FORGET IT, MOM! I'M TOO ORDINARY FOR ANYONE TO WANT TO MARRY!
WELL THEN, WE'LL JUST HAVE TO TRY SOMETHING EXTRAORDINARY.
LIKE WHAT?
LET'S HIRE A DRAGON.

ACKNOWLEDGMENTS

This book has been several years in the making, and there are so many people to thank who have helped me along the way. First of all, thanks to Professor Goto for helping me develop the story. It has changed a lot from my time at SCAD, but I'm grateful for all your insight! Thanks to my editors, Rachel Roberts and Jenny Blenk, for seeing Princess Basil's potential and helping me hone the story even more. Thank you to the comic queen of my heart, Lisa Morris, for your unwavering support and encouragement, and for reminding me of what's really important. And thank you to my family, both here in Portland and back home in Washington. I love you all and I couldn't do this without you.

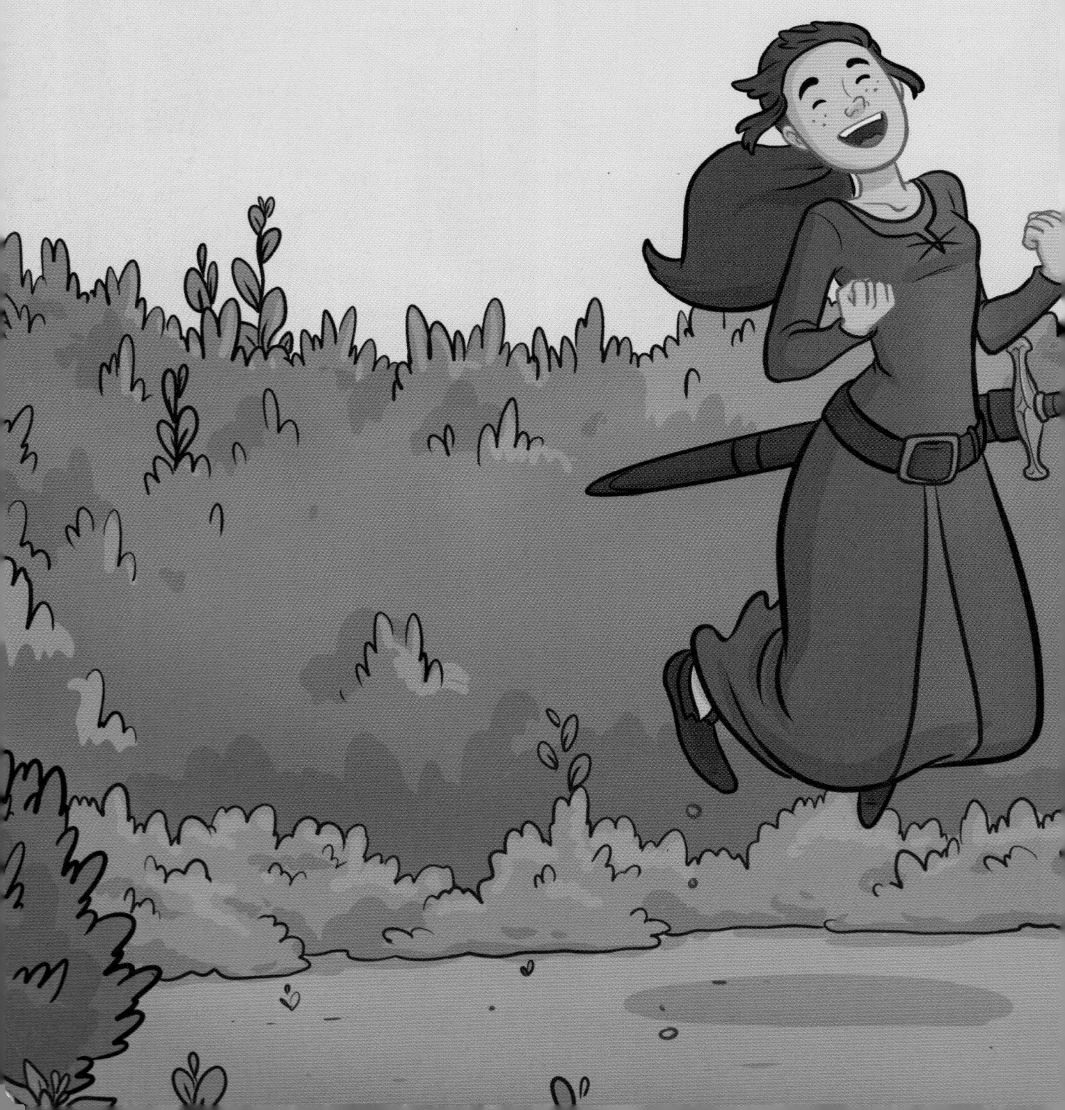

ABOUT THE AUTHOR

Cassie Anderson is a freelance illustrator and the artist behind the graphic novel series *Lifeformed*. After earning a degree in sequential art (read: comics) from the Savannah College of Art and Design, she moved to Portland, OR, where she currently lives. When she's not drawing comics, she can be found baking tasty treats or exploring the great outdoors.

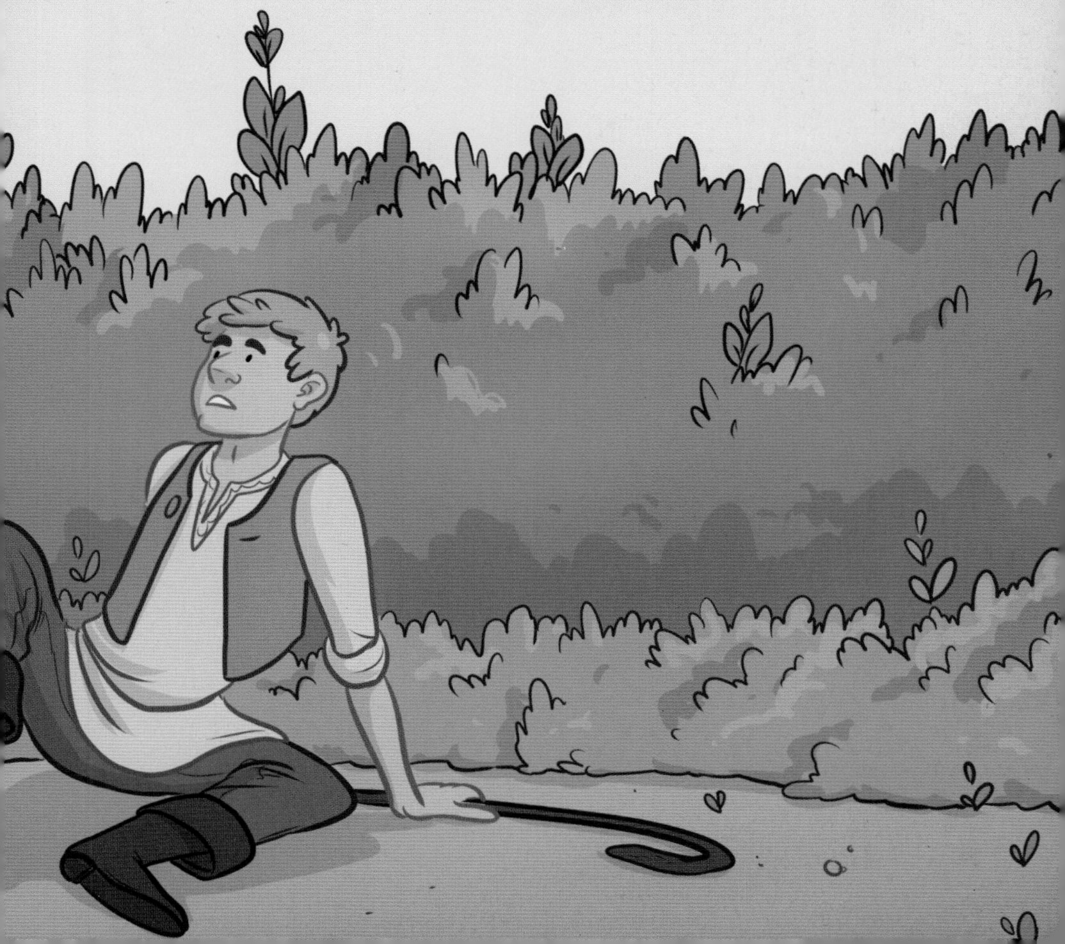

ALSO BY CASSIE ANDERSON!

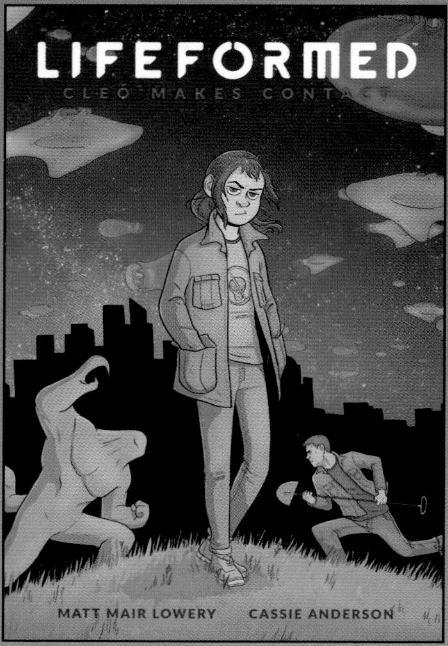
LIFEFORMED
CLEO MAKES CONTACT
MATT MAIR LOWERY
CASSIE ANDERSON

LIFEFORMED: CLEO MAKES CONTACT TP

978-1-50670-177-6 | $12.99

In the wake of an alien invasion—and her father's death—a young girl must fight for the future of Earth. Aided by a shape-shifting rebel alien posing as her father, the unlikely pair bond, fight back, and ponder what it means to be human.

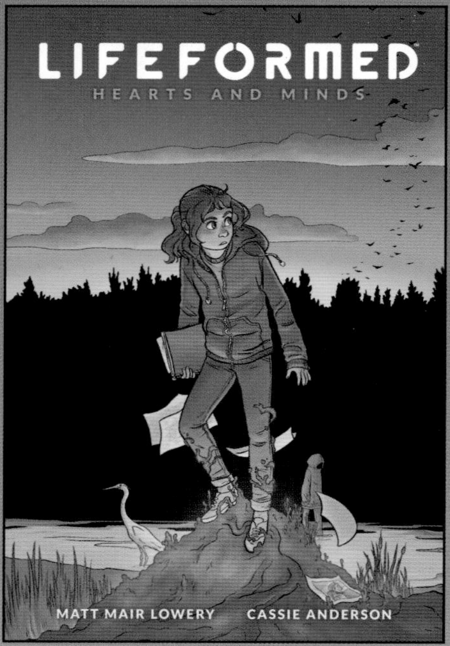
LIFEFORMED
HEARTS AND MINDS
MATT MAIR LOWERY
CASSIE ANDERSON

LIFEFORMED VOLUME 2: HEARTS AND MINDS TP

978-1-50670-937-6 | $12.99

Cleo and the shapeshifting rebel alien posing as her father make a fearsome team in a guerrilla war against the invaders. However, she cannot escape her past and an adversary she thought she'd seen the last of is out for revenge, determined to ruin Cleo's life.

lifeformedcomic.com

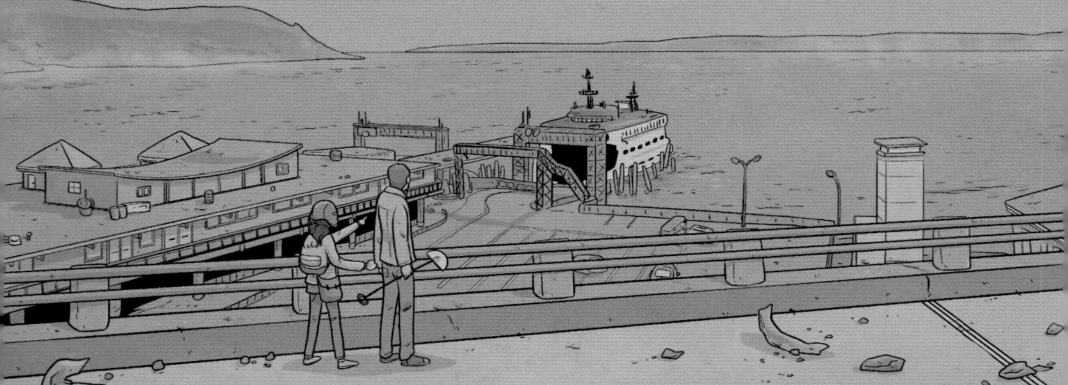